About the author

John Martin spent most of his working life in the financial services sector, but since retiring as a company director has written three children's books: *The Magical Tales of Alfie and Frank*, *The Fun-Packed Adventures of Alfie and Frank* and *It's Party Time for Alfie and Frank*.

He has now turned his hand to fiction with this, the publication of his debut novel: *Just for ME*.

He is married, with two grown-up daughters and lives in Gloucestershire.

JUST FOR ME

John Martin

JUST FOR ME

Vanguard Press

A CIP catalogue record for this title is
available from the British Library.

ISBN 978 1 784653 31 6

Vanguard Press is an imprint of
Pegasus Elliot MacKenzie Publishers Ltd.
www.pegasuspublishers.com

First Published in 2018

Vanguard Press
Sheraton House Castle Park
Cambridge England

Printed and Bound in Great Britain

Acknowledgements

Thank you to my wife, Nicola, for reading the early drafts, for her patience and support throughout the editorial process and thank you also to my daughter, Victoria and Michael Grant for their encouragement and advice.

Dedication

To Alexandra, with all our love.

Chapter 1

David Lane was orphaned in his early teens as his wealthy stock-broking parents died in a tragic plane crash when returning from a business trip to Zurich in 1983. A combination of fog and low cloud, with a faulty instrument panel, were the published findings of the board of inquiry, set up to investigate the accident. Apparently the private jet should never have been in the air, as the changing weather conditions were unsuitable for such a small, light aircraft and sadly the crew and two passengers paid the ultimate price.

His early years were harrowing and traumatic, to say the least, as the stark reality of his parents' untimely death haunted him day and night. The young adolescent was often inconsolable, living on his nerves in a state of abject fear and anxiety as he struggled to adjust to a world of isolation, devoid of love and affection. Still in mourning and suffering from dramatic heart-wrenching flashbacks, fate conspired to cast another shadow over his wretched existence. Shortly after his parents' funeral, the vulnerable youngster was dragged unceremoniously from the familiar family home in Richmond and sent to live in Hastings in the care of his spiteful, uncaring cousin, Carol Jones.

She was a sadistic woman who disliked her new charge from the word go, regularly subjecting the freckled-faced teenager to prolonged periods of torment and mental abuse. This was at a time when the fragile, nervous youngster pined for love, compassion and kindness, and the occasional pat on the shoulder, but instead the teenager was ridiculed, mistreated and made to feel unwanted. He was relegated to a life of loneliness and despair where hatred and fear walked arm in arm and dogged his every waking moment.

Life at the local comprehensive was little better and in stark contrast to the exclusive private school he'd attended in South London. David was victimised, beaten and attacked in an orchestrated campaign of terror led by an overbearing thug, called Martin Conway. He was a big, fat bully, with a chip on his shoulder the size of a dustbin lid, who took great pleasure in hurting the youngster whenever he could. Conway was an ugly brute with unsightly gaps between his badly stained teeth, while clumps of grey matted hair tried to escape the confines of his protruding ears, sticking out like oversized door mirrors. He was short and stumpy, with large fat hands and a head shaped like an onion with squinty little eyes that peered out beneath two bushy grey eyebrows and an acne-stricken forehead.

This horrendous period of terror and fear, supplemented by bouts of deep depression and sleepless nights, was so different to the privileged life he'd enjoyed in his formative years. Love, warmth and tenderness had never been in short supply and the adulation of his caring, devoted parents formed the basis of his happy childhood days. It was idyllic. So this timid, frightened youngster was forced to live on his nerves, never knowing when the next abusive onslaught, or verbal tirade would descend on him. David's teenage years were a battle for survival; just getting from one day to the next was a constant challenge, while any vestige of hope or optimism remained firmly on the back burner as a far-off distant dream. Paradoxically, there were times when things got so bad that he blamed himself for his own predicament, empathising with his callous tormentors, believing it was his fault; he was somehow responsible for his nightmare existence and only had himself to blame. Over time he became conditioned to periods of unprovoked cruelty, took it in his stride, thought it was normal and part of the pattern of everyday life. Being shouted at, for the slightest reason, by his crusty, bad-tempered cousin and kicked, as part of the evening's entertainment by her different drunken partners, was par for the course, something that just happened like eating, sleeping and going to school.

Carol's ear-piercing shrieks would forever haunt him, squealing her foul-mouthed orders, with a copious sprinkling of profanities, up the staircase of their three-bedroom semi, while the frightened orphan hid in his poky first-floor bedroom, pondering on his fate at the hands of Cruella de Vil, wondering whether his undernourished body could take much more physical abuse from his malicious relative.

"If I catch you stealing food again, you know what'll happen to you. Now get to sleep, you little brat, I don't want to see you until the morning."

Her heartless words were usually the prelude to a night of heavy drinking, loud thumping music, followed by shouting, swearing and untold arguments between drink-sodden inebriates and legless junkies. Sometimes the police were called by distraught neighbours and shortly after a black police van took up position on the gravel drive. Then a motley crew of unsightly lowlifes trooped out of the house, off to the local nick to dry out and make restitution with the magistrate the following morning, before repeating the same mind-numbing routine several days later.

David's answer to this inane pattern of drunken debauchery was to lock his bedroom door, slip underneath his tawdry discoloured sheets on his rickety single bed, and cover his head with his outstretched arm. He then grabbed a few hours' shut-eye, as his mother gently stroked his forehead, before Martin Conway picked up the baton in the morning and continued the cycle of abuse. The teenager often tried to escape the shackles of anger and hate by immersing himself in the world of superheroes and sword-wielding adventure stories. Here his mind was transported by the turn of a page to another place where thrills and spills, fun and fantasy were on the agenda, offering a welcome respite from the trials and tribulations of his life that so characterised his early years in Hastings.

David was fascinated, enthralled by Arthur Conan Doyle's riveting stories of Baker Street's famous detective – Sherlock Holmes. *The Hound of the Baskervilles* captured his imagination as did: *A Scandal in Bohemia, The Valley of Fear and A Study in Scarlet*. Here he embarked on a series of action-packed tales of escapism and adventure, many miles away from the pernicious life he endured in his solitary prison cell.

The gripping tales were compulsive page-turners for the avid reader. He imagined the antics of the super-sleuth and his medical companion when they deployed their well-honed detective skills in their relentless quest to outwit the criminal mind and bring the wrongdoers to book. But sadly David was often dragged back to reality when Carol's alcoholic ravings swept through the semi-detached house, like a giant tidal wave, sending torrents of fear crashing against the high-gloss walls and painted ceilings, up the winding wooden staircase – and straight into his first-floor hellhole.

Concerned neighbours sometimes enquired about David's state of health, particularly as he often looked gaunt, shabbily dressed and clearly undernourished. But the threat of violence and intimidation from his quarrelsome, cantankerous guardian was enough to unnerve the locals to the point of hiding behind their settees, fearing for their lives. They knew, from past experience, that retribution of some kind was inevitable if they opened their mouths, and dared to warn the authorities to the youngster's miserable plight.

Like a revolving door, the cycle of cruelty continued unabated. The weak, self-centred residents turned a blind eye to his suffering, carried on mowing their pristine lawns, putting out their recycling bins every Tuesday, clipping their privet hedges and doing their weekly shop at Sainsbury's. It was as though nothing was amiss. David Lane was invisible. He didn't exist.

Carol's cruelty knew no bounds, often venting her anger and uncontrollable bad temper on her young charge for no apparent reason. She'd often burn his arms and shoulders with lighted cigarettes and beat him with a thick wooden cane, only stopping her brutal assault when David screamed so loudly, she feared a passer-by would alert the police.

Most of his wretched existence was spent alone in his room, out of sight, out of mind, always fearful of attracting the wrath of his demented cousin. He'd snatch a quick meal from the kitchen cupboard when the coast was clear and hide modest supplies under the wooden floorboards, taking every care not to arouse any suspicion. The defenceless orphan was forced to stockpile food for his own self-preservation.

Apparently a healthy monthly allowance was paid to his guardian for his education, upkeep and general well-being, but sadly David never saw a penny of it. The troubled schoolboy didn't benefit at all. Instead vast sums were squandered on lavish interior decorations, valuable porcelain ornaments and on unlimited supplies of alcohol for Carol's rowdy drinking sessions and frequent late-night parties.

It was David's strength of character and stubborn determination that got the frightened adolescent through those five harrowing years of hell, suffering daily at the hands of his sadistic tormentors who wallowed in his misery and woe. But thankfully there was a light at the end of the tunnel. Things were about to change for the better. His eighteenth birthday was looming large and it couldn't come soon enough for the teenager who'd been ticking off the days, putting a thick black line through the months and crossing out the endless years with a bold felt-tip pen, while time crept ever closer, ever nearer towards the day when his pitiful life would change forever. His detailed diaries of life at 5 Dewhurst Road were a graphic testament to the endless reign of terror he suffered on his own, out of sight and out of mind. They documented a harrowing catalogue of physical and mental torture, offering a tear-jerking insight into his lonely ordeal at the hands of his abusers. The page-worn diaries were carefully stored in his trusty old suitcase, shedding light on those dark days when he often cried himself to sleep at night, thinking about his beloved parents and how much he missed them. When he was very low, very desperate, he'd write a short note to his mother saying how much he loved her, that he always cleaned his teeth at night and brushed his hair before going to sleep. This gave him some comfort, however brief, while the tears rolled down his cheeks onto his sullied sheets and badly discoloured pillowcase.

But at last the big day arrived. The birthday boy felt happy, elated at the prospects ahead and, with an anxious smile, left his smelly, dingy box room, clutching just a few precious possessions under his arm. David ambled down the newly carpeted staircase, holding onto the banister for support, accompanied by the droning sound of passing cars and yappy dogs barking in the distance, before stopping at the foot of the stairs to quietly savour the moment when freedom beckoned the other side of the solid oak front door.

He reached down and picked up the letter that was addressed to him lying innocently on the thick doormat with the word, WELCOME, firmly inscribed in the centre. How ironic, he thought. A firm of local solicitors had written to him a month earlier asking David to look out for an important letter in relation to his forthcoming eighteenth birthday.

So, he'd completed his sentence and he could now close the book on that sordid chapter in his early years and look to the future with some optimism. David wiped his damp cheeks with the sleeve of his jacket, as the enormity of the occasion got to him. He glanced along the freshly painted corridor, with its array of fine art pictures and expensive porcelain ornaments proudly displayed in the two ornate wall-mounted glass cabinets. This wealth and extravagance was a far cry from the austere existence he'd endured in his squalid, seedy room, with its old worn-out furniture, flaky, tarnished paintwork and lines of peeling paper hanging from its damp walls.

David was jittery and unsure of himself when, with a strong sense of trepidation he took a deep breath, pulled open the door and prepared himself for the day ahead and the next stage in his turbulent, unpredictable life.

Strangely enough he wasn't vengeful, or angry towards his cruel tormentors, even though they'd contrived to wreck his teenage years and make suicide a realistic option on a number of occasions. Carol Jones and Martin Conway were two names he'd never forget, their sinister faces were forever etched in his psyche. As the tears continued trickling down his cheeks, he wondered why he'd been singled out for such hateful treatment and why life had dealt him such a lousy deck of cards? But now, for the first time in his life, he was in charge of his own destiny; he could make his own choices. He'd take control and do precisely what he wanted. So the hapless teenager, with a touch of acne, a collection of nasty scars on his back and a dodgy right ankle, left 5 Dewhurst Road on a warm sunny day in July, with the morning sun beating down on his back and a pleasant welcoming breeze sweeping across his grey, ashen face.

Wearing a moth-eaten dark suit and an open-neck frayed tartan shirt and clutching a battered old green suitcase, stuffed with diaries and a handful of treasured possessions, he left the front door wide open at Miss de Vil's house of horrors and ambled head-down towards the main road, over the newly laid gravel drive with the chunky ill-shaped chippings protesting loudly under foot.

Chapter 2

The journey into Hastings took ten minutes on the local double-decker bus, which gave David time to study Mr Crawford's letter again. It was intriguing, to say the very least.

The solicitors' offices were in an old Victorian building on the resort seafront, enjoying attractive, uninhibited views of the pebble beach and wavy coastline that stretched as far as the eye could see. Mr Crawford was quite elderly, very slim and well-groomed, dressed smartly in a pinstripe suit, with a matching shirt and bright floral tie. His office was light and airy and his solid oak desk, in the centre of the room, was covered in piles of loose papers and bulging brown folders. He offered David a comfortable seat in the bay window. The suave articulate gentleman, with a passion for rugby judging by the number of framed pictures hanging on the office walls, explained that his legal firm had been his family's lawyer for many years and that the Richmond and Hastings offices knew his late parents very well.

Mr Crawford was shocked by the manner of their death, particularly at such a young age, and offered his heart-felt condolences for David's loss. His rather shy-looking client, with tears in his eyes, smiled and nodded.

"Please tell me about yourself young man, and what you've been up to?" asked the friendly solicitor with a warm, reassuring tone.

"Well, I went to Larkhill Comprehensive sir, until a couple of years ago. I found it very difficult and quite lonely. I was ignored and left on my own most of the time. I didn't have any friends, you see. Then I got a place at the local college, but I didn't like it, missed lots of classes, just messed about and left in the end. Carol, my cousin, got ill, probably because of her excessive drinking and I had to help with some of the cooking and cleaning, even though we never got on. She disliked me. Don't know why. She's not a nice lady really, Mr Crawford. Quite cruel, in fact."

"How are you feeling now?" asked Mr Crawford, clearly concerned by David's appearance and general demeanour. The nervy young lad was timid and reserved and seemed unwell, rarely making eye contact with the elderly solicitor, who became increasingly worried for his client's state of health the longer they chatted.

"Okay. I feel much better now I'm eighteen," said David, slowly looking up from the carpeted floor with a slight smile as he bit his bottom lip. He then rubbed the knees of his shiny dark trousers and gazed at the solicitor in a doleful way, appearing ill at ease in the unfamiliar surroundings. His cold blue eyes were empty and unfeeling: just staring ahead, motionless without blinking.

"Well, I've got some very good news for you young man, which we'll come to shortly," explained Edward, glancing over his reading glasses at the forlorn character sitting just feet away. He wished David a very happy birthday and thanked him for coming in as they sipped their freshly percolated coffee and ate ginger nut biscuits from a crimson-coloured barrel, perched on the edge of a circular glass-top coffee table.

Eventually, after some courteous chit-chat, Edward got down to business and walked the inquisitive teenager through the terms of his parents' will. He peered over his horn-rimmed glasses, from time to time, to see whether his rather bedraggled, unkempt companion had any questions. There were none. David felt too nervous, too unsure of himself to even cough, let alone interrupt the legal beagle in full flight.

David knew his late parents were wealthy and that he'd be comfortably catered for, so long as he survived his incarceration with the wicked witch. But he never imagined in his wildest dreams that the estate was so vast. He could only listen intently, often open-mouthed, whilst the family lawyer, in his fetching floral tie, reeled off stacks of numbers like a deranged bingo caller on acid. He quoted investment trusts, unit trusts, stocks and shares, property bonds, government gilts, overseas investments and lots and lots of portfolios. None of this gobbledegook registered with the lad, he didn't have a clue what Mr Crawford was going on about. The badly dressed birthday boy was more concerned with his sleeping arrangements for that coming night, than the size of his extensive portfolio. Whatever that was.

However, towards the end of the lengthy explanation as David's attention was beginning to wane and his right ankle starting to throb, one figure stuck out as the eloquent solicitor paused for a moment and took a quick slurp of his luke-warm coffee. Edward peered over his glasses, perched precariously on the end of his nose, and relaxing back in his soft leather chair, grinning from ear to ear, said:

"So, young man, if you add up all the investments, the whole lot, the whole caboodle, it adds up to about sixty million pounds." There was a pause whilst he checked his notes again and reached for his calculator. "Yes, sixty, yes sixty million pounds. That's more or less the figure, give or take a few thousand or two."

David gasped, dragged his bruised hands over his face, rubbed his sweaty palms down his shiny trousers and stared at the high-pile carpet that engulfed his badly scuffed black shoes with frayed stitching and worn down heels. "Sixty million pounds," repeated David in a state of shock. "I can't believe it, Mr Crawford. Are you telling me it's all mine, are you sure? Don't you think, with all the muddles and paperwork you've got on your desk, you might be confusing me with someone else?"

Seagulls were squawking and circling overhead, car horns were blaring out from the streets below. Holidaymakers cavorted on the expansive pebble beach, adjacent to the seafront promenade, as the scruffy homeless millionaire gazed deferentially at Mr Crawford, waiting patiently for a reply.

Most of Edward's work was quite boring and often tedious to the extreme, but when he was waxing lyrical about the proceeds of a large estate to an expectant beneficiary, then the world was his stage. Here he teased his audience by slowly moving through the well-honed script to the inevitable final act when he explained, with flair and authority, the size of their inheritance. This was invariably delivered with great eloquence, just like an accomplished Shakespearian actor executing his lines with fluency and finesse.

"I can assure you, my lad, that it's true," replied Mr Crawford, rather abruptly and somewhat put out by David's less than subtle innuendo about his day-to-day working practices. Raising his voice he went on. "What's more, you're the sole beneficiary. It's all yours, every darn penny," said Edward with a confident grin, leaning forward in his posh leather high-backed chair and patting his bemused client gently on his shoulder. David winced.

"Another ginger nut, my boy?" he asked, waving the half-empty biscuit barrel under his nose.

"No, no thanks, Mr Crawford," said David hesitantly, gazing through the open window out to sea, while small boats and tall-masted yachts bobbed up and down on the white-crested waves. Time stood still, no clocks were ticking, as the enormity of his vast inheritance slowly sank in.

So according to the terms of the will, which the lawyer repeated several times, he'd have a healthy monthly allowance until he was twenty-one years old and after then he'd have full access to the estate, to do as he wished.

At least I won't have to sleep rough tonight, he thought to himself, grabbing a ginger nut from the barrel and drinking the rest of his cold coffee, before gently rising to his feet and bidding farewell to his legal adviser. David was in a bit of a daze, a bit of a quandary, when he shook Mr Crawford's hand on that eventful midsummer morning and sauntered along the jam-packed seafront, past throngs of excited holidaymakers and pale-looking day-trippers. He was trying to understand the implications of his good fortune and what it meant for the future.

After a few moments, he plonked himself down on a wobbly, wooden bench in a deserted circular bandstand, with his battered green case grasped firmly on his lap, watching the rolling white waves pounding against the nearby harbour wall. The date was 14th July, 1988. It was the dawn of a new age; a new chapter in the roller-coaster life of the young immature teenager. He checked his rotary watch, with its badly scratched face, for the umpteenth time and leant back against the old creaky wooden structure, with its flaky paintwork and early signs of woodworm, while some bloated seagulls waddled past, gorging themselves on a free meal, courtesy of an overflowing refuse bin.

Then, with case in hand he shuffled to his feet, much to the annoyance of his plump feathered friends, still stuffing themselves on tasty scraps and little titbits, and went off in search of Cavendish House that according to Mr Crawford was situated at the end of Parabola Road. He vaguely remembered some of the solicitor's garbled directions when he got into the lift, closed the wobbly steel-framed door and descended to the ground-floor exit, to be treated to a shard of bright dazzling sunlight and the thumping sound of passing traffic.

In the distance David saw the impressive four-story building with its vibrant eye-catching window displays of ladies' and gents' fashions. Its commanding seafront position stretched right around the corner of the busy main road, no doubt a magnet for the serial shopper and the fashion-conscious holidaymaker with money to burn. Mr Crawford was right. There was a dazzling array of colourful international flags swaying proudly on the roof, standing adjacent to the store's illustrious rooftop restaurant that boasted mesmeric views of the celebrated south coast. The shy youngster was gratified to see the familiar smiling face of Miss James, standing on tiptoe outside the illustrious store's main entrance, waving her arms frantically in the air. They'd already been introduced to each other at the end of David's meeting with his solicitor as the daunting prospect of entering such an august building, on his own, with its revolving doors and smartly dressed doormen, made the introverted teenager shake in his second-hand boots.

"Hello!" she yelled. "Let's go inside and have a look around and see what you'd like to buy. It'll be great fun, you wait and see." Susan was just like a small child let loose in a sweet factory, jumping up and down and smiling in anticipation of the spending spree ahead.

David didn't have chance to reply and was whisked into the store before he even had time to catch his breath. Susan quickly assumed the role of personal shopper and guide and took him under her wing, like a proud mother hen. She directed her wealthy client from floor to floor, with boundless enthusiasm and a warm beaming smile to match. It was like a fashion parade with David the star of the catwalk. Susan chose a number of shirts, umpteen pairs of trousers and various items of underwear, as well as bright, colourful socks, linen and tweed casual jackets, with matching belts, plus packets of cotton handkerchiefs and several pairs of expensive cufflinks. The assortment of goodies for the man about town was quite mind-boggling.

David's impetuous assistant was on a roll, on cloud nine and hadn't had so much fun in years. The attractive, bright-eyed solicitor grabbed the moment, throwing herself headlong into the task, directing the young lad to the various changing rooms like a police officer on point duty, grappling with their numerous shopping bags that were soon brimming full of new colourful purchases.

Susan kept scuttling off around the store in her manic quest to smarten up his image, only to return moments later, often slightly out of breath, clutching a new selection of clothes with matching accessories for his perusal. For Miss James, this assignment was far more invigorating, much more fun than handling boring mortgage applications, writing tedious wills, or conducting dull, tiresome probate enquiries. She'd been freed, for a few magical hours, from the mind-numbing shackles of legal paperwork and humdrum tax affairs and relished every moment of it. It was bliss.

"There you are, David. After an exciting shopping spree we've done it, we've bought lots and lots of fantastic clothes by tip-top designers for you to wear in your new posh abode," suggested Susan, bouncing up and down like a puppet on a string, waving half a dozen bulging shopping bags in the air that were stuffed full with shirts, trousers, jackets and jeans.

"I hope I'll live up to the billing," he said ruefully, peering enviously at the impressive labels displaying images of trendy, well-groomed men in smart designer clothes, looking rather cool and very suave. But before he had time to catch his breath or take stock of his new purchases, he was racing along behind his personal shopper, towards the nearby lift with footwear firmly in their sights.

"Once we've seen what their shoe department have to offer, we can call it a day," announced Susan excitedly, falling backwards into the unoccupied lift with arms bursting with goodies and gripping hold of their prized possessions as though their very lives depended on it. True to her word, a few moments later, the couple returned to the claustrophobic confines of the store's wobbly lift. This time laden with several pairs of casual shoes and soft magenta slippers all boasting fine handmade stitching and leather soles. The ensemble was complete.

So after an hour or so of high-octane shopping, with regular changes of clothes that made David feel punch drunk, his frenzied companion suggested they take a pit stop for lunch in the store's swanky top-floor restaurant, famous for its waiter service and pristine white cotton tablecloths.

Being a bit of a foodie, Susan salivated at the thought of the scrumptious mouth-watering meals on the menu and, still in charge, ordered steak and kidney pies, with all the trimmings, to be followed by her favourite sticky toffee pudding and finished off with a tray of the restaurant's speciality petit fours and fresh ground coffee. She was in heaven. Meanwhile her shy, retiring client smirked to himself behind his hand, watching his confident, erudite chaperon tucking into her lavish meal at his expense.

Not surprisingly, David was still in a state of shock, trying to come to terms with his new found wealth and prosperity, whilst his highly-strung companion was either racing about like a woman possessed, grabbing armfuls of exciting new clothes for his delectation, or devouring great mounds of food as though she hadn't eaten for days. David had been parachuted into a world that bore no resemblance to the existence he'd suffered for so many years. The impulsive shopper, with an unquenchable thirst and sweet tooth, didn't appreciate the turmoil he was suffering as she calmly devoured a second helping of sticky toffee pudding and ordered two speciality coffees with cream.

Susan was a charming, petite girl with shoulder-length blonde hair and pale green eyes and wore a cream figure-hugging dress, that showed off her slim sleek curves. During his high-speed shopping spree, he became increasingly enamoured by her striking good looks and natural charm and was most impressed by the way she took charge and made things happen. But in contrast to the frenetic antics of his overzealous colleague, the eye-catching views of Hastings' golden shoreline afforded a sense of peace and much needed serenity for the weary shopper, sitting quietly immersed in his own private thoughts.

"I've really enjoyed myself today David. Thank you very much," remarked his affable, easy-going companion, quickly dabbing some blobs of cream off her lower lip with her white crumpled linen napkin and getting to her feet.

"You're welcome Susan, and thank you for your help and for all the amazing clothes. I won't have to buy any more for years. I'm really kitted out. But could you tell me where I'm staying tonight, please?" he asked anxiously.

"It's all in hand. Don't worry. I'll take you there now," she replied. Just then a couple of familiar faces from the Men's Department came over to their table, collected up their bulky shopping bags and pushed them on a silver-framed trolley towards the waiting lift with instructions to deliver the items to the nearby Imperial Hotel.

David's hotel room was spacious, well decorated and furnished to a high standard, with a generous en suite bathroom, all the mod-cons and a gorgeous oval-shaped balcony. He was lost for words, struggling to understand how his dreary, pitiful existence had been transformed, changed out of all recognition in just a few short hours. He pricked himself to make sure he wasn't dreaming. Thankfully, he wasn't.

His luxurious accommodation offered uninterrupted views of the town's dramatic coastline with its wide expansive pebble beaches and miles of open water. The blue, tranquil sea was home to a number of sailing crafts. Sleek green and white ferries could be seen on the far horizon, plying their way up and down the English Channel. Single-masted yachts huddled together in the foreground, practising their seafaring manoeuvres under the watchful gaze of their megaphone-laden instructor shouting out his nautical instructions over the sound of breaking waves. Tall majestic yachts tacked their way towards the distant headland, bringing style and elegance to the seafaring shenanigans, appearing aloof and somewhat superior to the churlish antics of their smaller, noisier cousins. Hired motorboats and private launches coughed and spluttered their way through the undulating swell with fishing rods at the ready and fresh bait close at hand.

Standing on his spacious balcony, he was greeted by the captivating sight of the pale blue sea, cloudless skies and a warm pleasant breeze, accompanied by the familiar sound of noisy gulls squawking overhead.

David was most impressed by his new surroundings and thought Mr Crawford had done him proud. There was a comfortable double bed and a spacious wooden mahogany wardrobe for his collection of new clothes and trendy modern footwear. The lounge area comprised a simple writing desk, a modern twenty-four-inch television, a low-level coffee table, long slim settee and two matching reclining chairs. The generous-sized room was painted in magnolia which made it bright, friendly and quite homely. Some framed prints of local landmarks and places of interest in Sussex and neighbouring Kent adorned the walls giving the suite a warm, welcoming feeling, which was very much to his liking.

Later that day, on her way home, Susan popped in to see how her client was settling in, to give him his new cheque book and some cash and also her private telephone number, just in case he needed anything when their offices were closed.

The assistant solicitor was a few years older than David and lived with her elderly parents in the town where tedium and humdrum had been her constant companions, with monotony running a very close second. But that had all changed. It was quickly swept away thanks to the unexpected arrival of the fresh-faced birthday boy on 14th July, 1988. Their innocent lives had suddenly become intertwined and their relationship slowly blossomed and grew in the months and years ahead. Fate had conspired to bring the two lost souls together and life would never be quite the same again for Susan James now that David Lane had rolled into town and taken up residence at one of the most impressive addresses on the Sussex south coast.

The bracing sea air and stunning vista from his top-floor suite conspired to delight and enchant the well-heeled guest with every turn of his head, every beat of his heart. It was magical; a far cry from the turmoil he'd endured just a few short miles away. He loved it. David was quickly seduced by his new home and its cosy ambience and intended thanking Mr Crawford and Susan for their kindness next time their paths crossed.

Chapter 3

Edward Crawford was sat with his elderly wife on their veranda at the rear of their imposing Georgian house, sipping a glass of freshly squeezed orange juice and resting back on their matching garden chairs. They were enjoying the early evening sun on their faces with the gentle sound of birds chirping in the nearby hedgerow. In the distance, they could hear the occasional motor launch spluttering as it passed along the meandering coastline of small beaches and quaint sandy coves.

"Do you know something Doris? I think I've let a young man down very badly. You see, this rather downtrodden lad came into the office this morning so I could talk him through the terms of his parent's sizeable will. They were very wealthy and I met them once or twice many years ago, but I've failed them badly, very badly indeed. Now hear me out," said Mr Crawford, anticipating an unwelcome interruption from his forthright, often uncompromising wife, renowned for her strong views and straight talking. "You see, I assumed that Miss Jones, his legal guardian, had taken good care of the young man, as agreed in a settlement some five years ago following the death of David Lane's parents. Well, I was wrong. Very wrong. It looks as though he's been maltreated for some considerable time.

"I received regular letters from Miss Jones, which are all on file, giving me glowing reports on his progress which always sounded okay, very reassuring, or so I thought. But I think I've been spun a pack of lies, complete twaddle and I blame myself Doris. I should have checked on him personally, but I had no reason to suspect anything. It's a huge error of judgement on my part for which David Lane, my client, has paid the consequences and I've let him down badly."

He sighed very loudly. A deep frown appeared on his forehead and, with both hands shaking profusely, he wiped his eyes with his crumpled handkerchief while wrestling with his conscience, trying to come to terms with his lack of care and professional oversight towards a vulnerable client.

"Now listen here, Edward Crawford. Because we live in Littlestone, we're not privy to the local gossip and tittle-tattle and it's very difficult, my dear, to make house calls when you're so far away," replied Doris, in a firm, yet conciliatory tone. "You're a very busy man and you can't do everything Edward, so stop beating yourself up for goodness sake. You'll have another heart attack, if you're not very careful. Stop being silly, d'you hear?"

He wasn't convinced by his wife's cursory, almost dismissive explanation of events, but was flattered by her generous support and unwavering loyalty, even if it was somewhat misguided.

The elderly lawyer's ashen face reflected the torment and anguish he was undoubtedly feeling as pangs of guilt reverberated throughout his tortured body. He continued. "You see, David lived with his parents in Richmond and then, following their untimely death, came to Hastings to be cared for by his cousin. There was no alternative. It was either that, or local authority care, so the family option was the best choice, or so we thought. During our meeting today, this frightened young man, looking as though he had the problems of the world resting on his shoulders, took a scruffy piece of paper out of his trouser pocket, looked straight at me and read this little ditty, as he called it. It won't win any awards at the Cheltenham Literature Festival, it's not highbrow enough, but as a piece of simple prose, it really tugs at your heartstrings, brought a lump to my throat, I can tell you.

"I've done my time, done my bird, served my five year term,
Seen it through in good or ill, got nothing in return,
My body aches, my arms are numb, my head feels really sore,
But still I'm here, can walk and talk, can't ask for any more.
I really hope you'll stop and chat, say something nice to me,
Will speak my name, pat my back, I think I'm plain to see,
But then I wonder if I'm here, perhaps it's just a dream,
Do I exist, d'you really care, life seems so very mean."

It went very quiet and even Doris, with her lively intellect and quick wit, was speechless wondering what kind of damaged soul could compose such a tear-jerking insight into their innermost feelings. The distraught solicitor slouched back in his seat and, grasping his head between his hands, continued in a soft, submissive tone, sounding increasingly upset and distressed.

"But just imagine for one moment, my dear. You're only thirteen years old without a care in the world, living a life of wealth and privilege, when all of a sudden, everything you held dear is snatched away from you. Then, in a state of abject fear, you end up in a strange town, in a strange school, with unfamiliar surroundings and, to make matters worse, much worse, you have to put up with years of neglect and abuse at the very time when you needed love and attention. I can't bear thinking about it, Doris. It upsets me so."

He wiped his eyes, blew his nose and after a quick gulp of chilled orange, continued with his voice quivering as the emotional words tripped off his tongue.

"You see, this all happened at the time of my heart attack and I wasn't in the best of health, so I asked Peter Barma, one of our senior partners, to check on David from time to time, make sure everything was okay.

"Peter asked David's guardian to provide monthly reports of his progress and general health, which she did in glowing terms. I thought that would be sufficient, but sadly it wasn't. Miss James reckoned he'd be all right after a good hearty meal and a warm bath, but I'm not sure Doris. He looked such a drab, sullen specimen clutching onto his old battered suitcase and rubbing the knees of his shiny trousers. He was thin, frail and definitely undernourished. A sad sight, I can tell you."

"Now stop talking like this Edward. It's all turned out for the best in the end and you mustn't hold yourself responsible," she retorted, in an impatient, somewhat stern manner, with her red hair blowing in the breeze as if to reinforce the sense of irritation felt by the straight-talking octogenarian.

The lawyer was a pitiful sight strolling across the patterned flagstones of the marble patio at the rear of their six-bedroom house and over the recently mowed grass that squelched softly underfoot, following a recent downpour.

Leaning against the trunk of an elegant silver birch that hung gracefully over the manicured lawn, he wondered what he could do to rectify the situation. How he might change things for the better. Sadly, Edward's sleep eluded him that night. The vivid nightmares he'd suffered during his long convalescence, following his heart attack, returned to haunt and upset the elderly gent.

In subsequent days Doris, who was terminally ill and not in the best of health following a severe bout of shingles, made discreet enquires about Carol Jones. On the surface she was quite a normal, ordinary, everyday person, who was well regarded at her workplace and around the town and seemed to have an unblemished reputation. However, upon closer inspection, Doris was flabbergasted by Miss Jones's notoriety in her local community. Apparently her anxious neighbours lived in fear, often scared of what she might do if they complained, or questioned her in any way. Her extensive investigations revealed that she was a nasty piece of work. The retired magistrate, a victim of abuse herself, was horrified to hear of the alleged cruelty perpetrated by this Jekyll and Hyde creature on her shy vulnerable cousin, but decided to spare her husband the gory details, knowing it would only add to his health problems and put further strain on his failing heart. Instead, Doris put her many contacts to good use as her name was still influential in the close-knit legal community. Doris was determined to bring Miss Jones to book, if it was the last thing she did. She'd make her answer to the law for the years of neglect and ill-treatment she had meted out in an orchestrated campaign of terror directed at the vulnerable young man in her care.

Chapter 4

David ate his three-course dinner in his salubrious hotel room on his own, feeling too self-conscious to join the other guests in the ground-floor restaurant, whilst still reflecting on how his life had changed so dramatically in just twenty-four hours. He'd gone from rags to riches at the speed of light, waving goodbye to the poverty that symbolised his teenage years, to greeting his newfound wealth with open arms and a self-satisfied smile.

Instead of the house of horrors with the rantings of a drunken spinster, he now lived the life of Riley in a prestigious top-class hotel, where exquisite food and exotic mouth-watering drinks were the norm. During the main course, he fancied a glass of red wine, after all it was his birthday, but he quickly realised his error when a white Chardonnay was delivered on a stainless-steel tray by a friendly well-dressed waiter, with a strange foreign accent and a bad cold. On his earlier whirlwind shopping spree with his madcap colleague he bought a simple notebook and pencil from the stationery counter, encased inside a soft blue leather cover, with the store's monogram emblazoned on the front. Here he made copious notes and random jottings of experiences and events as they happened. So Chardonnay was duly recorded under the heading of white wines with Rioja listed as red.

As David sat there in his new red dressing gown, new slippers and new matching pyjamas, gazing out across the bay from the vantage point of his balcony, the sun was slowly setting against a bright flaming red sky, promising good things to come for all the local shepherds. It was a cool sultry July evening with just the constant drone of vehicles trundling along the main road whilst weary, red-faced holidaymakers made their way back to their overnight billets, clutching buckets and spades and bright colourful towels, after another day of thrills and spills on the fun-loving Sussex coast.

He remembered playing with his parents on Oddicombe beach, years earlier, collecting small seashells and tiny crabs in the many rock pools that bordered the golden sands. Of enjoying endless games of football and cricket, hearing the sound of the nearby funicular railway conveying droves of cheery holidaymakers up and down the sheer cliff face. He loved chewing gooey toffee apples and licking huge sticks of fluffy candyfloss that invariably stuck to his nose. David often helped his enterprising father build rows of misshapen sandcastles which they carefully decorated with seashells, urchins and flimsy paper flags bought from a nearby market stall. He'd dig a deep, oblong hole in the damp undulating sand and race backwards and forwards to the water's edge with plastic buckets brimming with clear seawater in an attempt to create a beach-bound water feature, but sadly it wasn't to be. To his dismay and consternation, the liquid always disappeared when his back was turned and he was never able to solve the plumbing problem. These were fond memories of his early childhood when innocent family fun was always on the menu and laughter and enjoyment the name of the game.

All of a sudden, a car hooted its horn at the traffic lights below, disturbing his daydreams as lines of tears trickled down his moist cheeks in sympathy while the sun finally gave up the ghost, disappearing behind a small blanket of dark clouds. The gaunt, tired-looking figure celebrated his birthday alone, toasting himself with another glass of wine from the freshly opened bottle of Rioja he'd ordered earlier from room service, before busily munching his way through a packet of salted peanuts. A savoury treat after his hearty meal of steak, chips and green beans. One of his favourite songs was by Buddy Holly, *Raining in My Heart*. The lyrics always struck a chord, and brought a tear to the eyes of the reluctant millionaire as he peered over the wrought-iron balcony towards the town's landmark pier glowing vividly in the distance, while dark grey skies enveloped the horizon bringing another summer's day to an abrupt end.

I love those words, he thought, quietly humming them under his breath. They capture my feelings and say so much about my life and my tragic loss. I pray to God for it to cease, for my agony and torment to end and for me to be reunited with my beloved parents and my nightmare to be no more.

As the drink took effect, his mind started to wander. He reflected on his vast inheritance; his sudden untold wealth. David tried to imagine how tall sixty million pounds would be if he stacked five pound notes on top of one another from the street many floors below. I bet it would be a huge tower, several metres high, he surmised, gazing over the balcony at the noisy bustling scene beneath him. But sadly as always, his cheery light-hearted mood was temporary, short-lived, when the enormity of his tragic loss, that had brought him his good fortune, returned to haunt him, making David wonder whether life was really worth living when isolation and bereavement were his constant bedfellows.

With due reverence, David lifted the gold locket wrapped in some soft crinkly paper in his old green suitcase and placed it on the bedside table. He then collapsed back onto his spacious double bed and gazed up at the ceiling longingly. Inside the precious heirloom were pictures of Louise and Jeremy Lane, his wonderful parents. Looking at their familiar smiling faces, he wished they could be with him to celebrate his big birthday, to enjoy the special occasion, but sadly it wasn't to be. The crestfallen teenager cried himself to sleep that night, something he'd done for many months. He was still trying to come to terms with his miserable existence, understand why he was spared an early grave. As always, the prospect of joining his parents in heaven was a far better proposition than the pitiful life he'd been forced to endure. He wondered why he was snatched from a life of love, warmth and kindness, to be orphaned at thirteen years of age, left to fend for himself in the so-called care of his evil demented cousin with a penchant for cheap booze and leather straps. But then as if by magic, like the flick of a switch, his life changed dramatically on his eighteenth birthday when a smart, debonair gentleman in a pinstripe suit with a passion for rugby told him, as he nibbled on a ginger nut, that he was a multi-millionaire, he was a lucky young man and the world was his oyster. Well it was the stuff of legends, like a far-fetched script in a cheesy soap opera, or a piece of cheap teatime fiction. Unfortunately, however, David Lane's life wasn't a fantasy or a fable, it was reality and he had the emotional and physical scars to prove it.

Later that night, stumbling his way back from the bathroom after being sick yet again from the rich food and red wine, he gawped at himself in the ornate oblong mirror, hanging from the wall between the television and the coffee table. What a sad-looking specimen, he thought, with his dull sour expression, spindly undernourished frame and an unruly mop of hair that had a will of its own. Gazing at his bleak sombre reflection, he swore he'd never celebrate another birthday on his own and, with his fragile stomach intact, the birthday boy climbed back into bed under the freshly ironed cotton sheets, smelling sweet and fragrant and very soft against his skin. He then caressed the gold locket with his outstretched fingers, and drifted off to sleep.

Chapter 5

During the next three years, David met Mr Crawford on a twice-weekly basis, availing himself of his business counselling and support services. Here he learnt about financial management and general day-to-day budgeting, all of which filled great gaps in his knowledge, giving him a good basic grounding in preparation for the many challenges ahead. He kept copious notes of their meetings, which he filed and indexed for future reference and were carefully stored away in a series of large lever-arch files.

David used his spare time to broaden his understanding of world affairs, economics, history, geography and English literature and was a regular visitor to the town's library. There he spent many an afternoon studying and recording information in his bulging files and notebooks.

Invariably his mornings were set aside for keeping fit and building up his body strength. He'd jog around the streets of Hastings for an hour or two at a time, but when the weather was wet and windy, you'd find him using the hotel's impressive facilities, either pounding the treadmill, or swimming up and down in the well-equipped state-of-the-art sports centre. The attentive hotel staff was well accustomed to their wealthy guest traipsing backwards and forwards with mounds of books, folders and periodicals. The bookworm took his education very seriously, knowing he'd very soon be master of his own destiny, responsible for managing his many portfolios, whatever they were.

He'd have to stand on his own two feet in a hard-hitting, uncompromising world that took no prisoners according to Mr Crawford. Needless to say his thirst for knowledge, his obsession with learning, was a double-edged sword. It stopped the student dwelling on the past, thinking about his family's misfortunes, and at the same time allowed him to acquire the necessary know-how so he could take full control of his affairs following his twenty-first birthday when the stabilisers would come off. The first few weeks were difficult trying times for the loner, who often felt isolated and insecure, but thanks to Mr Crawford's gentle reassuring words, he gradually became more positive and upbeat about the future.

However, David's quest for self-improvement was taken to a more personal level with the timely intervention of Susan James. On Tuesday, Thursday and Sunday evenings, she added a bit of spice and pizzazz to his world of academia by introducing him to raunchy sex, Hastings style. This was a real bonus as far as the teenager was concerned, adding some much-needed zest to his rather boring, pedestrian existence. So needless to say the spotty-faced youth seized the opportunity with both hands, throwing himself into their saucy evening encounters with great relish and uninhibited enthusiasm.

Then late one afternoon, when he was relaxing in the hotel lounge after a demanding session under the duvet, which left parts of his nether regions feeling sore and tender, he had an unexpected visitor. David was wondering whether to struggle out of his comfortable leather armchair and have another gentle soak in the hot tub before dinner, when an elderly lady with a noisy walking stick approached him.

"Excuse me, young man. Are you by chance, David Lane?" she asked in a confident, direct manner.

"Yes, I am," he replied.

"I'm sorry to interrupt you unannounced, but I wanted to meet you and as I was in town doing some last-minute shopping, I thought I'd pop in on the off chance."

"Please take a seat," said David, standing up and pointing his visitor in the direction of the adjacent chair whilst placing her walking stick in the umbrella stand directly behind her seat.

"Can I offer you something to drink or eat?" he asked politely.

"No, thank you. I'll get straight to the point if I may. My name is Doris Crawford, my husband's your solicitor and no doubt well known to you."

David smiled and nodded his head several times, but was unsure where the conversation was going.

"I've heard so many glowing reports about you from Edward that I feel as though I know you, but I wanted to meet you in the flesh, so to speak."

Not another one, thought David, gently rubbing his thighs and adjusting his seating position as the cheeks of his bottom felt as though they were on fire, ready to explode at any moment.

"I know you've had a tough time and forgive me for being forward, but I wondered whether there's anything I can do to help. Edward's always singing your praises, my dear."

David smiled quizzically, looked over his shoulder in the direction of the adjoining cocktail bar, thinking how best to respond. It was a long time since anyone had taken a real interest in him and for some strange reason he seemed at ease, even comfortable in the old lady's company.

Eventually, after a few moments' thought he turned to face his elderly inquisitor who was dressed in a plain tweed suit, smart beige shoes and a green silk scarf with a mop of long flaming red hair resting untidily on her broad shoulders.

"My parents died in an accident a long time ago. It still haunts me and I guess it always will. I don't think I have the right to live and spend their money on myself. Everything seems so unfair. I miss them so very much."

Doris was ill-prepared for this sudden heart-rending outburst after just a short time in his company, but unperturbed leaned forward in her easy chair, resting her arthritic arms on the wide curved wings and said. "Now listen to me. There's always a reason for things. Sadly your parents died when you were young, but they loved you very much and thankfully made provision for your future. Surely you owe it to them to do your best and not let them down? My husband says they were a happy, fun-loving couple, who worshiped and adored you and the last thing they'd want to see is you moping about feeling sorry for yourself."

She rested back, wondering whether she might have been a tad too direct, too forthright for the hapless young man, particularly as they'd only just met and didn't know each other at all, so she bit her lower lip and waited anxiously for his response.

For David, it wasn't the reply he was expecting. He was rather put out by her hectoring tone of voice and lack of sympathy for his plight, but as he reflected on her stern insensitive comments decided, rather reluctantly, that she talked sense even though her style was a little brusque for his liking.

This first rather unconventional encounter was the prelude to a number of weekly chats where she would meet David to talk about anything that came to mind. Doris implored her companion not to mention their meetings to her husband as it would only serve to worry him and put more pressure on his failing health. David was more than happy to oblige. For the first couple of months, he was reluctant to open up and confide in her, so these sessions were brief quiet affairs of limited value. But slowly and surely, as he trusted Doris more and more, so David's confidence grew and he became increasingly animated and more vocal. He talked with passion and emotion about his early childhood, explaining with great fluency his love and adoration for his mother, describing how they'd spend many happy hours together in local parks and playgrounds laughing and joking and messing about when his workaholic father was away on long business trips.

He reminisced about their many family holidays abroad, their precious times together and waxed lyrical about the majestic lakes of northern Italy, the enchanting scenery that captured his imagination, the wonderful food and the warm, welcoming people. Famous places, such as Stressa, Garda, Riva, Malcesine, Peschiera, Verona and Venice tripped off his tongue as though he'd been a recent visitor to Italy and had returned in the last few days. The sweeping coastlines of the Cote d'Azur, the enchanting Bay of Naples and their exciting family trips to Paris and Barcelona, conjured up many timeless memories which he loved to talk about and relive time and time again.

David became really animated and sometimes tearful when he mentioned their favourite resorts in Devon and how his energetic father would drive the long journey from Richmond to Babbacombe in their posh sleek 3.2 litre crimson-coloured Jag, with cream-coloured leather seats and a mahogany drinks cabinet in the back. During the long, tedious journey on the A303, they'd laugh, joke and play endless games of I-spy, before checking into their hotel suite with its splendid panoramic views across Lyme Bay while the world famous Jurassic Coastline and Chesil Beach were only a stone's throw away.

David sometimes talked about life at the hands of his sadistic bullies, describing how they would beat and burn him for no apparent reason. On one occasion, much to Doris's surprise, he even showed her the scars on his back and shoulders and his permanently bruised right ankle, thanks to Martin Conway, that throbbed if he overdid the exercise. These were the trophies of his tragic youth, as he called them. However, the teenager was invariably reluctant to spend too much time talking about that dark period in his life, often evading any direct questions for fear of opening up old wounds and revisiting bad memories.

"Carol could be okay some days. I'd have a hot meal when I got home from school, she'd talk about her day and what she'd been up to. She worked part-time as a checkout at the Co-op in Bexhill about five miles away. Carol's quite tall, with short cropped hair and quite muscular arms and legs. She rarely wore make-up and always dressed in trousers and loose-fitting tops and is about fifteen years older than me," he explained.

"But then most days when I arrived home she'd be shouting at the current boyfriend, drinking bottles of cider and beer and falling all over the place. That was the signal for me to disappear; do a runner. So I'd grab a quick sandwich, some pieces of fruit and anything else I could find in the fridge and beat a hasty retreat to my salubrious hotel suite on the first-floor." He smirked when he said it.

"She was evil, crude and bad-tempered and often took out her anger on me by burning my back and shoulders, or beating me with a stick, or an old leather strap she kept hidden under the stairs. When she was really upset her face went bright red, like a fresh ripe tomato and her cold, heartless eyes stuck out as though they were on springs. She looked evil, I can tell you. Her ugly pear-shaped head was ready to explode at any moment and her strong muscular arms and big manly hands shook when the rage took hold and her whole body seemed possessed by the Devil. She was evil, really evil. I'm glad I'm rid of her. Do you know something Doris? My last night at number five was a case in point. Outside I could see from my tiny bedroom window the old witch sky-high on drugs and swigging scrumpy out of a plastic bottle, shouting all manner of obscenities at a bunch of shocked Jehovah's Witnesses quietly conferring at the end of the drive. That was what she was like, most days.

"Here's a funny thing. I discovered quite by chance that she hated mice and spiders and was frightened to death of anything that crawled. So I'd bring things home from school, let them loose downstairs and every couple of days, I'd hear her loud piercing shrieks, followed by the sound of broken crockery. I'd chuckle to myself, knowing that she'd found one of my little hairy friends. That was fun and it brought a bit of humour to my daily routine. I also found out that she was scared of fire, something to do with her childhood, but I don't know what. I also found out from one of the nosy neighbours that the wicked witch hated water, which was a strange thing considering we lived in a coastal town. Carol always refused point blank to go anywhere near the sea. Apparently she nearly drowned when she was on holiday once on the Algarve so trips around the bay were a no-no. She was a bit of a wreck, really," reflected David with a sinister grin.

To Doris's surprise, David sometimes even joked about the house of horrors and Carol's antisocial behaviour, but said his abiding memory was the loud, thumping music. It was a big part of his teenage years and even though it often got between him and a good night's sleep, many of the tunes had remained with him to the present day.

"It took my mind off things and made me feel happy," he said. "Harry Chapin's *WOLD* was a firm favourite and so was Mick Jagger's *19th Nervous Breakdown*. The irony of the Beatles' chart topping single, *All You Need is Love*, made me chuckle to myself. But I shall never forget *Green Onions*. The thumping bass made my wobbly bed vibrate and the old wooden wardrobe didn't stand a chance, shaking in protest in the corner. Jimmy Page's relentless journey on his *Stairway to Heaven* had a similar effect on my rickety furniture and dodgy central heating pipes. The Four Tops always got my vote with *Reach Out I'll be There*. I loved that rhythmic melody. It always made me smile as I pranced aimlessly around my prison cell, happily singing along. This musical escapism helped me to keep sane, survive my ordeal," he explained with a wry smile.

And so it was. David's regular fix of high-octane rock and pop music, late at night, brought a splash of colour to his dull and dreary bedroom. He took temporary solace on his magical mystery tour, in the exulted company of the Beatles, Sting, Fleetwood Mac and Led Zeppelin, with the drunken witch spinning the 45s, rolling around downstairs, half-cut, hardly able to stand.

Doris sat for hours listening intently to David, often not fully understanding what he was talking about, but that didn't matter; it wasn't important. For many months, she was afforded a privileged glimpse into his world and realised that even though life had been tough and uncompromising, devoid of any warmth and kindness, David Lane had come through the ordeal, relatively unscathed. During their time together, she was gratified to see her husband's counselling sessions had paid off, witnessing firsthand his gradual transformation from a shy, introverted, badly dressed teenager, to a confident more self-assured young man.

There was one salutary, unforgettable moment that Doris would always remember until her dying day. It was on a cold and wet morning in late October, a week before Halloween, when the wind and the leaves had a will of their own and the outlook for the weather leading up to the celebrations wasn't good. The pair were quietly drinking Earl Grey tea and munching their way through a plate of freshly baked scones in the hotel's impressive orangery when, without warning, her impulsive companion dropped his china cup and saucer onto the glass-topped coffee table with an almighty crash, making horrified guests peer over in surprise.

David turned and looked straight at her with streams of tears slowly rolling down his cheeks and, in a trembling voice said, "Whatever they did to me Doris, whatever they said, however they hurt me, they couldn't take my memories away, my sacred memories of my beloved Ma and Pa. They're so vivid, so real that I can almost imagine they're still alive. They're buried in my heart and soul. Precious, timeless gifts that they bequeathed to me and I shall cherish them forever until one day, God willing, I shall meet them again. Oh, I miss them so much Doris, so much."

It was a poignant moment in their relationship charged with raw emotion, such that Doris, the tough, retired magistrate, with a forthright manner and tongue to match, was forced to take refuge in the ladies' ground-floor toilets if only for the sake of her reputation and professional dignity.

On her return, having regained her composure, but still dabbing her eyes with a paper tissue, she sipped her luke-warm tea in silence and gazed at the brave young man sat opposite, imagining how Jeremy and Louise Lane would have felt if they could have seen their only son. How proud they would have been of his strength and resolve against the unrelenting powers of evil and hatred, when all the odds were so heavily stacked against him. He was a credit to them.

But there was a strange thing that often mystified the elderly counsellor when she quietly relaxed in her garden at home, reflecting on her recent session with David. She sometimes noticed during their chats, many of which were highly charged encounters, that his thighs and lower back were clearly giving him trouble, judging by his uncomfortable wriggling and strange facial expressions when he moved about in his soft leather chair. Doris put it down to his overzealous exercise regime without thinking, for one moment, that her husband's legal assistant was responsible for his physical discomfort as part of his ongoing initiation into the wild, unforgiving world of *the Kama Sutra*.

Chapter 6

Then one day, the top-floor resident at the Imperial Hotel had some special visitors. David had been languishing in the luxurious surroundings of the imposing four-star hotel for some time, gradually settling into his lavish lifestyle when a strange thing happened as the leaves were falling, the nights drew in and the cold winter months beckoned just around the corner.

Unannounced, the local police made a visit to his salubrious hideaway and, because of the seriousness of their mission, they asked Mr Crawford to join them. His imposing guests sat around his highly polished wooden coffee table, looking uncomfortable and rather glum. The two police officers removed their leather-bound notebooks from their breast pockets and Chief Inspector Campbell explained the reason for their early morning call.

He was short, overweight and bald, with bristly facial skin that was dark and seemed in need of a shave. He had pitch-black eyes, with badly bitten fingernails and dark brown shoes that hadn't seen polish in ages. He was accompanied by Constable Parry, a young raw recruit of a similar age to David. He was slim, fair-haired and appeared nervous, sitting quietly alongside his boss, no doubt learning the ropes.

The inspector coughed, cleared his throat, then glanced up from his official notebook and said. "I'm sorry to intrude upon your time, but unfortunately I have some very bad news for you David, and I've asked Mr Crawford here to join me as I understand you know him very well."

David frowned, nodded and looked on intently whilst massaging his lower back, promising to have a quiet word with Susan next time they met following her overzealous antics with his bare buttocks the night before.

"Unfortunately, there was a serious fire at 5 Dewhurst Road yesterday evening and I regret to say your cousin, Carol Jones, died in the house from smoke inhalation. I'm very sorry for your loss, it must come as a terrible shock for you. I can arrange for Constable Parry here to stay with you if you want any support," remarked the inspector in a soft, conciliatory tone. It all went quiet with just the obligatory sound of squawking seagulls and noisy car engines in the background. The trio waited for David's response; his reaction to the devastating news which they knew would come as a terrible shock, be very upsetting for the smartly dressed hotel guest who, judging by his pained expression, was clearly in a great deal of discomfort.

"I don't need any help, thank you. I'm okay," replied David. He tried to appear concerned, even distressed by the unexpected revelation of his cousin's untimely demise but, if truth be known, he found it difficult to control his emotions and play the part of the bereaved, distraught relative.

David was duty bound to look upset by the devastating news that should have cast a dark cloud of despair across the room, reduced him to a snivelling wreck, sending him reaching for the paper tissues to soak up the endless flood of tears. But in actual fact, all David wanted to do was race around the suite shouting and cheering at the top of his voice, doing cartwheels from wall to wall with the pulsating sound of *Green Onions* blasting out in the background, and swigging umpteen glasses of expensive champagne to toast his cousin's timely reunion with the Devil. But that didn't seem quite appropriate, especially in such exalted company, so the celebrations would be on hold and the amateur dramatics would have to continue for the time being.

"As you'll appreciate, David, our enquiries are at an early stage at the moment, but I will let you have further details of the tragedy when they emerge following the fire service's examination of the scene and our own investigations," explained the grim-faced inspector with his partly chewed biro dangling precariously in the corner of his mouth. "Before I forget. I'd like to ask you one thing, if I may. Did your cousin ever mention her wishes in the event of death? Forgive me. I know it sounds very insensitive to raise the issue at this difficult time, but as you're the only living relative, we wondered whether she'd ever mentioned the subject. I'm sorry to have to ask you, but I'm sure you understand our predicament and the situation we're in," explained the inspector rubbing his neck with both hands and appearing embarrassed.

The shell-shocked relative reflected on his time at the hands of his vile cousin who he despised with a passion before gazing across his hotel room towards the open double doors and the welcoming balcony that had been the venue for many of his infamous late-night drinking sessions.

After a few moments quiet contemplation, David said, with a quiver in his voice, "I remember her joking one day, she liked to laugh and joke you know, saying that she wanted to be cremated if anything ever happened and her ashes spread across the sea. Carol loved to stroll along the beach and spent many a happy hour walking the coastal paths and sitting on the pier. That was one of her favourite spots, just sitting quietly in a deckchair listening to the waves breaking on the seashore. I can almost see her now. Those were her wishes, as far as I can remember, and I think we should respect them if at all possible," said the distraught relative, dabbing his eyes with his index finger, gently sucking his bottom lip, all the time making sure he didn't make eye contact with Mr Crawford.

The inspector made a quick note in his book, glanced at the solicitor and, sensing David's discomfort, the anxious-looking visitors stood and slowly ambled towards the door, glancing back as they did, making sure the bereaved teenager was okay and not too upset by the tragic turn of events.

"Oh, one thing before we leave, David. I nearly forgot to mention it. As you're the only living relative and Miss Jones died intestate then the house will be yours, to do as you wish," said Mr Crawford, opening the door and shaking his hand before wandering down the corridor towards the nearby lift.

David's ornate lounge mirror was the only witness to his broad beaming smile that stretched across his face. He jumped up and down with tightly clenched fists raised towards the heavens shouting Yeah! Yeah! Yeah! at the top of his voice. He raced around the room clapping and cheering, celebrating her demise with the powerful, hypnotic sounds of 'Booker T' blasting out in the background.

I hope she likes the funeral arrangements, it was the least I could do after all she'd done for me, he chuckled to himself. The rogue slumped back into his comfortable easy chair, plonked his feet on the coffee table with a resounding thump, before slowly running his manicured fingers down the hotel wine list, searching for the most expensive bottle of champagne with which to celebrate the end of Miss de Vil.

"Should I give David a call in a couple of days?" asked Constable Parry, as the lift slowly descended to the ground floor.

"No, I think he's all right, he didn't seem too upset by Miss Jones's death. Do you agree, Edward?" asked Inspector Campbell when the squeaky lift juddered to a grinding halt on the ground floor.

"Yes," replied the solicitor, grinning. The party then strolled towards the long narrow reception desk where the hotel staff were busily handling the mid-morning check-outs and taking telephone bookings from holidaymakers hoping to savour the many delights of Sussex's premier coastal resort. "He's put up with a lot in his short dramatic life, but the loss of his cousin won't concern him too much, I can assure you," explained Mr Crawford, with a cheeky smirk. He then bade a fond farewell to the local boys in blue and walked briskly along the seafront, in the direction of his grand palatial offices, dodging between bustling crowds of tourists out enjoying the warm, autumn sun and the town's holiday atmosphere.

That David Lane never fails to amaze me, thought Edward, shaking his head and laughing to himself just as a young toddler with a yellow sailor's hat and an orange bucket and spade careered straight into him.

"Sorry mister," he mumbled, after a bit of hasty prompting from his bad-tempered mother with a bright red face and a cigarette butt hanging from the corner of her mouth. Edward bent down and picked up his walking stick and carried merrily on his way, still thinking about the artful dodger's one-man show that he'd just witnessed at the Imperial Hotel. It was truly memorable and deserved an award. It was that good.

The funeral took place a week later, but the distraught relative was too upset, too distressed to attend the church service and made his excuses which everyone fully understood, with the exception of Mr and Mrs Crawford. They thought that following his Oscar-winning performance with the police, he'd probably find it difficult keeping up the sombre pretence of the grieving cousin throughout the one-hour ceremony. But David felt duty bound to make an appearance at the cremation, if only to witness Carol's safe passage to the after-life. However, his choice of music at the beginning of the service was quite distasteful according to Mr Crawford. He sat rigid throughout, completely traumatised with embarrassment when Elvis Presley let rip with his chart-topping single, *His Latest Flame*. Then to make matters worse, knowing the deceased's heart-felt fear of the sea, David chose a medley of sea shanties featuring *Whiskey*

Johnny, Bully in the Alley and *The Drunken Sailor.* These were played as the coffin disappeared behind the dingy, grey curtains before long lines of mourners trooped out of the church. Some were predictably glum and upset, leaning on each other for support, while in contrast, a large number of the congregation appeared cheerful, even uplifted by her sad demise, walking with a pronounced skip in their step towards a seafront bar with the promise of light refreshments and a well-earned glass of bubbly, thanks to the kindness of her only living relative.

Later that day, the solemn scattering of the ashes took place at the end of Hastings Pier and David looked on with delight when her powdery remains landed on a gooey mass of engine oil and soggy debris, then floated up and down on the choppy waters before eventually dispersing into tiny waterlogged fragments on the outgoing tide.

The incorrigible Mr Lane was a class act. He'd duped the chatty, affable vicar, with a narrow pointed nose and freckles, into believing that his dearly departed cousin loved the sea and the memories it evoked and that she also had an overwhelming passion for the soft dulcet sounds of Presley's wavering vibrato. But sadly, it couldn't have been further from the truth. The visiting cleric, from nearby Battle, was unaware of the circumstances leading up to Carol's untimely death in a smoke-filled room in a quiet suburban backwater, otherwise he'd have disallowed the music on the grounds of bad taste and gross insensitivity.

So ended one of the sad chapters in David's troubled early years. He felt rejuvenated, even invigorated now that his cousin's name was consigned to history and her memory a mere blot on the landscape.

Things settled down in the weeks ahead and David returned to his books and fitness training with increased urgency. Then, for some reason, Doris stopped calling on him and he wondered what was up and, during one of their business sessions, Edward mentioned that his wife was seriously ill, confined to bed and the prognosis wasn't good. Sadly, he never saw Doris again and apparently she died some months later. David was very much indebted to her for her blunt outspoken advice, her candid uncompromising opinions and for never letting him feel sorry for himself. He was frequently annoyed by her forthright views and her boorish attitude. But it worked, it helped him accept his lot; his roll of the dice and, in doing so, turn his back on self-centred feelings of remorse and, instead, look to the future with optimism and real hope.

David smiled to himself when he remembered some of her quirky, off the wall expressions, very much reminiscent of a bygone age. At one meeting, he took the bull by the horns, enquired about her age. Well she was really put out by his cheeky impudence and told him in no uncertain manner. "It's for me to know and you to ponder," was her angry retort.

It was as though Doris was quoting a passage from a nineteenth-century Dickens novel, or a chapter from *Wuthering Heights*. It was priceless and symbolised Doris to a tee. He'd never forget the rather plump, stout lady with blazing red hair who was no doubt a formidable presence when passing sentence on some poor quivering wreck shaking in the dock. Apparently grown men, with a history of wrongdoing, would quake in their boots at the mere mention of her name, such was the fear of her caustic, razor-sharp tongue. Rumour had it that she was a committed supporter of capital punishment and would welcome the return of the birch for many minor criminal offences, such as fouling the streets, failing to pay council tax on time and parking on double yellow lines, but that was all conjecture and never proved.

Doris was his guardian angel and confidant when he really needed one. He'd always remember her gushing smile, her animated hand gestures and words of wisdom, some of which were captured for posterity in the lad's extensive filing system. Doris would always have a special place in David Lane's heart. A very special place indeed.

Chapter 7

During the three years David stayed at the hotel, Susan called on him regularly. As well as indulging in a hearty three-course lunch with all the trimmings, the enthusiastic solicitor threw herself into an array of sexual antics with boundless energy and unbridled enthusiasm. The memory of their unrestrained encounters often lingered for days after. David invariably felt sore and strangely uncomfortable in places he never knew existed, such was the ferocity of their lovemaking. Many's the time he'd choose the creaky hotel lift for the return trip to his suite in preference to climbing the stairs, as the prospect of scaling the north face of the Eiger promised to be an uncomfortable experience for any moving parts below the waistline.

There were times when the immature teenager was angry and frustrated and took out his wrath on the poor, hard-working hotel staff, who always tolerated his unpredictable mood-swings, knowing he was a troubled soul in need of support rather than finger-pointing and criticism. Sometimes the miscreant overdid the alcohol, got legless, even blind drunk, and then feeling ebullient, treated late-night revellers and passers-by to a montage of rock and pop songs, delivered with great oratorical passion from the sanctuary of his stylish, top-floor balcony.

However, there was one part of David's intensive education that was sadly lacking. He was devoid of any moral compass, any sense of propriety and, following his raunchy encounters with Susan, imagined that all women were fair game and uninhibited sexual gratification was par for the course. The norm. There was a period when he entertained prostitutes in his room, much to the disgust of the hotel management. But thankfully it was only a passing phase as Miss James stepped up her evening visits, at the behest of the hotel manager, keeping her sex-mad client fully occupied in the trouser department.

The exuberant youngster sometimes attracted the wrath of nearby guests late at night when he sang along with Steve Winwood and Gerry Rafferty, or tried imitating Mick Jagger whilst gyrating around the room in front of the mirror with the bathroom backscratcher acting as a makeshift microphone and the Bosch CD player blasting out on full volume. But when the performer's mood was more melancholic, more downbeat, then the top-floor guests were treated to the classics in the guise of Debussy's *Clair de Lune*, Bach's *Air from Suite No 3*, or the smooth melodic strings of Elgar's *Nimrod from the Enigma Variations.*

Away from his impromptu, often drink-fuelled night-time shenanigans, the musical maestro continued spending hours in the hotel lounge studying and writing up his notes. On these occasions he'd sometimes look up from his work, take a breather and be surprised to see how badly dressed the male population was sauntering past his discreet vantage point. He imagined there'd be very little difference between their day-to-day clothes and the garments that adorned their bodies when they were mowing their lawns, or pottering about in their garden sheds. This made him think as he sipped his percolated coffee and observed many of his male contempories dressed slovenly in their old-fashioned, ill-fitting clothes often with poor body postures. To make matters worse, some of the ungainly male residents boasted flabby stomachs that hung over the tops of their trousers, stretching their overworked elastic waistbands to breaking point.

So the wise young man with a sophisticated musical ear, a stack of money under the bed and an immature streak that sometimes got him into trouble, came to a salutary conclusion. If he was to make his mark in life, stand out from the crowd, then he had to dress well, really well. His manners had to be impeccable, his diction near perfect and his general knowledge had to be better than most. David believed these qualities would ingratiate him with the opposite sex, give him a head start over the tiresome, badly dressed, beige and greys. They may be better connected and more streetwise than me, he agreed, but if I work on the things that count, am more colourful, more fun than the scruffy, chubby-faced competition, with the dress sense of an orang-utan, then the world should be my oyster. Of course his untold wealth gave him the edge, was a sure-fire winner in the love stakes, a guaranteed passport to a lady's heart. So if he splashed the cash like stardust in the breeze, dressed in the finest designer clothes that money could buy, then the bright-eyed playboy would have the fair maidens rushing to his door, swooning at his feet, or so he thought.

The teenager knew he had to keep fit and alert both mentally and physically. For part of his rigorous exercise regime, he enjoyed running through the Alexandra Park that snakes its way alongside the town's bustling streets and hectic thoroughfares, down towards the open sea with its breathtaking views of the English Channel. He'd occasionally take a breather in the square-shaped peace garden, where he'd admire the splash of seasonal colour displayed in well-stocked borders and flower beds. In the summer months, when the sun was at its highest, the fragrant smell of scented roses floated on the breeze as the athlete's muscular legs pounded passed on the uneven gravel surface.

David spent many hours in the hotel lounge, with its enchanting views of the renowned wall garden, its long winding arbour and beautifully manicured lawns. It was light and airy, with large imposing chandeliers hanging from the pale blue ceiling at opposite ends of the room. An array of comfortable settees and easy chairs allowed their pampered guests to sit and chat and enjoy the snacks and refreshing drinks from the neighbouring cocktail bar. The atmosphere was convivial and peaceful, very much conducive to private studies and people watching – both of which were amongst some of David's favourite pastimes.

For relaxation, he sometimes sat back in his customary soft leather chair, with its wide swooping wings and patterned bronze buttons, indulging in some light-hearted reading care of Mills & Boon. Even though he often found the story lines a bit far-fetched for his taste, he nevertheless enjoyed escaping into a fantasy world of passion, love and betrayal. It sounded quite provocative.

The avid reader also got hooked on Tom Sharpe and was bowled over by his wicked, irreverent sense of humour. The page turner sometimes laughed out loud, much to the surprise and annoyance of the elderly guests who sat resting, or sleeping peacefully, nearby. Poems were a regular feature in many periodicals and local newspapers, which interested the wordsmith very much, inspiring him to put pen to paper, try his hand at composing little ditties, as he called them.

The staff, as always, were at his beck and call. He only had to raise a finger, or nod his head and a cup of piping hot coffee with freshly baked biscuits would arrive on a silver tray, whilst the transient hotel guests took second place to the needs of the well-heeled millionaire, with deep pockets and a penchant for generous tips.

There was an occasion, in the spring of his second year at the Imperial, when David was admiring the curvaceous figures of the female staff sweeping passed when he had a sudden brainwave; an idea for a poem. He quickly snapped closed his lever-arch file, grabbed his fountain pen and A4 pad and after about twenty minutes of frantic scribbling, with much huffing and puffing, he'd composed a piece of romantic rhyme:

She's a wine to be savoured,
A romantic melody,
A soft blend of pure compassion,
Choirs sing in harmony.
She personifies perfection,
Stands out for all to see,
And that is why my darling Sue,
Is just the one for me.

A few moments later, David manoeuvred himself out of his comfy chair, feeling quite pleased with himself, gathered up his files and umpteen textbooks and staggered towards the ground-floor lift. Anne, an attractive happy-go-lucky waitress, called out to him. "Excuse me sir, but you've dropped something." She bent down and picked up a carefully folded piece of A4 paper lying on the carpet underneath the low-level mahogany coffee table. "Is that a poem? Can I see it please?" she asked.

He nodded, but then much to his embarrassment the pretty giggly girl, with a short stubbly nose and petite figure, grabbed her reading glasses from her pinafore breast pocket and read it out loud.

"That's very good, how clever of you. I wish I was clever and could write like that."

"Thank you, but I don't think it's finished yet," he replied, looking rather bashful at hearing such gushing praise for his first attempt at rhyme.

"I may carry on with it later today," remarked David, grabbing hold of his bulging collection of textbooks and folders. Seeing the resident scholar's predicament, Anne gently slid the piece of paper under his chin that was resting on top of a stack of novels and dashed towards the lift and pressed the button with her thumb.

Rumour had it that Anne was recently caught in a compromising position with the wannabe poet, following one of his late-night drinking sessions, but the suggestion was strongly denied by David. Outrageous was his only response, when challenged by the nervous deputy manager, fearing the wrath of their esteemed resident when questioned on such a delicate matter.

Anne, however, kept quiet about the alleged encounter refusing to confirm, or deny anything, but her red blushes and frantic nail biting were viewed as an admission of guilt by her streetwise colleagues, fully aware of the warning signs and what their young impressionable colleague had been up to. As the lift doors slammed shut with a resounding thump, she called out. "By the way, congratulations on passing your driving test yesterday sir, well done!"

After a bit of awkward fumbling, the ham-fisted guest managed to push open the door to his room, whereupon he threw his bulky cargo across the double bed, slipped out of his green moccasins and collapsed back against the deep crimson headboard. A poet, eh? he thought to himself. That would be another string to my bow, give me the edge, he surmised, as his head sank into the soft, fragrant pillow and Keats' youthful protégé promptly drifted off to sleep.

Chapter 8

When the multitude of birthday cards landed on his mat, from his many well-wishers, the shy forlorn character that crossed Mr Crawford's threshold some years earlier had been transformed into a more self-assured, more confident young man, looking well-groomed in a pair of freshly ironed white trousers with a razor-sharp crease and deep blue slippers. His pale blue, short-sleeved shirt was tucked neatly into his trousers and a cream leather belt fastened firmly around his slim waist, a testimony to hours of exercise and a balanced, fat-free diet.

So thanks to Barma, Higgins and Crawford, and some frisky hands-on input from the exuberant unabashed Miss James, his education was complete. The good-looking guy with a hefty bank balance and a penchant for the better things of life was ready to take on the world. The high-roller had languished in the august Imperial Hotel for over three years, living the good life, enjoying the trappings of wealth, but shortly after his twenty-first birthday the inscrutable Mr Lane checked out of his temporary home, shook hands with the affable general manager and kissed one or two of the attractive female staff, looking on with tissues at the ready.

"We shall all miss you very much," said Mr Clarke, with a saucy grin and wink of the eye as the pair stood at reception waiting for the HP printer to spew out his final receipt. The suave hotel manager with a slight lisp and red birthmark across his neck was always well dressed in his customary three-piece lounge suit, colourful eye-catching tie and highly polished leather shoes.

"It's been a great pleasure having you as a guest and we hope you've enjoyed your stay and will return to see us. I know we've had our little ups and downs, but that's all behind us now and I hope things work out for you, which I'm sure they will."

"Thank you, Mr Clarke," replied David. "Yes, I've had a great time, your staff are a credit to you and thanks for all your help and forbearance. I feel ashamed when I look back at some of my childish antics and I appreciate your understanding. I'll never forget those late-night parties, with the local girls, drinking bottles of bubbly and singing nosily on the balcony and that time when the police were called and I spent a night in the local nick for fighting with the guests. I'm deeply sorry for the trouble I've caused and I'm forever in your debt," said David, looking red-faced and embarrassed while the memories of his misspent youth returned to haunt him.

"We shouldn't talk about these things, put it down to experience," replied Mr Clarke in a quiet conciliatory tone. "It's all part of growing up, you had a rough time before coming here. But thankfully, you've turned the corner, become a more mature, more responsible adult."

David sensed he was being told off, but ignored the less than subtle innuendo and shook the manager's hand firmly as another chapter in his roller-coaster life came to an abrupt end. The confident millionaire strolled out of the hotel, waving to the staff like a well-known celebrity on a red carpet. They'd congregated in two wavy lines outside the imposing entrance and treated him to a rendition of *For He's a Jolly Good Fellow* followed by a rousing chorus of three cheers. Feeling slightly overcome, David thanked them for their cards, presents and goodwill messages, as Anne was seen wiping the tears from her eyes, knowing her well-heeled first love was walking out of her life forever and their paths would never cross again. The birthday boy then wandered along the heavily congested seafront, reflecting on some of his memories of his time in the seaside coastal town. In the distance was the battered bandstand with its familiar squawking seagulls and a brown signpost pointing in the direction of the sprawling Alexandra Park, which brought a wry smile to his suntanned face.

He popped into Mr Crawford's offices to express his gratitude for everything they'd done over the last three years, before catching the late morning train up to London and then onto Cheltenham, his soon-to-be adopted second home nestling at the foot of the wonderful, scenic Cotswold hills.

He thanked his solicitor for getting council approval to change the status of 5 Dewhurst Road from a residential dwelling to a refuge for battered women. Edward had lived through months of mindless objections, lengthy inquiries and tedious petitions from angry local residents, nimbys and vested interests of all types before eventually clinching the deal and signing on the bottom line.

"A hefty contribution to the pier restoration fund may have helped sway things in our favour," David suggested, clasping a mug of hot coffee and nibbling his way through a ginger nut. "Before I forget, could you please organise the delivery of doormats for all entrances to the property and ensure the initials CJ are boldly imprinted in the material so the evil one will always be remembered every time the gallant ladies wipe their dirty feet?" remarked David with a smirk.

The solicitor, seemingly perplexed, nodded his head and smiled at his young charge when recording his strange request on his open notepad. "In all seriousness, it upsets me when I read about these women who are abused, beaten, even murdered at the hands of their husbands and boyfriends and no one does anything about it, no one lifts a finger. No one gives a damn, in fact people do all they can to put barriers in your way. How ludicrous is that? It's wrong and number 5 is my way of supporting these women, it's a national disgrace. If you look at the stats they're quite disturbing. Hundreds of women a year are beaten, abused and hospitalised, through no fault of their own and two a week, yes, two a week, die at the hands of their partners. So number 5, once the house of an abuser, is now a refuge for the abused. Quite ironic isn't it? I intend to set up more of these bolt-holes around the country and, with your help, we can make a difference, get the upper hand and help these women live a more normal life. We owe it to them."

A determined expression was etched on his face when he dabbed his sweaty cheeks with the back of his hand, stood and looked straight at his trusted companion with a piercing glare.

"I'm not going to ignore it, not for one moment sir," he declared. Edward leaned forward, gently patted him on the shoulder, trying to reassure his troubled client and put his mind at ease.

"You see, your words have not been in vain, our sessions have not been a waste of time. Far from it. I've listened to your wise counsel for the last few years, you've really influenced my way of thinking, which I appreciate very much. Thank you for everything, Mr Crawford. You've been like a father figure to me sir, a real father," said David. His chin wobbled and he felt a large lump in his throat as he tried to swallow.

The lawyer was quite overcome by David's heart-warming compliments, knowing how he treasured his father's memory and held him in such high esteem. He was forced to turn away to save his blushes and maintain his professional image.

"It's a first in the area and something I'm really proud of. It will definitely give the hedge trimmers and the curtain twitchers something to think about, as their new neighbours let off steam, celebrate their hard-fought freedom from the clutches of their cowardly abusers. Everybody wins, Mr Crawford, I mean everybody," remarked David, shaking hands with his mentor and patting him firmly on the shoulder.

It was a poignant moment in their relationship when the straight-laced lawyer smiled with pride at the young confident twenty-one-year-old. It was like a scene from the *Pretty Woman* movie, released a year earlier, where Julia Roberts was changed from a downtrodden prostitute, without a penny to her name, into an elegant, sophisticated woman with style and class, thanks to the love and adoration of her knight in shining armour – Richard Gere. David Lane had pulled off the same trick, he'd changed dramatically from the spotty, self-conscious teenager who wouldn't say boo to a goose, to a mature, sophisticated man with excellent dress sense and strong personal presence.

Edward Crawford was quite overcome when he bade a fond farewell to his client and wished him all the best for the future, promising to keep in touch and check on his progress from time to time.

For Susan, David's departure was a bit of a shock when her flamboyant boyfriend announced, quite nonchalantly over dinner, that he'd be leaving Hastings for pastures new. Susan's circumstances meant she couldn't leave the Sussex coastal resort even if she wanted to. Her frail elderly parents relied on her as their live-in carer and would no doubt be taken into local authority care if she trundled off into the sunset.

Anyway, the legal assistant loved her job very much and was hoping to be made a partner when Mr Crawford retired later in the year. She'd already been given a nod by Mr Higgins, the senior partner in the firm, so the future was quite rosy for his oversexed girlfriend with an ambitious streak to match. As their relationship was more lust than love, she was happy to indulge in the occasional romp in the sack, patiently biding her time until Mr Right rode into town on his white charger and swept her off her feet.

Her wealthy boyfriend would always keep in touch with his first love and, even though he'd move out of the district and settle down in one of Cheltenham's leafy suburbs, he'd still rekindle their relationship, from time to time, by meeting her at the Imperial Hotel for a scrumptious three-course dinner with the promise of a little something extra for afters. The arrangement offered benefits for both parties.

And so it was on a sultry summer's day in late July 1991, David Lane took his leave of the quaint unspoilt Sussex town, his home for over eight years, to begin a new life with optimism and hope and a little trepidation.

Chapter 9

In previous months David had visited Cheltenham on a number of occasions, quickly fell in love with the place and, with the help of Mr Crawford's dedicated staff, bought a palatial Regency villa in a prominent position in the centre of the spa town. Mr Clarke arranged for his personal possessions to be packed up and shipped to his new address in Gloucestershire and, as the previous owners had emigrated to Australia and wanted to sell the property fully furnished, the arrangement was perfect for the enterprising bachelor.

David decided to visit London en route to his new abode where he did some shopping on New Bond Street, followed by a light lunch at Fortnum and Mason. He then took a leisurely stroll up the famous Burlington Arcade before catching the five thirty p.m. cross-country train from Paddington to his new residence in the shadows of the rolling Cotswold hills. An attractive, well-spoken young woman from Elgar's Estate Agency met him from the train and drove David to his new home some two miles away.

"Did you have a pleasant journey, Mr Lane?" asked the thirty-four-year-old divorcee with sleek dark hair that draped seductively across her shoulders, and wearing a deep blue business suit, white blouse and pink chiffon scarf, tied around her slender neck.

"Yes it's gone very well, thanks," replied David, sinking into the soft-textured leather and surveying the passing scenery from his comfortable front seat. The car radio regaled stories of John Major's ongoing machinations with his party over Europe and his alleged infidelity with a certain cabinet colleague, which brought a saucy smirk to his suntanned face. Then, following the short journey, the small saloon car swept into Pavilion Avenue where the excited passenger was treated to a line of majestic beech trees in full bloom, providing welcome shade and privacy for the prestigious Regency homes standing proudly on either side of the town's number-one avenue.

"Here we are, Mr Lane. Didn't take too long, did it?" remarked Shirley, glancing inquisitively at her fresh-faced client sat innocently alongside her, appearing slightly apprehensive in his unfamiliar surroundings.

"Have my cases arrived safely at the house and my food shopping done as I requested?"

"Yes," she replied, rather irritated by his brusque manner. Shirley then drove up the steep, gravel drive and handed the door keys to David, wondering how someone so very young could afford such an impressive property in one of the town's most exclusive locations.

"Great, and while you're here, get rid of the *sold* sign. It looks awful perched at the end of the drive," he snapped impatiently, fumbling with the front door keys.

"And another thing, stop looking at me like that. You're not my type. I can assure you of that. You're batting way outside your league, sweetheart, so just do what you're paid to do and we'll get on fine, okay? So get rid of that bloody sign."

Shirley was caught off guard, shocked and upset by his cruel, heartless comments that tripped off his tongue with such apparent ease. The normally high-spirited, bubbly estate agent felt as though she'd been kicked in the stomach, insulted for no apparent reason. With both hands shaking, she grabbed the leather steering wheel to steady her nerves.

"Yes, I'll organise it today," she called out in a quiet quivering voice through the car's open window as the black Audi slowly slipped down the drive. Shirley glanced in the mirror, convinced that her battle-scarred appearance was due to the recent acrimonious divorce from her adulterous two-timing husband, otherwise the posh boy would have been putty in her hands.

Sadly, however, a pile of damp paper tissues lying scattered across the front seat of her car, with a strong smell of burnt tobacco, was testimony to the damage David had done. For the rest of the day, after her acrimonious meeting with Mr Lane, the hard-nosed agent was still recoiling at the vitriolic words reverberating throughout her body. It reduced the tough, resilient saleswoman of the year to bouts of tears and an overwhelming sense of low self-worth that stayed with her for days to come.

Meanwhile, David was gratified to see his four bulging designer suitcases from Harrods and numerous tea chests, bursting with textbooks and lever-arch files, standing in the cavernous hallway at the foot of the imposing spiral staircase. It was then when the emotion of the day took over as the exuberance of youth got the better of him. One minute he was charging around the beautifully designed kitchen bashing the copper saucepans together with his clenched fists and, the next, he was rushing through the lounge jumping from chair to chair and bouncing up and down on the handcrafted material settees. Without thinking, he then raced up the spiral staircase, past his first-floor office, before collapsing flat out on his king-size bed staring up towards the recently painted magnolia ceiling and laughing at the top of his voice.

After this outpouring of wild unabashed enthusiasm, the new homeowner sauntered back downstairs to collect his old battered suitcase. His legendary, well travelled moth-eaten suit and frayed tartan shirt were hung up in pride of place in the wardrobe alongside his scruffy old black shoes and threadbare socks. These were painful reminders of his time at Dewhurst Road and the reign of terror of the wicked witch who was now safely at rest with the crabs at the bottom of the English Channel.

Carol had a lot to answer for. When the family home in Richmond was sold and the house clearance people auctioned the furniture and contents, David was left with a few small boxes of memorabilia dating back to his parents' marriage on 5th September, 1965. At the time of the funeral, when the distraught adolescent was being looked after by the local authority, his evil cousin destroyed many remnants of his family history, leaving David with just his mother's gold locket that was found on her burnt body at the time of the accident in 1983. For reasons of security, his parents' friends and work colleagues were discouraged from taking photographs of David, so he had very little to remind him of their all too brief time together.

So his precious family heirloom was carefully retrieved from the inside pocket of his blue linen jacket and placed, with due reverence, on the small wooden side table, alongside his king-size bed. "I hope you like your new home," he mumbled under his breath. He polished their pictures with his cotton handkerchief, then positioned the open locket so he could see their smiling faces as he lay back on the bed.

The villa smelt of paint. No doubt the previous owners had quickly spruced up the place before departing. It was a grand, imposing Regency building, boasting a huge cellar and well-equipped games room below stairs. The ground floor comprised a large dining room with a polished mahogany table and eight matching chairs. There was a pair of slim, elegant sideboards standing proudly against two of the walls with four large chromium lamps in the corners of the room, providing additional lighting under the watchful gaze of the imposing chandelier. It dominated the centre of the ceiling, injecting a sense of timeless elegance and tasteful sophistication. The spacious, wood-floored kitchen had the obligatory island in the centre, where a variety of copper pots and pans were hanging freely from a wooden frame attached to the ceiling.

All the rooms were painted in magnolia and furnished to a very high standard as befitted a property of such distinction and style. The capacious lounge comprised two patterned material sofas, six easy chairs and a long narrow coffee table in the centre. The sweeping bay window afforded grand views of the recently laid gravel drive, manicured borders and carefully tended conifer trees that bordered the front of the property. The pale green curtains were decorated with pastel-coloured leaves which made the room look warm, airy and welcoming. Even though the house was large and quite overwhelming it still felt homely, restful and pleasing to the eye.

David Lane was happy with his choice. The previous owners had even left a forty-inch television and CD player in a stylish handmade cabinet in the far corner of the lounge, placed alongside an elegant, glass-fronted cocktail cabinet which made the affable playboy smile when he imagined it full of his favourite French bubbly. There was a deep-pile cream carpet snaking throughout the building, making it look light and welcoming with solid wooden flooring in the spacious utility room and storage areas at the rear of the property.

The remaining two upper floors accommodated four double bedrooms, with matching en suite bathrooms. They were exquisitely decorated throughout, giving the unpredictable socialite a sense of pride and self-importance when sauntering from room to room. Nearby was a fully furnished office with a new HP laptop and printer sitting on a shiny mahogany desk, while a Bang and Olsen television was built into the wooden panelling immediately behind his black high-backed leather chair.

The room overlooked the rear garden which had been turfed for ease of maintenance. Brightly coloured flowers were in full bloom in the well-stocked borders and a brick-built triple garage at the end of the property gave direct access to the road at the rear. It was a perfect setting and a far cry from the grubby box he called home back in the bleak days of isolation and despair.

In the weeks ahead, he gradually settled in to his new abode much to the amazement of his wealthy neighbours who were astonished to see the new occupant of number one looking so youthful, so confident and with lots of time on his hands. Being a private person, David kept himself to himself, steering clear of the busybodies, local gossips and malicious rumour mongers.

David enjoyed his regular chats with Mr Crawford, they helped keep him on the straight and narrow and face an uncertain future with some optimism, even though the death of his parents still hung heavy on his mind. Then one day, quite out of the blue, he had the call he'd always dreaded. Mr Barma telephoned to say that Edward had died of a sudden heart attack whilst visiting 5 Dewhurst Road.

It was a terrible shock for David, affecting him badly for days, often drowning his sorrows with a bottle of malt whisky, or anything else he could lay his hands on. The death of his close adviser highlighted his lonely, rather reclusive existence, devoid of friends and companions. It was something Mr Crawford had warned him about repeatedly and it had now come home to roost. He attended the funeral in Hastings which was a drab depressing affair, having to hold back the tears when the austere coffin slowly disappeared behind the curtains and his friend and ally took his leave for the last time. The sombre guests trooped out of the crematorium, looking very glum and tearful with the funeral march playing softly in the background. Mr Crawford was a wonderful man admired by so many, judging by the number who'd turned out to bid him farewell. Yet David knew that, even though he'd be terribly missed by family and friends, at least he'd be reunited with his late wife who'd no doubt organise his life in heaven, as well as she did on earth.

Chapter 10

In the months ahead, David made regular trips to Hastings. In their lighter moments, he joked with Susan about their passionate, sex-fuelled relationship, how she'd corrupted him over many years, taking advantage of his childhood innocence, leading him astray with dark untold pleasures of the flesh.

"You stole my precious virginity when I was most vulnerable. You seduced me when I was susceptible, weak and defenceless. But now you've wet my appetite, got me excited at the prospect of our illicit encounters to such an extent that I can't see why we should ever stop," said David, with a wink and a shake of his head.

"We have a good arrangement, Susy," he added, perched on the end of the double bed, trying to tie his shoelaces after another heart-pounding romp in the sack, while the prospect of a daunting 180 mile return journey in the Aston Martin, famous for its firm suspension, that jolts and jars on even the smoothest road surfaces, wasn't good news for Casanova's sore buttocks and thighs.

"I treat you to lunch, a lavish lunch I might add, and then we have some raunchy fun and games under the duvet before going back to our separate lives feeling refreshed and rejuvenated with just a few aches and pains. How wonderful is that?" he laughed, patting her on the bottom with his open hand, before climbing into the waiting lift and pressing the button for the underground car park.

Sometime after David's move to Cheltenham, Susan married Roger Sands, a smarmy jack the lad second-hand car dealer with piles of money, a dodgy background, strange North Country accent and a pronounced hairlip. Not surprisingly David refused to allow a simple thing like marriage get in the way of his sexual cravings and so, at his insistence, the pair continued with their adulterous escapades unabated. As their relationship wasn't going anywhere and it was just raw sex that drove them together, David wasn't troubled by her marital status so long as they could meet a few times a year and indulge in some risqué lovemaking behind her husband's back. That was the deal. It was the salacious nature of their adulterous affair that excited her randy boyfriend most, giving him an outlet for some of his sexual fantasies, but for the new bride with church bells still ringing loudly in her ears and the ink barely dry on the marriage certificate, their illicit liaisons were a source of great concern.

Susan was worried at the thought of her jealous, vindictive husband getting wind of her treachery and being booted out of the family home while the ensuing scandal would inflict untold damage to her legal career and undermine her hard-won reputation in the town.

The fun-loving playboy had never experienced true love as lust and gratification were his favoured bedfellows thanks to his seduction, many years earlier, by his amorous legal adviser. David enjoyed regular sexual conquests with a parade of different women, all without any strings. He sometimes had to splash the cash for the more erotic, more deviant, but that was par for the course for the good-looking bachelor with deep pockets and a sex drive to match. David was unashamedly content to drift through life, wallowing in the pleasurable comforts of the female form whenever he wanted to indulge his sexual fantasies and have a bit of harmless fun. It was ideal.

But sadly there was some bad news for the newlyweds. Susan and Roger would have to resign themselves to a childless marriage, where the pitter-patter of tiny feet was never on the cards. Apparently, the salesman's low sperm count and a history of erectile dysfunction was his downfall and a real body blow for his fragile male ego.

Needless to say David couldn't stop laughing when Susan, rather foolishly, broke the news of his shortcomings over lunch. With a sarcastic laugh and a string of rude unsavoury remarks, he promised to do what he could to compensate for her husband's sexual inadequacies. David wasn't known for his sensitivity and tact and wallowed mercilessly in Roger's misfortune and inability to satisfy his wife.

But then there was a change of fortune for the oily rag, as David christened him. He was tickled pink, ecstatic, in a state of abject shock when Susan told him she was pregnant while tucking into a bowl of muesli and drinking a glass of freshly squeezed orange. Their bewildered GP was very forthright in his prognosis and called her pregnancy a miracle, a real miracle, turning his head to one side and giving Susan a knowing glance.

David, needless to say, was over the moon at the prospect of fatherhood and chose his daughter's name in memory of his dear mother. Languishing in bed with his mistress one sultry summer's afternoon, his deep blue eyes filled up as he gazed longingly at the captivating photographs of the beautiful six-pound baby girl at her recent christening. Louise had inherited her mother's good looks and soft complexion.

However, the baby's pale blue eyes, slim fingers and cheeky smile were reminiscent of her father's striking features, something which her excited boyfriend was quick to point out, several times. David's rather nervous mistress, with badly chewed nails and deep frown, couldn't understand how she'd conceived a child after all the scrupulous precautions her errant boyfriend had taken to prevent an unwanted pregnancy. It was a mystery.

Louise was the married couple's pride and joy, bringing unexpected love and harmony to their boring, uneventful lives, where tedium and dullness were their constant companions in a relationship that had never lived up to its expectations, falling far short of its initial billing. Susan was determined to give her daughter a stable family upbringing and, even though she'd considered leaving Roger on numerous occasions, she decided to put her daughter's happiness first, knowing it meant sharing her life with a dreary nobody who was going nowhere fast.

Susan combined her high-profile job, as a partner in the town's premier law firm, with evenings and weekends in the company of her darling precious daughter and her obnoxious husband. That was her bed and she would lie in it.

Chapter 11

"I don't know why you have to work such long hours Suzy, particularly as you've been recruiting more staff recently," asked Roger in a grumpy tone of voice, grabbing another can of beer out of the fridge and munching a mouthful of cheese and onion crisps while bits of debris shot out of his mouth onto the woodblock kitchen floor.

"We have to spend a lot of time training people on our different procedures, but we'll be out of the woods by the end of the month and be up to full strength again, so life should be much easier then. Anyway, I told you all this yesterday, so why d'you keep asking me the same tedious questions?" retorted Susan angrily, as she removed the warm plates from inside the oven and started serving up the evening meal, frequently crashing the serving spoon onto the hot ceramic surface, incensed by her husband's monotonous questions about her job.

"Louise seems to have a bit of a cold according to the nursery so we'll have to keep an eye on her overnight, don't want her having a high temperature and another convulsion. The doctor at the hospital warned us it could happen again so best be on our guard and not take any chances," she yelled over the sound of the fan-assisted oven.

"If you didn't work such long hours then our daughter wouldn't be neglected and pushed from pillar to post like a ragdoll," Roger shouted, helping himself to some more chilli con carne and cutting up several slices of French stick which he plonked down on the edge of his oval plate. The fractious, ill-tempered couple sat at the breakfast bar, not saying a word, just peering out at the small well-cared for garden with its obligatory children's sandpit and newly painted swing.

"You're always like this when you've been drinking, Roger. You know Lou isn't neglected, she has the best possible care, so I don't know why you say these awful things, it's so hurtful."

"Oh, I nearly forgot. I saw Helen pushing a trolley load of Mothercare boxes and parcels the other day. What's all that about?"

he asked, crushing an empty beer can in his clenched fist and throwing it into the refuse bin alongside the kitchen sink.

Susan was used to his moody argumentative ways, his childish tantrums and selfish behaviour, but this unexpected question put her on the back foot. She had to come up with a convincing reply otherwise he'd be like a dog with a bone, going on about it every time he had a drink, which could prove embarrassing if they were entertaining important people from work. She had to nip it in the bud once and for all.

"Yes, I know. We've been collecting donations of children's clothes for the local charity shop on the front, next to BHS, opposite the pier. Mrs Collins approached us some time ago and, as a major player in the town, we want to do our bit for the community, so we donate what we can to help out. It's as simple as that."

"Um," he mumbled. "Pity you haven't got better things to do. If you didn't waste your time on these silly things, you'd have more time to spend with our daughter," he said, chewing noisily on a piece of half-eaten French stick.

Susan ignored him and carried on eating the hot meal, sipping her large glass of chilled Chardonnay, feeling her cheeks getting warmer and warmer and hoping to God her explanation sounded plausible.

"When we had dinner with Mr Barma the other day, he mentioned that one of your clients was the wealthiest you've ever had and you've been handling his affairs for some time. You never mentioned him. What's he like?"

"Well, Mr Crawford handled them initially until his retirement and then Mr Barma took over. I've helped out on some of the legal stuff from time to time. Not very exciting really."

"I said what's he like!" yelled Roger with a pained expression and slurred speech. "I'm not interested in your work, for God's sake. I asked about him as a person. Are you deaf?"

Susan coughed, cleared her throat and patted her flushed cheeks with a Kleenex tissue. "He's in his twenties, quite shy and insecure, rather immature for his age. Glad I didn't have to spend too much time with him," she explained, before suddenly catching her breath on the hot chilli peppers and then quickly swallowing a glass of cold tap water to ease her dry throat.

"Have you ever met him in his hotel room since we got together?" asked her husband with a sinister sneer.

"Of course not. It would be inappropriate and unseemly for me to do such a thing. You know that. Can we please change the subject and eat our meal in peace? It sounds quiet upstairs and we ought to take the opportunity to enjoy our chilli before Lou Lou stirs and wants her nappy changed."

"I didn't know he lived at the Imperial for over three years and you went to see him there. Were you lovers before I came on the scene?"

"Look Roger, I shall have to go to bed if you carry on like this. It's very unfair. I've got a big day tomorrow with all these new staff members and I don't want to spend the whole evening arguing," she shouted indignantly, slamming her fork down on the breakfast bar with a resounding crash and downing the rest of her wine in one big gulp as her face took on a deep red glow. Her years of legal training taught her that attack was always the best form of defence. The bright, ambitious lawyer adopted that fail safe approach every time with her grumpy, bad-tempered husband, hoping to cut him off at the pass, outwit him before he got up a head of steam and stop lengthy discussions on contentious topics that could land her in hot water.

Sensing he might have overdone things and upset his hard-working wife, the inebriate got up, kissed her on the forehead, collected up the dirty cups and plates and dropped them into the dishwasher, before wiping the surfaces with a clean dishcloth. The overweight car dealer with an unsavoury streak then sauntered into the lounge next door, relaxed back in his comfy leather armchair, picked up the evening newspaper and promptly went off to sleep.

Chapter 12

Meanwhile the enigmatic playboy was fired up at the prospect of fatherhood and, in his drive for physical fitness and self-improvement, his imagination knew no bounds, throwing himself head first into a number of exhilarating body-toning pursuits in his unyielding regime of strict dieting and relentless exercise. Health and general well-being were firmly on the agenda for the new father. He kitted out the games room with all the latest gizmos, joined the local gym, where tiresome, insecure middle-aged men with big stomachs insisted on telling him how successful they were. He swam regularly at the local baths, perfecting the front crawl and breast stroke, following a series of intensive one-to-one lessons from the in-house female coach who, much to David's delight, turned out to be a real sport, in more ways than one. He was often seen running through Cheltenham's idyllic parks and wide open spaces dressed in a bright red jogging outfit and matching shoes, with a fetching floral bandana tied around his head. His scenic route took him across Montpellier Gardens and Imperial Square, down the Promenade and out onto the main Evesham Road towards Pittville Park and the iconic Regency Pump Rooms. He'd then sweep passed the world-famous racecourse and through the village of Prestbury before returning to the sanctuary of his palatial abode, about forty-five minutes later.

With fatherhood firmly in his sights, Mr Lane was a regular visitor to the local Mothercare store on the Promenade. Here he proudly filled up a trolley with piles of pink baby clothes, toys and games of all descriptions and anything else that caught his eye. The whole lot was then dispatched by courier service to the solicitors' offices in Hastings. Susan's confidential secretary was well versed in the antics of their extrovert client. She would pop the array of parcels and boxes onto an office document trolley and push it along the uneven pavement to the nearby charity shop. Here she'd hand over the bundles of goodies to an enthusiastic store manager, who'd welcome the assortment of brand new gifts with open arms. Mrs Collins was a big, stocky woman, in her late fifties, with strong muscular arms and funny shaped teeth, giving her the appearance of a rabbit when she smiled.

Susan knew her daughter would enjoy many of the toys and games that her mercurial father had sent her. She'd look gorgeous in some of the pretty, dainty dresses and little tops that matched her colouring perfectly, but she couldn't take any chances of arousing her jealous husband's suspicions. It wasn't worth the risk.

In the meantime, David's insatiable zest for speed and bottom-clenching excitement was assured when the boy-racer splashed out on a Harley Davidson motorbike, got dressed up like James Dean, his boyhood hero, and took off into the countryside with its plethora of quaint unspoilt villages and Cotswold stone pubs. Sat proudly astride his majestic black machine, with its deep guttural drone and elegant lines, he looked like a god on wheels, weaving to and fro at breakneck speeds, down narrow country lanes and along winding dusty farm tracks. Meanwhile, the top of the range soft-top Aston Martin was safely housed in the triple garage at the foot of the garden. It was his pride and joy, guaranteed to impress the ladies with every turn of the soft leather wheel, every press on the throaty throttle. The sound of the throbbing six-litre engine was a real head-turner, a magnet for the fair sex. His cool, smooth image was in stark contrast to the hordes of drooling men standing with eyes on stalks, salivating at the Aston's sleek elegant lines gliding past like a sophisticated screen goddess in a Hollywood blockbuster. His jealous male contemporaries could only dream of owning such a prestigious machine as it rolled down the celebrated tree-lined Promenade purring like an angry lion, leaving a cloud of smoke in its wake every time the show-off pressed the feisty throttle. The word envy was firmly emblazoned on every speed-freaks' forehead within earshot of the raging beast, growling under the deep blue shiny bonnet, yearning for the open road.

In those early months, the bachelor kept up to speed with his daughter's progress and continued keeping the local courier service fully employed, driving backwards and forwards to the Sussex coast with van loads brimming with goodies for the town's lucky under-fives.

He also visited some of his old childhood haunts in Richmond, but as it brought back painful memories, opened up old wounds, he decided to give the place a wide berth, preferring to look to the future rather than wallowing in the past. With a cheeky grin, he remembered Doris' wise words and the many good times they shared together at the Imperial Hotel, drinking Earl Grey tea and putting the world to rights.

Private studies were still a big part of David's life and bulging files and jam-packed bookshelves in his new home were evidence of his insatiable thirst for knowledge. Poetry still interested him greatly. Here, he'd often put pen to paper whilst relaxing in the nearby Imperial Gardens. The pleasing sound of young children playing in the background and the familiar aroma of freshly mown grass, making him sniff from time to time, kept the enterprising scribbler company as he tried to compose his latest offering. A deep frown and umpteen pieces of crumpled paper, lay strewn across his favourite park bench, showed how difficult it was for the aspiring poet to capture his thoughts in perfect rhyme.

The wordsmith even tried to get his work published. But sadly it wasn't to be. He had a hoity-toity letter from Faber and Faber spraying torrents of cold water on his latest rendition, saying their sophisticated customers preferred carefully crafted prose rather than the simpler, less refined alternative. So David reconciled himself to composing rhyme and verse for fun and pleasure, nothing else. The prospect of being captured in print was a dream too far, but their stern rebuttal didn't dampen his ardour, far from it. His tongue in cheek reply summed up his feelings. It was aptly entitled *I'll Be Back*:

A letter of rejection makes you feel so very ill,
For a fluent wordsmith, it is a bitter pill,
Your words conveyed a message, brought tears into my eyes,
But I'll never stop my writing, till I achieve my prize.

Feeling fairly confident in his ability to write simple uncomplicated rhyme, he searched for local ideas to stimulate his latent talent. Cheltenham's famous love affair with horse racing grabbed his imagination early on.

He was also enchanted, even captivated, by the town's leafy streets, landscaped parks and beautifully maintained gardens that changed so dramatically from one season to the next, inspiring the would-be poet to put pen to paper and compose two poems while sitting on his familiar park bench.

Gold Cup Fever

Town comes to life in springtime, to the sound of spurs and whips,
Guinness-laden punters press for the latest tips,
Meetings are frenetic, go on till nearly dark,
We all applaud the racing, that's at our Prestbury Park.

Sleek trains unload their cargo as punters weave their way,
Along our leafy tree-lined streets, to a park where they can play,
See fleets of race-day buses, jam-packed cabs and Learjets,
As they convey expectant crowds to the park to place their bets.

Gold Cup's the star attraction at this annual equine show,
Crowds are hoarse from shouting, if their fillies run too slow,
They jostle for position, as they cheer and watch the race,
With levels of excitement, stamped firmly 'cross their face.

Park is really buzzing when the horses run and jump,
Sound of bridles clanking, as they charge and sometimes bump,
Place becomes a haven for fashion, style and fun,
Cheltenham's at its best right now, as it welcomes everyone.

Town for All Seasons

Spring flowers start to blossom and trees are in full leaf,
We love the floral vista that is beyond belief,
Our town becomes a beacon for travellers far and wide,
Shopkeepers get excited; their joy can't be denied.

Summer is upon us; the sun is at its height,
Pretty floral gardens, display a tranquil sight,
People are excited, they're out to have some fun,
The hot and sultry weather, a treat for everyone.

Clumps of snow lay sodden on the frozen squelchy ground,
A boy discards his bicycle and walks his paper round,
The autumn wind is blowing and the cold has made its mark,
Only brave Cheltonians are out when it's so dark.

As we're drawn to Christmas, bright lights reflect our mood,
The season is upon us to taste exotic food,
We gaze with eyes wide open at its culinary delights,
And gasp in sheer amazement at the wondrous Christmas lights.

With an eye on the future, the studious young man began to realise there was more to life than just reading, writing and studying. So taking dear Mr Crawford's advice, he decided to widen his social network. For the bachelor, with time on his hands, this meant one thing. He hooked up with a string of girls and young women he met in pubs, clubs and seedy hotels, who he wined, sometimes dined, but quickly got bored of. His vast wealth and risqué reputation went before him and made him a magnet for the social climbers, the money-grabbers and local dimwits, of which there were many. This gaggle of women, of all shapes and sizes were attracted to him like bees to a honeypot with their gaudy coloured fingernails, silly high-heeled shoes and giggly voices that grated every time they opened their mouths. When the young socialite got bored with soppy girls, wearing narrow belts for dresses, he decided to change tack, broaden his horizon by ingratiating himself with some of his wealthy, upper-crust neighbours. So one summer's evening, a handful of the locals trooped into his prestigious residence for drinks and nibbles. Here they fluffed up their chests, talked about their wealth, telling everyone several times how successful they were.

The young couple from next door were good value. They talked in glowing terms about their young daughter, Mercedes, boasting about her academic achievements, her sporting prowess and her natural beauty that would undoubtedly have the male population drooling at her feet.

"So, you named your offspring after a German car manufacturer?" was the host's cheeky retort as they wittered on, with their noses in the air, about the virtues of private education when compared to the inadequate state system and its longstanding courtship with mediocrity. The posh knobs, as David christened them, took umbrage at his rude comments. After all, she was a senior Geography teacher at the local prep school, used to laying down the law, so he imagined she might box his ears at any moment, or at least make him sit on the naughty step at the foot of the spiral staircase.

Standing in the corner of the room out of harm's way was a slim, boring, know-it-all with hair escaping from his nose and ears and looking grossly undernourished in his ill-fitting clothes. The social pariah's wife, by contrast, was a short, shy woman who enjoyed her food as her hard-pressed blouse buttons and elasticated skirt would testify. Other guests chatted, mingled and walked in and out of the downstairs rooms as though they were in an art gallery, frequently passing judgement in whispered comments, on the landscape paintings and portraits, while the exquisite collection of crystal glass figurines and china ornaments, that adorned the light spacious ground floor rooms, didn't escape their scrutiny either.

The impressive spiral staircase with its imposing chandelier that sparkled and glittered in the light was the star of the show, a real head turner for the nosy neighbours who ignored their young host, choosing instead to huddle together in small groups to compare notes. The length of rope straddling across the bottom step, stopping anyone climbing up the staircase, was an amusing addition to the decor and a source of annoyance for those who'd hoped to rummage around the palatial property exploring every nook, every cranny from top to bottom. With the incessant whispering and general chit-chat between his envious guests, weighing up the pros and cons of each item, David imagined an auctioneer from Sotheby's might appear at any moment with catalogue in hand and her trusty gavel raised in the air. As the wine flowed and the atmosphere became more convivial so the inquisitive guests, green with envy, couldn't resist the temptation and, like bloodhounds searching for their quarry, asked several intrusive questions of their host in their resentful quest to establish the source of his unbridled wealth.

This was manna from heaven for the cheeky rogue. It allowed the twenty-something to wax lyrical about his array of imaginary business interests and enter the world of fantasy, fun and make-believe by exploiting his guests' sense of insecurity and jealousy. David was brimming with ideas. He was like an incendiary device waiting to explode at any moment, or a wildcat preparing to pounce on its unwary prey. So the stage was set, the audience was primed. His wild imagination was being fuelled by several glasses of chilled Moet and a large cognac, and served up with an overwhelming sense of self-confidence. It was an explosive cocktail.

Successful poet of international renown sounded good for starters. The proud recipient of many prestigious accolades and awards for his literary talents also sounded impressive. It was a strong opener. A professional gambler had them thinking and a club baron was believable, judging by the nods and winks, but as the drink took hold so his world of make-believe gathered pace with ideas tripping off his tongue like water spraying from Neptune's fountain. As David was saying goodbye, shunting his dull, tiresome guests towards the open door after an hour and a half of mind-numbing tedium, the fantasist discharged his salvo, with such precision, that even his literary hero, Tom Sharpe, would have been impressed.

He stood on the top step, like Julius Caesar issuing a proclamation to an expectant crowd of subservient onlookers, and announced with great oratorical presence, to his inebriated guests stumbling about on the uneven gravel drive, that his latest business venture was into the highly lucrative world of hard porn.

"Apparently the *Bonking Bitch, Throbbing Robin* and *The Lusty Lessies* are the three top-selling videos!" he yelled at the top of his voice. This particular tasty titbit was directed straight at Mercedes' mum careering ungainly towards the roadway, looking ashen-faced and deeply embarrassed by the lewd suggestion that she, of all people, would be interested in watching such obscene material. After all, she was a pillar of society, a respected parish councillor, devoted charity worker and a lifelong member of the Conservative Party. Surely those credentials alone should mark her out as a person of propriety and repute with no interest whatsoever in such unsavoury goings-on?

As the smiling host collected up the empty glasses and plates and turned on the television, he toasted Edward with a glass of his finest Moet, thanking him for opening his eyes to the benefits of socialising.

The incorrigible playboy enjoyed the rest of the evening gloating to himself, while planning another drinks do later in the year once the dust had settled. He knew his cards were marked, he'd be a social pariah for some time to come after his disreputable behaviour, but that was only to be expected. I think my idea of spiking their drinks was a good touch, he laughed to himself, placing the half-empty bottle of vodka back in the drinks' cabinet, with a reassuring pat.

In a matter of days, the local gossipmongers came up trumps, as evidenced by a parade of scantily clad teenage girls, smiling and wiggling provocatively outside his palatial residence, hoping to get a glimpse of Mr Porn and the opportunity to get their kit off, flaunt their bits in the latest lads' magazine. Dodging his young admirers, David often strolled into town, doing some window shopping, hoping to get inspiration for another bit of poetic rhyme.

However there was one occasion when giving a cursory glance into Elgar's Estate Agency window, a young woman approached him from behind.

"Can I help you, sir?" she said in a slow, sexy drawl. It was Shirley, boasting a saucy grin, clutching a pile of brown folders with several broadsheet newspapers clasped under her arm.

"No, thank you," he said, pushing open the glass door to let her through. "But I'd like you to join me for lunch, if you would."

The attractive estate agent wasn't sure how to handle his pert invitation, but decided to call his bluff and accepted his pushy offer with a confident whisk of her hair. And so, after a shaky start and a great deal of trepidation on Shirley's part, their relationship blossomed and grew over the weeks ahead. The couple spent time together walking, talking and eating at some of the best restaurants around the town and wider afield, but as always something seemed to go wrong in David's topsy-turvy world and, sure enough, fate reared its ugly head and dealt him a real body blow. After numerous meals, several trips out in the Aston and two or three designer handbags, with matching shoes, the estate agent dropped a bombshell. Without any warning, quite out of the blue, she called off their relationship, much to David's surprise. Apparently he wasn't her type and Shirley took great delight in telling him in no uncertain terms.

Things were going well, or so he thought, so being dumped was a terrible shock for the confident, erudite playboy, leaving him feeling depressed and distraught and his fragile ego lying in tatters. He'd never experienced rejection before, believing that life was on his terms, people were at his beck and call and he only had to flick his fingers for his demands to be met. For the naive young man, used to calling the shots and getting his own way, this was a flagrant departure from the script and, as he saw it, something quite unheard of. But then looking back, several days later, still licking his wounds and feeling very sorry for himself, he began to appreciate Shirley's point of view, recalling his rude off-hand behaviour when they first met that was totally uncalled-for and which he'd regretted ever since.

David learnt a painful salutary lesson about relationships and, in particular, how to treat women. Though the episode shattered his self-confidence, making Shirley a target for his anger and frustration, it made him a better man, more aware of the needs of others and less inclined to fly off the handle when he didn't get his own way.

Then one day, quite unexpectedly, when he was busily planning another social gathering for the local posh nobs, thinking how best to spike their drinks, he had a call from the estate agents saying that Shirley was very ill in hospital, unlikely to survive and had asked to see him.

The public ward wasn't to David's liking so the patient was quickly transferred to a nearby private hospital where the treatment was of the highest standard, with specialist twenty-four hour care. Shirley's room was festooned with goodwill cards from family and friends, while the pleasant fragrance from the many bouquets of flowers afforded a sense of love and hope at a time of deep sadness. All the intrusive tubes and wires had been removed and the monitors on both bedside tables switched off, the screens were eerily blank. Lying with her head nestled on a pure white pillow, she slept peacefully, hardly moving, rarely making a sound with the occasional muffled murmurings in the adjacent corridor reminding the solemn crestfallen visitors that life goes on, even in the most tragic circumstances. Sadly Shirley died, shortly after her admission, cuddled up in the arms of her doting parents, who couldn't understand why their beautiful daughter had been snatched from them in the prime of her life with so much to live for. A tearful David Lane couldn't fathom it out either and wondered why, with all the money invested in her recovery, had Shirley not been saved from an early grave. This was the second salutary lesson, in so many weeks, that the wealthy Londoner had had to face up to, making him wonder what the hell was lurking around the corner and whether life was really worth living.

He was learning that things can be tough, unpredictable and often unfair with no cast-iron guarantees for the future, even if you've got a big posh house, the latest Aston Martin and bundles of cash hidden under the mattress. Why, he asked himself later that night, wallowing in self-pity with a bottle of French cognac for company, have all the people I love deserted me? Ma and Pa started the trend, then Mr and Mrs Crawford picked up the baton and now, just when things were going well, Shirley's turned up her toes.

In the months ahead, things got much worse for David as his life took a serious nose-dive and Shirley's untimely death continued to haunt him. He experienced a plethora of failed relationships, embarked on some stupid, ill-conceived business ventures, lost vast amounts to the revolving table, whilst the four-legged nags either refused to jump, or preferred to act as back-markers for their fellow equine friends. Life was bleak, very bleak. He blocked the world out, drew the curtain on life and took refuge in the bottle, drowning his sorrows with copious amounts of alcohol and spending days at a time in a semi-comatose state as the lure of the grape took its hold on his wretched life. David was often admitted to a rehabilitation centre to dry out and receive medical support for his addiction, whereupon he'd discharge himself after a period of intense treatment, try to get his life back on track, only to return to the clinic when the demon drink got the better of him. His sad, dreary life was just like a revolving door with no end in sight.

Chapter 13

The millionaire took a real interest in Louise's development, making financial provision for her future and all the time promising one day he'd claim his prize and be reunited with his precious daughter. Even though he smiled when he said it, saying he was only teasing, Susan felt his words were threatening and unnerving, often making her feel vulnerable and defenceless against the wishes of her powerful, headstrong boyfriend. David Lane held all the trump cards, was in the driving seat. But being aware of his unpredictable temperament, Susan chose to bide her time, keep him sweet and gradually convince her errant boyfriend that it would be in Louise's best interests to stay with her mother, rather than sharing an empty, inconsequential life with her mercurial father and his long-standing courtship with the bottle.

During the times when alcohol was under some control, David became more hands-on, took charge of his finances, met his accountants to check on his extensive portfolio of investments and review his long-term business plans.

Even though his interest was often very fleeting and cursory, it showed the clever number crunchers that the millionaire playboy had his finger on the pulse and could enter into rational discussions about his extensive business affairs, for some of the time anyway. He was gratified to know, even with his philandering and litany of failed business ventures, that thanks to the fastidious management of his finances, his original investment pot had increased dramatically since 1988. The extensive portfolio in commercial and residential properties, started years earlier by his resourceful grandparents, had paid off dramatically and the revenue stream from that source alone was mind-boggling.

"I don't need to get a job then," he joked on the phone to Lawrence Stevens, the senior accountant from Whites, the London-based wealth management company. It had handled the Lane's family fortune for over fifty years and had worked closely with Barma, Higgins and Crawford since the 1970s as their legal advisers.

"No, not unless you want to, sir," was the snooty reply from his suave gravel-voiced adviser proudly boasting a mouthful of plums.

During the good times David immersed himself in the music of the eighties as groups like Soft Cell, Queen and the Communards stole the scene with their fresh brand of music that seriously rocked the establishment and dared bring sexual equality to the fore. His musical taste was quite eclectic, often indulging his passion for the classics in the revered company of Grieg, Dvorak, Rossini and Debussy. But sadly David was often preoccupied elsewhere, fighting a desperate battle against the demon drink that haunted him day and night, threatening to destroy his way of life and bring him to his knees. In the lighter moments, when temptation was on the backburner, he'd stroll around the town's many open parks, its inviting lawns and tranquil lakes and, for relaxation, sit and admire the well-tended gardens with their abundance of beautiful flowers, exotic shrubs and plants. He'd meander down leafy avenues, along hectic bustling streets, seeking inspiration and ideas for his next poetic offering, sometimes making random notes and jottings on his pad before finally relaxing on his favourite wooden bench in the Imperial Gardens under the restful shade of an overarching horse chestnut tree. It was bliss.

Here the solitary scribbler would gaze longingly across the sweeping lawns and manicured flowerbeds as young boisterous families and groups of gregarious students sprawled on freshly mowed grass, eating large packets of crisps and gulping down cans of fizzy drinks with disjointed idle banter and shrieks of raucous laughter. He sometimes heard the sound of the revolving door at the entrance to the salubrious Queens Hotel, accompanied by the noise of clinking glasses and popping champagne corks, as fun-loving revellers enjoyed an afternoon tipple in the secluded private garden.

Then it would happen, without warning, the craving, the overwhelming yearning for alcohol sweeping over his body like a giant tidal wave. He'd run back home as fast as he could, dodging parked cars and passers-by. Here he'd race up the stairs two at a time, often losing his footing and crashing into the banister rail, before taking refuge in a long, gushing cool shower, followed by umpteen glasses of cold water as the demons pleaded with him to submit to the tantalising pleasures that fine wine and malt whisky could offer.

With hands shaking and feeling sick, lightheaded and unable to think, he'd struggle to his bed and with his heart pounding louder and louder, he'd cry out for some relief from the torment ripping through his young battered body attacking every bone, every sinew. Curling up like a ball, he'd hide under the white cotton sheets before drifting off to sleep – only to be haunted by gruesome flashbacks of his parents' burning bodies flaying about in a smoke-filled aircraft as it plummeted relentlessly down to earth.

During the times when the wicked demons won the day and alcohol was in charge, David often crossed paths with the law over minor misdemeanours which inevitably led to further periods in rehabilitation. After one such lengthy confinement he decided, quite out of the blue, to up sticks and discharge himself and return to the sanctuary of his opulent home in Pavilion Avenue. He'd had enough of quacks, shrinks and do-gooders to last him a lifetime and elected to take responsibility for his addiction, come what may.

The French doctor who'd handled David's treatment for a number of years wasn't convinced by his patient's ill-informed diagnosis and, as he waved him goodbye, Dr Pierre Sharon knew his irrational behaviour and serious addiction to alcohol wasn't under control, far from it, and he'd be darkening his doors again. It was merely a question of when.

Chapter 14

Fortunately for David, fate came to the rescue in the guise of a minor road accident. Following a heavy drinking session late one afternoon in a chic Montpellier wine bar, he got behind the wheel of his brand new Aston Martin and decided to return home for a well-earned sleep. After several failed attempts, he finally managed to press the ignition button, whereupon he dropped the car into gear and promptly reversed into the side of a passing Ford Fiesta. The dishevelled drunk then levered himself out of his car, totally oblivious to his surroundings and unaware of the chaos his stupidity had caused. A crumpled, unbuttoned, tartan shirt hung loosely over his scruffy denim jeans revealing the elasticated band of his off-white underpants and a bloated belly. He wobbled and swayed to and fro, as though he was facing a force nine gale, flopped back against the curvaceous side panel for support before kicking the door closed with a hefty wallop. The drunk then reached, rather shakily, for the chrome door handle, lost his balance, stubbed his foot on the high kerb, tripped, fell backwards and landed flat out across the windscreen of his silver machine.

He then slid down the sloping bonnet, just like a cobra slithering around the trunk of a tree, rolled over the polished radiator grill and bumperbar, before coming to rest underneath his personalised front number plate. Here he curled up into a ball, put his grubby thumb in his mouth and promptly went off to sleep. The outraged female driver ranted at her drunken assailant when she surveyed the extent of the damage to her precious little car. She was incensed by this unprovoked attack on her sweet, innocent Betsy, especially as the scruffy yob was blind drunk, out for the count, not concerned in the slightest by her predicament. She paced around the crumpled wreck several times, looking on in horror at the shattered glass and mangled bits of bodywork. As she quietly calmed down and became more composed, she peered at the sad, dejected object lying on the pavement and, for some strange reason best known to herself, took pity on the poor wretch, even though the selfish lout had wreaked havoc and destruction. Some nosy onlookers offered a helping hand, as great clouds of dark smoke belched out of the badly crushed bonnet and side panels and a black oil slick surrounded the front of her poor wretched machine. Many suggested she call the old bill, make the drink-sodden blighter pay for the damage and distress he'd caused.

Poor Betsy had come off badly in the altercation with the super-car and would probably spend her final days in a dingy, dank scrapyard before meeting her end in a giant steel crusher. Claire was shaking like a leaf and clearly suffering from shock, when a podgy guy with tattooed arms and stapled ears picked up sleeping beauty and, in one brisk movement, threw the damp bundle onto the front seat of his luxury motor. Fortunately a passing busybody recognised the number plates, knew where the reprobate lived and, once the car keys had been retrieved from the driver's wet trouser pocket, one of the chubby, well-fed onlookers volunteered to drive him home.

Later that evening, feeling a little better after a couple of nifty cognacs and bottle of Rioja Reserve, David sat up in bed and, with a shaky hand, wrote a little ditty which he thought just about summed up the day.

Never drink while driving; the mess goes everywhere,
Bits of fruit stick in your teeth, with cherries in your hair,
You try your best to chill the wine, but this is just too much,
Then you're forced to brake real hard, as ice cubes freeze your crutch.

In the weeks that followed, Claire became a regular visitor to number one, helping David get his life back on track. It was a very bumpy ride to begin with. There were lots of fractious, irritable arguments with bouts of crockery thrown and doors slamming, accompanied by tedious shouting matches and endless tantrums, often stretching her nerves to breaking point. But Claire was determined to give it her best shot, not give up on her belligerent, uncouth boyfriend who could test the patience of a saint. Eventually though, after months of endless battles, childish outbursts and silly crying matches, her valiant efforts were rewarded. David at last took full responsibility for his addiction and was determined to take control of his life and move forward.

But then, out of the blue, there was an unexpected turn of events that threatened to destroy their fragile relationship for ever. One lunchtime, shortly before Christmas in 1998, just after they'd decorated their eight-foot pine tree and placed numerous greetings cards from well-wishers in the spacious bay window, all hell let loose. For no reason, no reason at all, after months of resisting the booze, David grabbed hold of an unopened bottle of whisky, stored in the nearby glass cabinet, and gulped down several swigs of the single malt in rapid succession. Feeling rather pleased with himself, he turned and sneered at Claire, just like a naughty boy when he knows he's done something wrong – baiting you, teasing you to react. She was fuming, enraged by his infantile behaviour. Claire could have smacked him across the face there and then, such was the anger she felt bubbling up inside, only made worse when he sniggered, smirked and waved the empty crystal glass in the air as if he was holding a trophy to symbolise success; a proud achievement.

Most women would have packed their bags, called it a day and wondered off into the distance without a second thought. But not Claire. She was made of tougher stuff and was determined to confront the bully boy head on, not let him get one over her. Without thinking, she grabbed hold of the precious gold locket with the framed photographs of David's parents and pointed at their faces smiling back at her. Then shouting at the top of her voice, gave him both barrels as the paralytic drunk slumped backwards on the floor, like a large sack of potatoes, dropped the empty glass, scattering fragments of tiny pieces everywhere before messing his trousers and throwing up on the new Wilton rug.

"What would they say if they saw you now, you worthless piece of shit? You make me sick. What have you done in their memory, you selfish prick, other than drinking yourself silly and urinating in your trousers? If Jeremy and Louise Lane were standing here now, they'd regret ever bringing a selfish sod like you into the world. They'd be disgusted by your degrading behaviour and the shame you've brought upon their proud family name. They'd never forgive you. You should be ashamed of yourself."

Claire was normally a relaxed sort of person, quite easy going, someone who took life in her stride and very rarely got rattled, or upset. So her intemperate language and frenzied rage was completely out of character, a real shock for her lumbering inept partner struggling to get to his feet, busily removing small shards of glass lying embedded in his dirty bloodstained palms. Her hands were shaking and floods of tears were rolling down her flushed cheeks when she raced out of the house and plonked herself down in a wicker chair on the patio, holding her head between her damp, soggy hands while crying uncontrollably into a handful of crumpled paper tissues. David Lane's girlfriend was distraught, inconsolable and clearly at the end of her tether thanks to the selfish, pig-headed antics of her drunken partner.

He was shocked and angered by her loud-mouthed rantings and vindictive comments about his beloved parents. "I hate that woman, she's no good for me, she'll have to go," he mumbled under his smelly breath, still struggling to get to his feet. For some reason, his trousers had taken on a red blotchy sheen and his legs refused to work, so standing upright was a bridge too far. Eventually, after much huffing and puffing, the villain of the peace stumbled up the steep staircase, using the sturdy banister rail for much needed support, but when the going got really tough, he was forced to revert to all fours. After what seemed an interminable time, he arrived at the guest room, collapsed fully clothed onto the bed feeling very sorry for himself like a spoilt petulant child. As an encore, a climax to his afternoon's ignominious performance, he then vomited several times into the Waitrose waste paper basket sitting innocently at the foot of the bed.

David's thumping headache threatened to rip through his skull at any moment and his stomach ached and throbbed with every excruciating movement. Sleep was in scarce supply that night as he gazed tearfully at the pictures of his beloved parents, sitting on the adjacent side table, that he'd safely retrieved from his girlfriend's grasping clutches.

But then, something quite extraordinary happened during the long bleak hours of darkness as David drifted in and out of sleep, often waking with a jolt and sweating profusely, such that when the mercurial character rose the next morning he seemed to have gone through some kind of transformation. The engaging playboy, with the endearing smile, was on show looking his very best while the dishevelled bully was nowhere to be seen. David showered early, drank several cups of black coffee before taking a brisk walk into town dressed in his favourite Armani suit, with a smart blue shirt, pink tie and expensive handmade shoes bought recently from the prestigious Cavendish House shoe department. He looked the ticket.

On his return, after his early morning jaunt and looking a bit jaded, he cooked breakfast with umpteen rounds of brown toast and two large cups of espresso coffee. Then holding his parents' treasured locket firmly in his grip, promised Claire, with tears welling up in his eyes, that he'd behave himself in future, he'd never let her down again. It was a poignant moment in their turbulent relationship and David, to his credit, kept his word, kept his side of the bargain and never allowed alcohol to rule the waves again. His girlfriend's stern, unyielding words really hit home, making him take a long hard look at himself and recognise the impact his selfish uncaring behaviour has on other people. Sure, at night he continued to see horrific flashbacks of his tortuous days at the hands of his sadistic abusers, and the sound of his parents screaming at the porthole windows of their plane often plagued him during the hours of darkness. But gradually the tide turned, the cravings reduced, his dependency on alcohol diminished and the insufferable nightmares started to recede. He built up his energy levels and body strength through a disciplined programme of swimming, running and power walking. It was modest to begin with, but as he progressed and saw the benefits of his hard work, so he raised the bar, pushed his body even further. Regular exercise improved his posture and physique as well as his general health and well-being. He invested a great deal of time and money on his bumpy road to recovery, but with Claire's unwavering support the bedraggled drunk, with smelly breath and a podgy stomach, was confined to history, a thing of the past.

Shirley's death had hit him hard and made him think. It showed how little can be done to stem the tide once a serious illness takes hold and that much more needs to be done in the field of diagnostics to prevent such precious lives being wasted in the future.

On examining a raft of medical statistics, studying lengthy articles and reading various papers in *The Lancet,* and others, he was shocked to see how many people fell prey to a catalogue of nasty, often incurable cancers. How hundreds of lives were blighted each year by a number of serious illnesses. Kidney disease, liver failure, heart attacks, diabetes and strokes all made the top ten. David Lane knew he was lucky compared to the rest, he had a trusty helpmate, a privileged lifestyle and some money in the bank. But what about the less fortunate, what did they do?

Several days later, having patched up his relationship with Claire and feeling much more at ease with life, he took his customary stroll into town. His favourite bench was slightly damp after a short sharp shower, but that didn't faze him. As he sat there, he thought about what his mother had said during that memorable night when he lay in bed drunk, nursing his sore head and feeling very sorry for himself.

She told him he was a star, a brave young man who was on the cusp of something great and he should use his talents for the benefit of others, make the family name great again. He gazed longingly at her photograph, inside the gold locket, and with a steely determination vowed to fulfil his mother's heartfelt wishes. Louise Lane was the catalyst for change on that unforgettable cold winter's night when her son swore to denounce his self-centred existence and follow in her redoubtable footsteps.

In the weeks ahead, it wasn't plain sailing for the recovering drunk, far from it. The irritable playboy lived on his nerves, often venting his anger by shouting and hollering from the upstairs landing, or by smashing and breaking things when the cravings, the pull of grape, got too much to bear. But he didn't falter, he didn't succumb to the temptations of the bottle, knowing that a drink-fuelled existence was a recipe for doom, the road to ruin. So with his mother's wise words still ringing loudly in his ears, he picked up the gauntlet, deciding that fitness and healthy living were the best route to recovery, the only positive way forward.

After all he was fit and active in the past and, with gritty determination and self-control, he could recapture his youth and do it all again. So his well-equipped basement gym and games room were his regular haunt. Here he pounded the treadmill, sweating buckets in the process, pumped iron till his arms nearly fell off and worked out on Jordan, his exercise bike, until he could hardly stand. This punishing regime kept him sane, kept him on the straight and narrow. He took each day at a time on his slow road to recovery, with the promise of better things to come when drink would cease to be his master and he'd be in charge of his own destiny, once again.

Chapter 15

"I know the guy very well. If it wasn't for you, he'd be dead by now, I can assure you. Your life hasn't been worth living for years, thanks to the antics of the drunk. He's run you ragged. I think you deserve a blasted award after what you've put up with. He's neglected you, reduced you to tears many a time, made your life intolerable so you definitely don't owe the guy anything," Pierre retorted angrily.

"I'm sorry, but I feel awful doing things behind David's back, especially now that he's much better. He's a complicated man with unpredictable mood-swings. He flies off the handle for the slightest thing. If he ever found out about us, he'd go mad, life wouldn't be worth living, I can tell you. When he's angry or feels threatened, he's at his most dangerous and it's best to give him a wide berth; keep well out of his way."

"Oh, I think you're exaggerating. He's like all men, rather selfish, full of his own importance, likes to be in control of everything. They're all the same. I don't know what you're worrying about. We've all done our bit to help him and you've gone the extra mile." He reached out, patted her gently on the leg of her pale blue designer jeans.

"You need to think about yourself for a change, do what you want to do. I really love our time together, Claire," he said with a broad grin, weaving his arm around her waist, gently pulling her towards him before kissing her tenderly on her deep, red lips.

"He doesn't deserve you. Just think about your boyfriend for one minute. You've turned down his many offers of marriage because he's silly, childish and does daft things. He'll never change. Do you remember when the idiot decorated your car from top to toe with 200 red roses and then it rained? So what did he do? He ordered another 200 the next day and did it all over again, but this time the nutcase hired a gazebo just in case. How dumb was that?"

Claire remembered it well and turned her head to disguise her smile.

"Then the lunatic traipsed into the Cadena Coffee Shop on the Prom dressed as an old lady, sat down and chatted to you and your friends for about ten minutes before the rogue removed his clever disguise and revealed all. That must have been a terrible shock for some of your more elderly companions. Whatever was he thinking of?

"And then, if that wasn't enough, your errant partner told a Jehovah's Witness that he was gay and enjoyed the carnal pleasures of the flesh as he stood on his doorstep, in his bright red dressing gown, fondling a sex toy with an empty bottle of whisky lying at his feet. Oh, and what's the idea of the *Colonel Bogey* doorbell blasting out that incessant racket every time someone calls at the house? It's just not in keeping with such a luxurious property. He'll paint the darn place pink next, you mark my words. David Lane takes eccentricity to the next level. The man's mad, years of hard drinking have addled his brain, surely you can see that? The sooner you pack your bags and leave him the better," he retorted angrily.

She smiled to herself when Pierre regaled some of David's bizarre antics, covering her crimson complexion with her hand, trying to stifle her laughter and any fits of the giggles.

"Yes, he's a rogue all right, definitely doesn't take himself very seriously. David's life is always shining bright, glistening and glitzy with sparkling colours everywhere. His world is full of vitality and energy, where happiness and humour are his constant bedfellows. He has no time for the beige and greys," she mumbled, trying to shield her mouth with the back of her hand.

"You need someone who's dependable, conscientious, doesn't mess about and acts his age. A mature person who knows where he's going," he said in a superior tone of voice.

"I suppose you're right," said Claire, rather hesitantly, mulling over some of the other impish things her mischievous, fun-loving boyfriend had been up to which her serious, more mature male companion was unaware of.

"Now let's change the subject, think about something nice. Let's take your sports car out for a spin, put the roof down, treat ourselves to some lunch and take things from there. What's wrong with that? How about the Broadway Hotel? You've always liked going there."

Claire smiled, grabbed his hand. The couple then strolled arm in arm out of his posh modern offices in Charlton Kings, a quiet salubrious suburb to the east of the Regency spa town.

"Okay, that sounds nice and perhaps we can browse around the designer shops and quaint little delis in the High Street, have coffee at the Lygon Arms and then call in at Winchcombe on the way back and have a look around Sudeley Castle? That would be great fun. Having studied history at university, I love visiting places of historical importance and Sudeley's always been one of my favourite haunts ever since I was a young girl," said Claire.

She sounded very perky and upbeat at the prospect of a few hours away from Pavilion Avenue and as Mr and Mrs Millins, their live-in housekeepers, were out for the day and David was in London attending a big charity board meeting, she wouldn't be missed. A close friend of his from Barcelona would be there and, as they had a great deal to talk about, she didn't expect him home until late evening when he'd catch the last direct train from the capital.

Sadly for Pierre, things didn't go as well as he'd hoped. In fact, it went pear-shaped before they even finished their fish starters. His supercilious jibes and endless criticisms of David was like a red rag to a bull and instead of driving a wedge between the pair, as he hoped, it made Claire even more infatuated with the man she'd shared her bed with for the last few years. So when the sports car came to a sudden halt outside the doctor's surgery, Claire let rip, telling her patronising front-seat passenger exactly what she thought about her good looking boyfriend.

"Do you know something, Pierre? David proposed to me again this morning and guess what, I've decided to accept his offer of marriage. I know he's very unpredictable, highly-strung and can be quite annoying, but I wouldn't swap him for the world and now the drink's behind him, he's a totally different man. By the way, for the record, I like red roses; I can't have enough of them. I hate Jehovah's Witnesses and *Colonel Bogey* is one of my favourite tunes. Dressing up as an old lady isn't my bag, but what the heck, each to his own. It made me giggle. You see, David Lane is a free spirit and, with all of his little idiosyncrasies, he makes me laugh every day. He makes me feel valued, he makes me feel very important. That's all I want."

Before Pierre Sharon had time to respond to Claire's emotional outburst, she raced around to his side of the car, opened his door to let him out and then raced off the tarmac drive, leaving great plumes of white smoke in her wake and two black lines of Pirelli rubber. She was going to call her man, once she got home, tell him that nine was his lucky number!

Chapter 16

Claire was David's guardian angel, injecting order and focus into his dysfunctional life. First of all as his personal assistant, confidant and best mate, but then slowly over time their tetchy, often fraught relationship, blossomed into something more serious, more permanent culminating with the sound of wedding bells in 2009. For Claire, the prospect of marriage to a reformed drunk, with a mercurial temperament and a strange take on life, seemed a daunting prospect fraught with problems and uncertainties. She questioned David's maturity and commitment and wondered whether he'd ever break out of the playboy lifestyle that had been his mantra for most of his adult life or, even worse, allow his demons to drag him back to the dark drunken days of his recent squalid past.

But it was his dedication, even obsession, with charitable work that was his saving grace. His social conscience and benevolent attitude towards others finally convinced Claire, after much heart-searching, that he was the man for her.

So Claire eventually succumbed to his many marriage proposals. They swopped twenty-two-carat gold rings at a private civil ceremony in a lavish top-floor suite at the awe-inspiring Meridian Hotel in the wonderful coastal city of Barcelona. The newly-weds enjoyed their first meal together as a married couple on the balcony of their hotel room with the sound of laughter and mayhem on the pavements below, and birds chirping in the blue skies overhead.

One of the defining moments of their happy union, the following day, was hearing the soulful voice of Aretha Franklin on a car radio as they strolled arm in arm down the Ramblas oblivious to the world around them. A shaft of light got in on the act, shining down on the rowdy outdoor restaurants and street cafes, offering a vibrant tribute to the happy couple. David looked into his bride's blue eyes and said, "Those simple lyrics say so much about my love for you and how you've helped me so.

"When my soul was in the lost and found, you came along to claim it," he quoted, gazing longingly into the tearful eyes of his new wife as the warm sun peered through the overhanging branches, gently swaying in the early morning breeze.

Claire smiled at David while the pulsating melody captured the mood of the moment, making her feel quite emotional. It was then, she recalled the day before when a beautiful bouquet of flowers were delivered to their luxurious hotel suite with a handwritten note clipped to the corner of the polythene. Her gallant, chivalrous white knight then read the message on bended knees:

I feel this growing passion, as my eyes rest on your face,
Your tantalising beauty, is never out of place,
You look so very graceful, your figure so divine,
When I go on bended knees, please say you will be mine.

Funnily enough, Claire remembered reading the very same cheesy poem in an anonymous Valentine card she'd received earlier in the year, but she didn't let on. Just made her smile.

Leaning forward and whispering in his ear, Claire had the final word on that memorable day in Spain's second city. "Do you know something David Lane? I've always been a fan of Aretha Franklin since my university days and you, you alone, make me feel like a natural woman, you really do." For once in his life, David Lane was lost for words. Speechless.

Chapter 17

The dawn of a new century was a turning point for the enterprising businessman. He'd crushed the demon drink that had dogged his life for many years, often making suicide a serious option and, through self-discipline and bloody-mindedness was in control and master of his own destiny.

David joined the management boards of many established charities, sharing his sales and marketing expertise that he'd developed over the years under the watchful eye of Edward Crawford and by attending various specialist business seminars and evening classes. Here he helped raise substantial funds for an array of research projects and good causes and built a reputation for his philanthropic pursuits throughout the charitable sector.

Spearheading many major new initiatives and schemes, he took on a hefty workload that often meant burning the midnight oil. His altruistic streak also reached out at grassroots level, making anonymous donations to many heart-wrenching causes that caught his eye and where he felt his intervention would make a difference, very much in accord with his mother's sacred wishes.

But then the debonair entrepreneur began to tire of the desk job and yearned for a new venture, a new challenge, where his keen money-making talents could be put to even better use. David Lane's vision was simple. He'd bring together a group of wealthy philanthropic individuals who would attract large donations from cash-rich companies and opulent private benefactors, in return for them pitting their wits against the elements through a series of high-octane cycle rides at prestigious locations across the length and breadth of Europe. After umpteen phone calls, texts and emails by David and Christopher Parker-Wright, his close friend and partner, they managed to coerce, corral and gently bully some of the wealthiest people in Europe into joining their international crusade.

So in the summer of 2009, David Lane, with his flamboyant companion, launched the much vaunted Pedal Power Programme at a glitzy gala dinner at the prestigious Ritz Hotel in central London with as much pomp and razzmatazz as the colourful duo could muster. They'd achieved the impossible. In a matter of months, they'd formed an elite, high-profile squad of famous faces from across the continent.

These rich well-heeled guys were household names in their own countries, synonymous for their extravagant lifestyles, but who after some smooth talking and gentle persuasion by the programme founders, were prepared to donate their time to a series of exciting highly publicised cycling adventures. Their reputation alone guaranteed huge commercial interest and untold marketing opportunities as droves of baying fans flocked to their TVs and various tablets in awe of their heroes, wanting to share in the daring exploits of their iconic pin-ups. David's compatriots courted publicity at every turn. They cherished the limelight and the constant click of the TV camera or the photo lens, often baiting the paparazzi to keep up such was their quest for fame and recognition. Team 30, as they were called, lived the high life, splashing the cash on prestigious houses, private planes, luxury yachts, fine art paintings and expensive jewellery. The healthy-hunks often appeared in glossy magazines and in salacious articles in the tabloid press as opulence and self-indulgence were their constant bedfellows.

The public admired, often envied the glamour and the glitz that followed these super-stars knowing the world they inhabited was something most people could only dream of. But their generous followers took these privileged thrill-seekers to their hearts for one reason and one reason only. The Team, over the years, used their fame and fortune to help others less fortunate which put them on a pedestal, making them celebrities and real-life heroes in the eyes of their doting fans. These altruistic qualities endeared them to their many corporate sponsors and wealthy benefactors as well as the man in the street, who was happy to part with his hard-earned cash, do his bit for charity, knowing they collected millions of pounds each year by riding a series of gruelling cycle rides often in arduous weather conditions. Their loyal fans often turned a blind eye to some of their outrageous excesses and raunchy antics that regularly made the headlines in the tabloid press and on social media.

Christopher Parker-Wright was a good example. He was born in England, educated at some of the finest schools in the country and a close friend of David since working together as board members for two well-known charitable companies. He was a middle-aged bachelor, living in Barcelona on a 1000-acre estate with his wealthy parents and a bank balance as long as your arm. He spent about one million pounds a year maintaining his lavish jet-set lifestyle. He wore £5,000 Savile Row suits, adorned his feet in handmade shoes costing in excess of £500, ate at some of the finest restaurants in the world, drove expensive first-edition super-cars and swanned around Europe in a private jet with his glamorous hairdresser in tow.

But here's the rub. This flamboyant playboy, who's addicted to Rolex watches and handmade shirts, attracted vast sums each year for the Pedal Power Programme. Because of his sex appeal and stunning good looks, he also acted as a roving ambassador for his family's vast global business interests in oil and gas, banking and the hotel sector, all of which benefitted quite significantly from his regular, high-profile presence in the media. So PW, as he's often called, felt that even though he enjoyed an extravagant way of life, he did his bit and according to his eminent partner, he really made a difference and that was good enough for him.

Chapter 18

He smiled longingly at his attractive wife as he drank his glass of Diet Coke and grabbed a handful of salted peanuts, leaned forward across the glass-panel coffee table at the prestigious Carlton Hotel and kissed her tenderly on her softly powdered cheek. She smelt good, very good.

"Well, this'll have to stop for a start," she said with a flick of her auburn hair.

"What do mean?" asked David, rather indignantly.

"No more fizzy drinks and nuts for you until after the big day, okay?" she replied, smiling.

He nodded, pouted his lips, looked down and scuffed his polished leather shoes through the plush crimson high-pile carpet just like a spoilt child when it fails to get its own way.

"Yes," he said. "I totally agree. I need all the help I can get. I can tell you."

David opened his Apple iPad and scrolled through the many eye-catching pages of the psychedelic Pedal Power website. It looked very impressive.

They sipped their drinks and he explained the rationale behind the extensive advertising campaign for Sunday's big race around the lake, saying with real emotion in his voice, that Facebook was already buzzing with excitement at the prospect. Messages of support and goodwill were pouring in from all over the place and he'd had tweets galore from fans and excited well-wishers. It was incredible.

The thirty cyclists were all well-known business owners and playboys of repute who'd attracted a rich following of generous patrons, even hero worshippers, such was the team's iconic status across Europe.

He brushed some wayward salted nuts off his pristine deep blue trousers and said. "This event will raise the profile of this Cinderella illness, get people talking about it and bring in pot loads of money to help fund research. We must raise the profile of this dreadful illness, Claire. It's been ignored for years as though it doesn't exist and I can't understand the reason ..."

"Can I take your glasses please Mr ...?"

"No, go away!" shouted David angrily, waving his hand dismissively at the frightened waiter, looking very annoyed at being disturbed in mid-sentence. Claire felt sorry for the poor guy having had the audacity to interrupt her husband's train of thought and attract the wrath of his wayward tongue.

"Come back later," he bawled out. His face took on a red glow and his eyes glared unashamedly at the miscreant who quickly scooted off, not wishing to upset their esteemed guest any further.

"Where was I? Oh yes. We must crack it Claire. There's thousands suffering as we speak, as we sit here in our comfortable little bubble. It's not good enough to say we tried, we did our bit. We've got to succeed and this ride will help to put ME/CFS firmly on the map."

He crashed his fist down onto the coffee table with an almighty thump, making the china crockery shake in fear and trepidation. Claire didn't budge, she daren't.

"It's going to be our best ride yet. It will be a festival of colour, with miles and miles of bunting and streamers, with happy, smiling faces and lots of flag waving. There'll be vibrant banners and flamboyant advertising awnings everywhere proclaiming their message of goodwill all around the iconic lake. It will be a great occasion and our best ride yet."

Claire saw raw passion and real determination in his eyes. She knew that Team 30 were going to do something extra special that weekend and with David Lane at their helm, success was very much in their grasp. So the adopted Cheltonian finished off his Coke, slumped back in his easy chair, swallowed the last nutty morsel and handed his empty glass to Claire, with a mischievous grin and submissive nod of the head. He closed his iPad, left a crisp ten-pound note on the table, waved to the red-faced waiter, who'd taken refuge behind the lounge bar and guided his attractive wife towards the hotel exit. Here they were greeted to a warm summer breeze as groups of young girls, dressed in smart green uniforms from Cheltenham Ladies' College strolled past, laughing and joking on their way towards the town centre.

"Francois' team have excelled themselves this time, you know. They've pulled out all the stops, really engaged with the locals, been doing lots of interviews on TV and radio. The Italian press are buzzing with excitement at the prospect of us rolling into town. Because of the reputation of many of the riders, we've attracted even more interest than ever. It bodes well for ME. This is our opportunity Claire, which we must grasp and exploit to the maximum.

"Right, let's get home my love. I've an early start tomorrow. I shall need all my strength for the challenge ahead," remarked David, as the gooey-eyed couple slowly wended their way up the road towards their majestic Regency villa, standing proudly at the brow of the hill. It must have been all of 200 yards! Moments later, they turned the key in the lock and ventured in. The word *wow* was always uppermost on their lips even though the couple encountered the awe-inspiring sight every day. They never got bored of it, not for one minute. There always seemed to be something new to marvel at, to savour and enjoy. The entrance alone was grand and imposing, oozing wealth, style and elegance wherever you looked. It was quite overwhelming with its tall endless ceilings, dazzling chandeliers sparkling in the artificial light and the strikingly bright magnolia walls, that were adorned with expensive first edition watercolours and fine art paintings. The grand swirling spiral staircase brought a smile to your face when you gazed up the sweeping gallery, reminding you of a bygone age, as the enthralling eye-catching centrepiece to their Regency abode made the uninitiated gasp in wonderment at the beauty on display.

Later in the evening, having packed his suitcases, they tiptoed up the wooden hill like a pair of naughty teenagers, holding onto the winding wooden banister for support. With polished shoes in hand, they sneaked passed the first-floor rooms, listened at a nearby bedroom door and heard the reassuring sound of the doting duo snoring in peaceful harmony. It was just after ten p.m. and Mr and Mrs Millins, their live-in housekeepers, had had an early night and were clearly fast asleep. The Lanes' spacious bedroom was tastefully decorated in fresh magnolia emulsion, with expensive landscape watercolours and one or two light-hearted family photographs, encased in gold picture frames, hanging on the lofty walls of their exquisite private paradise. They quickly undressed, washed in their his and hers sinks and prepared for bed in the company of Sam Smith's haunting melody, *Stay with Me*.

David, often the clumsy one, did his usual party trick. In his haste to get under the white, silk sheets, he managed to stub his toe on the foot of the bed and spent the next few minutes caressing the bruised digit. Meanwhile his unconcerned wife, oblivious to his night-time trauma, turned over in bed, took the lead from their first-floor employees and very soon was snoring with great gusto.

After days of intensive training, David was back in the saddle again, in fine fettle and raring to go. He'd endured lengthy, sweaty workouts in his basement torture chamber under the watchful eye of Harry, his sadistic personal trainer, and completed umpteen timed cycle rides on a purpose-built track in the town. He'd survived countless intensive sessions on Jordan, his old exercise bike that had been with him since the dark days, when alcohol was his only friend and sobriety a mystical dream. That was David's gruelling training programme since his sudden bout of flu confined him to his king-size bed at the end of May and so, thankfully after a period of arduous workouts, with a carefully controlled diet, he was fighting fit and Harry's punishing campaign had paid off dividends. Tanned legs and well-honed, muscular arms and thighs were testament to his high level of physical fitness. David knew, from past experience, that long distance cycling in challenging, arduous conditions took no prisoners and you were facing disaster head-on if you were unfit, or even slightly under par. In recent weeks, he'd been riding twenty miles or more most days, all the time testing his strength, stamina and mental fortitude to the limit. He was now stronger than ever, much more agile and 100 per cent focused on the daunting task ahead.

At last he'd lost the excruciating pain that had plagued him for about a week, attacking his lower back and neck and making sleep and rest almost impossible. So Claire's extrovert husband, with a passion for extreme sports, was a rejuvenated specimen, keyed up and fully charged for the tough ride ahead. But as always, the athlete's overriding concern before embarking on any charity venture was failure; the fear of letting people down and not delivering on a promise. David's recent health problems had dented his confidence somewhat, exposed his vulnerability to illness and brought into question his ability to step up to the plate. But that was all behind him now. Thanks to the unflinching support of Claire and Harry, he was positive and upbeat and looking forward with cheery optimism to the challenges ahead.

Chapter 19

And so on an unusually damp, soggy morning in July, 2014, David kissed Claire goodbye and said he'd miss her terribly standing there in her sexy tight-fitting denim jeans and loose top, leaning provocatively against the half-open front door to their palatial Cheltenham residence. She looked good, very good and smelt even better.

"When you stand like that, you remind me of Paul Bettany you know, but you're much better looking of course," she called out, as her husband turned and descended the steps with his luggage bumping clumsily over the concrete slabs behind him.

"Don't forget to oil Jordan, get Mr M to do it," he suggested coyly. The revitalised athlete, with a very slight limp, sauntered down the gravel drive dragging his wheeled suitcases close behind him. "See you on Monday evening!" he called out, shaking the taxi driver's outstretched hand and glancing back over his shoulder for a last glimpse.

Flopping into the waiting car, with Ken Bruce's dulcet tones for company, he waved longingly through the misty rear window and sank into the comfortable soft cream leather. The deep blue BMW then sped out of town, up the busy M5 motorway on its way to Birmingham International Airport, with Graham, the diminutive driver, at the controls. An hour later, David joined a snake-like queue of about twenty people checking in for the late morning British Airways flight. He looked slim and dapper, strolling confidently through security control in his freshly ironed designer jeans, open-neck white shirt and casual red jacket. He was frisked a couple of times by a miserable, overbearing official before passing the test and being given the all-clear. Apparently, it was the collection of keys in his jacket pocket that caused the trouble, making their security machines go bleep, bleep, bleep.

It was a Friday in the peak holiday season and the international airport was quickly filling up so he retreated from the noise and hullabaloo of the concourse, taking solace in the solemnity of the executive lounge with its familiar posh leather seats, friendly ambiance and attractive panoramic views of the airport runways. He checked his mobile phone for messages, ignored most of them, knowing Claire would handle any urgent issues and, with time to spare before the flight, decided to take an early lunch.

The fitness fanatic munched his way through a portion of crinkly lettuce, chewed on some thin slices of cucumber and tomato, with slithers of green and red peppers and finished off his calorie-controlled banquet with a couple of hard-boiled eggs and a few rounds of bread and butter. These tasty morsels were washed down with several cool glasses of ice-cold water that really hit the spot and helped stave off any underlying hunger pangs. As always, prior to any ride, he'd eat lots of carbohydrates and proteins to help build up his energy and stamina levels, and as it was less than forty-eight hours before the starting gun, he needed to manage his food intake very carefully.

David noticed, with much relief, that the white windsock was draped loosely around the pole alongside the main runway, a signal that boded well for a fairly comfortable take-off. The frequent flyer was not a fan of air travel. The take-off invariably caused sweaty palms and flushed cheeks, while the flight itself and the actual landing weren't to his liking either. The sound of tyres screeching on the tarmac as the aircraft decelerated and lumbered to a halt was music to his ears, confirming his safe return to good old terra firma.

Glancing around the lounge, engrossed in his own private world, he daydreamed about his lovely wife, thinking how much he loved Claire, her quirky little ways, her funny smile, infectious laugh, and her positive outlook on life. But sadly this image of love and trust had been seriously dented over the last few weeks. He'd begun to have serious doubts about her fidelity and had been made aware of some tell-tale signs that could jeopardise their future happiness together. The next few days would bring the issue to a head and hopefully his fears would be allayed and life could return to normal.

Sometime ago, David noticed on Facebook that a young woman in Cheltenham had undertaken various sponsored activities in support of ME/CFS, a debilitating illness affecting seventeen million people worldwide, including over 250,000 in the UK. The lady in question had worked tirelessly for the charity and had raised considerable amounts of money over a number of years for the ME Association. It was this selfless story of dedication, and his subsequent research into the distressing illness, that inspired David to propose dedicating the proceeds of the Lake Garda ride to ME research.

The story was even more amazing when, following further investigation, he discovered that the girl had suffered from ME/CFS for over twenty-five years and, rather than worry about herself and her own problems, had dedicated her time to help fellow sufferers. Her compelling story of compassion really pulled at his heartstrings, making David determined to do what he could to raise the profile of the illness and get people talking about it. The monies from the Italian ride would finance further research and hopefully lead to a cure for the millions of silent sufferers scattered around the globe.

When David launched the Pedal Power Programme in 2009, he wanted it to be bigger and bolder than anything that had gone before, to capture people's imagination such that they rushed to their wallets, cheque books, credit cards and purses in their eagerness to get involved and make a difference. It was organised on strict business lines with a Committee of well-qualified individuals, drawn from the world of finance and commerce, overseeing the smooth running of the Programme. Based in Paris, it organised five high-profile cycle rides in Europe each year. They selected one charity per event and all donations were subsequently channelled to that single cause.

Their duties weren't onerous, or particularly time consuming, but David wanted to guarantee transparency in their working practices and reassure their generous supporters and benefactors that everything was above board and beyond reproach. This was very important bearing in mind the average purse, per event, was often in excess of five million pounds. Previous rides had targeted a range of serious illnesses and social issues. MS, AIDS, kidney, liver and heart disease, various cancers, child poverty, mental illness, alcoholism, drug addiction and domestic abuse were included. But much to David's annoyance, ME/CFS had never been raised as an issue at board level, let alone made the cut, but that was soon to change. Clearly the millionaire had some clout and influence over the charitable projects selected by the Committee and so, after a bit of arm twisting and gentle lobbying, he won the day and that summer's charitable ride was dedicated to the illness. He made an impassioned plea on behalf of the charity, complaining that ME was a silent illness, often ignored and very much overlooked when compared to other life-threatening ailments and disorders.

He suddenly jerked to life, noticing on the overhead television screen that his flight was called and that was the signal for him to rush to the nearest loo. He'd overdone the Evian water and his sensitive bladder was now paying for it.

Shortly after his ten-second experience with the Dyson air-blade hand-dryer, he joined his fellow travellers, waiting expectantly at gate forty-three, to board their British Airways flight. They appeared tense and ill at ease, gripping their passports and boarding cards. This wasn't good news for the nervous flyer. However, half an hour later they were all strapped in, cruising effortlessly at 36,000 feet towards the snow-capped Swiss Alps and the enchanting city of Verona. The take-off was a dream, he didn't even notice it. David prayed that the landing in two hours' time would be equally kind to his delicate stomach and sensitive disposition.

He'd sampled the delights of Verona before and remembered fondly its gentle flowing rivers that meandered around the metropolis under an array of fine historic bridges. He recalled a majestic Roman colosseum dominating the centre of the city, a reminder of its barbaric past when death and cruelty were part of everyday life. But today, in contrast, the very same building was a hot spot on the tourist trail, a renowned venue for operatic concerts, international recitals and Shakespearian plays. Its friendly, congenial neighbours included raucous shopping malls, chic hotels and classy Michelin star restaurants. David could almost smell freshly cooked sardines on the grill, with the poignant waft of garlic on the breeze, making his mouth salivate at the very thought of it.

A broad smirk drifted across his face when he recalled a middle-aged guy called Arthur. They bumped into him while enjoying a weekend break in Italy's premier city. He was an intriguing character with great clumps of grey hair sticking out of his ears, a strange accent and a pronounced bent back that made him lean forward when he walked. Apparently he was a regular visitor to Riva, on the northern shores of Lake Garda, and saw himself as a bit of an authority figure, an aficionado, when it came to Italian history and its culture. He was enamoured with Claire from the outset and couldn't keep his beady eyes off her see-through chiffon top, particularly when it floated freely on the breeze, giving tantalising views of her curvaceous figure. The hobbit tried to ingratiate himself by offering her some practical local advice and, with a Birmingham accent, he pointed out that the main gate and walls in Verona, built by the Romans about two thousand years earlier, were leaning very badly. The walking guidebook suggested it was unwise to sit too close to the structures as the porous cement might disintegrate and cause the walls to collapse at any moment. Claire couldn't believe what she'd heard; she turned her head away and covered her face with a hanky to stifle her giggles. Well, needless to say the poor unfortunate hobbit became the brunt of many a late-night joke at dinner parties and social gatherings when Claire regaled his extraordinary tale as the wine flowed and champagne corks were popping.

Then near journey's end and making their descent, the aircraft suddenly experienced turbulence. This unnerved David, who was prone to air sickness and bouts of nausea for the slightest reason. In his blind panic, he inadvertently grabbed hold of the man's arm sat quietly resting next to him. This was most embarrassing and the remaining fifteen minutes of the British Airways flight were somewhat uncomfortable, to say the least. His new flying companion seemed flattered by the unexpected attention lavished upon him and proceeded to wink every time their eyes made contact. This episode was most disconcerting for David Lane who relished the company of attractive, beautiful women and cringed if a man attempted to hug him, let alone wink. The sound of the landing gear being deployed couldn't come soon enough, was music to his ears. Thankfully the gods had listened to his earlier prayers and their gradual descent onto Italian tarmac was smooth, uneventful and without any further dramas. That's exactly what David liked.

With his stomach intact, and still chewing a strong Polo mint to stop his ears popping, he quickly homed in on his luggage lying precariously on the edge of the revolving carousel. Under the watchful gaze of his travelling companion, he dragged his two red cases towards the customs desk with several pieces of bright pink ribbon tied to the handles and fluttering gently in the air. In the light of his recent embarrassing altercation, the colourful bits of lace weren't such a good idea, but it definitely wasn't the right time to start messing about with bits of frilly ribbon in full view of his secret admirer. His pre-booked cab was ready and waiting, parked up in the shade outside the terminal building, alongside a row of resplendent foreign coaches with their diesel engines switched on and air-conditioning belting out at full blast. He was quickly whisked away from the noisy, bustling scene of hot sweaty travellers dragging their bulging cases and heavily laden trolleys, and was soon resting back in the cool, capacious comfort of the Mercedes, gliding effortlessly towards his luxury hotel some twenty-five miles north. Sweeping along the tranquil unspoilt shores of the beautiful Lake Garda that glistened in the late afternoon sun, he was treated to fields of yellow lemon groves, bright red and pink camellias and soft rolling hills, an idyllic, unforgettable scene seemingly untouched by the passage of time and a welcome sight for the English visitor.

He rang Claire from the comfort of the S-class Mercedes while the glaring airport flood lights and traffic control beacon got smaller and smaller and finally disappeared only to be replaced by rows of vineyards, brown parched fields, terracotta roofs and small quaint villages. Here old nineteenth-century houses and small local shops hugged the narrow roadways making passing difficult, often reducing their speed to a mere snail's pace. David talked about his flight and the unexpected turbulence, knowing his wife would understand his discomfort and, towards the end of their crackly conversation, he mentioned his new flying companion and their embarrassing coming together. However, he soon wished he'd been more circumspect, had kept tight-lipped, as it allowed his mischievous wife to unleash her wicked sense of humour, tease him mercilessly for the rest of the forty-five minute journey through a constant barrage of saucy texts that weren't at all to his liking and Claire knew it.

Chapter 20

Now David's not your typical, archetypal playboy who coveted the high life, squandered obscene amounts on lavish, vulgar trivia or surrounded himself with young, soppy girls. No, such tawdry trinkets didn't appeal to the self-educated Londoner with a family name to uphold. He inhabited a more discerning, more modest world, where taste and style were his best mates and class and elegance always close at hand. However, this was in stark contrast to some of his jet-setting contemporaries who treated cash like confetti, throwing it wherever the fancy took them as self-indulgence was their mantra and brash, over-the-top opulence their way of life. Sure, he relished some of the finer things in life. His two million pound home with all the expensive trappings was testament to that and he didn't shy away from splashing out on things that captured his imagination, or appealed to his impulsive, hot-headed nature. He adored well-tailored designer clothes, loved the feel of soft hand-stitched shoes on his pedicured feet, collected expensive Swiss watches as if they were going out of business and basked in the luxury of fast supercars and powerful German motorbikes. Classical music by Elgar, Chopin and Beethoven and earthy rock by Led Zeppelin, Steve Winwood and the Stones were his staple diet, but he was never happier than when he was engrossed in a serious historical novel, or gripped by a modern crime thriller by Lynda la Plante, his favourite novelist.

His romantic fantasies were normally satisfied through the explosive, often feisty pages of a Mills & Boon novel, but he'd never admit to such tasteless vulgarity amongst some of his well-educated peers, who talked of Keats and Shakespeare with such iconic reverence and would turn up their noses to literature of that ilk. David had a fondness for quality wines from the Loire, was partial to the occasional glass of Rioja with his evening meal and savoured the delights of a Moet reserve whenever his heart desired. In recent years, he'd learnt to manage his cravings and consumed alcohol in careful measures, always aware of the dark days in his past and the need to exercise moderation and restraint. But away from the world of alcohol and all that evoked, there were two insatiable desires that tormented his soul and never went away. We're not talking about drugs, or any such things, it's much more profound than that. You see, this fun-loving, childlike sports fanatic adored, relished, even worshiped vacuum-packed salted peanuts. He loved them with a passion. David also had another guilty secret which was equally damaging to his waistline. He was on cloud nine when he had a mouth-watering packet of soft-textured wine gums resting in his hand. It was fair to say he was in heaven, chatting with the angels, when he was sharing time with these two no-nos. But sadly they were taboo, banned, never talked about during periods of intense training or prior to any of the big five cycling events he was committed to each year.

But once the season ended in September, the curtain was drawn on another year in the saddle and the precious bicycles were safely under wraps, then the party began with a vengeance. David's desires were unleashed as he devoured these banned substances to his heart's content in fits of selfish, unashamed indulgence. At last, after months of restraint, he could savour the illusive crunchy peanuts and chew his way through a packet of soft, tender wine gums without any feelings of guilt or regret. It was paradise.

Chapter 21

It was late afternoon when David arrived at his Garda hotel, nestled quietly above the quaint sun-drenched town, boasting panoramic views of the lake and lush green rolling hills and mountains. Bright sunlight glistened against the steep rock faces of the surrounding slopes that shone and sparkled in the unforgiving glare. The next thirty-six hours was an opportunity for the visitor to acclimatise himself to the prevailing conditions, get used to the sweltering heat and intense humidity knowing these two cruel accomplices threatened to dog his every step on Sunday's gruelling ride.

Lake Garda was a beautiful scenic setting for the fourth ride of the year, promising to be demanding both on body and mind. He quickly checked in, shook the concierge's hand firmly and kissed the tanned cheeks of the female staff who knew him from previous visits. The Italian lovelies flocked to greet him, drawn by his stunning good looks and infectious charm, before the embarrassed Englishman took the hotel lift to his luxurious, top-floor presidential suite to prepare for the big day ahead.

The first night, as always, was spent resting and relaxing and, as the weather forecast didn't bode well, the athlete decided a quiet evening in the private seclusion of his hotel suite was a good antidote to Sunday's challenge. Feeling refreshed after his hot shower, he tucked into a medium rare steak with salad and plenty of carbohydrates for added muscle strength and stamina and finished off his high-protein meal with fresh fruit and several cups of herbal tea. This was his staple diet before a ride and was a routine that worked very well for him.

He thought about Claire, pondered on his doubts about her infidelity, wondering whether the woman he loved was involved with Francois, particularly as they spent a lot of time chatting on the phone, texting and emailing each other. Mrs Millins, his trusty housekeeper, had discreetly mentioned the issue to her employer, not wishing to talk out of turn or spread malicious gossip, for which he was very grateful. As he rested back on the bed he picked up his mobile and called home.

"Hello Francois, thanks for calling back," said Claire, grabbing her phone off the kitchen table.

"It's me my love, not Francois. Sorry to disappoint you. You're now confusing me with the Frenchman, Claire. Whatever next," snapped David in a bombastic tone.

"What do you mean?" she yelled down the phone. "I was expecting him to return my call, it's as simple as that and I thought it was him. What's your problem, David?"

Claire wasn't thinking when she picked up her mobile, her mind was elsewhere. The lady of the house felt embarrassed for making such a stupid mistake, knowing she'd be in the firing line from her jealous husband, who was always on his guard, wary of any indiscretion.

"I thought I'd call to see how you are. Obviously I'm not uppermost in your mind and, as I've got some reading to do, which won't be of interest to you, I shan't waste any more of your time. I'm sure you're eager to get back to your friendly Frenchman," he shouted sarcastically, ending the call abruptly.

David walked onto the balcony, grabbed hold of the metal rail with both hands and gazed, unflinchingly, towards the picturesque towns of Salo and Gardone, resting peacefully on the west side of the shimmering lake. His hands were shaking with rage and his white knuckles clenched hold of the rail that shuddered under the pressure of his vice-like grip. The phone call convinced him, as if there was any doubt, that his wife had betrayed him, making him look foolish in the eyes of others. According to Mrs Millins, a Frenchman regularly rang the house when he wasn't there and that, together with his own suspicions, was testament to his wife's infidelity. Claire had a lot to answer for, but that would have to wait until Monday when he returned home. David's mind was elsewhere, there were much more important issues at stake than the future of his marriage.

The auditor's critical report covered several pages of detailed financial analysis, pulled no punches in its scathing assessment of the company's finances and concluded with a list of recommendations requiring immediate attention by the Committee. It cast a huge shadow over the future of the Pedal Power Programme.

He was aware that something untoward had been going on for some time, and it was the reason why he'd personally commissioned the inquiry in the first place. Sadly, the report confirmed his worst fears. Apparently the Pedal Power Programme had been a target for fraud over a number of years and a considerable amount of money had been misappropriated and couldn't be accounted for. His recent meeting in London, with Christopher Parker-Wright and their company auditors, highlighted many financial irregularities in their business practices. As part of their internal enquiries, the auditors also identified potential company insiders who may be implicated in certain fraudulent practices. This was all very worrying for the founder as David knew that the slightest whiff of scandal would have their loyal supporters deserting them in droves, putting the future of the prestigious Programme in serious jeopardy and causing irreparable damage to his own hard-fought reputation. He was determined to do everything in his power to safeguard his charitable endeavours and bring the perpetrators to book, but sadly time wasn't on his side.

David knew that once the fraudsters suspected something was up and he was onto them, they'd quickly up sticks, disappear from the scene and no doubt resurface sometime later and set up camp in another unsuspecting company. That wasn't going to happen according to Mr Lane, so speed and secrecy were of the essence. He had to catch the blighters in the act, hand them over to the boys in blue, keep a lid on the whole sordid affair and carry on with business as usual. That was the plan in a nutshell.

So there he was, quietly relaxing in the early evening, as though he hadn't a care in the world, when he was only a matter of hours away from the punishing Garda 150, with the future of his precious Pedal Power Programme hanging in the balance and his marriage floundering on the rocks. Now most people faced with this scenario would be reaching for the whisky bottle, swallowing valium by the bucket load, but not Mr Cool, that wasn't his style. Very few things got under his skin, or fazed David Lane. He used the peace and quiet of his hotel suite to plan his next steps and also quench his insatiable thirst. Freshly squeezed orange with large cubes of ice were a welcome late-evening drink for the flamboyant playboy sitting on the balcony of his room, dressed in a long white robe with red slippers and the wind rustling through the nearby Cyprus trees.

The darkening skies offered a welcome respite from the glaring sunlight that had been a feature of the day's scorching hot weather, pushing the mercury up to record levels but promising to return with a vengeance the following morning. He gently closed his eyes and listened to the sound of birds chirping on high, with just the occasional ferry chugging past on the lake and the droning sound of traffic in the far distance. It felt like paradise to the new arrival. The relentless heat of the day had been exchanged for a peaceful sultry evening where you could escape the problems of the world and quietly drift away in your own private thoughts. By nine p.m. David was sleeping like a babe under the thin cotton sheets of his king-size bed with just the soporific murmuring of the air-conditioning unit for company.

Then in the early hours, he suddenly shot up with a jolt when the enormity of Claire's adulterous affair woke him from his restless sleep. He was sweating profusely and, even though the air-conditioning had done its job, his short cropped hair was damp to the touch. His face looked ashen and strained and his teeth were clenched tightly together as the thought of Claire's betrayal haunted him. But then he slowly settled back down to sleep, trying to put his wife's infidelity to one side, and concentrate his energies on Sunday's big ride. It was a restless night that followed. David's strength of character was tested to the limit and at one point he became so incensed, so jealous, that he decided to ring home and confront his wayward partner there and then, but after a few moments he thought better of it and went back to sleep. He'd learnt self-control as a route to conquering his alcohol problems years earlier and it was his impenetrable willpower that the gritty, single-minded athlete called on that lonely night, in Garda.

Chapter 22

During his first full day on Italian soil, David relaxed by the hotel swimming pool, soaking up the atmosphere and reading a novel by Tom Sharpe. As he squeezed *The Great Pursuit* back onto the hotel's crammed bookshelf he smiled to himself when he reflected on some of the author's outrageous comments and saucy storylines that symbolised his witty satirical writing.

With the glaring sun for company, he took a mid-morning trip on the *S.Martino* twin-deck ferry to Lazise. Not surprisingly, it was jam-packed with boisterous holidaymakers and excitable locals all drawn like magnets to the town's well-publicised Saturday market, offering bargains galore for the thrifty, streetwise shopper. It's one of his favourite places on the lake, evoking happy childhood memories of holidays past, with its striking red-stone terracotta buildings, quaint narrow walkways and expensive designer shops hoping to entice the day trippers to part with their hard-earned cash. Lazise was unspoilt with its ancient walls, embattled towers and historic churches reminding you of centuries past when the pace of life was much slower. Small spluttering motor launches, driven by brown bare-chested hunks with permanent grins, treated their excited visitors to some wonderful awe-inspiring views of the magical hamlet that gently hugged the picture-postcard waterfront.

David meandered casually around the mass of sprawling market stalls pitched up all the way along the water's edge, busily selling a range of bright colourful clothes, leather goods of all description and an array of household utensils. It was mayhem. However, he soon tired of the constant jostling and hurly-burly, deciding to make tracks and return to base camp. He joined the afternoon ferry that was swarming with locals and jubilant sun-tanned visitors weighed down by bulging carrier bags full to the brim with clothes, all manner of footwear, fresh fruit and other local produce. The elegant ferry slowly snaked its way along the eastern shoreline, stopping briefly at Bardolino. Then as it chugged through the tranquil water around the next peninsula, David was treated to a tantalising glimpse of Garda perched below the surrounding hills draped in lush green vegetation, with its line of sweeping trees along the sprawling lakeside promenade. The well-known promontory called *La Rocca* was gleaming brightly in the sunlight, reaching up to the fluffy white clouds that appeared motionless, almost glued against the sky's deep blue background. The scene was so provocative, so exciting that David felt the sudden urge to put pen to paper and capture his thoughts for posterity.

Apparently Louise Lane was a prolific writer and poet in her twenties and, even though none of her work was ever published, David knew his mother was a very talented wordsmith and she got a great deal of pleasure in expressing her thoughts in poetry and prose.

At the time of his parents' death his jealous, vindictive cousin destroyed masses of precious photographs, memorabilia and paperwork in her sadistic attempt to eradicate all vestiges of their family name. Sadly, this mindless act of vandalism meant his mother's literary work was reduced to ashes along with many remnants of his family history. So David thought by composing short poems he was in some way rekindling her memory and immortalising her name through the written word.

On his return to terra firma, he plonked himself down on a white plastic seat, underneath the awning of a large grey umbrella, ordered a glass of fresh orange and started to scribble. Garda's lakeside restaurants were packed to the rafters with noisy boisterous tourists competing for attention amongst a generous sprinkling of locals. Many were eagerly tucking into pasta dishes, slim tasty pizzas and scrumptious mouth-watering ice creams built like tower blocks, generously garnished with exotic sauces and thin slender pieces of fresh fruit.

They quenched their thirsts on fine wines and chilled beer and the friendly, carnival atmosphere brought a broad smile to everyone's face. He felt the hot sun on his back, heard the jibber jabber of different languages and dialects as he reached for his notepad and biro and started to capture his thoughts in rhyme. Then after a few minutes, he glanced up and noticed Francesca from his hotel sauntering casually towards him. Her shapely hips glided effortlessly from side to side, much to the wonderment of the passing males whose heads turned in adulation at her shapely, curvaceous figure. She was gorgeous. Francesca served him drinks shortly after his arrival. She felt sorry for David sitting on his own, looking lonely, surrounded by young families and love-struck couples and so she spent time chatting to him between serving other guests around the hotel's swimming pool.

"What are you doing?" she called out, slumping into the chair opposite and rewarding him with a sexy shake of her head.

"I'm trying to write a verse about my time on the lake," he shouted over the guttural sound of about twenty Harley Davidson motorbikes driving past in a long wavy line ridden by a group of overweight middle-aged men in black leathers, with dark beards and ear studs. "Sometimes I use poetry to record my recollections of a place, rather like a diary," he explained, chewing the end of his biro that was hanging from the corner of his mouth. "When I return home I can then imagine the scenery, the sights, the sounds, even the people I met and then relive my memories. I'm not very good at it, but I find the experience most satisfying. It's also a bit of fun and it makes me use the old grey matter which is a good thing at my age," he added coyly.

"Can I hear it?" she said, leaning forward and perching rather precariously on the front two chair legs of her white plastic seat that wobbled under the strain.

"Okay, but it's not very good," he replied. "Here goes. Promise you won't laugh?"

Francesca nodded her agreement and smiled adoringly at the forty-something and then looked straight into his deep set blue eyes, waiting patiently for the poet to begin his impromptu lakeside recital.

"I haven't decided on a title yet," David mumbled under his breath. He coughed, cleared his throat and gazed down at his slightly crumpled notebook.

Red roofs of terracotta fringe this tranquil lake,
Perfect place to spend your time, that well-earned summer break,
Saunter 'cross smooth pathways at Salo's harbour-side,
Soak up the unspoilt vista that affords such local pride.

Church bells peal out their welcome as you breathe the fragrant air,
You're tempted to an ice-cold drink, or taste the local fare,

Sleek harbour fronts, lakeside paths caress the water's edge,
See fledgling birds, as they retreat, beneath a sun-drenched
hedge.

You taste a slice of heaven as you slowly disembark,
Riva's narrow walkways, well-kept gardens, lakeside park,
Eat bits of fresh cooked pizza in noisy street cafes,
Quench your thirst on lemon tea as the sun burns off the haze.

Ferries ply their cargoes, zigzag from shore to shore,
Cut through the blue fresh water, hear engines spit and roar,
Ice cream-laden loved ones press for a scenic view,
Your eyes enjoy the sight of the lake that's painted blue.

"I like that," she said, swaying from side to side on her chair and grabbing a quick slurp of her chilled drink. "You're very clever with words, sir. I think it's great. Why not call it, *The Blue Lake?*"

"That's a good idea," he replied, pushing the notepad back into his shirt's breast pocket and dropping his biro onto the white plastic table. To be quite honest, David was more captivated by her quirky little smile than the title of his latest offering but, nevertheless, he thanked her for her kind words of encouragement.

Francesca looked very much at ease with life, nothing appeared to faze her which appealed to her male companion very much. Her long, black, shiny hair was swept back over her shoulders and her sunglasses were perched on her forehead. Her slightly faded blue jeans and pink chiffon blouse were figure-hugging, emphasising every contour of her eye-catching figure. She asked about Sunday's ride and said she'd be there to cheer him off. That made David feel good, really good. Half an hour later, they were still sipping cool lemonade drinks, laughing and joking and spearing little green olives with bits of stick, acting as though they'd known each other for years, seemingly relaxed in each other's company.

Francesca talked about Garda, its local sights and sounds saying how much she loved the warm summer months by the lake when the tourists returned in their droves and the weather was on its best behaviour.

Meanwhile her silent admirer leaned forward, like a love-struck teenager, hanging onto her every word that tripped off her tongue. She was like a tonic, a breath of fresh air, transporting her foreign guest to another world, a world devoid of fraud, greed and infidelity, where innocence and beauty were the only things on the agenda. Then with a sudden jerk, Francesca noticed the time and cried, "I must go. I'm on duty shortly. I shall be in trouble if I'm late again." She grabbed her battered handbag, dangling on the back of her seat and, as she raced off, shouted thanks for the drink. "I'll see you tonight, ya? Like the poem very much. Don't forget my suggestion for the title. Ciao." Then she was gone.

David nodded, waved and watched longingly as her slim, sylphlike shape slowly disappeared out of sight, just leaving her soft fragrant perfume lingering provocatively in the still air. With a self-satisfied smile, the fledgling writer crafted the finishing touches to his scenic ditty, wallowing in the approval of his female admirer with its title written in bold capital letters at the top of the page. He pushed his chair back against the bulging trunk of a large magnolia tree and, just as he was quietly dozing off with the sound of water lapping gently against the concrete harbour wall, he heard the throaty, roaring rumble of an expensive supercar, changing gear in the distance and heading his way.

A few moments later, he peered over his Armani sunglasses that had slipped to the end of his nose and dabbed the droplets of sweat from his face with his soft cotton handkerchief. Then a bright yellow machine growled into a nearby parking bay, roaring like an angry cat searching for its prey, with the driver buried in the cockpit, strapped tightly inside a pair of red safety belts. Once the beast was tamed and the engine put to rest a throng of open-mouthed onlookers congregated around the shiny curvaceous Lamborghini. She was a beauty; a high-octane fantasy for the macho male with very deep pockets and an ego to match.

"D'you fancy a spin up the road before dinner, my friend?" called the heavily tanned driver sporting a pair of pure white shorts with a pink linen T-shirt, and blue-framed sunglasses tucked neatly inside his breast pocket.

"Of course," came the reply from his fellow petrol-head who owned a collection of expensive cars himself and wouldn't miss the opportunity of a high-speed thrill especially in such a prestigious location. After shaking hands with Christopher Parker-Wright, the middle-aged boy-racers strapped themselves into the cockpit and were soon charging north towards Torri del Benaco, a quiet, rather genteel lakeside village a few miles north of Garda.

The yellow peril shot up the road like a bullet out of a gun and with such G-force as to push the two show-offs crashing back in their cream-coloured sports seats. Every corner, every turn, was a frantic tussle; a battle between driver and machine with Chris grappling with the leather-bound steering wheel, trying to keep the car on the smooth tarmac surface whilst the low-profile Pirellis squealed in protest, discharging great clouds of white smoke in their wake. Peace and tranquillity was dashed with every flick of the flappy paddle as the sleek dream machine screeched and roared towards the unsuspecting village quietly nestling beside the lake. On arrival, the driver performed a mind-boggling handbrake turn amidst clouds of burning rubber much to the delight of the throngs of enthusiastic onlookers, cheering and waving their approval when the hare-brained show-off performed his well-rehearsed party trick. The return journey to Garda wasn't for the faint-hearted either. It was a similar white-knuckle ride, a guaranteed tummy churner for the uninitiated when Chris put the supercar through its paces, yet again, with every heart-stopping gear change and turn of the high-tech steering wheel. Eventually, the restless beast snarled to a grinding halt with the tyres squealing in protest in a great plume of smoke as the Pirellis stamped their trademark signature on the smooth Italian roadway, while crowds of animated well-wishers greeted them on their return.

"That was fantastic Chris, she's an incredible car. The speed's awesome, that was an amazing experience. I shall have to get one," laughed David wrestling with the red safety belts, trying to manoeuvre himself out of the tight passenger cockpit. The two pals liked each other's company very much and chatted for a few moments about their mutual love of fast cars before slowly wandering up the steep slope towards David's hotel. Here they enjoyed a cool refreshing drink and some snacks, care of the hotel's excellent room service, before turning their attention to the auditor's report and its disturbing accusations of fraud and corruption within the Pedal Power Programme.

"Our instinct is to lash out, attack those that do us harm and bring them to their knees, but that won't work this time. We must be more circumspect, more cunning than our adversaries otherwise we'll lose the battle. Cool heads is what's called for," explained David.

Chris agreed and was equally angry at the revelations highlighted in the report and was determined to do what he could to capture the culprits. He was incensed that someone close to them would seek to undermine their philanthropic efforts and put the future of their prestigious international Programme in jeopardy.

The Pedal Power Programme had captured Chris's imagination from its inception, injecting a sense of purpose in his life, so the thought of someone trying to undermine his efforts outraged the millionaire as though it was a personal attack on him and his family. Chris was the son of a highly successful family dynasty where he enjoyed untold wealth and the opportunity to indulge in fast supercars, expensive properties, lavish designer clothes with a constant supply of beautiful women. In amongst all this opulence, however, the forty-seven-year-old donated vast sums each year to charitable causes and medical research projects. His father was British and his mother Spanish. Shortly after leaving Eton, Chris worked in one of his father's factories, but after a couple of weeks he found the hours too onerous and, to protect his health and general well-being, took early retirement and had never regretted the decision. However the inscrutable playboy did earn his crust. His lively personality and attractive good looks projected a clean-cut self-assured image to the press and media who flocked to him in their droves. Chris was articulate, confident and a great ambassador for the family's worldwide business interests, so the engaging, fun-loving old Etonian felt justified in receiving an allowance of £1,000,000 a year as recompense for the pressure he endured as a hard-working international emissary.

That evening David had dinner on his own in his suite where he enjoyed a front-row seat watching nature perform a magical twilight trick as the sun slowly set above the shimmering, breathtaking lake against the backdrop of a bright red sky. Surely this was God's back garden, he surmised, strolling into the bathroom and smiling to himself at the startled looks on people's faces when they shot past at speed and did an amazing 360°-turn in the middle of the road. As he lay there luxuriating in his bubble bath, he wondered when Francois would call to talk through the arrangements for the following day. The Pedal Power Committee was well known to David; it was his baby, and over the last five years he'd undertaken a series of challenging fund-raising ventures on their behalf. As usual, Claire had done all the important leg work for Sunday's ride, ensuring the administration was up to scratch and everything went smoothly, but now the spotlight was on him. It was time for David Lane to complete his side of the bargain and deliver the goods. As predicted, the Frenchman rang at eight p.m. just as David was drying himself off with a large fluffy towel and sipping a glass of orange. After the pleasantries, which David found very difficult to handle in view of his suspicions, they discussed the route for the Garda 150, the timings and the security arrangements.

As usual there were thirty riders in the group and the total sponsorship was already in excess of £0.5 million, which was good news for the designated charity – ME/CFS. David was pleased to hear that things were going well and was optimistic about securing more donations in the days to come and achieving their target with ease.

"We start and finish the ride by the ferry point on the quay in Garda and I'll be there at seven a.m for the off at eight a.m. Details of the ride have been left at your hotel and should cover everything as usual," Francois pointed out.

"I'll see you in the morning," said David, quickly ending the call and continuing with his intensive body-pampering. He sprinkled Johnson baby talc on his feet to prevent chaffing, then studied the route around the lake noting the various stop-off points for refreshments. It was a mere 150 kilometres in thirty-five degrees heat, starting and finishing in Garda whilst circumnavigating the largest freshwater lake in Italy. No problem, he smiled to himself, leaning back against the red, padded headboard and watching John Wayne talking perfect Italian on his Sony television. He sent a short text to Claire explaining his plans for Sunday, slumped down into bed and promptly went to sleep. She didn't reply.

Chapter 23

It was an eerie sight that greeted the lonely cyclist strolling down the steep slope from his chic hotel to the main road overlooking the iconic lake shining undisturbed in the early morning mist. David stopped momentarily to savour the moment. This was nature at its best, with the tranquil blue strip stretching out before him like a perfectly laid piece of soft pile carpet, with just a glimmer of the yellow globe slowly rising over the distant shoreline. His special handmade cycling shoes clanked on the cobbled footpath as he walked gingerly down the road in the direction of the official meeting point. Suddenly, a foolhardy grey tabby cat threw caution to the wind and shot across the busy road only a matter of inches in front of a lumbering eight-wheel Mobil oil truck that was racing at breakneck speed towards the town centre. I wonder how many lives you've got left, thought David, with a wry smile. The driver didn't apply his air brakes, didn't even attempt to slow down as the frightened moggy scuttled away with his tail between his legs, happy to be in one piece, but no doubt minus another precious life. It was Sunday 13th July 2014 and the location was Lake Garda. It was slowly waking from its slumber under the watchful gaze of the nearby alpine range. A popular playground for people of all ages, famous for its olive groves and lemon trees, its fine local wines, exotic ice creams and scrumptious wafer-thin pizzas and delicious pasta treats.

Very soon you would hear the reassuring sound of church bells ringing out along the winding shoreline, inviting worshippers to celebrate communion and Mass, while hungry hotel guests languished in the warm, pleasant breeze, tucking into their cooked breakfasts, al fresco. The 13th July was a unique date in the calendar. That was the day of the much vaunted, much publicised Garda 150, when thirty strong, determined riders from across Europe would toil in the heat in their quest to complete the gruelling circular ride and secure five million pounds for ME research. That was the goal.

As David turned, looked down the steep road towards the town centre, he wasn't prepared for the sight that greeted him on that warm sticky morning. It was beyond his wildest dreams, far more impressive than anything he'd ever witnessed before. His ears were bombarded by the raucous sound of bongos, drums and trumpets, playing by the water's edge, with crowds of frenzied onlookers spilling onto the road, like a river bursting its banks, causing the local police to push them back behind specially constructed steel barriers. It was absolute mayhem. Well-wishers shrieked and hollered, waving streamers and flags and even ordinary everyday handkerchiefs to celebrate the triumphant arrival of Team 30 in their midst.

Bold eye-catching posters, vivid, vibrant banners and all types of colourful bunting were draped across the main road, hanging from trees and lampposts, injecting a frenetic carnival atmosphere to the festive occasion. The stunning red and white slogan, 'Just for ME' attacked your eyes everywhere you looked. Large glitzy flags hung from open windows, twirling freely in the air. Giant posters in dazzling eye-catching colours proclaimed their support for the charity, fluttering and flapping in the soothing breeze.

Wherever your eyes rested, wherever you looked, there was an outpouring of infectious enthusiasm by rowdy holidaymakers and locals alike. The occasion seemed to have captured everyone's imagination, pushing the decibels to ever greater heights. Emotions were on red alert amongst the throngs of headstrong bystanders clambering to get closer to their cycling heroes, share in the pageant that had swept through the unsuspecting town like a giant tidal wave. David was gobsmacked, speechless, overwhelmed by the scene of euphoria and genuine affection for his courageous colleagues and the charity they so warmly supported. It was even more amazing when he glanced down at his watch and saw it was only seven a.m.

The founder of the Programme stood in awe, hardly able to move, traumatised by the cacophony of sound that attacked his eardrums. It reminded him of street parties in the past, carnival parades in Richmond as a child and the infamous Mardi Gras, such was the atmosphere of passion and emotion that engulfed Garda's sweeping bay and its enchanting tree-lined promenade. Cars, lorries and vans of all shapes and sizes got in on the act, hooting their ear-splitting horns and banging the sides of their vehicles with clenched fists as they weaved their way between throngs of milling crowds. Animated drivers waved frantically through open windows, shouted words of support in different languages while rows of smartphones captured the moment for posterity. After all, it was a day like no other day and would be remembered by young and old for years to come. It was the day when the famous Team 30 roadshow rolled into town, accompanied by all the pandemonium and razzmatazz their well-disciplined publicity machine could muster. David walked slowly towards a cluster of brightly clad riders, chatting together by the ferry point, waiting eagerly for their erudite leader to make an appearance. Then when the red and white cyclist arrived on the scene the noise level went up several notches. Eager red-faced fans recognised the famous David Lane, the man behind the revered Pedal Power Programme, and rushed to greet their gallant hero with the customary phones held aloft.

The burly security staff, dressed in high visibility jackets, were well versed in crowd control, ushering the bewildered playboy through a gap in the barriers to be met by Chris, who welcomed his friend with a broad, beaming smile and a firm slap on the back.

"Well this is incredible. I never expected anything like this!" yelled Chris, as crowds of raucous supporters, with a forest of outstretched hands, tried to attract the guys' attention and capture their famous faces in 'a once in a lifetime' selfie.

"It's fantastic, Chris. It's an amazing sight, this is brilliant news for the charity. I'm overwhelmed!" shouted David at the top of his voice, gripping hold of his space-age helmet and walking towards his other brightly clad colleagues standing just a few yards away. They were happily greeting one another with firm handshakes and lots of hugs and laughter, but that all stopped when their celebrated leader strolled onto the scene. They became more animated, even more vocal, treating David to a barrage of hearty pats on the back and an outpouring of emotion that only he could attract, such was the impact his personal presence had on those closely associated with him.

Like him, they were staggered, bowled over, by their warm reception and equally overwhelmed by the expressions of encouragement posted on social media. Facebook, Twitter, YouTube and emails were all buzzing at the news of their arrival in Italy. Outpourings of praise and adulation dominated the airwaves which lifted Team 30's spirits and buoyed them up for the challenges ahead.

Local hacks were united in a common cause. The news-hungry media clamoured to record the group's well-publicised reunion on the shores of Italy's premier lake, with the noise of clicking cameras dominating the scene on the congested promenade and along the adjacent promontory. Here, the baying press shouted out the riders' names hoping to gain their attention. A plethora of long lenses jostled for position in search of that exclusive shot that would mark them out from the rest of the crowd, put a feather in their cap in the eyes of their tough unforgiving news editors. Seasoned camera clickers knew their hard-fought photographs would be hitting the news-stands in a matter of hours, be gobbled up by devoted fans and hero worshippers. Time was of the essence if they were to meet their editors' tight deadlines and satisfy the adulation of the news-hungry public and their insatiable quest for topical pictures of their pin-ups.

On hearing about his quest the night before, some of the early-risers from the Excelsior Hotel put breakfast on hold and congregated under the branches of a tall magnolia tree to show their backing for David's brave, possibly foolhardy adventure. At one point, the intrepid cyclist caught their eye and waved to his fellow guests who seemed overwhelmed by the exuberant scenes of enthusiasm being enacted along Garda's normally peaceful, Sunday-morning shoreline.

Meanwhile David's cycling colleagues, in their figure-hugging outfits, mingled at the start point admiring their precious racing bikes and making minor adjustments to their machines before the off. The well-honed security staff ushered the press to one side to give the stars of the show a breather from the media hurly-burly and the constant barracking from the unruly newshounds. Friendly banter and mutual words of encouragement were the order of the day for the daredevil adventure seekers, who looked eager to enter the fray and put their well-honed bodies to the test. As always, the excitable, highly charged group of adrenalin junkies loved the limelight and pandered to the baying press and crowds of fans, but in this media melee, the guys also knew there was a serious side to their endeavour and they had to step up to the plate and fulfil their part of the bargain.

There was a sprinkling of top-notch company directors and business owners who wouldn't be missed as they indulged in the limelight, broke out of the shackles of corporate life to spread some joy and happiness through their outrageous cycling adventures at some of the most picturesque locations in Europe. The Pedal Power Programme gave a bunch of freethinking attention-seekers the opportunity to let off steam, exploit their talents for the benefit of others, keep themselves fit and have some fun into the bargain. Everyone was a winner according to their eminent group leader. Many European nations were represented in the elite squad, including the UK, Ireland, Italy, Spain, Germany, France, Portugal, Austria and Holland. There was a sprinkling of strong committed riders from the Scandinavian countries who were more circumspect, less vocal than their boisterous, over-the-top counterparts. The blond fair-skinned Nordic riders preferred to spend the last few moments before the starting pistol making final adjustments to their flamboyant headgear and body-hugging attire, rather than ingratiate themselves with some of the young female spectators, who were bedazzled by the good-looking bronze bodies and muscular physiques on display.

All the guys knew one another from previous backbreaking encounters and some were even close friends, best mates and business partners. They repeatedly put their legs on the line for the benefit of others, frequently subjecting their bodies to lengthy periods of pain and discomfort. Facing each cycling challenge with enthusiasm and some trepidation as the harsh elements often contrived to do them harm, and stop them in their tracks.

Already that year, the squad had ridden in three tough events. Barcelona was first of the 2014 season and was like a baptism of fire for the uninitiated. The March weather was unexpectedly hot and oppressive and sapped the strength of even the fittest team member. The 200-kilometre route was arduous and punishing, taking the riders along a purpose-built roadway on Chris' sprawling family estate and then onto local roads and byways. The terrain was bumpy, hilly and difficult to negotiate, made much worse by the blistering heat and strength-sapping humidity that goaded them from dawn to dusk.

Predictably, the thirty-strong contingent took it all in their stride even though they hadn't expected such a gruelling, agonising test of their stamina so early in the year. The gutsy riders were not daunted by the severe conditions, showing determination, grit and unwavering resolve. The MS charity was the beneficiary of their valiant efforts and a whopping £6.2 million cheque was presented to their tearful chief executive at a spectacular gala dinner later that month.

In late April, the team experienced torrential rain, high winds and storms in the Bavarian capital. It added a punishing dimension to the exhausting event, causing two experienced competitors to temporarily withdraw from the Munich 200 after coming a real cropper on the wet slippery road surface. The brave guys untangled themselves from the wreckage, staggered to their feet and, after some quick medical attention, jumped onto their replacement bikes with the elusive chequered flag uppermost in their minds. So with bloodstained bodies, bruised and battered heads and torn skin suits, the fearless Frenchmen re-joined the fray, ignoring the frantic protestations of the medical team urging them to have treatment for their many cuts, scrapes and serious abrasions.

The dynamic duo from Nice and Bordeaux wouldn't hear of it, giving up was not in their Gallic vocabulary. The two plucky athletes continued the final exhausting forty kilometres with the constant, unremitting glare of several television cameras capturing every agonising move, every throbbing thrust of their battle-scarred legs. Invasive shots of their ordeal were transmitted in vivid detail by a news helicopter hovering closely overhead, stalking every step of their heart-wrenching journey towards the finishing line. Chris kept a watchful eye on the progress of his two brave compatriots who looked in a bad way after their accident, but was most impressed by their unwavering determination to complete the ride, come what may. However, Mr Parker-Wright quickly realised the commercial opportunities following their misfortune, as anxious teary-eyed viewers watched in horror at the live pictures being beamed across all platforms, showing in graphic detail, the grimace-strewn faces of the riders as their tired bodies garnered every ounce of energy to push their wheels over the line.

Eventually, the resourceful Frenchmen completed the backbreaking ride to the rapturous applause of their colleagues and the acclamation of the press and social media. George and Henri were immortalised, were national heroes, were elevated to iconic status for their unstinted courage and tenacity and their selfless determination to succeed in the face of such overwhelming odds. So in the best traditions of Alexandre Dumas – all for one and one for all – the cavalcade of drained, shattered bodies, with George and Henri at the helm, swept over the finishing line to the adoration of cheering crowds lining the streets five deep on that memorable wet and windy spring afternoon. They'd witnessed an heroic spectacle of physical endurance that reflected the ethos and strongly held beliefs of the renowned Pedal Power Programme. The event was enormously successful in raising the profile of their charitable endeavours and George and Henri's sad misfortune added a bit of spice and unexpected drama to the Munich 200. Needless to say, Mr Lane was very pleased with their day's work, especially as the designated charity was better off by a cool £5.6 million. This was thanks in part to a huge increase in text and telephone donations from distraught, panic-stricken fans who'd seen first-hand the injuries suffered by the brave resilient Frenchmen, overcoming pain and physical discomfort to complete the gruelling ride in such an impressive way.

In late May, the cavalcade ventured west setting up camp in gay Paris. The 200-kilometre ride around the outskirts of the capital was relatively kind to the guys, in stark contrast to the ordeal they'd endured near the Alps some seven or eight weeks earlier. Towards the end of the challenge, there were one or two minor mishaps on some of the cobbled roads when the crew found the damp, greasy conditions difficult to handle following a sudden, unexpected downpour. However, the Paris 200 was deemed a tremendous success and the riders were heartened by the cordial reaction of the French public and gratified to see the five million pound target was smashed early in the day. As always, Team 30 were eternally grateful to social media for their warm words of encouragement and support which kept them going when their thighs and arms were ready to drop off. The scorching globe beat down on their backs for most of the day, giving the feisty thirty a taste of high temperatures and sticky, airless conditions, which stood them in good stead for that day's grilling in the Italian oven.

Against this history of success in the saddle, there was often a tinge of jealousy in Francois' voice when he spoke about the riders' extravagant lifestyles. His unsavoury comments were often at variance with the philosophy of the Programme and his high-profile role as head of communication. When he'd had a few drinks he'd let his guard down, often referring to Team 30 as the silver spoons, which sounded rather arrogant and condescending. David took issue with him on a couple of occasions explaining that, unlike many of their wealthy peers who saw self-indulgence as their God-given right, his colleagues were different. They chose to harness their wealth and influence for the betterment of others stressing that amongst the noisy, sometimes juvenile banter and carefree attitude, the guys had a common bond that welded them together like glue. Team 30 were passionate in their mission, their altruistic quest, which ingratiated them to the wider public and inspired people of all ages to contribute to their campaign. He knew his views fell on deaf ears and that Francois's ingrained jealousy was deep-routed and whatever he said he had little chance of changing the Frenchman's blinkered outlook.

David was seen as the father figure, the head of the pack. He was cool where Chris was brash, undiplomatic where his chum was confrontational; he was mercurial, where Chris was transparent and highly predictable. But stick them together with a common purpose and they were a formidable force for good. They were at the vanguard of charitable giving, projecting a bright, glowing beacon of hope that excited, even mesmerised their generous supporters such that many yearned to come on board, join the revolution and make a real difference to the lives of others.

As David clonked along the quay, towards the starting point, a text pinged on his smartphone.

Now what's that, he thought? It must be urgent. He reached into his breast pocket and sure enough it was a message from Claire, no doubt wishing him good luck. He glanced at the screen and smiled with delight.

"Congratulations, you clever devil, you've been selected as a candidate at the next general election. Mike says you were always the frontrunner and the party deserves someone like you. Have a good ride. Talk tonight. Keep away from other men, lover boy! Claire."

In amongst the milling crowds and jaunty bystanders, David finally reached Francois's outstretched hand. "Hello!" he called out. "Nice to see you again, hope you're fit and well and raring to go?"

"Yes," replied David, in a strong, confident tone of voice. "Never felt better. It promises to be a hot, sweaty day, but we'll do our best to come through unscathed and take home the booty. It's all for ME this time out."

"I understand congratulations are in order, you could be an MP come the next election. Well done. That's another string to your bow," said Francois carefully removing David's distinctive racing bike from the adjacent storage rack, and giving it a quick look over and a cursory flick of the handlebars with his silk handkerchief, before walking off to talk to the waiting press.

David was surprised that the Frenchman had heard of his good fortune before he did, but chose not to mention it. It wasn't the time or the place, but he had a pretty good idea as to the source of the leak and where he'd got his information from. The dapper forty-year-old was sporting a smart clean-cut image in his well-pressed pale blue Armani suit with matching open-neck shirt, and breast pocket handkerchief. He looked very much the part, like a master of ceremonies, projecting a confident distinguished air, quickly checking on the progress of his staff, making sure everything was on schedule. Francois was a stickler for detail and woe betide anyone who messed up and failed to meet his exacting standards.

The all-important bikes had been carefully stored in the specially designed eight-wheel transporter parked up about a hundred yards away. The impressive vehicle was a magnet for the milling throngs of enthusiasts clambering with phones in hand, trying to capture pictures of Gary, the stout middle-aged driver, standing proudly alongside his imposing vehicle, adding a bit of engineering pizzazz to the august occasion.

Both sides of the massive transporter were dominated by colourful attention-grabbing pictures of brightly clad cyclists in psychedelic skin suits and avant-garde helmets racing up a hilly terrain with the emblematic words, 'Pedal Power Programme' emblazoned in stunning red characters across the bottom of the vehicle. Open-mouthed fans gazed in admiration at the beautiful lines and sheer elegance of the famous juggernaut that always grabbed the limelight every time it hit the road with its cargo of expensive special edition bikes safely housed on board. The stunning design was the brainchild of a member of the backup crew scooping many awards and accolades in the trade press, as well as attracting a strong committed following on social media, making Victoria, their in-house artist, a bit of a celebrity in her own right and a much admired member of the support team.

David's special edition bicycle, with its shiny chrome wheels, wafer-thin tyres and a featherlight red frame, made it a striking symbol of his altruistic endeavours gleaming unashamedly in the early morning light while, in memory of his dear parents, he always wore the obligatory skin suit in a distinctive red and white combination, with matching helmet.

An assortment of high-end, top-notch carbon fibre machines, for the serious sports enthusiast, were on display. Slim finger-thin wheels, white-walled tyres, sparkling chrome handlebars, shiny oil-free spokes and featherweight frames dominated the picturesque setting on that memorable morning in mid-July. Specially designed bikes costing thousands of pounds, including Pinarello Dogma, Boardman, Trek Madone and Cannondale were on parade. Their owners coveted their pristine charges, polished and wiped their psychedelic frames, making them sparkle in the shimmering light, acting as a magnet for the cycling geek looking on in awe at the magnificent collection of expensive state-of-the-art bicycles. They would have given their eye teeth to have owned any one of the prestigious two-wheeled dream machines.

Francois watched with interest when David attached the precious family locket to his chrome handlebars. As always, the heirloom took pride of place, a tribute to his beloved parents. When he was on the open road, battling against the elements, gripping hold of the handlebars, he often felt close to his mother, imagining her applauding his efforts, sharing in the accolades that were so warmly bestowed on the Lane family name following his many money-making ventures.

Chapter 24

There were two specially equipped BMW support vehicles in the convoy; one at the front and the other following at the rear of the peloton. Francois was at the head of the line and, with the aid of a handheld radio, could communicate with the guys giving them periodic updates on road conditions, details of refreshment stops and the all-important up-to-the-minute reactions on social media to their thrilling adventures in the saddle. The Garda authorities agreed to close the roads at intervals and to deploying teams of volunteers to designated road junctions, busy intersections, pedestrian crossings and other hazards that might impede the riders' safe passage. Both estate vehicles were kitted out with an assortment of specialist tools and spare parts as well as numerous bicycle chains, wheels and tyres. Half a dozen replacement bikes were strapped to their roofs just in case things went really pear-shaped. The BMW at the rear was Alison's base throughout the event. As a state-registered nurse, she kept a keen watchful eye on her charges, tending to any cuts and bruises but, as always, she hoped her skills wouldn't be called upon, that she could just sit back, have a rest, savour the captivating views as they gently cruised around the beautiful, sun-drenched lake.

David's saddle was too high so he quickly adjusted it before taking up his position with the rest of the group. Leaning back, adjusting the Velcro straps around his designer shoes, he caught a brief glimpse of Francesca some way off. She was dressed for work, wearing a smart green pleated skirt, cream loose-fitting blouse and belt. This modest, rather plain get-up didn't detract from her simple good looks as her long sleek black hair and cheery smile competed for attention with Garda's stunning tree-lined promenade and sweeping bay. The young hotel waitress suddenly caught David's eye, stopped talking to her workmates and looked straight at him with her piercing deep-set eyes. She treated the athlete to a jaunty wave of her arms as he carefully adjusted the strap on his helmet and pushed his Pirelli sunglasses into place. He raised his gloved hand in acknowledgement. Meanwhile David's flamboyant colleagues chatted to one another before weaving between the narrow gap in the specially erected steel barriers when their names were called out by the company's official recorder. He was an elderly gentleman with a freckled face, long straggly neck and dressed in a badly fitting yellow high-visibility jacket and was sat perched on a wobbly shooting stick, ticking off their names on his clipboard as they freewheeled passed. The final act before the off was the formal picture of the group. This was taken at the beginning of every ride as an official record of their many sorties in the saddle.

"That's good," said Francesca's tattooed boyfriend, lifting up his grubby, paint-splattered jeans over the top of his portly waistline. "Mr Lane's rather taken with you, you've done a good job. Your cheery smile and silly wave had the idiot really thinking. He likes you, my girl, and that's exactly what I want to see. Right, let's get off and you can come back later when the gormless millionaire returns from his silly cycle ride."

She grinned to herself, while walking briskly up the steep slope with her scruffy boyfriend in tow, heading towards the impressive Excelsior Hotel standing on the brow of the hill, watching over the picturesque resort town below.

Meanwhile, the intrepid cyclists chatted between themselves. They adjusted the straps on their space-age helmets, zipped up their tops and exercised their fingers, sheathed inside leather-bound cycle gloves. They were ready for the starting pistol. It was eight a.m. Designer shoes were clipped onto bright chromium pedals, posh sunglasses were adjusted for protection from the glaring sun and creams applied liberally to exposed parts as little pesky insects often seemed quite partial to the taste of pampered playboy. The group slowly freewheeled off the quay heading towards Bardolino. David glanced over his shoulder, peered between the riders at the rear, but sadly she was nowhere to be seen. The relative peace and tranquillity of the early hour was soon disturbed by the clanking sound of boisterous pedal pushers cruising passed shuttered homes blissfully unaware of the cavalcade of colour weaving about in their midst. Outdoor restaurants and street cafes lay deserted under dingy grey awnings flapping freely in the breeze, and plastic chairs leant against circular tables waiting patiently for their first customers of the day. A flock of bloated gulls squawked in protest, scattered skywards when the meandering snake surprised them as they gorged themselves on pieces of damp bread and cold, sodden chips.

In a few hours' time, the still-muted scene would be transformed into a foodie's paradise when young, energetic waiters quickly scurried between tables delivering scrumptious thin-crusted pizzas, fishy treats and traditional exotic ice creams dripping with mouth-watering fruit sauces and freshly whipped cream. Sometimes this frenetic madcap activity proved too much for the local oldies dressed in shiny long trousers and casual shirts, choosing instead to snooze the morning away seduced by the strumming guitar of an overweight busker, aided and abetted by several glasses of freshly-chilled Perone.

The route from Garda to Bardolino was about five kilometres and took them along a straight purpose-built cycle lane that caressed the soothing eastern shores of the deep, cavernous freshwater lake. In their information packs they were asked to ride in single file and watch their speed as they might frighten the natives by the sudden, unexpected arrival of the thirty-strong racing roadshow.

The intrepid band rode alongside the calm idyllic lake that was glistening in the early morning sunlight with rows of tiny waves quietly lapping against clumps of motionless reeds and boulders, while small rocks and shale lay scattered along the peaceful waterfront. It was paradise, a perfect setting for a Sunday-morning saunter with fields of olive groves and lemon trees set against a backdrop of rolling hills and blue cloudless sky. The only sound they could hear, over the clanking of revolving cycle chains and friendly banter, was a solitary passenger ferry spluttering around the headland, chugging across the lake towards Salo and Gardone gently hugging the distant western shore. This initial stage was a pleasant easy-going jaunt, designed to acclimatise the team to the oppressive conditions, slowly ease them into the saddle and prepare the hearty souls for the endurance test ahead.

Advice was freely given by old hands who'd experienced the blistering heat of the Italian sun before. Even at that early hour, it was close, sticky and very humid. As the long bendy-bus wended its way passed lines of tightly packed caravans and family-size tents they sometimes got the tantalising whiff of fresh coffee and fried breakfasts with bursts of noisy chitter-chatter and hoots of raucous laughter. This was often interspersed with snippets of hideous music, reminiscent of the Eurovision Song Contest, invariably accompanied by some dodgy Italian singing. Many of the riders were already quenching their thirsts and wiping great blobs of sweat from shinny damp chins and steamy sunglasses. Knowing glances were exchanged between fellow riders as they peered up and down the peloton, checking on the welfare of their fellow competitors.

"This is going to be very hot," said David, glancing over his shoulder, while adjusting the damp material strap to his red and white cycling helmet.

"I agree," replied Hans, riding closely in his slipstream and tilting his water bottle to his parched lips before rubbing streams of sweat off his red blotchy cheeks with a cursory swipe of his riding glove.

"We're in for a grilling today, you know. It's already over seventy degrees, but it's the damned humidity that's our biggest enemy. It really saps your strength."

David nodded and reached into his breast pocket for an energy bar. He was over six foot tall, slim and weighed in at about twelve stone. A perfect specimen for a competitive cyclist. He loved the thrill of the sport and thrived on the adrenalin rush when he was pitting his wits against the unpredictable elements. His agile, well-toned frame and firm upright body posture exuded an air of inner confidence, no doubt a legacy from his parents who were single-minded in their determination to be the very best at whatever they did. The self-assured playboy had an obsession with his appearance dating back to those sad dark days when drink was his master and he its indomitable servant. Nowadays he was always well groomed whether suited and booted, or in everyday casual attire. David always looked the part with his short, tightly cropped hair, slightly grey and thinning on top. This annoyed him greatly and was something his wife liked to tease him about when it took her fancy. His pronounced jawline, unblemished skin, steely blue eyes and a flamboyant demeanour were the distinctive characteristics of this philanthropic playboy. The only imperfection was a slight limp in his right leg and various cigarette burns on his shoulders and back, all legacies of the brutality and abuse he suffered in his early teenage years in Sussex. Since his traumatic battle with the booze in his twenties, he'd never allowed the bottle to dictate his way of life again and, against strict medical advice, enjoyed the occasional tipple between periods of intensive training.

Over the last five years, the Pedal Power Programme had become an unwavering obsession for the reformed drunk, replacing his thirst for fine malts and the lure of the grape. David proved time and time again that he was the master of his own body, strong-willed enough to overcome the pull of the pint and any alcoholic temptation that life might throw at him. The local AA group were amazed at his self-control and applauded his determination to combat the demon drink, knowing his long history of addiction and lengthy periods in rehabilitation. But the group leader chose not to share his remarkable, highly unorthodox story with other class members, thinking that an occasional tipple for a reformed drunk was a dangerous path to pursue, fraught with many untold dangers for those less strong-willed and more easily tempted.

Even though David was a driven man, always striving for perfection and never accepting mediocrity, he always exuded warmth and kindness to those less fortunate, remembering the days when he'd fallen from grace and needed a helping hand to get him back on the straight and narrow.

Riding towards Bardolino, the peloton was greeted by a plethora of vibrant 'Just for ME' posters and banners tied to lampposts, draped around tree trunks and on top of road signs. It was a carnival of colour, a celebration of their cause. Francois had done well. He'd really pulled out the stops in raising the profile of the chosen charity, pushing the forgotten illness to the fore. The litany of eye-catching bunting took your breath away and a show of raised clenched fists, in response to the charity's attention-grabbing placards, was a great sight to behold. The guys waved at the fun-loving crowds that had skipped breakfast to join in the excitement and offer their support for the peloton gliding effortlessly along the cycle lane towards its first port of call with their 'Just for ME' armbands proudly on display. David was overjoyed by the sight of red and white streamers flapping in the breeze knowing the publicity, in such an iconic venue, would make a huge difference to the charity's profile and attract large donations from all across Europe.

"I'm sure I wouldn't get out of bed at seven a.m. to get a glimpse of a bunch of cyclists racing by!" yelled a German rider chewing on an energy bar and spitting the empty paper wrapping out of his mouth.

David was not impressed by Gerhard's antics but, knowing his large financial contribution to the event, bit his tongue, smiled out of politeness and took a hefty drink from his half-full water bottle.

The outskirts of Bardolino was a welcome sight even that early in the ride. The athletes wiped the floods of perspiration from their hot clammy faces and necks, while the unrelenting glare of the sun beat down and burnt their exposed lower legs and arms. The team swept gracefully under a long arbour of grey olive trees draped across the cycle path giving them some temporary relief from the intoxicating heat.

Jorgen, a veteran of many previous outings, was the chosen lead cyclist for their grand entrance to the town. The Dutchman was humbled by the honour bestowed on him by his peers and, judging by his frenzied handwaving and persistent jumping up and down, you'd have thought the man from Amsterdam had won a major stage in the prestigious Tour de France. National flags waved their approval, fluttering freely from lofty white poles along the water's edge, looking down on the peloton as it glided towards the centre of the town. The group followed behind their spirited leader towards the Catholic church, standing at the top of the slope with its marble, tiered steps and tall imposing spire. The grand building offered a religious haven for its devoted worshipers and an architectural treat for its many international visitors. You could smell the early morning heat, as the trailblazers continued past traditional gift shops and exclusive high-end boutiques, boasting fashionable tailor-made designer suits and the season's latest frocks. The road surface was flat and smooth so they sat upright in their saddles to alleviate any pain in the lower back and give their legs a bit of a respite, while soaking up the welcoming atmosphere of the much revered lakeside resort.

Crowds of well-wishers screamed and shouted in a cacophony of different languages, injecting a cosmopolitan atmosphere into the celebratory parade, as the animated convoy waved their gloved hands in response before disappearing through a deserted park and onto the busy main road. Here both support vehicles were parked up in a lay-by with their diesel engines belching out great clouds of exhaust fumes, clearly ready for the off.

On seeing Francois perched patiently on the BMW's bonnet, the riders quickly pushed the plastic plugs into their ears and, after some crackly adjustments to the frequency, were treated to the dulcet tones of the silver-tongued Frenchman.

"Great to see you, guys. Hope you enjoyed the scenic route. We had to settle for the boring main road which wasn't anywhere near so much fun. Remember, Alison's at the rear in case of problems. It's going to be hot on this stretch so keep emptying those water bottles. We can restock when we stop. Don't forget to keep two abreast and watch out for oncoming traffic. But looking around I suggest we have a few minutes break before carrying on."

Chapter 25

Just then David's phone pinged and, thinking it might be important, he glanced down at the text message from Claire. She sounded angry. Apparently Mr Millins had upset the neighbours again. "He's been leaning over the garden fence, teaching next door's twins certain rude words. He's taught them bitch, piss, crap, todger and buttocks and those are just the words the children can remember without referring to their notes. As if that wasn't bad enough, the linguist has shown them how to emphasise the meaning of words through strong hand gestures and crude voice modulation. The twins have shared their newfound knowledge with their innocent chums at their exclusive £7,000-a-year prep school, teaching them an array of expletives that would even make some adults blush. You can imagine playtime can't you, when words like balls, shyster and cock trip off the tongues of the sweet tiny tots following any minor dispute, or argument? Must do something on your return to stop the corruption of the local posh knobs, otherwise we'll have to move to bandit country the other side of the M5. It's that serious! See you Monday. Love to PW, Claire."

The soulful sound of *Wonderful Life* by Black was playing in a nearby street cafe when David, with a cheeky grin on his face, leaned across his handlebars and showed the text message to Chris. PW was in stitches, he couldn't stop laughing while gently adjusting the straps on his bright blue helmet and clipping his pure white shoes back onto the chromium pedals.

"He's really something your Mr M, isn't he? Imagine little innocent kids in carefully ironed uniforms running around in the playground of their exclusive school, yelling todger and cock at the tops of their voices and upsetting the great and the good at their snooty candle-lit parties. Well done Mr M, you get my vote every time!" said Chris still laughing behind his gloved hand. David ignored the text from his unfaithful wife, dropped the phone back into his breast pocket, zipped it up and freewheeled behind his colleagues onto the main road.

Now David loved his gadgets and boys' toys, as Claire called them. His luxury top-of-the-range Boardman bicycle cost thousands and was no exception in his obsession with modern leading-edge technology. The six-inch square screen dominated the centre of the polished handlebars, perched upright like a car's sat nav waiting patiently for its master's instructions.

At the touch of a gloved finger, the high-resolution display would spring into action. Lying in wait behind the discreet brown-tinted glass were more megabytes than NASA had when it dropped the first man on the moon in 1969. It was like a roving encyclopaedia where David could learn about prevailing weather conditions, potential road hazards, the mechanical status of the bike, tyre pressures and even the condition of the chain. This was supplemented by an array of mind-boggling stats and data that only an engineering graduate would understand. His fellow thigh-thumpers looked on in amazement at the technical wizardry on display only inches away from the playboy's inquisitive fingertips. But all this expensive state-of-the-art technology paled into insignificance when compared to the heart-shaped gold locket strapped by his right hand on the edge of the shiny handlebar. It held the precious photos of his beloved parents, taken on the last day of their fateful trip to Zurich all those agonising years before. Amazingly the temperature was over seventy-five degrees. It had risen dramatically in just the last thirty minutes. David tapped the tinted screen with the fist of his gloved hand to check the authenticity of the data. It was right; there wasn't anything wrong with the reading at Jodrell Bank.

On the occasions he'd taken to the saddle in Italy before, he'd never known it that hot and so oppressive at such an early hour. It didn't bode well for his fellow riders who seemed oblivious to the potential dangers ahead, as they continued their journey south towards Lazise and on to Sirmione, their first station stop at the most southerly point on the lake. The road surface was kind. It was smooth, comfortable and easy to ride on offering no resistance to their thumping thighs. They peddled at an even pace past Cisano, with the sun's blazing rays beating down, threatening something worse to come.

The guys knew that it wasn't a competitive ride, there weren't any trophies, garlands of flowers, or a podium to prance about on while being kissed by pretty young lovelies in tight-fitting skirts.

They weren't the stars of the show. As always the designated charities were the focal point of their efforts, not the antics of the individual riders. It was a team effort. It was in everyone's interest to work together, share intelligence and hopefully complete the gruelling challenges in one piece, thereby attracting the maximum sponsorship money from the great and the good while publicising the name of the chosen charity to the wider world.

Alexandre Dumas' wise words always resonated with Mr Lane. In one simple sentence, it captured the quintessential beliefs behind their athletic endeavours; it personified everything they stood for; it characterised the philosophy and ethos of the Pedal Power Programme.

In the early stages, David tended to ride in the centre of the group and as they progressed, he moved slowly through the pack checking on the welfare and general health of his friends. Riders were comfortable with this style and felt motivated by his support and personal presence. From time to time, he'd glance down at his specially designed Rolex watch moulded within his left-hand glove, like a Formula One racing driver's timepiece, checking their progress and the timing of their next station stop. Since 2009, David had cultivated a reputation as a generous philanthropist and a compelling spokesman for good causes. He worked tirelessly for those less fortunate and expected nothing less from those participating in his beloved Pedal Power Programme. Hence his interest in the well-being of his chums, knowing full well that his altruistic conquests relied on their doggedness and resolve, as his plans would never leave the drawing board if it wasn't for them and their unflinching loyalty.

Riding south in the middle of the pack, his mind started to wander. He thought about his candidacy and the likelihood of electoral success. The local party's standing in the polls was excellent due to the hard work and influence of the incumbent MP, who was standing down at the next election after thirty years in Parliament. David stood a very good chance of retaining the seat on the back of the outstanding achievements of his highly respected predecessor. He was somewhat surprised, however, to have been shortlisted as there were a number of strong note-worthy candidates for the safe seat with impressive backgrounds in commerce, finance and the public sector. He put his good fortune down to his well-publicised charitable work and no doubt his substantial donations to the party over the years may have swayed the selection panel in his favour.

"Hi guys, just to let you know that there are street marshals in position along the route warning you of any impending danger so keep your eyes peeled," yelled Francois into David's earpiece. "We don't want any mishaps this early in the ride. We'll soon be passing Lazise, so look out for a series of tightly-bunched pedestrian crossings and mini-roundabouts along the zigzag roadway. They can be dangerous as you well know."

Chapter 26

"Damn thing won't start!" shouted the tattooed man. He kept turning the ignition key in his old battered Fiat which responded with an annoying series of solid clicks. He shuffled out of the dingy grey tin can, looking angry and hot under the collar, before kicking the front tyre and slamming the dented door closed with a deafening thump.

"I'll be saying goodbye to this heap of junk tomorrow once I get my hands on that lovely money," he grinned while dangling his hairy tattooed arm around Francesca's shoulder and glancing skywards. She smiled as her unkempt boyfriend kissed her tenderly on the cheek and patted her bottom.

"Now don't forget the plan, we've gone over it lots of times. By tomorrow you'll be a woman of wealth, I promise you," he whispered in her ear. Her eyes dilated at the prospect. She kissed him passionately on the lips and strolled the short distance from the car park towards the white-walled hotel entrance, seemingly unperturbed by the intense morning heat with her imitation Radley handbag, minus the dog, swaying loosely on her sleek, tanned shoulders.

Francesca sauntered into the hotel when the automatic glass doors swished wide open to greet her, then wandered passed the deserted marble reception desk and along the expansive passageway towards the cool capacious lounge. Here some scantily dressed new arrivals were mingling about in small family groups preparing to subject their pale, unblemished bodies to the vagaries of the sweltering Italian sun.

Francesca had hitched up with Midge a few months earlier and had grown fond of his funny, quirky ways and easy-going attitude. It was his carefree, relaxed manner that attracted her most to the fun-loving clown. Midge wasn't fazed by life's little challenges and took everything in his stride, except for the unreliable antics of his ageing rust bucket that made him shout and kick out when it failed to perform. Sure, he was a scruffy sod with a violent streak that often frightened her, had miles too many tattoos and was devoid of ambition and drive. But strangely enough, she felt at ease in his company and that was all that mattered for the time being. They were in their early thirties, drifting through life on a journey to nowhere, with chips on their shoulders the size of a satellite dish.

Most of their contemporaries had made something of their lives, however modest, but these two ne'er-do-wells had jogged along aimlessly, parked up in a dreary cul-de-sac for most of their adult years, watching their friends move up the greasy pole and, all the time, blaming others for their pitiful existence rather than pointing the finger of blame at themselves.

 Midge lived with his retired parents in a rundown tenement block just outside Garda, where drab, dull and dirty were the closest of friends and lived in hapless harmony together. Life had given Francesca a better throw of the dice in the guise of a prestigious top-notch hotel where she languished for the summer months, enjoying all the trappings. When the season drew to a close in September and the curtain came down on another hectic six months, she'd just pack up, move north to the ski resorts where she'd wait at tables and work as a wine waitress before wandering back down the slopes in early spring when the jaunty holidaymakers returned to the shores of the famous blue lake.

This repetitive, revolving-door existence had been her lot for longer than she could remember, often pandering to the needs of disgruntled hotel guests, sometimes being the brunt of rude jokes and bad manners and even having to endure their drink-fuelled attempts to grapple with her native tongue.

Francesca felt a little guilty stringing the Englishman along, particularly as he'd been so polite and charming, showing her every courtesy since his arrival on Friday. But he was a wealthy businessman, dressed in stylish designer clothes with an expensive Breitling Chronomat watch strapped to his wrist so he definitely wouldn't miss the odd thousand or two. Her conscience was clear and anyway, the plucky waitress wasn't going to let a rich aristocrat, languishing in a 400-euro-a-night hotel suite, get in her way – to stop her fulfilling her dreams of a new life, a fresh start elsewhere. Once the spoils were shared out, she'd be on her toes, over the white-crusted Alps as quick as her flip-flops could carry her, waving goodbye to the boring humdrum lifestyle that had been her mantra for so long.

This was her big break, her big opportunity. The attractive senorita was determined to grab it firmly with both hands and turn her miserable life around once and for all, even if one or two innocent people got hurt in the crossfire.

Midge said the boss's plan was fool proof, all they had to do was follow it to the letter and they'd be set up for life. It sounded wonderful, almost too good to be true. Back at work, Francesca fantasised about the future thinking what she'd do with her share of the booty, as she busily collected up the remaining dirty glasses from the night before and loaded them into the large dishwasher, hidden discreetly behind the circular, restaurant bar.

Chapter 27

Meanwhile Team 30 charged past Lazise, with David still pondering on his career prospects, when the momentary lapse in concentration nearly caused a collision with an outstretched flag being waved across the centre reservation by a well-meaning, red-faced marshal. That was a close shave, he thought, dodging the swirling ensign and the protruding raised manhole cover. Some of his close neighbours turned their heads and glanced at him knowingly.

By now the big yellow globe was doing its worst, bearing down on their sweaty bodies and aching limbs. The limited breeze and high humidity promised to raise the bar, challenge their fitness, making the journey to the foot of the lake increasingly arduous. Once they arrived in Sirmione and turned north, the convoy would face a much tougher, even more energy-sapping ride up the exposed west side with its winding roads, frequent mini roundabouts and punishing inclines before it finally reached Riva del Garda at the top of the lake, a hundred tortuous kilometres away.

The cavalcade was constantly reminded of the beauty of Lake Garda as the shimmering waters tracked their progress south, offering some breathtaking vistas of paradise on earth while green sun-drenched hills touched blue cloudless skies, as crowded ferries plied their trade between towns and small lakeside hamlets. Sweeping south the peloton saw signs to Peschiera del Garda, well known for its busy industrious harbour and a popular base for visitors to nearby Verona, while the more romantically inclined could sample the delights of Venice, a few miles to the east, nestling beside the waters of the imposing Adriatic Sea.

Eventually the thirty-strong snake, with its sea of outrageous headgear and psychedelic outfits, pulled in for a planned pit stop at the spacious central coach park just outside Sirmione. The security cordon was already in place holding back the boisterous, high-spirited fans who'd heard of their progress on social media and rushed across town, with phones at the ready, hoping to catch a glimpse of their hunky heroes before they chased north.

The keen, efficient staff in the two support vehicles threw their car doors wide open and sprang into action, performing their well-rehearsed routine with great precision. They quickly distributed supplies of high-protein biscuits, crunchy snacks and bunches of bananas to eager, outstretched hands, as sweaty, fraught-looking bodies, slumped back under a row of trees dotted along the perimeter edge of the coach park. Thankfully nature was temporarily on their side, treating them to a brief reprieve from the intensive heat that had stalked them since leaving Lazise. Anyone thinking this challenge was a pushover would have a rude awakening in the next few hours. It would test even the fittest in the group. The guys would need to dig deep, draw on their reserves if they were to complete the challenge in one piece and return home on Monday relatively unscathed.

The team rested in the cool refreshing shade, wiping streams of sweat and grime off their tanned faces and limbs with the emblematic red-and-white-striped towels, before swigging great gulps of chilled Evian water and flavoured drinks. Some even doused their heads in water in an attempt to cool down and invigorate their hot, clammy bodies.

After a few minutes, their batteries were fully recharged and the guys were chatting and laughing and teasing the young female support staff as they topped up their water bottles and handed out extra bananas and energy bars to the handsome prima donnas. David wandered through the throng of bodies, bikes and bottles, patting them on the back, handing out fresh towels and waving his gloved fist to a crowd of excited onlookers, standing expectantly behind the steel barriers some distance away.

"At least we haven't got the damn wet stuff that plagued us in Munich, god what a ride that was," remarked Eric when he caught PW's eye. Chris grinned.

"How d'you feel?" asked Chris, flopping down next to David on the uneven gravel surface and taking a hearty swig from his half-empty plastic bottle. The journey south had taken its toll judging by the pained expression on his face.

"Not so bad thanks, but it's the hottest I've ever known at this time of day, so make sure you keep drinking my friend otherwise who knows what might happen, especially at your age," David remarked with a cheeky grin, glancing down at his impressive

Rolex watch firmly embedded within his hand stitched leather red and white cycling glove.

"Guess what? It's twenty-nine degrees, yes, twenty-nine degrees, no wonder I'm feeling a tad hot and sweaty."

"Wow!" yelled Chris, raising his arms from side to side to stretch his upper body, before slumping back against the trunk of a tree and waving to Alison ambling past with a tray crammed full of bandages, plasters and creams.

"Do you know something? In some ways Alison reminds me of my Elena with her trim figure and saucy little wiggle but, of course, she's much older, more battle weary too," Chris whispered with a snigger behind his gloved hand.

"Now don't be rude, PW. You don't know when you might need the lady of the lamp, so be careful what you say. She's the last person on earth you want to upset right now, I can tell you. We have to trust her. But things are sometimes not how they appear, we can be easily deceived by those close to us and who we trust. Blind to their deception in many ways," he replied, glumly.

Then like a flick of a switch, David quickly snapped out of his pessimistic mood. He jumped to his feet and bolted down the remains of his half-eaten banana while one of the cheery helpers, dressed in skimpy shorts and T-shirt, climbed between the mountain of luxury bikes checking on their protégés before the off. By this time Team 30 were gearing themselves up for the next stage, feeling revitalised after their short break, when the charismatic Frenchman blew his whistle to get their attention. Leaning against the BMW's shiny bonnet, dressed in an open-neck shirt, perfectly ironed trousers, with an expensive pair of designer sunglasses perched on top of his head, he looked very much the part as the master of ceremonies.

"Right guys, we're now moving on our way up to Riva. The roads will be marshalled all the way and the police will make sure the road's clear, but remember to watch out for oncoming traffic. As you know, from your information packs, Alison will act as backmarker stopping any vehicles overtaking from the rear. Now, it's much too hot to hang around here so unless you've got any questions, I suggest we hit the road. Remember to follow Chris. He's the main man for our exit out of Sirmione so don't let him out of your sight. Best of luck."

There were no questions. Quite frankly, the stars of the show were too busily involved with their gear to take too much notice of Francois's briefing. As seasoned athletes with umpteen rides under their belts, and some bumps and scrapes to prove it, all they wanted to do was get off, make tracks before they melted on the tarmac.

A stream of bright sparkling machines gently freewheeled down the narrow slip road towards the main highway. Riders sat upright in their saddles, stretching their long narrow fingers inside their tight-fitting leather gloves. With designer sunglasses firmly in place and creams applied to exposed parts, the convoy moved off two abreast serenaded by the familiar sound of crackling in their ears while Francois adjusted the radio signal from the comfy vantage point of his air-conditioned BMW.

"We're off to Salo then!" said Chris gently patting his best mate on the shoulder and snatching a quick slurp from his water bottle that was strapped halfway down his bike's pale blue frame.

"I wish we could have rested longer, especially as I'm one of the oldest in the pack. Fifteen minutes doesn't seem enough to me," he remarked.

"I'm not sure," argued David. "It's probably best to get going before the sun gets any hotter so we do need to make waves, my friend. I'll talk to you later. I must move back along the peloton and keep an eye on the guys."

Then, as if on cue, and without any warning, the pied piper raced off like a scared rabbit out of a trap, allowing no time for his colleagues to flex their muscles and ease themselves back into the saddle after their short break. PW was unpredictable, often impulsive and frequently prone to irrational behaviour, but his selfish antics were outrageous even by his standards. The incorrigible rogue was making his mark, putting his stamp on the ride, sending a huge salvo across the bows of any doubters who thought he'd had his day, was over the hill and ready for the scrap heap. Chris was out of the saddle, pounding his peddles for all they were worth, riding fast enough to be closing the gap on the lead BMW followed by a stream of brightly coloured heads bobbing up and down in his wake. Undaunted by the chaos he'd caused, he continued to raise the pace knowing there was a series of tight bends to come, then a sudden steep incline. Within a matter of minutes, the peloton was stretched out into a long straggly wavy line.

Angry, red-faced riders were forced out of their saddles, peddling as fast as they could, fearful of losing contact with their belligerent headstrong leader. Eventually the road levelled out, the going got easier and PW rested back in his saddle. He was pleased with himself for keeping within the BMW's slipstream, for setting a brisk pace and not faltering on the uphill slope even though the steep gradient was a real test of his fitness, making the backs of his thighs hurt like hell. Not bad for an oldie, he mumbled under his breath, quietly sniggering like a Cheshire cat at his chums who, judging by their contorted facial expressions and the slowness of their assent, were not enjoying the climb one little bit. Needless to say, the atmosphere between PW and the others was very fractious for the next few kilometres, but he didn't care, not a jot, even though David admonished him for his childish prank, telling him to grow up and treat his colleagues with more respect. Barcelona's main man had proved his point, he'd shown his contempories that he hadn't lost his edge and was still a force to be reckoned with. Chris was slim and stocky with muscular shoulders and a square jawline. He was fitter than many which wasn't surprising. The multi-millionaire playboy spent a small fortune on personal trainers, health boffins and nutritionists and admitted, when under the influence, to the occasional nip and tuck in his relentless quest to slow down the passage of time.

His recent forty-seventh birthday was a case in point. The sombre event was commemorated on his own, hidden away from family and friends. There were no fanfares or popping corks, not even a card or two to mark the occasion such was the sense of foreboding he felt with the chiming of the midnight hour and the unedifying prospect of another waxed candle on the proverbial cake. It wasn't until his bubbly, vivacious hairdresser consoled the aging juvenile in her own inimitable way, that he decided life was worth living and perhaps forty-seven wasn't such a big number after all.

The heat seemed more intense as they pounded along the southern section of the lake before slowly turning north towards Salo and Gardone, with the busy, bustling town of Desenzano nearby. The roads were smooth and comfortable, kind to their buttocks and backs with only a few unexpected jolts and sudden judders to their nether regions. An unwavering cocktail of heat and humidity contrived to bring the riders to their knees, stop them in their tracks, but with clenched teeth and plucky resolve the guys pressed on determined as ever to defy the elements and achieve their goal. Their flagging spirits were constantly raised by the countless number of red and white ME flags flapping freely in the breeze from lampposts, window ledges and street signs bordering both sides of the road.

Endless rows of banners, billboards and eye-catching streamers welcomed the arrival of Team 30, who raised their gloved hands in unison to acknowledge the shouts and ear-piercing screams from banks of sun-drenched well-wishers lining the streets sometimes two or three deep. Energetic supporters even ran alongside the convoy on the steeper slopes hoping to catch a close up of their heroes or, better still, a precious selfie to show off to family and friends.

Inquisitive motorcyclists sometimes came alongside, beeped their horns and yelled muffled words of encouragement, while diving into the frequent gaps between the healthy hunks. Some mindless idiots got too close for comfort but thankfully, most of the time the convoy was given a wide berth, treated with respect and both parties got on well together. Meanwhile, their Gallic cheerleader didn't hog the airwaves with mindless chatter, only using the radio to talk about up and coming stops, explain the changing road conditions and often remind the thigh thumpers of the perilous dangers of dehydration. They appreciated the prompt.

The black support vehicles also joined in the fun and pageantry, with banners and stickers plastered along both sides of the estate cars; with countless ME flags flapping about on the bonnets and roofs promoting the chosen charity to the excitement of the baying crowds. The sleek shiny BMWs, draped in their colourful livery, sometimes attracted as much attention as the sea of helmeted heroes that were spread between them like a tasty filling in a gigantic sandwich.

Without warning, a very strange thing happened. Half an hour into the ride, a swarm of airborne insects appeared from nowhere and latched onto the group, like barnacles on a flat-bottomed boat. Francois was caught off guard. He couldn't work out why they were attracted to the cyclists and told the bewildered riders to keep their mouths shut and cover up any exposed parts, which was easier said than done. Moments later, a number complained of nasty bites, stings and itchiness to their legs and forearms with many of the riders flaying their hands and arms about in the air trying to rid themselves of the pesky little parasites.

Passing motorists coming the other way wondered what the hell was going on when the meandering line of cyclists swerved from side to side, shaking, waving and wriggling about. Yet before they knew it, the swarm of creepy-crawlies disappeared, were nowhere to be seen and the poor pampered playboys were left to lick their wounds and ponder their plight.

Alison had a theory that seemed credible. Her pride and joy back home was a yellow mustard-coloured hatchback which often attracted flies, wasps and other insects. Now, as many of the riders had yellow in their distinctive outfits, she thought that the colour might have been a magnet for the pesky beggars and the reason for their frenzied attack on the bouncing beauties.

This part of the ride lived up to its billing. It was an exhausting stage, with the weary cyclists peddling behind the lead vehicle at about twenty miles per hour in ninety degrees heat. The sound of cheering crowds, smiling faces and the constant waving of banners and bunting continued to lift their spirits, but you could see that as they approached the halfway stage, some were finding the going very tough.

A constant throbbing in David's right ankle was a distressing reminder of his cruel treatment at the hands of Martin Conway and the bully boy's predilection for kicking people's legs, often being on the receiving end of the yob's violent streak in the school's dimly lit bicycle sheds.

The unexpectedly high temperatures and humidity were taking their toll on the squad. Progress up the west side was hard going and the unyielding conditions made life difficult for the guys, who'd already emptied most of their water bottles and were eagerly looking forward to a break in Salo and the opportunity to replenish their dwindling supplies. The mercury was slowly creeping up and it was far hotter than anything they'd experienced before. David's Rolex was boasting ninety-two degrees when he drifted up and down the peloton checking on the welfare of his chums, dishing out bottles of water from his limited supplies. Because of the uncertain terrain, it was deemed too dangerous for the rear support vehicle to drive alongside the convoy, making dehydration a real threat to the success of the venture. It was also considered unsafe to bring the peloton to a standstill on the narrow roads, so the support teams kept their fingers crossed and hoped for the best knowing that Salo was only a few kilometres away.

Friendly marshals, with flags in hand, did their bit to keep the riders moving, but even they couldn't patrol every traffic hazard and busy road junction. Frequent mini-roundabouts, dotted along the route, added to the torment, forcing the peloton to sometimes come to a near standstill. Tired limbs were then forced to climb out of their saddles and, with clenched fists, they gripped hold of the handlebars and peddled as hard as they could to get back up to speed before repeating the strength-draining exercise time and time again. The unrelenting incline merely added to their torture and a gallery of gaunt, stress-lined faces said it all.

'Just for ME' banners and flags were hanging everywhere all the way along the route, showing unflinching support for the cause, draped prominently in shop windows, stuck on billboards, outside chic restaurants and garage forecourts and even dangling from clothes lines, car aerials and motorcycle helmets. It was madness, pure madness, but tremendously uplifting for the guys with parched throats and legs that wanted to rest.

Boisterous crowds cheered, clapped and shouted from every vantage point, standing two or three deep on sharp narrow bends and crumbling pavements, enthralled by their heroic quest. Young and old celebrated their arrival on home turf and joined in the once in a lifetime spectacle when their cycling idols passed in their midst, no doubt boasting for years to come of the day they brushed shoulders with the internationally famous Team 30. The unrelenting, ear-splitting racket of beating drums, squeaky trumpets and high-pitched whistles was a huge fillip for the guys, making them forget their tired muscles that were constantly telling them to stop, call it a day, return home post-haste to their revered world of wealth and privilege. But Team 30 were made of tougher stuff, not put off by a bit of heat, showing craft and guile on their journey to the chequered flag proving, to any doubters, they were a real force for change and were not just a collection of pretty faces with a few bob in the bank.

Chapter 28

At last, after what seemed like an eternity, the lakeside town of Salo was in their sights with its carefully manicured parks, beautifully laid out gardens and expensive designer shops pandering to the well-to-do and anyone with money to burn. The lead rider, Pierre La Blanc, guided the team towards the town's main thoroughfare, through hordes of exuberant onlookers, to a shaded area adjacent to the ferry point where cool drinks were distributed at speed from the rear of the two cavernous estate cars. Expensive top-notch bikes and loud gaudy helmets lay strewn across the marble surface and hot perspiring bodies lay sprawled flat out, exhausted and drained. Others just flopped back against the town hall's cool, shaded columns, tipping bottles of Evian water over their soaking wet heads and taking great swigs of the wet stuff to quench their voracious thirsts. Then after a few moments bodies were rejuvenated and the sound of laughter, joking and idle banter filled the air. Francois and members of the support team sauntered between the motley crew distributing fresh, fluffy towels and checking on their health and general well-being.

Thankfully they all seemed okay, albeit a little tired and rather frayed around the edges, which was only to be expected. Alison was fully occupied treating the stings and sores left by the pesky little devils earlier, while the lads gulped down bottles of cool water and munched on bunches of bananas and high-protein energy bars. She was also looking for any signs of heat stroke or dehydration, or anything else that might signal danger. Flora, as the riders' nicknamed her, was an integral part of the group, spreading help and kindness in her own inimitable way. Knowing they were pushing their bodies to the absolute limit, testing their fitness to the extreme, it was reassuring for the guys to have a qualified nurse on hand just in case something went wrong.

Alison was surprised to see how much damage the insects had done, causing blood to rise to the surface and creating horrible red weals on vulnerable exposed parts. She applied a combination of creams and lotions to reduce the swelling and irritation, and alleviate the awful itching that tormented many of the riders. Bjorn, one of the cheeky Dutch contingent with a wicked sense of humour, said that he felt something wriggling inside his lycra bottoms and invited her to investigate the source. Now Alison was streetwise, had been around the block several times, and was used to the mischievous banter of exuberant males, so needless to say she wasn't taken in by his suggestive comments.

Lying sprawled out across the ground, trying not to itch their exposed bits, the lads chuckled at the Dutchman's bawdy banter, but cheered loudly when Alison got her own back by squirting a tube of ice-cold liquid into Bjorn's skin suit. He shrieked and hollered and jumped about in a frenzy as the freezing moisture slowly seeped down his chest towards the parts in question. It was then when Francois, still laughing at Bjorn's predicament, blew his whistle.

"Gentleman. I hope you're fully refreshed. Once we get to Gargnano, we enter the tunnels which, you'll recall from your notes, are a constant feature all the way up to Riva. It's too dangerous for vehicles to pass us southbound so the police will close the road, guaranteeing us safe passage all the way up. Any questions? Right, let's move out before we bake to death."

So the team regrouped and rode off across the expansive town courtyard towards the congested ferry point where a long winding queue of oriental visitors hid under rows of dainty, ornate parasols trying to protect themselves from the sun's blistering rays. But when Team 30 appeared on the scene, all hell let loose.

The sedate diminutive group suddenly burst into action with an explosion of clicking cameras and smartphones, capturing the once-in-a-lifetime moment when they came face to face with David Lane's famous thirty. Throwing caution to the wind, and ignoring the perils of the sun, they yelled, cheered and shrieked with unbridled delight at the sight of their famous heroes. Looking slightly shell-shocked at their over-the-top reception, the guys duly responded with a series of cursory waves and broad beaming smiles which would no doubt be the stuff of legends in years to come when, thousands of miles away, the cheery oriental visitors regaled the story to their children and grandchildren of the day they met Team 30 in all its glory.

The slow, easy-going ride took them through peaceful, shaded streets, alongside rows of traditional white Italian houses standing in the shadows of their vibrant terracotta roofs, while the sound of dogs barking could be heard some way off in the distance. A light wind wafted off the lake, offering a refreshing treat for the guys before returning to the rigours of the open road and the blistering heat. But suddenly, misfortune struck. They hadn't even settled back into the saddle, or got into some kind of rhythm, before Francois explained on a crackly line that a minor mishap had occurred at the rear of the pack.

Apparently two stragglers were so engrossed in their own private conversation that they collided with each other and ended up face down in a dirty, dank water-logged trench bordering the main arterial road to Gardone. Other than their pride and their bedraggled appearance, no serious damage was done and the Portuguese duo soon re-joined their unsympathetic mates, who treated them to a surfeit of rude jokes and coarse remarks about the dangers of ditches and dykes.

Meanwhile Anton, the lead cyclist, was the first to see the sight. It was absolutely overwhelming. He'd got separated from his chums when the meandering snake came to a sudden standstill at a set of traffic lights a couple of hundred yards back up the road. But when the peloton finally caught up with their front man, they were also captivated by the scene that greeted them. It was just like a guard of honour at a wedding, with rows upon rows of happy smiling faces standing on either side of the pedestrian walkway that ran parallel to the lake and stretched far off into the distance. Crowds stood behind makeshift steel barriers, cheering their arrival like a welcoming party for a famous celebrity, or an important dignitary. Throngs of animated locals dressed in 'Just for ME' T-shirts and similar headgear were jostling for position, trying to catch a glimpse of their heroes while frantically shaking flags and banners and calling out the names of their favourite pin-ups as they cruised by, just yards away.

Any feelings of tiredness were long gone; dismissed without a second thought. The guys were invigorated by the infectious outpouring of warmth and geniality that the kind-hearted townsfolk showered on them with unbridled enthusiasm. Riders' arms were raised skywards and kisses blown to young hysterical girls in short skirts and bikini tops jumping up and down with excitement, chanting their names and offering undying love to the shapely six packs, whose pictures and posters no doubt adorned their bedroom walls. At the end of the long walkway, bordered by a string of bars and street cafes, was the imposing Gardone Hotel, a stylish landmark retreat for the wealthy, gently caressing the waterfront, looking calmly over the proceedings below. The peloton slowed to a crawl before stopping next to the town's bustling ferry point where, to everyone's surprise, Anton was presented with a bouquet of fresh flowers by a short stocky gentleman dressed in a dark pinstripe suit wearing a bright yellow tie and boasting an impressive chain of office hanging loosely across his broad shoulders. Standing bolt upright on a wooden rostrum with his chest out and a beaming smile, he looked very important as the town's mayor and leading dignitary. He shook Anton's hand vigorously, posed for a couple of press photographs, then kissed the handsome German on both damp cheeks before waving the peloton on its way to the frenetic sound of cheering and clapping ringing loudly in their ears.

Moments later Francois's calm, reassuring voice took over the airwaves. "I hope you enjoyed that little treat!" he yelled into their earpiece. "You deserved it, guys. I don't know about you, but didn't the dwarf with the big shiny chain have more than a striking resemblance to Ronnie Corbett, my favourite comedian of all time?" The British riders chuckled to themselves as they adjusted their gear and sunglasses as the rest of the group looked on, somewhat bemused, wondering who the hell was Donny Sorbit and why were the silly Brits giggling over a soppy name?

In the distance the black support vehicles were lying in wait, under the shade of the hotel's awning, ready to guide their valuable charges to their next stop. After a brief chat with the local police, Francois was ready for the off. The Garda authorities were committed to the cycling challenge from the word go, falling over backwards to do everything they could to support the prestigious event. When the phone call came in 2013, telling them they'd been chosen as the venue for the fourth ride of the 2014 season, they couldn't believe their luck, it was beyond their wildest dreams. They knew the publicity alone would have a dramatic impact on the local economy for years to come, bringing much-needed income into the region that relied heavily on the vagaries of the tourist trade.

For reasons of safety, adjacent roads were closed for short periods and traffic marshals placed at intervals around the lake. Italian drivers were reasonably patient, driving in line behind the cyclists, knowing the group would periodically pull into specially set up lay-bys to allow them to pass. It was very well organised. After the team's warm reception in Gardone, they were soon back in their stride, pounding the pedals with even greater enthusiasm, but somewhat oblivious to the dangers of the blistering heat and scorching temperatures that continued to follow in their tracks.

"I understand the road ahead is free of obstacles and any dodgy hazards and hopefully we should make good time. Keep drinking as much as you can. Dehydration is a real threat today," shouted Francois into their earpieces.

David rode towards the front of the convoy behind a group of Dutch riders, who waved their gloved hands in the air when he entered their slipstream. Jack, a wiry fair-skinned athlete with strong broad shoulders and a muscular physique, with an international reputation in the world of landscape design, patted him on the back as he stretched upright in the saddle and gazed in awe at the beautifully tended gardens lying peacefully along both sides of the narrow winding road.

A quick glimpse at the stylish state-of-the-art consul in the centre of David's chrome handlebars confirmed his worse fears. The temperature was ninety-four degrees and the humidity was also perilously high at just over ninety. A daunting proposition for the fittest of seasoned riders who'd no doubt find the going pretty tough, let alone a bunch of guys the wrong side of forty who were not as agile as they used to be. The enigmatic leader was finding this challenge more difficult than he'd imagined. Even though he'd ridden longer distances in the past, it was the ruthless, unforgiving heat and stifling humidity that was sapping his strength, making every thrust on the pedals increasingly difficult.

But thankfully after a few more arduous miles relief was on the horizon. There in the distance was Gargnano, resting on the edge of the lake, surrounded by towering hills and grand awe-inspiring mountains, decorated with zigzag pathways climbing relentlessly towards distant summits and blue cloudless skies. It was idyllic. They freewheeled through a series of gentle bends, basking in the panoramic views, while sitting back in their saddles, relishing the constant rush of cool air dousing their hot bodies before finally coming to a halt in a dust-laden lay-by on the outskirts of the town.

Extra supplies of water were taken on board and energy bars stuffed into breast pockets. It was well known that the main road around Lake Garda was cycle-friendly and relatively easy to negotiate until you reached Gargnano. Here it changed into a series of sharp bends and dark unforgiving tunnels, which were a feature of the remaining miles up to Riva. So to guarantee their safe passage, the police closed the road both ways with the stipulation that the team finished that section of the route as quickly as possible. After a brief comfort break, the guys continued their journey north, but very soon the clammy oppressive weather, that had dogged them since Garda, was gone as the single-line convoy entered a series of cool intermittent tunnels. Interestingly, years earlier the smoking tyres of James Bond's growling Aston Martin shot into the very same tunnels that now offered temporary solace from the scorching rays for the multicoloured centipede. Here the chilly air swept over their hot sticky bodies bringing little goosepimples to the fore. No one complained; it was bliss; it was manna from heaven.

Everything was going smoothly, going exactly to plan and they were making good progress towards their lunchtime stop until disaster struck. Cristiano, a veteran of many previous outings, clipped the steel barriers with his front wheel and lost his balance. The Spaniard then crashed to the ground, skidded across the smooth greasy surface before coming to a halt tangled up in the spokes of his bent front wheel, lying prostrate in the middle of the dimly lit highway. Apparently the man from Madrid was adjusting his gloves, made slippery by the water dripping through the roof of the tunnel and lost his grip on the handlebars. Fortunately, there were no other casualties and the cavalcade managed to swerve around their fallen colleague before stopping about a hundred yards further on, huddled together in the dark, dank tunnel. In the meantime, the two BMWs came to a screeching halt with their yellow hazard lights flashing on and off in the gloom. Fortunately a series of breaks in the perimeter wall allowed the sun to shine through so their favourite nurse dispensed first aid to her blood-stained patient lying traumatised against the adjacent steel crash barrier. Time was clearly of the essence and, following some frantic treatment to his injuries, Cristiano stumbled to his feet and, against strong medical advice, lowered himself gingerly onto the replacement bike's uncompromising saddle. Then after a bit of irritable fumbling with the Velcro, he slowly moved off with a bandaged wrist, badly swollen knee and a collection of red insect bites scattered liberally around his grazed neck and legs, testimony to his earlier misfortune.

He was a sorry sight in his torn skin suit and dirty oil-stained gloves, with badly scuffed shoes and bent helmet, looking as though he'd come off the worst in a charity mud fight instead of competing in an exclusive cycling challenge around a legendary Italian lake. Five minutes later, the peloton was back up to speed again, a fact that was much appreciated by the impatient Italian horn-honkers waiting in line at the entrance to the tunnels.

As they moved off, David waved to Sebastian May, a Belgium rider and playboy son of a wealthy pharmaceutical tycoon. At forty-one years of age, he was the youngest member of the team and this was his second season on the Programme. The millionaire was dark-skinned with short black hair and deep piercing brown eyes which, together with his magnetic charm and seductive smile, attracted women like bees to a honeypot. He'd appeared on cable TV in short acting roles that were never very stretching and had featured in some reasonably successful TV adverts for cosmetics and luxury cars. Sebastian was a regular contestant on daytime game shows where he didn't do particularly well, but as his mere presence sent audience figures through the roof, no one really cared. The playboy's salacious affairs and extramarital conquests were front-page news in the tabloids and sleazy magazines, making even the most broad-minded blush at some of his raunchy antics. Mary was his fifth wife of seven months and the Belgium bookies weren't offering very good odds to her being on payroll for their first anniversary later in the year.

Chapter 29

David drifted up and down the cavalcade of colour and recognised the guys that had ridden with him on a number of occasions before, giving their all for a catalogue of good causes. He smiled to himself recalling some of the rude nicknames they'd bestowed on one another. There was Blanks. Sadly, Harry had a low sperm count and couldn't have a family and, lacking any kind of sensitivity or compassion towards his plight, the team often teased him and joked openly at his expense. There was Ping. He was constantly bombarded by an endless stream of text messages, but somehow Simon, the nimble-fingered Swede, had the uncanny knack of being able to reply to his many ardent followers even when charging along on his custom-built Trek Madone. It was remarkable to see. Then there was Pinky. Whatever the conditions the jocular, easy-going Frenchman, with a pronounced lisp and jug-like ears, never got a suntan, not even a slight blemish of the skin. While his fellow riders took on a deep bronze sheen as the season progressed, looking increasingly healthy and fighting fit, Pinky's skin remained a resolute whiter shade of pale whatever the conditions. Then there was Gerhard. How could he forget him? A strong, strapping powerhouse from Helsinki, with huge shoulders that never seemed to end, large muscular thighs and hands and a neck the size of a tree trunk. True to form his mates were totally oblivious to the meaning of political correctness and nicknamed him REO – rear entrance only. Fortunately for them their gay colleague thought it was amusing, and not in any way offensive, otherwise his irreverent chums would have had to choose something less provocative if they didn't want to attract the wrath of the fearsome Fin. But then there towards the middle of the peloton was the star of the show, the guy who took the most ribbing from his mischievous cycling cohorts. Tim was a carpet hugger; a vertically challenged guy from Essex and christened 'the dwarf' because of his closeness to the ground. His specially designed bicycle frame was smaller than the others in the squad and had two blocks of solid wood firmly bolted to his pedals, giving the midget from Maldon some extra height and more control especially on the steep slopes. Tim was often the brunt of many a rude caustic joke about his stature, but the diminutive well-to-do stepson of a wealthy shipping tycoon took it all in his stride and invariably gave as good as he got. It was fair to say this was a unique bunch of guys none of whom would have looked out of place on the expensive bits of a monopoly board.

Okay, they were filthy rich, with privileged backgrounds and most of them had never done a serious day's work in their lives, but these exciting adventures captured their imagination, transformed their predictable lives, giving them a real sense of purpose. Their happy, carefree expressions draped across their slightly tired faces said it all and was confirmation, if needed, that they enjoyed their cycling escapades, their relentless tussles in the saddle and the binding friendships and camaraderie their energetic exploits evoked.

Even though they were feeling the strain, Team 30 were still fully committed to the task, determined to fulfil their promise to the ME Association. Failure for this intrepid band of angels, who thrived in the theatre of hope, was never an option, never in their vocabulary.

At last after pounding through an endless string of dark, monotonous tunnels with the occasional shaft of light breaking through the gaps in the concrete walls, they were rewarded by the captivating, mesmeric view of Riva beckoning them on the horizon. The resort town stole the show perched at the head of the lake, languishing beneath a string of breathtaking mountain ranges and steep sloping hills with peaks that reached up to the deep, blue sky as tiny clumps of fluffy white clouds floated on the gentle summer breeze. It was magic; it was heaven on earth.

Chapter 30

Back in Cheltenham, Claire was busily organising the do for David's return on Monday evening and the Millinses were getting under her feet as usual, not helping in the slightest. The elderly housekeepers had been with David for a number of years as the four-bedroom villa, stretching over three floors, was too much for him to maintain on his own and, because of his many charitable ventures and regular trips abroad, he needed some kind of live-in help. It was the Millinses that came to the rescue in his hour of need with bus passes in one hand and crumpled plastic macks in the other.

A highly respectable employment agency organised a series of job interviews for the important housekeeping role, one warm summer's day in late June. A date that was forever etched in David's memory. As the afternoon drew to a close, and he was thinking which oily fish to eat with his salad for dinner, Mr and Mrs Millins trooped into the lounge unannounced dragging a squeaky battered green suitcase and holding a couple of Tesco carrier bags full to the brim with bulky items of clothing and several well-leafed women's magazines.

He'd already seen four couples earlier in the day, none of whom came up to scratch and was feeling pretty depressed by the whole affair. But even at that late hour, when food was on his mind, the homeowner was intrigued by the amiable pair who'd just sauntered nonchalantly into the room and plonked themselves down on his Duresta Lansdowne sofa. Mrs Millins gazed over towards David with a broad smile on her face and said in a soft quiet tone, "How nice it is to meet you Mr Lane, thank you for inviting us. You have a wonderful home sir and the decor is truly magnificent. Isn't it Cyril?" Her husband grinned and nodded his head.

As David sat there perched on the edge of his deep red Belton chair wondering what the heck was going on, he very soon realised that the old biddies were under the misapprehension that they'd already secured the position; it was in the bag and that meeting the nice Mr Lane, as they called him, was a mere formality, a rubber stamp. Mrs Millins reached into her bulging handbag and, after a bit of rummaging about, retrieved a crumpled piece of paper with a list of handwritten questions to raise with her would-be employer.

"I'd like to ask you one or two things if I may Mr Lane, if that's okay with you?" David, looking perplexed, nodded in agreement. What else could he do? So with the aid of her slightly bent reading glasses she read out the questions from her well-prepared script. Following each of David's replies, the couple conferred by trading glances and, if they nodded and smiled in unison, this was good news for Mr Lane, implying that he'd provided a satisfactory answer and it was worth proceeding to the next.

Meanwhile George Medley, the dapper, well-dressed agent in a pinstripe suit, blue shirt and tie with highly polished black shoes, couldn't believe his eyes. He'd never seen anything quite like it before and didn't know where to look. He cowered in the corner of the room, hoping to be swallowed up by the floor, as his well-to-do client took part in an impromptu quiz programme, that had a striking resemblance to an edition of *Mastermind*. In fairness David didn't falter once, or appear fazed by the Q and A session. In fact he took it all in his stride, played his role remarkably well. At one point he even poured them a glass of freshly squeezed orange juice and handed them a plate of Hobnobs while the interview panel were busily conferring.

After about five minutes of gentle grilling, punctuated by frequent nods and smiles by the seventy-year-olds, the piece of A4 paper was shoved back into her handbag and Mr Millins, who'd been relatively quiet throughout the interrogation, leant forward and asked, in a soft, calm tone of voice, if he had any questions? David hadn't given any serious thought to the subject, he was still trying to work out what was going on and where things were leading. Then Mr Millins took a hearty swig of his drink and explained they were both dog-tired after the long tedious coach journey from Bournemouth and they'd like to have a little nap before catching up with their soaps later in the evening. To George's absolute amazement, David shook his head, smiled and said he'd show them to their room shortly.

He seemed spellbound, even captivated by the nice unassuming pair that had just strolled into his life, set up camp on his new sofa and laid down the terms of their employment. It was priceless. He liked their cheeky impudence, their friendly sociable manner and simple innocence. David loved how they communicated with each other by little gestures, knowing glances and the occasional tilt of the head. It was wonderful, magical and he grinned and chuckled to himself every time they did it.

David Lane could be a softy sometimes and on that late afternoon in June, with the sun slowly disappearing and dark, menacing clouds forming on the horizon, he was like a piece of soft chiffon gently fluttering in the air, fascinated by the charm and kind-hearted geniality of the Dorset duo. He chatted to them about the job, explaining what they'd have to do and how he liked things organised. They talked briefly about their work experience and David smiled when they argued over dates and different places they'd lived. The atmosphere was warm and friendly. Both parties seemed relaxed and at ease in each other's company as though they'd been friends for some time, but the climax to their meeting was unbelievable. As the Millinses sipped their lattes, thanks to George Medley, and finished off a second plate of Hobnobs, Mrs Millins bent down and opened one of her bulging Tesco carrier bags.

"Thank you for your kindness Mr Lane and for the opportunity to work as your housekeepers. Before we go to our room, we'd like to give you some gifts to show our gratitude."

Rather shakily, she handed her employer a leather cigar case and two pairs of pink socks with broad, black diagonal wavy lines. Apparently she bought them from Primark in the lower high street earlier in the day and handed him the till receipt just in case he wanted to change them for a different colour, or size. She also gave her new employer a small retractable umbrella in a plastic sheath that was sponsored by E-on, which Mrs Millins thought was a real fashion statement for any man about town and something to be cherished. She apologised for not wrapping up the presents, but her arthritis was giving her gyp so messing about with sticky cellotape and bits of ribbon was a non-starter for the old girl. As the inaugural meeting came to a close, it was a poignant moment. Mr Softy didn't have the nerve to upset the interviewing panel, dash their hopes of gainful employment, so Mr and Mrs Millins squeaked off to their quarters and they'd been with him ever since.

The somewhat unusual presents had remained undisturbed in pride of place on a side table in his first-floor office sharing a landscape view of the rolling Cotswold hills. They acted as a light-hearted reminder of the day he was successfully interviewed by his doting, elderly housekeepers who remained his trusted companions and friends ever since.

Sadly, over the years a combination of arthritis and two dodgy knees made the spiral staircase a no-no for Mrs Millins. So at some expense, David had a lift installed to their first-floor suite, giving her aging limbs a break and treating his elderly housekeeper to a bit of TLC. The luxury lift with panelled walls, soft lighting and folding mahogany seats guaranteed the short journey would be a comfortable, easy-going experience for the elderly lady. It was fair to say that Mr L had a soft spot for the Millinses, who he viewed as surrogate grandparents and treated them accordingly. So with the touch of a dimly lit pale blue button, the housekeeper hailed her cab and the lift took the strain, allowing her to move around the home quite easily, dishing out help and advice to the often fraught and frazzled lady of the house even when she didn't need it. In the early days of their tenure at number one, Mr Millins kept the palatial gardens up to scratch and even drove his employer to local business meetings. But sadly the years caught up on his aging chauffeur, who found it increasingly difficult to perform the simplest of driving tasks. He did his best to maintain the sprawling rear gardens to Claire's exacting standards, but in the end they had to employ another gardener during the spring and summer months to help keep the expansive lawns under control and make sure the borders were well stocked, weed-free and at their colourful best all year round. Mr Millins was promoted to a supervisory role in the household. That was how David sold the idea over a large glass of his favourite Madeira sherry. After all, he didn't want to hurt the old boy's pride and make him feel unwanted.

Claire was constantly annoyed by her husband's misguided loyalty and felt the oldies should be shipped out, pensioned off and replaced by a dynamic go-ahead young couple to reflect their important social standing in the spa town. Already, David was a leading light in the Conservative Party and there was a very good chance he'd be an MP come the next general election. God knows what the local movers and shakers would think when greeted at the door by a pair of old geriatrics, with the social skills of an orang-utan, as she so cruelly put it when complaining to her husband about their lack of breeding. However, Mrs Millins was never outgunned and had a very special trick up her sleeve. It was her saving grace;

her raison d'être. She was an excellent cook, capable of creating the most amazing flavours and sumptuous treats that tantalised and excited the taste buds. Mrs Millins was the Lane's live-in master chef, she was that good. Every time Claire was at breaking point, ready to throttle the pair and face the rope, she delivered one of her infamous knockout blows.

Seemingly out of thin air, the cunning old fox would produce a special mouth-watering flan, or a to-die-for thin pizza with a tempting array of warm toppings, or cook Claire's favourite dish, a simple bread-and-butter pudding baked just as she liked it. Mrs Millins knew which button to press and her timing was impeccable, she should have been on the stage. The tasty treats and enchanting smells, emanating from the luxury high-tech kitchen, reminded Claire of her early childhood and as she tucked into a scrumptious slice of freshly cooked pizza, complemented by a cool glass of Chardonnay, any immediate thoughts of murder went out of the window. A reluctant reprieve was granted by the lady of the house until the next inevitable crisis erupted when Mrs Millins's life would, yet again, be on the line. After one memorable heated argument, Claire bought her veteran housekeeper a DVD of *Downtown Abbey* as a goodwill token, not appreciating the implications her generosity might have on two impressionable minds who were determined to keep on good terms with their tetchy, highly strung employer. The elderly couple were instantly besotted by the mesmeric storyline and the characters that literally jumped out of their forty-inch HD television screen. In their wisdom, they thought that was how Claire wanted them to behave when fulfilling their domestic duties; and so being obedient, dutiful servants, they duly obliged.

To begin with, they insisted on remaining in the dining room when the couple had dinner, standing bolt upright throughout each course which was a tad difficult for Mrs Millins's dodgy knees. When David, or Claire, left the room for a call of nature on their return they were helped to their seats with a hefty shove of the chair under their bottom. The last straw was when, as an act of deference to their employers, they insisted on walking backwards with their heads down when leaving the dining room. After a couple of days their antics got too much for Claire's sensitive nerves and so David was told to sort things out. Late one evening, in the company of Mrs Millins's favourite sherry, the prospective MP explained that they were an integral part of his life, they'd always be welcome at the villa and be looked after in their dotage. However, he went on to explain that they'd be cast adrift, dismissed immediately, if they carried on making him feel like a bit-part actor in their favourite Sunday evening costume drama. It had to stop. They laughed as they sipped their drinks and ate some of David's favourite caviar. She was embarrassed, even a bit tearful, but promised to mend her ways and not be so silly in the future, whilst retreating backwards from the room holding their empty sherry glasses in her shaky, arthritic hands. David had to laugh to himself.

Chapter 31

Something was wrong. They knew that as soon as they coasted towards the dull grey power station with the Hotels Sole and Bellavista dominating the shoreline and the early afternoon passenger ferry spluttering from its moorings. Francois had made an almighty cock-up. Tired eyes were treated to the sight of a huge street carnival in full flow parading raucously along the harbour front, forcing the team to come to a grinding halt at the foot of the town's magnificent clock tower. It was almost impossible to push their bikes between the heaving masses, let alone ride them, as crowds of excited revellers scuttled along the jetty and up and down the surrounding narrow walkways. It was mayhem. This wasn't on the agenda, mumbled Chris under his breath, glancing at his crestfallen colleagues shoving their way through the maze of marauding locals, searching for some shade and a place to regroup in preparation for the final push south. It was hot, very hot and extremely claustrophobic, not the kind of reception they were expecting. Not at all.

Meanwhile the two support vehicles swept along the adjacent main road to the north of the resort and came to a grinding halt in a car park on the east side of the town. An agitated red-faced Frenchman jumped out of the lead vehicle before it even stopped, and darted in and out of the manic crowds hoping to catch up with his irate colleagues who were frantically trying to negotiate the town's busy main square.

"What the hell's all this about?" yelled David, waving his arms in the air, pointing at the crowds of people milling about and throwing his bike and helmet to the ground in disgust. "We're never going to get through this lot and the sight of thirty bad-tempered riders isn't going to help our cause is it? What a bloody mess."

Panting and gasping for breath the flustered Frenchman shouted over the din. "I don't know what's happened. I thought the damned carnival was next week. Well that's what they told me. Sorry, I know it's a bloody cock-up, but I'll sort it out, leave it to me."

"Don't be stupid," shouted David. "What can you do? You've done enough already. Go back to the cars. I'll lead the guys through the town somehow and we'll meet you there. PW will follow at the rear, making sure we don't lose anyone." Chris nodded. Meanwhile, Francois knew better than to argue with David so he took to his heels, looking very hot and bothered, dabbing his forehead with some crumpled paper tissues and dodging between the bustling crowds.

"Right guys," shouted David over the racket. "Follow me." With a look of thunder emblazoned across his face, he picked up his stuff and pointed his unhappy band of followers towards the east of the town.

Visitors to Riva know that in the afternoon, this traditional lakeside resort was blessed with a strong north-westerly wind that swept over Mount Baldo, an expansive mountain range to the north, offering a welcome respite, a temporary relief for the townsfolk from the summer's scorching temperatures. The best place to savour the Ora was in the shade of the tall, chestnut trees clustered together near the water's edge where a chilly wind and goosepimples were on the menu for the fortunate few. But sadly their luck was out. Bands of streetwise families, with lots of rowdy kids put paid to that idea, swarming over the wooden benches and plastic chairs, sprawling out across the deep lush grass under the shade of some sturdy magnolia trees. Admittedly an unusually strong swirling breeze gave the athletes a bit of a break from the oppressive conditions, but the close proximity of lots of hot, sweaty bodies took the edge off things and meant they had to find relief elsewhere.

Unbeknown to them, Riva was embroiled in a celebratory carnival, an outpouring of civic pride that occurred every year in July. Here smartly dressed middle-aged men in their best Sunday suits, with bulging waistlines, fresh white shirts and dark-coloured ties, sauntered along through the maze of narrow streets and quaint walkways, with heads held high and smiles from ear to ear.

Their womenfolk, not wishing to miss out, also got in on the act, wearing eye-catching floral dresses, curvaceous summer hats and holding stylish parasols. They strolled arm in arm with their loved ones to the exuberant sound of blaring trumpets and thumping drums while excited locals and jubilant holidaymakers cheered them on their merry way.

Chris had grabbed a great bundle of 'Just for ME' flags from Francois's management folder earlier and charged across the open square, dishing out the red and white bunting to the highly-charged cavalcade, who duly obliged by waving them in the air while cavorting their way along the congested shoreline in front of a gallery of prestigious high-end hotels.

David gave him a hefty pat on the back.

"Well done, Chris," he hollered, struggling to be heard over the commotion. "At least you know what you're doing. Bloody Frenchman."

"Let's hope it does some good, but I wouldn't hold your breath," Chris shouted over his shoulder as he handed out the rest of the flags to a couple of inquisitive kids, from the nearby park benches, who rushed off frantically waving the famous 'ME' slogan in the sticky, humid air.

"Francois really let us down, you know. This is unforgivable. Sod must have known about the carnival. If I find out that this is deliberate then his life won't be worth living," retorted David angrily.

The difficult conditions that had dogged their every step since Garda was bad enough, but now this unexpected turn of events made the team even more disconsolate. They were annoyed by the total lack of publicity for their campaign, being upstaged by a local jamboree of no importance was a bitter pill to swallow. On top of that, Team 30 were dismayed by the shoddy indifferent reception they'd received in Riva and were anxious to bid a hasty retreat, get the remaining miles under their belts before the sun returned with a vengeance. Francois was sorry for his oversight, apologising repeatedly on the short-wave radio. His trademark planning skills had eluded him and his dejected colleagues were paying a heavy price for his manifest incompetence. His emotional act of contrition didn't cut much ice, merely fanning the flames of discontent amongst the disgruntled ranks. Fraught, cheerless bodies with heads down wheeling expensive, high-tech machines between hordes of hysterical fun-seekers said it all.

Very soon it was goodbye to picnics, parades and parasols as the team followed their angry talisman over the town's central square, zigzagging its way towards the park, away from the hullabaloo and ceremonial pageantry. Here, the peloton was treated to a riot of colour and the soft poignant smell of sweet peas and fragrant freesias wafting gently in the air. The beautiful eye-catching scene was in stark contrast to the mayhem, only a few hundred yards away, as the town's annual gala got into full swing and the volume shot up several notches more. The glum Frenchman caught a glimpse of the temperature displayed on the neon sign, hanging inside a brightly lit pharmacist window. Thirty-eight degrees was the number on display and then in the blink of an eye, it turned to thirty-nine. Not good news, he surmised, drying great streaks of moisture from his furrowed brow and rubbing his stubbly chin nervously. Things were going from bad to worse for the wily Gallic charmer whose deft touch had evaded him, disappeared in the mist of time, raising fundamental questions about his ability to uphold the fine exacting standards of the Pedal Power Programme.

All of a sudden, there was an horrendous crash outside the entrance to an adjacent hotel. An unfortunate holidaymaker had ended up spread-eagled across the ground with his plastic shopping bags and contents strewn everywhere. Apples, pears, grapefruits and several bunches of bananas saw their opportunity to escape and were lying scattered all over the square. Many ended their days squelched under the feet of the cheering masses drawn to the sound of the passing procession. Apparently the scorching orange globe had done its worst. The middle-aged shopper felt giddy, a tad unsteady on his pins and collapsed without warning, landing onto the unforgiving gravel surface with a resounding fifteen-stone wallop. The ungainly Brit was dressed in dull grey knee-length shorts and a gaudy T-shirt proclaiming his loyal support for Aviva's personal insurance products. Being scantily clad, with little protection from the elements, his tender exposed skin took the full force of his flight of fancy. The result of the contest was inevitable – solid surface one point, ungainly fat man nil. Alison witnessed the coming together at close quarters and rushed to his aid without a second thought. She dabbed his grazed, bloodstained forehead, checked his blood pressure and pulse, and revived the crumpled mass with the aid of smelling salts and two bottles of Evian water snatched from the rear pouch of her bulky backpack.

Some friendly bystanders took pity on the poor chap, thinking he'd been overdoing the vino at one of the local tapas and gathered up the fruit that had survived the assault and helped the bedraggled visitor to his feet. Two sturdy young Italians, garnished in tattoos with stapled ears and jet-black earlobes, propped the invalid up against the gleaming white hotel wall, in the shade of an overhanging magnolia tree. Flora did her bit, spreading healthy portions of tender loving care to her beleaguered patient.

Then, without warning, the weather suddenly changed. An unforgiving gloom cast a brief eerie shadow over the frenetic town square, while large pockets of deep black cloud raced relentlessly across the threatening skies at the behest of an angry north-easterly wind. But then, as if by magic, the sun, not wishing to be outwitted by its dull cohabitee, quickly got the upper hand, burnt off the dark foreboding clouds, turned up the heat and normal service was resumed. It was quite bizarre, no doubt a warning of dire things to come as knowing glances between old hands confirmed their suspicions.

Riding gloves and sunglasses were adjusted and minor changes made to seating positions as the team waited for Alison to return to the fold. But then glancing over towards the patient, David couldn't believe his eyes. The podgy casualty propping up the hotel wall was none other than Arthur from Verona. The same guy that warned him, all those years ago, of the dangers of leaning against old Roman ruins that had been around for over two thousand years. He'd been the brunt of many a joke at the Lane's stylish late-night dinner parties and drinks dos, ever since.

Wiping his chin with the back of his glove, he peered at the forlorn, overweight shape just a few feet away. David was pleased to see Alison had worked her magic and the guy was now sat upright, chatting and laughing with fellow holidaymakers, seemingly none the worse for his misfortune. Seizing the opportunity, he leaned over the handlebars of his Boardman and, with gloved hands, removed his damp sunglasses and looked straight into Arthur's bloodshot eyes and said. "Hi, remember me?"

Arthur peered in his direction, slightly bemused, before a broad grin slowly rolled across his face when he recognised the cyclist staring down at him.

"Oh yes. How are you? It's a long time since we met. I've had a bit of an accident as you can see, but this kind lady here has kindly patched me up."

"Good. I'm pleased to see you've recovered and you're better now," replied David with a grin. "I'd like to give you some advice, if I may though. It's very important, so listen carefully."

Arthur didn't know what to say. Drums and trumpets were still making an annoying din on the other side of the square when the curious invalid, with a headache, bent forward over his podgy tummy wondering what little titbit was coming his way.

"Well, brace yourself for a bit of a shock," explained David in a whisper, covering his mouth with the back of his hand. "You see, I wouldn't lean against that wall if I was you. Not for a moment longer than you need to."

Arthur leaned forward with his hands touching the ground, open-mouthed, and hanging onto every word that tripped off the cyclist's tongue.

"You see, this hotel has a real big problem. Bigger than you and I could ever imagine. You see it suffers from subsidence, bad subsidence, real bad subsidence and I understand it could collapse at any moment, any moment at all, so be warned my friend, be warned."

The patient's expression was priceless. His grazed jaw dropped to his chest and his top set shot out of his gaping mouth in a dramatic bid for freedom, just like his fruit had done only moments earlier. Then his bruised body crashed back against the solid wall when David's words hit home. He scrambled to his feet, grabbed his torn plastic bags and shot down a nearby alleyway like a sprinter in a hundred-metre race. The playful playboy resisted the temptation to look back and savour Arthur's torment, choosing instead to gently freewheel towards his exhausted colleagues, standing nearby in Riva's fiery furnace. Smiling to himself, he checked his high-tech console for up-to-date weather information, kissed the precious locket perched on the shiny, reflective Boardman handlebars and stretched his fingers inside his tight-fitting gloves preparing for the off. Alison chatted to Francois, as they strolled across the park, in the glare of the scorching sun. Here young and old were having a good time, licking tower-block ice creams drenched in gooey sauces and quenching their thirsts on chilled drinks. Others rested their sylphlike bodies on colourful striped towels and inflated beach lilos, basking in the heat of the globe's glorious rays. Fun-loving holidaymakers mixed with brightly clad football fans, waiting in earnest, in frenzied anticipation, for the big match that was kicking off just a few hours away, when German discipline would come face-to-face with Argentinean flamboyance in the eagerly awaited World Cup Final.

Walking side by side through the open park, Alison told Francois that some of the guys could be suffering from dehydration and muscle fatigue following their gruelling ride up the west side of the lake, and this wasn't good news as there was at least another thirty miles to go before the flag was lowered on their epic journey.

"They ought to be given the option to withdraw, Francois," she argued, shielding her eyes from the bright piercing sunlight. "It's the least you can do. I'm sure their sponsors will cough up if we explain the dangerous conditions and that we advised them on medical grounds to call it a day."

For the dedicated nurse, the high profile ride was quickly turning into a nightmare and, she felt duty bound to speak out in defence of the riders and the potential perils ahead.

"All the riders are over forty years of age, not in their prime of life and definitely not accustomed to the tortuous weather conditions that have engulfed the region over the last few days," she reiterated several times.

Francois pondered on their dilemma. Drying his face on one of the small red and white fluffy towels, he realised it wasn't his decision and decided to consult with the team, get their views before going any further.

In the meantime, the convoy had found a suitable spot to rest and recuperate and lay joking and laughing on lush cool grass under the welcome shade of two huge oak trees. They were taking on drinks and refreshments and topping up their empty plastic bottles for the next stage of the journey.

"First of all guys, let me apologise for the almighty cock-up here in Riva. I shall hold a full inquiry to find what went wrong and report back to you as a matter of urgency. Heads will roll, I can assure you," explained Francois, leaning against a tree trunk for support. No one said a word, not a dickey bird, but if looks could kill you wouldn't bet on the Frenchman making it home in one piece.

"Now, onto a more serious note. Gentleman the conditions aren't good, so please let me know, with a show of hands, whether you wish to continue with the challenge. There'll be no shame if you decide to hang up your helmets as this unusual weather presents a serious danger to your health and, according to a local forecast from David's high-tech console, it promises to get worse in the next couple of hours."

Droplets of water dripped off his chin. He wiped his damp neck with his cotton hanky, trying to soak up some of the annoying perspiration before it trickled down his back.

There was no hesitation; no delay; no debate. Thirty outstretched arms shot up in unison, pointing to the heavens above as though they hoped to grab hold of the dark unforgiving clouds slowly floating by. Francois smiled, he knew full well what their response would be and nodded with a smirk as Alison held her head between her clammy hands and flopped back against the solid tree trunk, hoping and praying she was wrong. Sheer machismo served up with bucket loads of male adrenaline drove the guys to go on. They didn't want to be seen as failures in the eyes of their peers and their generous supporters, or so she thought.

"Right guys, that's pretty conclusive," said Francois, gazing over to David and PW for confirmation to continue. They both nodded their heads and glared unflinchingly at the Frenchman busily wiping up the leaks from his forehead. "One other thing I need to tell you before we make tracks," explained Francois. A uniform groan of frustration filled the air signifying to the thick-skinned Frenchman that he was living on borrowed time and should get off the stage while he was just slightly ahead. He'd let them down badly, his Midas touch had gone walkabout and Francois was now pushing his luck and their patience to the absolute limit.

The lack of attention-grabbing publicity for the ME charity was an opportunity missed and the mood of disappointment was palpable, made even worse by the unruly crowds that had hampered their progress, reducing their illustrious ride to something of a sideshow. Sensing an atmosphere of dissension, the communications director raised his voice over the disgruntled mumblings and, with handkerchief in hand, tried to assert his authority, take control of the situation.

"Finally, please listen up. Don't forget the road from Torbole all the way down to Garda is closed because of the tunnels and your safety so you have a clear run back to base camp, which is good stuff. Another thing, I have some very good news, very good news indeed. I've just been told by Head Office that you've achieved the magical five million pound target and money is still pouring in. Congratulations, but there's something else I need to say. Apparently, you bunch of reprobates have caused a right stir here in Riva and our hotline number has been overwhelmed by telephone donations. Facebook and other social media are buzzing with excitement, are agog with the news of your arrival at the top of the lake, so again, well done, you clever sods. You've made more of an impact than you realise."

The pampered prima donnas couldn't believe their ears. They treated the unwary nurse to a sequence of hearty hugs and gooey kisses that had her gasping for air, as their barefaced passion and fiery fanaticism reached fever pitch. An atmosphere of overwhelming euphoria raged through the team like a fearsome firestorm. Mr Dijon rose from sinner to saint in the wink of an eye, such was his dramatic change of fortune. One minute there was talk of a lynch mob on the banks of the nearby lake, apt punishment for his blatant incompetence, and the next he was the man of the moment, someone to be admired, the hero of the hour. Words of praise and adulation were lavished on him like confetti at a wedding. So with a spring in their step, Team 30 sidled off in pairs, wheeling their trusty bikes through the park before joining the two support vehicles, waiting at the perimeter edge with great plumes of diesel fumes bellowing from their shiny, silver twin exhausts. A cheery-eyed Mr Dijon took up his familiar station at the front of the pack with the air-conditioning on full blast and displaying a confident grin from ear to ear. Alison by contrast was slumped, somewhat disconsolately, in the second BMW hoping her medical skills wouldn't be called upon and her doom-laden prophecy wouldn't materialise. Forty-five minutes after being engulfed in picnics, parades and parasols, the peddle-pushers were at last on the move.

Through a thin heat haze they could see that the cycle lane ahead was festooned with red and white banners. There were hundreds of 'Just for ME' flags, bright vibrant streamers and ribbons the colour of rainbows draped across the pathway while giant billboards and posters were pinned to trees and lamp posts, proclaiming Team 30's arrival on 13th July 2014. It was awe-inspiring and amazingly uplifting for Team 30 who'd wallowed in the doldrums for some time, feeling sorry for themselves, but now they were rejuvenated, firing on all cylinders, ready to face the challenges ahead with big hearts and equally large egos. Sombre, grim-faced miseries, on parade half an hour earlier, were cast aside, consigned to history, replaced by shouts of jubilation and exuberant back-patting. Feisty riders jumped up and down in their saddles, waving arms and hands in the air as they cruised alongside rows upon rows of vibrant eye-catching bunting, fluttering and flapping in their honour. Daredevil windsurfers added their voice to the celebrations, cavorting in the air with spectacular displays of agility and finesse. Passenger ferries hooted their horns at the aerial contortionists swarming along the water's edge, like brightly coloured butterflies, often taking to the air when sudden gusts of wind gave them flight, before propelling their sleek smooth craft at speed through the shimmering pale blue waters of the iconic violin-shaped lake.

Chapter 32

"The car won't start again, you idiot. You'd better come round and see what you can do. See you outside my parents' house in ten minutes," yelled Midge, snapping the phone closed and swallowing the rest of his lukewarm beer before crushing the empty can with his hand and throwing the crumpled tin into the litter bin perched at the end of the wooden bench.

A highly charged mood of anticipation engulfed Garda, sweeping across the lakeside town like an hypnotic drug searching for its prey. Media crews from all corners of the continent were milling around in their droves, some quenching their thirsts and eating great slices of pizza whilst others were seeking out the best vantage point to capture the momentous occasion when the fearless thirty rode back into town. 'Just for ME' T-shirts and attractive red and white shorts adorned the well-disciplined fresh-faced support team waiting anxiously at the water's edge. Copious supplies of cool refreshing drinks and energy bars were laid out on sparkling white tablecloths draped across three trestle tables lined up outside the Lido Garda Beach Cafe.

"Now remember, when your lover boy gets off his bike make a fuss of him, show him that you're impressed by his little jaunt in the sun, pander to his silly whims," smirked Midge, frantically searching in Francesca's canvas shopping bag for another can of cheap beer. "Wave, clap and jump up and down and even rush over and give the idiot a kiss. Don't overdo it though. Make it look natural, not false. I know these stupid millionaires are really dumb and easily taken in by beautiful women, but we shouldn't take anything for granted. He might be brighter than we think. It's important for people to see you together and for lover boy to be interested in you. You know what I mean? Let him get close and get him to even put his arms around you. I want everyone to see the smarmy prat looking at you and touching you up. D'ya hear? You must be convincing and, even though you don't like him, do your best and think of the money we'll be getting. It's easy, now don't forget what I say. I'll call you later to see how you got on and we can then plan the next bit. But don't worry about that now. We can then think about our new life together and how we're going to spend the money. Okay?"

Francesca grinned, nodded and rubbed her thin shapely hand through her long black locks while gazing skywards through her sunglasses, dreaming about the future, a life away from the drudgery of hotel life and boring, gormless holidaymakers who plagued her every working moment with their podgy stomachs, poor dress sense and uncouth remarks.

"I'll do my very best," she replied, with a smile and a casual flick of her wrist. She kissed her unkempt boyfriend on the lips and handed him another can of beer from the deep recesses of her scruffy material shopping bag. Then waved goodbye and sauntered across the road with a jaunty swagger.

"Hope your brother can mend the car," she called out over the drone of passing traffic. Francesca strolled up the steep slope in the direction of the prestigious Excelsior Hotel just as the gleaming white *Andromeda* passenger ferry moved gracefully from its temporary moorings towards Bardolino, a short distance away, with the ever-present sun sparkling brightly on the imposing Rock that dominated the far off headland.

Chapter 33

Green Onions was playing loudly outside one of the chic hotels bordering the lake when Team 30 glided along the purpose-built cycle lane towards Torbole. Hordes of enthusiastic well-wishers shrieked and hollered in competition with 'Booker T' when the renowned celebrity cyclists rode passed two abreast, laughing and joking between themselves. The thumping hypnotic sound brought back fond memories of David's early days in Hastings and Edward and Doris' unflinching kindness during a seriously low point in his life. He wondered what they'd think of him garnering huge sums of money for good causes, riding around Europe with a bunch of ne'er-do-wells, gaily pandering to the excesses of the overzealous press and media. Hoping they'd be proud of his accomplishments, he smiled to himself when recalling some of the mischievous antics he got up to at the Imperial Hotel, his salacious love affair with Susan and, of course, how could the old romantic ever forget his beautiful daughter, Louise – the love of his life. Then it happened, without warning, completely out of the blue. The accident sounded horrendous and it was. After only a few kilometres into their meandering journey south, casually freewheeling towards the east side of the lake, David came a real cropper when an unexpected cloudburst suddenly besieged the group just as they were entering Torbole, a popular holiday destination for young sporty types.

Great torrents of rain belted down like stair rods, quickly turning the road into a fast flowing river making the surface very slippery and extremely treacherous for their slim one-inch-wide Pirelli tyres. In a flash, visibility was cut to a matter of yards as the heavens opened and huge gushing plumes of spray filled the air. Soaking wet riders swerved in and out, trying to avoid the many deep puddles lying dotted along the greasy roadway. In the melee David lost his footing, clipped the rear wheel of the bike in front and crashed across the road with arms flaying about in the air and legs wedged firmly in the wheels of his precious machine. Fortunately, he was riding at the rear of the pack with no other cyclists in close proximity, otherwise it could have been even more serious. Once extricated from the mangled wreckage, he staggered precariously towards the nearby kerb looking gaunt and confused. Here he slumped down in a heap on the edge of the pavement, leaning against an adjacent lamppost for support. He was suffering from shock and feeling rather nauseous and light-headed as he tended to his bloodstained injuries, as best he could. It was then that a tall, wiry fellow cyclist dressed in a psychedelic orange skin suit and plastered in bits of mud and oily grime slipped alongside and offered to help. David's eyes stared in amazement when the deeply tanned athlete removed his gaudy multicoloured helmet.

His lower jaw collapsed wide open, exposing a set of highly polished white teeth and several new crowns that any self-respecting dentist would be proud of. Jolting back in horror he banged his head against the concrete lamppost. He was right, it was definitely him. It was Gary the Wink; his earlier flying companion, the guy with the strong muscular arms who insisted on watching him in a highly provocative way, becoming the source of many rude, rather coarse text messages from his adulterous wife back home. After the initial shock of their meeting up, Gary explained he was the new kid on the block. One of PW's fresh recruits for the final two rides of the season, a forty-five-year-old playboy, with bags of time on his hands and, to David's delight, very happily married with three kids and no interest whatsoever in the male form. Gary had felt unwell during the morning of the ride, but had managed to join the team in Limone and that was the reason why their paths hadn't crossed until then. Apparently his new chum thought he'd recognised David from a photograph he'd received from PW, but felt too embarrassed to introduce himself on the plane just in case he was wrong. Hence the misunderstanding. Strangely enough, Gary thought David had designs on him, especially when he grabbed his arm shortly before landing at Verona airport and then kept glancing at him out of the corner of his eye while waiting at the busy baggage carousel. Regaling the same story of misguided gay entanglement to his wife in Surbiton, she thought it was a memorable way of introducing himself to the founder of the exclusive, internationally respected Pedal Power Programme.

With crowds of onlookers gazing anxiously at the fallen hero, the black BMW mounted the pavement, juddered to a screeching halt on the damp, slippery surface, where upon Alison, dressed in shorts and a 'Just for ME' T-shirt, threw the door wide open and raced to his aid like a well-honed athlete shooting out of the blocks at the sound of the starting gun.

"I'm off," yelled Gary, climbing aboard his green Cannondale and quickly riding off to join his mates waiting patiently ahead. "Hope everything goes okay. See you shortly. Nice to have met you. Arrivederci, as they say."

"Thanks for your help," replied David struggling to his feet, trying to get the circulation moving again in his bloodstained legs. After a couple of dodgy strides, he plonked himself down on a low-level perimeter wall opposite a line of gift shops and hairdressers. Here several ladies in big chunky curlers peered out of the steamy salon windows seemingly concerned at his plight, while eagerly snapping photographs of the injured rider from all angles.

"Sorry for the delay, but we got held up behind a stupid car that had broken down right in the middle of the damn road," Alison pointed out as she rummaged through her bag of tricks, searching for her remedies and potions.

The flustered red-faced nurse surveyed the scene of carnage, cleaned and wiped her patient's battered legs and forearms as thin streams of blood continued seeping through his ripped and torn red and white cycling outfit. He was in a bad way.

"Nothing's broken thankfully, but you're badly cut and bruised. I don't like the look of your legs either. You've got umpteen deep lacerations and many nasty scratches and gashes which need further attention and time to heel, otherwise they could spell trouble," said Alison, handing him a bottle of water from her pack and quickly wiping away the splashes of dirt and debris from his forehead and around his eyes.

"How do you feel?" she asked. "Do you feel light-headed or nauseous?"

"I'm okay, thanks. I'll survive. It's my own fault. My mind was elsewhere. I was daydreaming, not concentrating on what I was doing," retorted David rubbing his lower legs and shoulders and swallowing great swigs of chilled Evian water.

"This should help, but it will sting a bit, so be warned," Alison explained as she applied dollops of cream to his battered body to help alleviate the discomfort and also prevent infection, which was her biggest worry. She then tied a large bandage around his upper thigh to stem the bleeding. Sharp twisted wheel spokes had done their worst, ripping and tearing the flimsy skin suit to shreds causing a series of nasty abrasions and deep cuts to his legs and abdomen. David was already sweating because of the oppressive conditions, so the sudden shock of careering over the handlebars onto a hard unforgiving surface put further strain on his body.

"Well, sadly that's the end for David," said Francois, when he called Alison on her mobile to get an update. "There's no way he can return to the fold. Give him a lift to Garda and I'll see him there," he hollered down the line.

"Rubbish," barked David, grabbing the phone out of Alison's sticky mits. "I've never failed to finish in any of my campaigns and I'm not going to let a stupid accident stop me today. Do you understand? There is too much riding on it. I owe it to the ME Association. No one's telling me what to do, d'ya hear?"

With a face like thunder and a temper to match, he thrust the phone back into Alison's hand. She wasn't expecting such an angry tirade and jumped back, frightened of what he might do next. His volatile behaviour was well documented and Alison knew it was more than her life's worth to cross swords with David Lane, who was capable of pretty well anything when provoked.

Francois, for his part, was pleased to be out of the firing line, safely out of harm's way. The director knew from past experience it wasn't wise to argue with the boss, especially when he stared at you with his cold piercing eyes, before unleashing his sharp caustic tongue, which invariably reduced even the strongest of opponents to a gibbering wreck. So as not to attract David's wrath, a replacement bike was lifted off the support car's roof rack and handed to him, rather gingerly, by an anxious member of the support team.

Undeterred, she glared dismissively at her dishevelled patient and, after a few deep breaths, plucked up courage and said, "I implore you to stop now. It's foolhardy and reckless and your intention to continue with the ride could be very serious, very serious indeed. Call it a day and allow me to take you to the nearest hospital for urgent medical attention." Oblivious to her protestations, David was sat astride his new charge adjusting his dented helmet and making some final changes to the height of the handlebars. Turning slowly in the saddle with his glasses perched on the bridge of his nose, he said. "Thanks for the help, now kindly shut up, get back in the car and do what you're paid to do. Get going now and stop interfering." His index finger pointed in the direction of the main road where a white plume of exhaust fumes was swirling in the air. Alison was shocked by his rude insensitive remarks, but not wishing to antagonise her bad-tempered patient any further, quickly retreated from the scene of the altercation, taking refuge in the back seat of the BMW as instructed. Now she's normally a quiet, reserved kind of person, who wouldn't say boo to a goose and wasn't accustomed to making hysterical outbursts, but some of the residents of Torbole were treated to a unique display of heartfelt emotion on that sweltering summer's afternoon in mid-July.

Holding the phone outside the car window to ensure good uninterrupted reception, she ripped into Francois like an animal devouring its prey, protesting at the sheer madness of allowing someone to return to the saddle when they're in need of urgent medical attention. He listened politely, with the phone held several inches from his ear, before the connection was lost, quite by accident, and her frenzied onslaught came to an untimely end.

Meanwhile Bernard carefully stored David's damaged bike on the roof of the support car, as the dishevelled cyclist perched gingerly on his saddle preparing for the off. He straightened his wonky red-framed sunglasses and moved off, making sure his scuffed leather shoes gripped the pedals this time. He wasn't taking any chances.

With damp tissues covering her lap, the nurse held her head in bewilderment as her headstrong patient slowly got into his stride. PW patted his chum warmly on the back when he rejoined the waiting pack parked up a few hundred yards ahead in a damp puddle-filled lay-by. David winced.

Ignoring his colleague, he caught Francois' eye as he leaned against the bonnet of the dirt-splattered BMW with his phone glued to his ear. "Let's get going," he yelled out rather irritably, quickly making some minor adjustments to the chin strap on his cracked cycling helmet.

Not wishing to upset Mr Big any further he jumped into the front seat, turned the air-conditioning to full blast and, like the renowned pied piper, led Team 30 back onto the road for its final push south. Very soon the peloton was cruising along at about fifteen miles an hour. Everyone was in a relaxed convivial mood waving at passers-by, cheering and joking and returning the kisses from their many adoring female fans who'd lined up to greet them with cameras at the ready. Long streams of vehicles were queuing along adjacent roads waiting for the convoy to pass, hoping to catch a glimpse of their illustrious heroes, with excited passengers waving arms out of open car windows snapping photographs of the winding cavalcade. The glitzy procession negotiated a few short innocuous tunnels and sharp bends, but these weren't a problem for the experienced riders, who took it all in their stride.

Since starting their epic journey the team caught glimpses of various ferries navigating the lake. The two catamarans – *Mantova* and *Freccia del Garda* were often in their sights as well as *Tonale* and *Brennero*, two capacious three-tier motor ships that trundled ungainly from port to port. But the ferry that got their vote, always made them smile was the *Andromeda* with its sleek sophisticated lines and glossy white livery. The lady of the lake was like the silver birch of the tree world, gliding effortlessly through the pale blue waters to her next scenic rendezvous, spreading serenity and elegance everywhere she docked.

Eventually the convoy cruised into Malcesine with Renoir, the eccentric Belgian billionaire, at the helm gesturing at the crowds with much heartfelt enthusiasm, as though he was conducting an orchestra and offering undying love to any female prepared to take a punt. They slowed at the main crossroad with the town's municipal offices on the right and where the steep roadway rolled down to the distant waters' edge bordered by rows of traditional gift shops. Bustling street cafes catered for the whims and fancies of the transient tourist trade. Terracotta roofs, bright blue and red buildings with narrow winding pathways and places of holy worship symbolised the town's history and its traditional way of life, unspoilt by the ravages of time. Nearby was a congested coach park packed with eager-eyed day trippers drawn to the magic of Malcesine's famous cable-car railway and its historic Scaligeri Castle. It was then that Francois had a further urgent call from the local police.

"As agreed the road will continue to be closed for the time being but because of the huge build-up of traffic behind the peloton, we can't keep it shut as long as we hoped," explained the inspector in a quiet doleful voice.

"There's the big football match tonight and we must clear the roads in the next forty-five minutes. I'm sorry, but that's our decision."

"Okay," replied Francois nervously. "I'll tell my colleagues but they won't be happy. We lost a lot of time in Riva because of the carnival and the heat and then one of our crew had an accident in Torbole."

"I'm sorry," said the policeman impatiently. "But my hands are tied. You must speed things up, or you'll have to finish the ride in Torri del Benaco."

A torrent of expletives shot out of the injured rider's mouth when the message came through on his earpiece. Shouting and smacking the handlebars with tightly clenched fists confirmed that their mercurial leader was not a happy bunny and his mood wasn't helped by the incessant throbbing in his legs and across his badly bruised shoulders.

"That means riding at about thirty mph in these energy-sapping conditions," David called out to PW riding alongside him at the rear of the pack. Downcast expressions on grey fraught faces were on display.

But a least there was some good news on the horizon. The earlier brief storm had receded, was long gone and the dark clouds had disappeared leaving the roads bone dry. Their good fortune was short-lived however, as the ever present sun took up its customary position overhead, promising a real grilling for the remaining miles and a heart-pounding test of strength and stamina for the gallant over-forties.

Chapter 34

Now some five years earlier, while swimming in the heart-shaped pool at the palatial Negresco Hotel on the Promenade des Anglais in Nice, David had a brainwave. It forced him to turn his back on the beautiful Mediterranean Sea and its white rolling waves, throw his swimming trunks, red and white jogging outfit and factor thirty sun lotion into his Seraplan suitcase and catch the first BA flight home. There was no time to lose. On his return to Blighty, he relinquished his directorships on various charitable committees, threw away the Parker fountain pen and board minutes and embarked on something totally different, something more exciting and, most important of all, something that promised to be much more fun for the resourceful philanthropist.

Richmond's illustrious orphan was the founder, the brains, the money-man, behind the innovative, forward-thinking Pedal Power Programme that quickly captivated the imagination of its many sponsors and benefactors across Europe. Here high-net worth individuals with time on their hands were coaxed, corralled and sometimes bullied, by the tenacious entrepreneur, into joining a new ground-breaking charitable venture, the likes of which had never been seen before.

Initially, David tantalised and teased the wealthy thrill-seekers with the promise of ever greater fame and stardom. Young gooey-eyed girls with short skirts and tight-fitting tops would stalk their every step, throw caution to the wind, shower them with love and adoration like confetti at a family wedding, as their affection and devotion would have no bounds in the pursuit of their hunky heroes.

But as the Programme got traction, captured people's imagination, so the jet-set thrill-seekers caught the charitable bug and marvelled at the genuine impact they had on other people's lives through their own simple, selfless pursuits. This was a shot in the arm, a real adrenalin rush for the posh boys and much more satisfying than anything they'd ever imagined, pushing their own sexual fantasies and desires of the flesh way down the pecking order, for the time being anyway. Here thirty impetuous, madcap riders from across Europe abandoned their celebrated lives of wealth and self-indulgence, hung up the keys to the prancing horse, tied the luxurious racing yachts to their private moorings and left the Moet on ice. Instead they donned body-hugging skin suits, shoved their manicured feet into handcrafted cycling shoes and stuck two fingers up to the elements as they took to the saddle, threw caution to the wind and joined forces for the benefit of others.

The prestigious, highly influential Programme comprised five gruelling cycle rides each year – March, April, May, July and September. The founder, to his credit, has been astride the saddle on every single occasion; he'd never missed one single outing in five years. The only other person to have achieved such a praise-worthy accolade was his friend and partner, the inscrutable Mr Christopher Parker-Wright. In between these flagship events, David also participated in other, less glamorous cycle rides in the UK, raising funds for charities that didn't always get the limelight, or the publicity they so rightly deserved, but the main focus of his time and energy was the Pedal Power Programme which raised the profile of many worthy charities and collected millions of pounds each year for an array of needy causes.

The Pedal Power Committee was the Programme's organising body, responsible for managing the finances, choosing the locations for the various cycle rides, doing all the administrative stuff and deciding on the charities for each high-profile outing. That was its remit. Francois Dijon, the debonair Frenchman, was the communications director, charged with organising the events and making sure everything went smoothly at each of their European venues.

It was true to say that David Lane was a true trailblazer in the world of charitable giving, attracting praise and accolades for his pioneering ideas and boundless energy. As always, he believed his success was down to the influence of his dear mother whose spirit lived on guiding and supporting her son in his many philanthropic endeavours. He often sensed her warm loving presence, particularly when his life was at a low ebb. As a teenager, he frequently cried himself to sleep after another bout of bullying and torment at the hands of Martin Conway and his fellow conspirators. During the small hours, he'd suddenly wake up in a hot clammy sweat, feeling nauseous and frightened following one of his frequent spine-chilling nightmares, but was soon comforted by his mother's soft hand soothing the back of his neck and brushing the damp curls from his deep furrowed brow. Of course, his mother wasn't averse to scolding her wayward son when he stepped out of line and his famous Christmas drunken episode was a case in point. Her scathing condemnation of his disgraceful behaviour forced him to ditch the alcohol and his selfish drink-sodden ways. And instead, to think about Claire and how she'd stood by him through thick and thin, never wavering in her loyalty and support particularly during his long protracted courtship with the dreaded bottle.

So David had fond memories of Nice as the inspiration for the Pedal Power Programme, but he always had a special place in his heart for his mother, who opened his eyes to Claire's unique qualities, kept him on the straight and narrow, gave him a purpose in life and an opportunity to make a real difference.

Chapter 35

Sensing failure, David knew there was only one thing for it. Fellow cyclists looked on in amazement when their indomitable leader sliced through the peloton to a chorus of raucous yelps and frantic cheers. Ignoring the pain and discomfort shooting through his body every time the bike jolted on the uneven road surface, David threw caution to the wind, racing headlong to the front like a young feisty gazelle. Renoir was holding things together at the sharp end, but couldn't believe his eyes when his fearless companion swept alongside with a determined grimace. Then in a show of brazen defiance, David swerved into the middle of the road and raised his gloved hand towards the fluffy clouds overhead before turning around in his saddle and yelling at the top of his voice the rousing battle cry. "All for One and One for All!"

Twenty-nine devoted followers replied in unison, shouting the same strapline several times with heartfelt passion. Then a loud rallying chorus of yelps and cheers swept through the peloton like a giant wave. Love him or hate him, David Lane could galvanise a team, bring out the very best in others, especially when the chips were down and the odds stacked against them. That was exactly what he did on that sweltering summer's afternoon when he welded his select team of extroverts into a strong fearsome fighting force with no regard for their own well-being, and with stark memories of the Negresco Hotel firmly fixed in his mind.

So a re-energised, highly motivated team got a second wind riding at speed through tight blind bends, over pedestrian crossings and around umpteen roundabouts thanks to the friendly faced volunteers who waved them on their way, blowing their high-pitched whistles to warn unsuspecting pedestrians of the peloton's impending arrival. There was a vibrant explosion of colour as the racing snake swept along the shiny tarmac to the sound of screaming well-wishers proudly waving their ME flags while their anonymous heroes, with space-age helmets and body-hugging outfits, pushed on towards their goal. Meanwhile, the beautiful scenery and the tantalising spectacle of the iconic lake with its numerous ferries zigzagging between ports of call, offered a mesmeric backcloth to their valiant endeavours. David was doing what he did best, beating the elements, rising to the challenge, not allowing anything to get in his way.

Even a blistering collision with a slice of Italian tarmac hadn't deterred him in his obsessive quest to achieve his target and raise the profile of his highly acclaimed Pedal Power Programme. After all, the forty-three-year-old was the only son of Jeremy and Louise Lane, who courted success throughout their working lives, kept raising the bar in their relentless push to be the best at everything they did and where disappointment and failure were never on the agenda, never an option. Very soon the peloton saw Torri del Benaco in the distance, and their friendly Frenchman confirmed the good news that they'd ridden fast enough, since leaving Malcesine, to negate the threat of any road closures and that a triumphant return to Garda was well within their grasp.

You could almost see the chequered flag wafting in the air, hear the victorious ticker-tape welcome from crowds standing ten deep, cheering and screaming as the team glided towards the finishing line like a flock of birds swooping on the breeze. Tired limbs were on autopilot, gloved fists grasped handlebars in a vice-like grip. But then, at last, the scene they'd been praying for came into view through the sheen of their perspiration-smudged sunglasses. Streams of swirling flags greeted the vibrant procession diving around the final bend, nearly kissing the kerb, with swarms of madcap spectators celebrating their triumphant return to base camp. A blaze of colour blitzed the white-lined tarmac when the jovial class of jesters shot alongside gentle tree-lined slopes, passed stone-walled gardens and busy, bustling hotels, as Garda's magnetic charm drew the fearless fortune-hunters ever closer to its welcoming shores. Overhead was the swirling sound of a helicopter's rotor blades with an intrepid cameraman hanging precariously out of the open door broadcasting live pictures to an expectant public clamouring for news of their progress. The Pedal Power Programme was a team enterprise, symbolised by Dumas' immortal words, where everyone strived for the common good in the name of the chosen charity and so, it was on that very day in mid-July that the fine estimable traditions of the Programme were upheld by the brave efforts of the band of thirty.

However, it's not surprising that a combination of testosterone-driven athletes and excitable onlookers was a recipe for a competitive sprint to the finish. Tradition has it that Francois's lead car was always removed towards the latter stages, giving the thigh-thumpers an open road, a clear run to the line, which for a feisty competitive male was like a red rag to a bull. So, as always, the dying embers of a ride were a hot caldron of male egos all vying for the plaudits of their adoring fans and the clicking cameras of the waiting press and hard-nosed paparazzi. That day was no different to any other when a group of eight riders charged over the line with the sound of jubilant crowds roaring in their ears while their more modest colleagues were happy to play second fiddle, trailing in their wake. David languished at the rear of the pack alongside PW and Gary the Wink, who looked a little weary after his first outing, raising both hands skyward in recognition of the vibrant applause from a group of young girls perched precariously on top of a hotel perimeter wall.

A uniform sigh of relief rippled throughout the team as the kaleidoscope of colour immersed itself in the glory and acclamation of their many ardent followers, while a group of hefty, overweight security staff, in obligatory high-visibility jackets, guided the sweaty prima donnas to their private enclosure alongside the Lido Garda Beach Cafe.

The venue for their happy reunion was normally a hive of manic activity for young late-night revellers when loud booming music echoed around the bay until the early hours. Hotel guests were often forced to take cover under skimpy bed sheets, with earplugs at the ready, trying to drown out the thumping sound and steal a bit of shut-eye before the familiar orange globe peeped between their curtains just after dawn.

The exhausted group sat subdued for several moments, leaning back in their white plastic chairs savouring their moment of glory in the relaxing shade of some welcome palm trees. Great gulps of chilled water quenched their raving thirsts and several bottles of liquid were doused over their damp heads and sunburnt faces before the guys got their second wind and joked and chatted about their long arduous day in the saddle.

Amazing scenes of triumphalism enveloped the esteemed holiday resort, like a giant tsunami, with hordes of people cheering and shouting behind steel barriers stretching several hundred yards from the modest Lido Garda Beach Cafe to the town's prominent ferry point.

By contrast David took refuge away from the hurly-burly, tending to his many cuts and bruises, and gazing fondly across the shimmering blue lake towards Salo as his mother dabbed his damp brow with her handkerchief and whispered words of encouragement to her brave young son. Then suddenly the peace and tranquillity of the moment was dashed when his energetic partner yelled out, "Come on! The guys want to hear from you. Stop messing about over there."

He jumped to his feet, wiped his eyes with the back of his grazed hand and followed PW to the sound of yelling and applause from the multitude of cheery faces and white glistening teeth lining the lakeside promenade. David loved this part of any ride, lapping up the plaudits from absolute strangers who'd taken time out to show their approval for his altruistic adventures. It gave him a real buzz, providing much-needed confirmation that he was getting it right. Feeling humble and emotional, and in some discomfort, he reflected on his mother's wise words before enjoying the praise and warm accolades from his loyal chums who stood in awe of their legendary cheerleader and front man.

Gallant riders were photographed by an eager press. Team 30 posed beside their trusty bikes, with familiar clicking cameras filling the air, as the ever-present sun, not wishing to miss out, peered through the leaves of the many elegant trees gracing the harbour front. David took up position on a concrete bench, like a conductor directing his orchestra, and explained through the mouth-piece of a borrowed megaphone the magnitude of their achievement and that the ME's research budget would be better off by a cool £6.1 million, thanks to the tireless endeavours of thirty tough men of conscience and resolve.

"Today we've ridden one hundred and fifty kilometres in very difficult conditions, but we achieved our goal and so Sunday, 13th July 2014 will always be a date to remember, forever enshrined in the proud history of your fair town. Garda should be congratulated for hosting such an awe-inspiring event, that's been an overwhelming success, a beacon for others. So thank you everybody for your help!" the imperious David Lane shouted out over the unremitting applause from droves of happy faces congregated along the curved shoreline. You could see from the beaming smile etched on his face, he was relieved that his brave chums had finished the ride in one piece, no one had come to any serious harm and, thankfully, Alison's dire warnings of Armageddon hadn't materialised. Team 30 could rest back on their laurels after another good day in the office.

A tired-looking nurse, with deep pronounced bags hanging under her eyes and an overwhelming sense of relief, slumped back against the bonnet of the lead support car, listening to David's poignant heartfelt words. She knew, from her medical training, how close she'd come to witnessing a real tragedy on that hot, steamy day, with many of her valiant charges running on fumes since before Riva. Age was never on their side as men twenty years their junior would have struggled in the daunting conditions, especially on the west side where the gradual unrelenting climb to Gargnano, with its endless roundabouts and the sweltering heat, would have felled even the fittest. But then a sinister smirk splashed across her sunburnt face when she imagined how much money had been secured by the hard-working silver spoons and where some of the lovely booty would eventually end up.

Climbing rather gingerly off the bench, David looked in pain following his tumble on the tarmac, but the leader of the pack was determined to hide his injuries, not hog the limelight, but instead focus attention on his tough, resourceful compatriots who'd fought tooth and nail to raise the profile of their chosen charity.

Seeing his discomfort, Alison came to his aid and, even though their relationship was rather strained, she wouldn't let her feelings of animosity prevent her fulfilling her medical duties even at that late stage. His bandages were changed, his injuries cleaned and further dollops of lotions and creams applied to his nasty cuts and bruises. They didn't talk, or even look at each other.

By contrast, high-fives, loud whoops and cheers of delight were on show as the hot sweaty riders removed their cumbersome riding shoes and thin lycra tops that gripped their soaking wet bodies like barnacles on the side of a boat. Team 30's fitness had been truly tested that day by an uncompromising Italian sun that took no prisoners. Even though they looked on their last legs, knackered and worn out, there was a strong atmosphere of camaraderie and true friendship radiating throughout the group and was no doubt the foundation on which their unrivalled success was forged.

Chapter 36

PW had to smile to himself as the 'lump' gorged himself on a bowl of crinkle-cut chips smothered in vinegar with great dollops of Heinz tomato sauce spread liberally over his 500-calorie snack. This was washed down with two glasses of ice-cold lager and a Gordon's gin and tonic. This was Alan's ritual after completing every outing, a poignant reminder of his unhealthy past when fatty foods and dodgy drinks were his staple diet and his life was hanging precariously on a very thin thread. His nickname had taken hold with the guys, even though he was now a slim, trim eleven-stone athlete with a well-honed body, strong muscular frame and a pronounced six-pack. Alan wouldn't have looked out of place on a London catwalk or appearing as a fashion model in a posh, glitzy male magazine.

The Pedal Power Programme was restricted to thirty riders and, because of its reputation there was an impressive list of wealthy extroverts waiting in the wings, biting at the bit, just yearning to join in the fray. If an established rider withdrew from the squad, it meant one of the lucky reserves was invited to join the select band of fitness fanatics, put their body through the mill and sign up for a backbreaking programme of punishing cycle rides across the length and breadth of Europe.

In September 2011, Alan Dawson's name rose to the top of the pile like a submarine bubbling up to the surface. The gregarious millionaire hotelier was duly invited to call Mr Parker-Wright on Skype to discuss his possible inclusion in the exclusive Programme for the forthcoming 2012 season. Sadly, the conversation didn't go particularly well for Mr Dawson.

"You aren't serious, are you?" said PW glaring at the great oversized object in his screen, boasting a huge double chin, great flabby arms and a bulging stomach that never seemed to end.

"I know I'm a tad overweight, bit out of condition, but with some serious dieting and regular exercise, you see, I'll come up trumps and be as good as the rest of you," replied Alan, rather indignantly, as his complexion took on a bright red sheen and his arms flapped about nervously.

The old Etonian wasn't renowned for his tact and diplomacy and tended to let people know exactly what he thought, often in quite colourful language. So true to form, not wishing to waste any more time PW leant forward, glared into the screen and let chubby cheeks have both barrels.

"Alan, let me cut to the chase. You're a great fat lump, you're clearly out of condition. I guess standing up unaided is a difficult proposition so riding a bike is a non-starter unless you're suggesting we rent a JCB to follow you around and scrape you off the road when you fall off your wretched machine. Now look, I've got better things to do than chew the fat with you. There are many guys waiting in the wings, much more capable of filling the vacant seat than you, so let's end the call now before I get nasty. If you're really determined to sort yourself out, then get on a diet, keep your mouth shut as much as possible and give me a call in a couple of year's time when you've lost half your body weight."

"Stop right there, posh boy!" retorted Alan, clearly upset by the torrent of abuse. "I'm a wealthy man, whose made his money in the hotel and leisure industry. My GP told me that if I don't lose weight, change my lifestyle pretty darn quick then it'll be curtains by the new year. So I'm having a gap year in 2012 and I'm dedicating myself to some top-notch charitable pursuits and I want to complete all five rides in your blasted Programme next year as part of my road to recovery."

Chris sniggered. "You're joking, aren't you? You must be mad. The fat has warped your brain, eaten all the clever bits. Look, we're an elite squad of stellar athletes who take our work very seriously, keep our bodies in tip-top condition all year round. We owe it to the people we support." Raising his voice, he went on. "Do you know how difficult it is to ride a hundred and fifty to two hundred kilometres in difficult, sometimes extreme weather, when even the fittest can fall by the wayside? Stop wasting my time, bye for ..."

"One-hundred-thousand pounds," shouted Alan, glaring angrily at the screen and thumping the desk with his chubby clenched fists causing a ripple of body fat to roll from his bloated stomach up to his double chin like the gentle swell of a tidal wave on a sea shore.

"I know the guys pay that amount each year, but I'll pay £100,000 for every ride I sign up for in 2012. You won't regret it, so get off your high horse and treat me with some respect. I'm a successful businessman who's created wealth from scratch, not a playboy parasite who's lived off his parents' good name, spending £250,000 on himself each year," ranted Alan banging the desk with his chubby fists and glaring angrily into the monitor with his bloated cheeks on red alert and rolls of fat wobbling in disarray.

Chris was shocked by the cruel vitriolic retort from his podgy adversary sat only inches away, glaring angrily at him. He took a couple of gentle sips of his hot lemon tea to compose himself while chewing his thumbnail and mulling over the options. Even though his ego had taken a bit of a hit, he was nevertheless quite impressed by Alan's bombastic manner. It said much about the fat man's self-confidence and determination as these were the qualities he'd need in bucket loads if he was to come up to scratch. His financial contribution to the Programme wasn't to be sneezed at either and was an important factor in the mix.

After a momentary pause, Chris said, "Right listen. This is what we'll do. If you can prove to me in five months' time you're fit and able to compete in 2012, then we have a deal. It's up to you. If you fail, as I'm sure you will, then you're out and you can get quotes for your funeral. That's it." He went on. "Oh by the way, it's one million pounds, not £250,000 that I spend each year. I suggest you get your facts right. I've got a young, attractive hairdresser to support whose addicted to handbags and expensive jewellery and thinks I'm Jesus in lycra." The call ended abruptly. PW didn't expect to hear from the hefty hotelier, with sweaty jowls and a dustbin for a stomach, ever again. But he was wrong, very very wrong.

So it was goodbye to kebabs, onion rings and Chinese takeaways and hello to a fresh new start in life. Alan's fridge filled up with copious supplies of red and green peppers, fresh-cut lettuce, Jersey tomatoes and chicken pieces, with umpteen crystal glass bowls scattered around his luxurious Surrey mansion like confetti, bursting with bananas, fresh oranges, grapes and juicy red Cox's orange pippins. They were his favourite. The couch potato was consigned to history, a thing of the past, as the fresh-faced-forty-three-year-old pounded the streets in the early hours, in all winds and weathers. He could be spotted shortly after dawn putting his jogging gear and Nike trainers through their paces at the local gym in his relentless race to get fit and regain some of his misspent youth. Membership of Slimming World was a sound investment. It kept him on the straight and narrow, never letting him falter from his mission as he religiously counted his syns and worked hard to achieve target at his regular Monday evening weigh-ins. For many years, the man peering back at him from his ornate gold-framed bedroom mirror had made him feel unloved and inadequate and the unsightly lumps of flesh bouncing about beneath an expansive double chin merely added to his torment. It wasn't the man he wanted to be, far from it and this was Alan's big chance to get a grip of his life and turn it around for good.

Against all the odds, the podgy hotelier shed four stone by Christmas 2011 and was looking a completely different man with his slim waistline, well-toned figure and an air of self-confidence following in his wake like a long vapour trail. Even his wife, who'd always rejected his clammy advances, often going elsewhere for love and passion, thought her revitalised husband was much more to her liking and was amazed by his dramatic transformation from a podgy, beer paunch to a beguiling body beautiful. But Alan didn't sit back on his laurels and put his feet up. He knew the job wasn't done by a long chalk, especially if he was to make the grade and meet PW's very exacting standards. So, determined as ever, he continued with his strict fitness regime of pounding the streets and thumping the tiresome treadmills, whilst counting the calories in his sleep and pushing himself to even higher levels of physical fitness all in preparation for the daunting challenges ahead.

So much to everyone's surprise, the former roly-poly with the bouncing belly successfully completed the first ride of the season in March 2012 and all the team applauded his valiant efforts and welcomed him to the fold with much praise and heart-warming handshakes.

Chris was staggered by the dramatic improvement in Alan's fitness and admitted he'd badly misjudged the guy and congratulated him on his remarkable success. It was an heroic effort. He knew all the cards were so heavily stacked against him, with failure a much more likely outcome, especially for someone with a track record of self-indulgence and poor diet stretching back many, many years. Since then the pair were the best of mates, often joking about their initial contretemps on Skype and the nasty, vindictive things they said to each other in the heat of the moment when emotions were running high and fragile egos on full alert.

So tradition had it, after every jaunt, Alan treated himself to a fatty fry-up, as a valuable reminder of the days when bulging waistlines and bursting buttons were his constant companions and bathroom scales his live-in tormentors. Since then, Alan always had 'Slimming World' emblazoned in blue around his cycling top, in recognition of those that helped him beat the bulge, fight the flab and evade the dreaded coffin that was looming large with every waking day.

The wealthy hotelier had always had a passion for golf ever since his childhood days when he played with his sporty parents at their local club, boasting an impressive handicap of eight as illustrated by a cabinet full of silver cups, engraved trophies and framed photos applauding his efforts on the fairway. But sadly those days of swinging freely on the greens, shooting under par and talking birdies in the clubhouse were a thing of the past once the waistline got out of control and the trouser elastic pushed to full stretch. Alan had adjusted to a sedentary lifestyle as a clumsy couch potato, often being the brunt of many snide remarks and sniggers. But thanks to the Programme and his redoubtable fighting spirit, his life had been turned around and his size nines were no longer in the shade when he teed off. He could dust off the woods, polish the irons, go chasing birdies to his heart's content. Sadly for Andrea, his wife, things hadn't worked out quite so well, she didn't make the cut, didn't even get past the first round to be precise. Alan's slender body shape was a magnet, a crowd puller for many a starry-eyed gold-digger, attracted to his new muscular physique and a hefty bank balance. So Andrea was treated to some of her own medicine, shown the door, cast adrift from her life of self-indulgence when the former fat man found solace, and much-needed affection, in the warm expansive arms of a buxom blonde hairdresser of his very own.

Chapter 37

Privately, the riders felt the Garda 150 was tough going with frequent periods of self-doubt and deep soul-searching, but their pride and alter egos wouldn't allow them to falter in their mission, or share their concerns with their elite chums. The constant supply of water and numerous tasty bananas helped quench their raving thirsts and raise their dwindling energy supplies. Precious machines laid discarded on the ground. Some of the guys were sprawled out across the concrete floor under the shade of neighbouring trees and cool white-bricked buildings. Francois' clever media planning had paid off brilliantly as the specially invited press and TV cameras were on site, milling about interviewing some of the more gregarious cyclists, trying to get an emotional insight into their ride around the blue pond. Some of the riders waxed lyrical as though they were auditioning for a film part, describing their time in the saddle with great eloquence. They embroidered the facts mercilessly so as to ingratiate themselves with the attractive female members of the press corps, who were jostling in the melee with iPads and microphones at the ready, hoping to tease out an exclusive slant that would give them the edge in the fiercely competitive world of the media.

By contrast, David and some of the other older hands fought shy of publicity. They left the media scrum in the capable hands of the Gallic extrovert, who as an experienced former hack, knew what buttons to press, how to exploit their gallant, foolhardy adventures for commercial gain. Sometimes the guys socialised after a ride. Here they'd share war stories in the company of young impressionable female admirers, who were out for a good time with their pin-ups and celebratory heroes. But that day was different, very different indeed. The unexpected conditions had taken its toll and the team agreed to put the customary 'after-ride' bash on hold until next time when they'd let their hair down in the Austrian capital; really paint the town red.

"We'll do it in Vienna when the weather's cooler," shouted Francois, standing on a concrete bench, using Alison's old megaphone to make his gravelly voice heard over the ear-splitting racket. "Don't forget Austria on 7th September for our end of season banquet," he yelled out in competition with the blaring car horns and throaty Harley Davidson motorbikes growling along the front towards the centre of the town.

The Frenchman congratulated the team on a fantastic ride that had raised lots and lots of dosh for ME while brandishing one of the official flags, to reinforce the point, which gave way to a cacophony of clapping and cheering from the milling crowds congregated alongside the water's edge. Some of David's cohorts were chatting to each other, or sharing selfies with their fans and admirers, while others chose to just rest back, savour a well-earned cold glass of beer and enjoy the moment. Meanwhile the party poopers took their leave, met their pre-arranged lifts, bade a bon farewell to their chums and departed from the scene in great clouds of diesel fumes and frantic hand waving. In the meantime, the promenade was chock-a-block with holidaymakers either queuing for private motor launches, or for ferries to their overnight billets, where they could quietly reflect on the memorable day when they rubbed shoulders, came face to face, with Team 30 doing what it did best.

"Until later," yelled Chris from the comfort of a soft-top Mercedes SL350, quickly speeding away in the direction of Bardolino with a young heavily tanned female at the controls, whose teeth were so dazzlingly white she'd never need to use headlights when driving at night. David nodded and grinned.

Alison glanced around the group, offering medical help to any remaining stragglers and then when the coast was clear, joined the support team for a well-earned drink under the awning of a quiet, secluded tapas bar. The experienced security team, still dressed in high-visibility jackets, removed the steel barriers and stored them away. Gary and his crew collected up the valuable bicycles and carefully loaded them into the eight-wheeled purpose-built transporter, where they were safely housed in rows of personalised cycle racks in preparation for the long journey north. In a few days' time the precious machines would be serviced, cleaned and polished by a specialist team, made ready for their final jaunt of the year when they'd be reunited with their masters and put through their paces, yet again, around the streets and cycle lanes of Austria's illustrious capital city.

At the post mortem, Alison was reminded by Francois that his middle-aged charges were experienced, mature riders with a number of testing rides under their belts and were quite capable of deciding whether to continue, or not. Hysterical outbursts were unprofessional, out of place and merely served to undermine their confidence and commitment to the cause.

He went on. "I shall ignore your unhelpful outbursts this time, but any repeat of your rantings will mean instant dismissal, so take it from me this is your last and final warning," barked Francois, thumping his empty beer glass down on the white, plastic table before checking his phone for any last minute text messages. Alison didn't take kindly to being dressed down in front of her peers, but would toe the line, do as she was told and be more circumspect in future. So she said.

In the powerhouse of masculine fortitude, it was David and the Wink who looked done in. Both of whom sauntered off, after a final check-up by Alison, to recuperate in a hot steamy bath and reflect on their day's work. David glanced around and noticed, through his tinted sunglasses, Francesca leaning provocatively against a broken branch of a tall towering Cyprus tree. He wiped his wet face on the sleeve of his ripped and torn lyrca top, while droplets of moisture continued leaking like a tap from every pore. His posh watch was bursting with information, showing thirty-four degrees in bold red characters and quoting humidity at over ninety, while explaining, as if he needed telling, that the air quality was excellent and there was a moderate northerly breeze.

Francesca wore a pale cream top with a pair of attractive, tight-fitting white shorts and dainty flip-flops. Her striking black hair was tied back in a bow and her blue-framed sunglasses were stuck on her forehead. The Italian beauty rewarded her secret admirer with a broad grin when her sultry brown eyes fell upon his. She sauntered towards him with a saucy wiggle, still showing off her signature smile. The unsophisticated hotel waitress was beautiful, naturally beautiful, oozing charm and charisma with every flirtatious stride, with every casual swish of her hair.

"How do you feel?" she asked, grabbing hold of his dented and badly scraped red and white riding helmet.

"Battered and bruised and in need of a long shower," he replied as they sauntered across the road, passed lines of foreign coaches with podgy overweight drivers resting face-down at the wheel, while the more energetic were seen having a crafty smoke at the back of the bus. The steep slope up towards the Excelsior Hotel was hard going, forcing David to stop a couple of times to get his breath and quench his thirst.

"I'll help you up the road, put your arm around me," Francesca shouted over the roar of passing traffic. David didn't have the strength to talk, let alone protest, so he just did as he was told, leaning on his young carer for support, accompanied by the sound of Francesca's flip-flops smacking down on the solid surface. His sore jaded limbs complained with every stride, with every agonising movement. He was exhausted after the day's heady challenge and, even at that late hour in the afternoon when the sun's rays were receding, Richmond's finest felt his energy reserves being drained with every tortuous step up the unforgiving incline. Francesca, fearing for the health of her companion, draped her arm around his waist to support his weight and it was then she noticed the injuries he'd sustained in his tumble on the tarmac. When the duo finally arrived back at the hotel, with the welcoming sound of the automatic glass doors sliding open to greet them, David seemed in a trance, almost oblivious to his surroundings. He was too exhausted to raise his arm, or even speak to the happy smiling guests standing patiently in the lounge to meet the returning hero. Ignoring them, he fell into the waiting lift, grabbed his battered helmet out of Francesca's hand and waved over his shoulder to his attractive companion before the doors slammed shut behind him.

Francesca wasn't too upset by his off-hand manner, knowing David was in a bad way and in need of a long hot bath and a well-earned rest. Anyway, she had more important matters on her mind than the posh boy's little cuts and bruises. Sadly for her things hadn't gone to plan and her gruff ill-tempered boyfriend wouldn't be happy when she explained that the millionaire playboy was too preoccupied with his own state of health to be interested in her. Fearing for her own safety, she knew she'd have to tread very carefully and cover her back as best she could.

Moments later, David collapsed in a heap on his wide king-size bed in his palatial suite and was chewing a soft fruity jelly left on his pillow by the hotel's chatty chambermaid. Here he remained sprawled flat out until his dreams were disturbed by the melodic chimes of Beethoven's fifth strumming out on his mobile phone. It was Francois.

"Sorry I couldn't talk to you at the end, but I got caught up with the press. It's been a tremendous success and we've made lots of money for your charity. Clearly the "Just for ME" campaign with the eye-catching slogan really captured the media's imagination and will be the lead story in many local papers and national news networks for the next couple of days. I understand some of the pictures and stories of the day have gone viral on social media. So it all bodes well. How are you feeling, by the way? Alison said you still weren't too good."

"I shall feel better once I've had a warm bath and soaked these weary bones," replied David drowsily. "That was a really difficult ride today. It's taken a lot out of me, I can tell you, but I shall soon be fighting fit again. You can be sure of that," he explained defiantly.

"We'll talk later. You should be very proud of yourself. I must go," said Francois quickly breaking off the call and grabbing a local newshound before he disappeared into a nearby bistro with a young female reporter in tow.

Struggling to move, David leaned back against the headboard, quietly reflecting on the events of the day, feeling pleased with the outcome and very proud of his courageous colleagues who'd done so much to make it a resounding success. Mulling over the names of the riders he thought how each of them, in their own distinctive way, had made a difference. They were all heroes in his eyes. But one of the unsung heroes of the day was Scotland's only representative, Michael Grant, a staunch supporter of the Pedal Power Programme since its inception and a renowned fitness fanatic. As one of the most revered riders in the pack, he was often seen moving up and down the peloton, offering words of encouragement to the guys when the going was tough and their confidence starting to wane. He was a real star.

Lying there, feeling too lazy to move and quenching his thirst on a cool glass of Evian water, a number of ideas came to mind and, quickly grabbing his iPad, the talented poet penned a moving tribute to his inspirational colleagues which he later called *A Sonnet to the Stars*.

It read:

One score and ten, such brave young men they rallied to the cause,
Attracted fans across the globe with smiles and loud applause,
They peddled on with gritted teeth, their legs cried out in pain,
Such was the quest that they pursued, hot bodies felt the strain,
Pampered playboys did their bit for those where life's unfair,
They toiled and sweat, they pushed and pulled, phones clicking everywhere,
My lycra lads fought hard and fast as fans screamed out their names,
While riding hard down soggy roads and winding country lanes,
From northern Spain to gay Paris the message was the same,
Keep peddling hard through rain and shine, ignore those aches and pains,
But when at last their ride was done; their mission was complete,
They rested back, a job well done, never thinking of defeat,
Dumas's words were ringing out, just like a clarion call,
The team had proudly done their bit, All for One and One for All.

Chapter 38

Later that afternoon, when the sun was slowly melting away, two people were sat quietly sipping a chilled glass of white wine and munching their way through a bowl of plain crisps and some tasty green olives.

"I can see Salo," said the man, holding a pair of tiny binoculars close to his eyes and peering towards the distant shoreline with its rolling hills and dramatic vista.

"To the right there's Gardone," he pointed with his outstretched arm. "It has a very impressive hotel of the same name that gently skirts the lakeside which, of course, you'll remember we saw it earlier today next to the town's modest ferry point. This is a beautiful place. It's like paradise with a beaming smile," the man remarked with a self-satisfied smirk before topping up their empty glasses and spearing a plump olive with the sharp end of a small wooden stick. Sipping her glass, she leant back, closed her eyes with the cool refreshing air wafting off the lake, offering a welcome respite after hours of relentless heat and kowtowing to the needs of the famous thirty.

With smug expressions on their faces, they pondered on their good fortune and how their cunning scheme would again line their pockets at the expense of the sick and needy. They would implement their usual plan and, with their reliable contacts in the accounts department, siphon off some of the funds from the day's adventure before the boffins calculated the final balance. It was foolproof, had worked like a dream for the last few years, nothing could go wrong. It was clever, undetectable and the callous, greedy duo knew it. Both were bitterly jealous of the high rollers, the lavish jet-set lifestyles they enjoyed and hankered for a taste of the good times for themselves. After all, they worked hard for little recompense and felt justified in taking a little something for themselves. So the thieves set up a small network of fraudsters, stealing about £100,000 per ride with the promise of much richer pickings between events when the monies continued to roll in unabated. It was a relatively insignificant amount in the scheme of things and too small to raise alarm bells from people in the know. Hence they could evade detection, hide their thievery from the authorities and put their grubby hands in the till with complete impunity.

One of their co-conspirators in the accounts department at the Paris head office recorded all the cheques, pledges and cash that came in for each charitable event. Donations came from company accounts, wealthy anonymous benefactors, members of the public, the riders themselves and through a number of other income sources. This all added to the melee, providing a rich feeding ground for the unscrupulous crooks. So a combination of convoluted financial transactions and slack auditing, with poor standards of governance, made for an ideal hunting ground for would-be thieves and embezzlers who'd ruthlessly exploited these apparent weaknesses and loopholes ever since the inception of the Pedal Power Programme some five years earlier.

The independent auditors had earlier highlighted a number of critical deficiencies in the company's accounting system, stressing its vulnerability to fraud, but as the suspected perpetrator of the deception held a key position on the Committee, the push for change was suppressed and therefore nothing was done to rectify matters.

The respected Pedal Power Programme had captured the imagination of many wealthy companies and philanthropic individuals across Europe. The excitement generated vast income streams that were much larger than David Lane and PW had ever imagined, with money pouring in between events like a swollen river bursting its banks, such was the impact Team 30 had on the public psyche. But sadly this exposed serious weaknesses in the administration of the project showing it wasn't fit for purpose and was in grave need of urgent reform.

The much needed changes, proposed by the auditors in a recent clandestine report to David, would have to be introduced with utmost secrecy, as the slightest whiff of wrongdoing would signal the death knell for David Lane's altruistic Programme, destroying everything he stood for and ruining the hopes and dreams of so many vulnerable people.

So, over a number of years, a network of unscrupulous thieves took advantage of the inadequate accounting procedures, set up dummy accounts for cash payments, stealing vast sums of money without a second thought for the consequences of their treachery and greed. However, the crooks knew they had a limited lifespan and the authorities would soon be closing in on them. The Viennese ride in September was the last time they could dip their thieving mitts in the till. The auditor's report, which they were aware of, would put the kybosh on their avidity, be the prelude to a range of new, fail-safe accounting methods designed to safeguard the Pedal Power Programme for years to come. Over the preceding five years, the callous thieves had stolen millions of pounds and, feeling satisfied with their haul, planned to disappear with their ill-gotten gains immediately after the Austrian ride and start a new life far away from the strong arm of the law.

"Can we have another bottle of the same?" he called out to the gaunt, podgy waiter strolling by with his order pad in hand who, sensing Francois' impatience, quickly scuttled off and very soon returned with a chilled bottle of Pinot Grigio and fresh bowls of plump green olives and crinkly crisps.

"We've got something to celebrate, my dear. In addition to today's haul, I've organised a little something extra to take the wind out of Mr Lane's sail, bring him down to earth with the rest of us," he laughed while charging his glass.

"What are you talking about Francois? I hope you aren't taking any silly chances at this stage. We've done very well over the years and we shouldn't be greedy and risk everything now," Alison replied, biting her lower lip and rubbing her damp clammy hands together with a couple of crumpled paper napkins.

"Don't be daft, trust me," he replied. "These guys are so full of themselves and their lavish lifestyles, they haven't the faintest idea what's going on under their noses. They are so dumb. Lane is a reformed drunk who's always up his own ass, throwing his money around as though he owns you. He's got the morals of an alley cat. Do you know something? They've even selected the prat as a parliamentary candidate. Could you believe it? It shows how desperate they are when they select a self-indulgent egotist like him, who thinks he's God's gift to women. He makes you sick.

"Who says money doesn't count, eh? His silly friend is just as daft. He lives on another planet, spending money like confetti and is as dim as him. The buffoon drives around as though he owns the place and talks as though he's got a plum in his mouth. Do you know he's never worked a day in his life? He's your archetypal parasite, but my dear, we'll always outwit the silver spoons, relieve them of their not-so-hard-earned cash and spend it on ourselves. Now, here's my little surprise. You remember Midge that little prick who's helped us out before? Well, I've got him to do something for us again which will net us a lot of cash and put him in the firing line if it goes wrong. I know where Lane is most vulnerable and Midge is going to exploit that and get his hands on a lot of money which no one will be able to trace back to me. But if there's a problem, then the hired hand takes the fall. It's foolproof. How clever is that?"

"I hope you're right, for our sakes; otherwise, we're going to clink for a very long time," Alison pointed out, as another glass of white wine disappeared down her throat, like water through a sieve, causing her to cough and splutter before eventually regaining her composure thanks to a couple of mouthfuls of water from her plastic bottle.

"Oh, by the way, I thought my public bollocking was a good ploy in front of the team. It put everyone off the scent, made them think we were just workmates, nothing more. Clever idea," Alison said.

"What makes you think it was a ploy?" he whispered in her ear, carefully spearing the remaining olive hiding in the corner of the curved glass bowl before tilting his head backwards and finishing his drink with a single swig.

Chapter 39

After luxuriating for some time in a hot steamy bubble bath, David dried himself off on one of the hotel's big fluffy towels before treating his many cuts and bruises to Alison's magical potions. He then stretched out on the bed gazing at the mellow, tranquil lake thinking about his beloved parents. There wasn't a day that went by when he didn't think about the wonderful times they shared together, playing football and cricket in their big sprawling garden that seemed to go on forever, or picnicking on a warm summer's day in one of Richmond's expansive parks with his mother's enchanting smile and father's infectious laugh for company. In his formative years, every day was an adventure, a new experience for the spotty-faced youth, with bruised knees, short grey trousers and a squiffy school hat, very much in the image of Crompton's *Just William*. Louise, his mother, was French from the Loire and his father, Jeremy, was born in London and educated at Eton and Cambridge where he achieved a double first in maths, the same as Louise. Their respective families were highly regarded in the world of finance with a distinguished reputation in international banking dating back several decades.

However, stockbroking in the square mile was where David's celebrated parents cut their teeth, stamped their mark on the industry and was the catalyst for their meteoric rise up the proverbial greasy pole. The high-powered duo joined forces on a number of major international projects and over time, a romantic relationship blossomed between the two young brokers, shortly followed by the sound of wedding bells and the swopping of expensive twenty-two-carat gold rings. In the summer of 1965, the perfect couple embarked on their new exciting journey together where the world was their oyster, life a flawless dream and everything they touched turned to gold, such was the charmed lives they so enjoyed.

David's arrival in July 1970 was a major turning point in their lives, with wealth and social prestige taking second place to the love and adoration they showered on their precious, blue-eyed son. He was everything they ever wanted and their comfortable, privileged lives were enriched by the little bundle of fun that smiled and gurgled from dawn to dusk. It was idyllic; it was manna from heaven, but sadly it wasn't to last.

Fate had other plans, conspiring to intervene in their lives, bringing their romantic fairy tale union to a sudden, dramatic end, when their light aircraft plummeted to earth in a massive fireball, leaving a trail of bellowing acrid smoke and untold heartbreak in its wake. The ill-equipped teenager was left to pick up the pieces, build a new life from scratch, knowing he'd never smell his mother's soft fragrant perfume ever again, or hear his father's raucous laugh at the resounding crack of leather on willow. Rows of tears trickled slowly down his cheeks when the enormity of his loss flooded back, serving to stalk the playboy's every waking moment. Even after all those years, his parent's death was still raw, like a deep jagged wound ripping through the stitches whenever their sacred memory simmered to the surface, offering little prospect of ever healing such were the ingrained feelings of anguish racking his tortured body.

Then, all of a sudden, he remembered the gold locket. In the pandemonium following his accident, he'd forgotten to retrieve the precious family heirloom from the handlebars of the twisted Boardman. With his hands shaking, he grabbed hold of his phone and called Francois in an agitated tone of voice who promised to contact Gary, the driver of the juggernaut, and retrieve the precious item before the lorry wended its way north early the following morning. David was exceedingly grateful and said. "As you know, I'm off tomorrow. I expect to be home late evening all being well. Oh I nearly forgot, I've got a pile of cash from some of the Scandinavian contingent who weren't able to pay the money into the company account. I'll leave it in the hotel safe so you can collect it tomorrow when you deliver the locket, if that's okay?"

"I'll be at your hotel for ten thirty a.m., so I'll drop off your locket and collect the cash then. Out of interest, how much is it?" asked Francois, in a jaunty, off-the-cuff manner.

"I'm not sure," said David. "I didn't count it, so perhaps you could do the honours? As you know, I'm not so good with money. There's a large envelope and a smaller one and judging by the weight, there must be over 50,000 euros, I'd have thought. I won't be back here at the hotel until after eleven a.m. tomorrow, so we'll miss each other, but thanks for doing this for me, you're a star. As you know, I can't leave the country without the locket, it's so valuable, it means more than anything to me. Please text or call me as soon as you have it. I shan't rest until I know."

A short time later, David had the good news he was waiting for. The heirloom was safe and sound, he could rest easy. He had a large tonic water to celebrate his good fortune and, turning on the telly, laughed out loud when he saw a very young David Jason, with his lanky undernourished brother, joking in perfect Italian while strolling through the damp shiny streets of Putney on a cold winter's day. It was quite surreal. This put him in a good mood.

Later wandering onto his balcony, shrouded in an over-sized, white knee-length bath towel, he glanced down at the oblong swimming pool below with its avid sun-seekers basking on their colourful beach towels and loungers soaking up the late afternoon sun. He sent a short text to Claire saying the ride had gone well and he'd be home early evening the following day. She didn't reply. David noticed a couple of feisty young teenage girls swimming up and down the pool, splashing everyone in close proximity. The playful adolescents stopped every couple of lengths for a giggle and a chat before resuming their aquatic exercises, much to the annoyance of some of the elderly guests who, judging by their sad forlorn expressions, weren't enjoying themselves at all which was at odds with the wonderful scenic paradise at their arthritic fingertips.

Seeing the girls enjoying some innocent fun made him think, reflect on his loss and the life he'd endured. Sure, his untold wealth had compensated in some ways, allowing him to indulge in various passions and expensive pursuits, but it could never make up for the absence of his adoring parents.

Leaning on the balcony rail, watching the bar staff below serving their guests with refreshing drinks and simple bar snacks, he thought about Louise. She was his only daughter, his own flesh and blood and sadly he'd missed seeing her grow up from a small, innocent child to a beautiful young woman that she was today. That pleasure had been denied him. Obviously, he'd seen lots of videos and photographs of her and had an extensive book of cuttings and memorabilia dating back to the time of her birth, but it wasn't like the real thing. He'd never met her, never kissed her, never held her in his arms. At the time of her birth David agreed, very reluctantly, to leave well alone, keep out of Susan's life and not interfere until

Louise was much older and able to handle things. But as he sipped his drink, peered out across the blue pond with its familiar ferries glinting in the late afternoon sun, a feeling of immense loss took over. So, without a moment's hesitation, David decided there and then it was time to act; time to stop living a life of lies. He would step out of the shadows and tell the world he was the proud father of the beautiful Louise Lane. After all she was entitled to know the truth about her parentage following years of pretence and deceit. He owed it to her, especially with her big birthday just around the corner.

With a wry smile and a quick slurp of squeezed orange, he sprawled out across his expansive double bed just as Del Boy was trying to offload some iffy goods to a sceptical bunch of East Enders unimpressed by Trotter's predictable sales patter. Then, while applying some lip balm to his dry cracked lips, David sent a short pithy text to Susan explaining how he intended celebrating his daughter's eighteenth birthday without giving a second thought to the impact it would have on the unwary recipient. Meanwhile the comedic antics of the television stars carried on unabated, filling the TV screen with bouts of laughter and applause, as the familiar hypnotic sound of bow bells chimed loudly in the background.

Chapter 40

Later, Francesca knocked on his door, and without waiting for a reply used her hotel key to let herself in which David thought was a tad rude, but he held his tongue especially as the new girl on the block was pushing a wooden hotel trolley laden with his favourite food. With a quick flick of her wrists she removed the two dome-shaped covers to reveal a piping hot bowl of vegetable soup and a mouth-watering piece of sliced pink salmon garnished with chopped crinkly lettuce, red and green peppers, shredded carrots, diced baby beetroots, dainty haricot beans and a sumptuous potato salad, just as he liked it. On the lower deck was a circular basket brimming with chunks of crusty brown bread and a crystal glass jug of freshly squeezed orange topped up with a mountain of misshapen ice cubes.

"How are you feeling?" she asked, tiding up his bed and collecting the empty glasses and coffee-stained cups lying scattered around the room.

"Much better, thanks," he mumbled, dipping a piece of bread into the warm, steamy soup and pouring himself a glass of orange.

"A soak in the bath helped soothe my back and legs and I've plastered my cuts and bruises in nurse's magical mix, so I should be much better after a good night's sleep. Thank you for the food by the way, just what I wanted."

Francesca had something special about her that made David feel comfortable; very much at ease in her company. Perhaps it was the way she tied her black hair up in a bow, or her sleek, trim figure and delicate neck, or just her sparkling brown eyes that drew the foreign visitor to her like a magnet. She was natural, didn't use much make-up, or cover herself in gaudy jewellery so it was this uncluttered simplicity that made her so seductively appealing to his wandering eye. Every time their paths crossed, David became increasingly infatuated, drawn to her quiet modest understated charm and innocence. Beautiful women with a bit of mystery and something special always got his vote, but this young girl with her carefree manner and relaxed style was in a league of her own, different from the others, very different indeed. Garda's little gem smiled at her hotel guest busily tucking into his salad and, not wishing to outstay her welcome, sauntered towards the door with her empty wooden trolley, promising to return later in the evening to collect his tray before he retired for the night.

From early evening, as the sun was having a well-earned nap, the tapas bars, lakeside restaurants and narrow, jam-packed streets were filling up with high-spirited revellers waving national flags with noisy exuberance and singing patriotic songs very badly, all waiting for the referee's whistle signalling the start of the World Cup final at nine p.m. local time.

David was drawn to the carnival atmosphere emanating from the streets below and so a short time later, feeling much better after his hearty meal, thought he'd have a nose around, stretch his legs and see what was going on. He quickly threw on a pair of white shorts, a freshly ironed blue T-shirt and matching trainers and sauntered casually out of his luxurious white-walled hideaway, along a steep pathway down towards the noisy town centre, hoping to sample some pre-match fervour first-hand.

The thought of animated Italian fanaticism joining forces with World Cup fever was a tantalising prospect too good to be missed. Very soon he was engulfed by groups of rowdy headstrong football fans, shouting and chanting in good-natured fun along the length and breadth of the iconic tree-lined boulevard while good old *Andromeda*, not wishing to miss out on the celebrations, quietly cruised into port as if on cue.

It was close, very muggy and quite oppressive with just a slight breeze blowing on his back. Feeling pleased with his day's work David chuckled to himself when he recalled his panic-stricken conversation, about the missing locket, with the light-fingered Frenchman earlier in the evening. A constant throbbing in his sunburnt arms and legs reminded the forty-something of the strain he'd put his body under. I'm getting too old for this, he mumbled to himself, as a couple of high-spirited German youths, draped in national flags, bumped into him and apologised profusely when the bolshie Englishman treated them to one of his famous penetrating glares. Gazing out across the dimly lit bay as little specks of light flickered brightly on distant shores, his mind was elsewhere, wrestling with a number of burning issues that had been the source of many sleepless nights. His Pedal Power Programme was at risk due to the fraudulent antics of some people close to him whom he'd trusted implicitly, had taken their loyalty for granted. He could hardly contain his anger at the thought of their treachery and betrayal.

But casting his personal feelings to one side, David was determined to rout out the culprits, bring them to book and do everything in his power to safeguard the future of his much-revered flagship Programme. That was his number-one priority. As he strolled between the heaving masses, a swarm of annoying midges and mosquitoes darted about in the humid air, attracted to the streams of artificial light and the prospect of a lakeside snack. But thanks to his repellent, sprayed liberally all over his body, the pesky bloodsuckers were kept at bay, even though some of the little devils were determined to top up their blood banks, whatever the risk, judging by the frequent frantic waving of his outstretched arms. David's casual evening attire and healthy tan gave the charismatic visitor a distinctive eye-catching glow, causing many female revellers to turn their heads as Mr Smooth glided by as if on castors. He loved being in the limelight. It made him feel good. The egotistical middle-aged tease often played to the gallery, raising his eyebrows, pouting his lips or just treating his victims to a series of deep seductive stares. However, that night things were different, he was oblivious to his many amorous admirers, their furtive glances and subtle turns of the head.

The wicked demons of deceit had conspired to steal the show; had colluded to take the edge off the day's victory parade, but he wasn't going to let them win. There was no way his beloved Programme was going to be derailed by a bunch of greedy, manipulative thieves who'd shortly pay for their heinous crimes when the full force of the law came to bear.

David was known for his hot-headed behaviour, especially with matters of the heart. His track record over many years was testament to that, with a long vapour trail of attractive women following in his wake, entering and leaving his life like a constantly revolving door. Sadly, he often applied the same casual, matter-of-fact approach to his charitable affairs, making quick, knee-jerk decisions that were devoid of serious investigation and scrutiny, often based on a whim, an urge, or just a sudden impulse. However, the entrepreneur knew this cavalier approach was his downfall and, for the sake of his beloved Programme, he had to shape up, be more cunning, more circumspect than his nimble-fingered antagonists if he was to expose the baddies and get his pet project safely back on track.

After a short time meandering around the bay soaking up the atmosphere, the rowdy behaviour got too much for the intrepid cyclist and his dodgy limbs, so he decided to retreat back up the slope to the safe haven of his luxury air-conditioned bolthole. It was then, quite by accident, that he noticed a podgy middle-aged guy with a pockmarked face and protruding ears chatting some distance away to a bunch of scruffy Brits. For some reason, it drew his attention. The fat rotund shape, in the dim light, seemed somewhat familiar, but he didn't know why. Following his instinct he decided to investigate and, taking his life in his hands, ducked and dived between the manic crowds of marauding football fanatics towards his quarry, leaning casually against the wall of an adjacent ice cream parlour. With every step, every jostle, every shove reality gradually dawned on him. His jaw dropped when he realised what he was looking at. It was completely unexpected; a real shock and a bolt out of the blue. With his mouth feeling parched, drained of moisture, just like sandpaper and grasping his flushed cheeks in his shaking hands, he stumbled back against an uneven stone wall for support. Tired blue eyes refused to blink once they recognised the harrowing object in their gaze, the cause of many tear-stained pillows, endless sleepless nights and the source of recurring nightmares that were still vivid today.

So there was David Lane quietly minding his own business, taking things easy, enjoying a bit of light relief in Garda's football fantasia, when just yards away was his callous teenage tormentor, Martin Conway. Memories of his traumatic schooldays came flooding back in great torrents while the gregarious bully boy chatted away oblivious to his presence, swigging a bottle of Pernod and tucking into thick slices of pizza. For some time David stared at his foe, rooted to the spot. Wiping his damp brow and feeling quite emotional, he slowly ambled across the roadway between milling throngs of inebriated youths hoping to get a better view of his long-time adversary. Yes, it was him all right, no doubt about it. Conway was still a fat little dumpling without any dress sense. David was gratified to see the years hadn't been kind, that the miscreant had lost most of his hair and his freckled face was lined with deep grooves and unsightly wrinkles. Thick black-lined tattoos were painted on his stubbly neck and lower arms as his floppy stomach hung over his dingy misshapen jeans, trying to escape the clutches of his ill-fitting T-shirt that had seen better days.

Time stood still for several minutes, allowing him to gather his thoughts, compose himself, think what he was going to do. But, after what seemed an eternity, David reached for his phone and, like any other innocent holidaymaker, took several photographs of the scene as excited football fans let off steam, chanted meaningless songs and verses as the grape and the hop cast their wicked spell. Anger, impulse and instinct were a dangerously toxic cocktail, compelling him, pushing him to confront the gormless goon there and then, beat the living daylights out of him before smashing his right ankle to smithereens. But even with his emotions running high, he thought better of it. It wasn't the time or the place for the revenge he so badly sought, especially as the promenade was swathed in colourful, majestic ME flags and banners hanging across the road and draping from rows of trees, lampposts and pylons. Powerful poignant reminders of a wonderful memorable day of high drama in celebration of a deserving good cause.

Thoughts of violence and retribution were clearly at odds with the messages of love and support so boldly reflected in the eye-catching bunting fluttering freely in the cool evening air. So with a fixed grimace and tightly clenched fists, he reluctantly stole himself away from his obese abuser and slowly ambled back to his pampered sanctuary with a heavy heart and a deep sense of regret.

The Englishman was still reeling on the ropes at the very thought of seeing Conway during his solitary evening stroll, when Chris' short punchy text came through saying he'd be at his hotel by seven thirty a.m. the next day to finalise their plans. PW was a man of few words; always straight to the point, a quality that endeared him to his partner very much. One of David's innate strengths, inherited from his parents, was his ability to compartmentalise issues, not fret or worry needlessly, but prioritise problems as they occurred, then address each one in a cool, calm, dispassionate way at a time of his choosing. That was how he handled the Conway confrontation.

Sometime later, he sat on his balcony, listening to the Beatles strumming away in the background, singing about the virtues of yesterday; of days gone by. It reminded him of his misspent youth when he'd shoot over to Malvern Link in his bright shiny Mercedes with the roof down and Mick Jagger boasting about his *Nineteenth Nervous Breakdown*. Here, the young rather immature Casanova turned on the charm that flowed unabated like the famous local waters, hoping to ingratiate himself with the feisty, female boarders, cooped up in the town's many exclusive boarding schools and trendy colleges.

Feeling hot and clammy after his little evening ramble, he decided to have a tepid shower and apply a further layer of Alison's magical mix to his wounds and injuries. Afterwards, he relaxed on his posh material settee and sent a series of text messages to his fellow riders expressing his gratitude for their gallant support which inevitably led to a raft of rude and witty responses. He called Claire to give her a brief update, ignoring the accidents and mishaps and some of the other issues of the day. She was busily tying up the loose ends, following the fourth ride in the season and preparing some of the groundwork for the final outing. Claire had set up a meeting with his party agent to talk about a number of things, including the campaign for the 2015 General Election. Mike was keen to start the ball rolling, feeling a Tory victory was very much on the cards as the polls were showing Labour support across the country slowly ebbing away.

"Have you spoken to Francois today?" he asked abruptly.

"No, why do you ask?" Claire replied, rather indignantly.

"Well you two always seem as thick as thieves, chatting to each other and sharing little titbits and secrets. I'm surprised you have time for anything else," he said sarcastically.

"What's the matter with you, David? You always talk like this when you're away. I have to speak to him as your PA, to keep everything on track. There's a lot to be done behind the scenes, which you don't seem to understand. You haven't got the faintest idea, have you?"

"Okay, let's change the subject," he replied impatiently, not wishing to get bogged down with trivia. "I've got things to do first thing tomorrow, but I should be with you early evening, all being well."

"Oh, are you flying from Verona as planned?" she asked, as an afterthought.

He pondered for a second. "Yes, I'll catch the flight straight through to Staverton with the usual private airline. See you tomorrow, all the best."

David dropped the phone on the bed. Claire knew from his snappy irritable tone that he wasn't happy, something was worrying him. Being a private person, he tended to keep things to himself rather than share them with his wife, which she'd always found difficult to handle. She hoped his birthday celebrations on Monday evening would cheer him up, lift his spirits and perhaps bring them closer together again.

Chapter 41

She was officially off duty when she returned to her pokey ground-floor room at the rear of the building, stuck next to the hotel's noisy air-conditioning unit. Francesca was startled to see Midge, with his formidable tattoos and unruly mop of hair, lying sprawled across her narrow single bed with his arms behind his head. Clara, an ex-pat and her best friend from their schooldays, couldn't understand what she saw in him, often describing her indolent boyfriend in disparaging terms, saying he was dense, dim and slow-witted, the sort of qualities you'd normally associate with a Kevin, or a Ken.

"I understand he'll be leaving tomorrow," she said with a shameless sneer and a slightly nervous quiver in her voice.

"Right, I'll do it tomorrow morning as agreed with the boss," he replied, bouncing off the untidy bed and tucking his beer-stained T-shirt into the frayed waistband of his faded jeans.

"I'll explain the plan when we're out so let's get off, have a few drinks and think how we're going to spend all that lovely dosh," he chuckled.

Joking and giggling, they strolled excitedly, arm in arm towards the town centre, drawn like bees to a honeypot by the sound of clanking bottles and tuneless singing by hordes of rowdy football fans out having a good time. The young lovers hoped their tedious uneventful lives would soon be a thing of the past, consigned to history, when their bank accounts moved from red to black and their pockets and purses bulged with crisp, unused euro notes.

An hour or so later, Francesca returned to the Excelsior and kissed her red-faced delinquent goodnight. Looking worried, she grabbed a room key from reception and raced up the winding staircase, two steps at a time. Not wishing to surprise David, she sneaked quietly on tip-toe into the suite, but the nervous sullen-faced waitress needn't have bothered with such subterfuge.

A tall solitary figure was sat on the half-moon-shaped balcony, dressed in a white bathrobe, drumming his thin manicured fingers on the oblong table to the thumping rhythmic sound of *Maggie May*. Rod's raspy voice was interspersed by clinking glasses and high-spirited laughter from bubbly late-evening revellers relaxing on the hotel's tiered patio below.

"How are you feeling?" she asked, plonking herself down on one of the white plastic chairs nearby. David looked up, a little startled by her presence. He never failed to be amazed by her carefree, unsophisticated manner. Without a bye your leave, his uninvited guest had just strolled nonchalantly into his private space and flopped down beside him as though they'd known each other for years, instead of just a couple of days. He was infatuated, besotted by her casual carefree manner and bubbly self-confidence. It made him chuckle to himself behind his hand as one of his favourite singers sang about the virtues of sailing and leaving home.

"Okay," he replied. "I'm taking the air for the last time before returning to Cheltenham tomorrow. I love this place you know, the wonderful food, the gorgeous scenery and, of course, the charming Italian people who have a very special place in my heart.

"You Italians never fail to amaze me with your noisy chatter and highly animated conversations," he remarked with a gentle grin, while peering straight into Francesca's eyes causing her to glance down at the floor to hide her embarrassment as her tanned cheeks took on a red sheen.

He went on. "But I adore Cheltenham. I never tire of it. I just love sitting in the Imperial Gardens of an evening, watching the world go by. It's very relaxing, you know, with Gustav Holst's statue in the foreground and the wonderful historic town hall nearby. I sound like an old man, don't I? I have a favourite bench; it's directly in front of a famous landmark hotel at the top of the town. It's the simple things I enjoy most and cherish at this time in my life. The gardens have always meant a lot to me ever since I pitched up in the town in the early nineties, after a few up and down years on the south coast. Cheltonians are friendly and welcoming and are fun people to be around. They love their festivals, street cafes and posh restaurants which are scattered all over the town, like stardust, catering for every palate. I'm an old romantic really, often spending my spare time just sitting, reading, making copious notes, languishing in my own little world, thinking how things might have been. If only. Those two simple words sum up my whole life, you know. But then, looking ahead, I might be an MP this time next year. That really would be a turn up for the books. I hope that a lovely couple I met in Hastings many years ago, who did so much for me, will be looking down and sharing in my success. I don't know where I'd be if it wasn't for them. They helped me when I was at a real low ebb. I still miss them a great deal and think of them most days," he said, dabbing his moist cheeks with a fresh white cotton handkerchief.

"Forgive me, I tend to ramble on when I'm with people I like, whose company I enjoy. I've forgotten my manners. Would you like a drink?"

His guest rubbed her bottom lip and, feeling thirsty, helped herself to a glass of water from a crystal jug perched in the centre of the highly polished redwood dining room table. Then with her hands shaking and tears welling up in her eyes, gulped it down in one swig and asked, "Have you got anything stronger?"

David looked slightly bemused, but pointed to the drinks' cabinet in the corner of the lounge, whereupon his worried-looking companion grabbed a bottle of Glenfiddich malt whisky and poured herself a large one.

After a hearty swig followed by a couple of wheezy coughs, the glamour puss turned and wiped her smudged lips on the back of her sleeve. He handed her a paper serviette.

"I've got a terrible confession to make," she explained, recharging her glass and leaning on the table for support before sauntering back onto the balcony. Unconcerned by her remarks, David helped himself to a handful of salted peanuts and poured another large glass of Evian water as the oppressive heat of the evening continued doing its worst.

"Well, what is it, what's this big confession?" he joked, glancing nonchalantly over the veranda at a crowd of hotel guests drinking by the open-air bar below. "Don't tell me. Let me guess. You're a member of the local mafia, or maybe a ruthless blackmailer with a devious cunning plan up your sleeve, or even worse, perhaps you've been recruited by a gang of local desperadoes as a drug mule and you want me to swallow some condoms before I fly home tomorrow?" He gazed teasingly into Francesca's bloodshot eyes, waiting for a response.

"Shut up, be quiet, and listen!" she screamed. "You keep wittering on and on, you don't know what you're talking about. For God's sake shut up," she shouted as a stream of tears raced down her face, causing her eye make-up to smear across her cheeks in rows of black wavy lines.

His mood changed in the wink of an eye. Mr Lane wasn't used to people yelling at him, they didn't dare. Shooting to his feet like a bullet out of a gun, he sent his flimsy white plastic chair bouncing straight across the balcony and crashing with a resounding thump against the wrought iron barrier. David glared at her with his stony cold eyes, gritting his white polished teeth together, as a fit of anger gripped his body like a volcano preparing to explode.

"This better be good," he barked, starring defiantly at the quivering wreck before him, his eyes slicing through her skin like a sharp knife through butter, making every bone, every sinew in her delicate size-ten frame shake in fear and trepidation.

People know it's never wise to antagonise David Lane. There should be a health warning emblazoned in bold strident letters on his chest, alerting unsuspecting folk to his fiery, unpredictable outbursts that can have even the toughest souls quaking in their boots. The self-educated Londoner was a frightening sight when threatened or provoked and Francesca had unwisely drawn back the curtains on this mercurial character and was in the front row of the stalls witnessing first-hand the dark, sinister side of the playboy's volatile behaviour that, once unleashed, knew no bounds.

In a quiet, trembling voice, she mumbled. "Tomorrow morning, my boyfriend will call you demanding 200,000 euros, otherwise he'll go to the police and report you for attacking me. He'll meet you in Garda, tell you to make a money transfer online. If you don't do it, he'll carry out his threat. Believe me, this is for real," she said, staring down at the floor, seemingly in a trance, gripping her head between her quivering hands with streams of tears rolling down her smudged cheeks.

"Report me for attacking you? What the hell are you talking about, you stupid woman?" he hollered. His deep bellowing voice was so deafening that some of the intoxicated guests below gazed up in surprise when the fiery fund-raiser went into a blinding frenzy, hurtling chairs and tables across the balcony. He demanded to know what he'd done wrong and why he was the target of a stupid hare-brained hoax cooked up by a couple of Italian halfwits.

"That you attacked and raped me in your room," she yelled. Her response was like a red rag to a bull. Her angry distraught assailant kicked two of the upturned chairs out of the way, grabbed her by the throat with both hands and threw her headlong onto the lounge settee. She screamed in protest, lashed out with her arms and legs before curling up like a ball, hoping to protect herself from the crazy rantings of her violent adversary. Punching, kicking and crying out in pain, the young damsel tried to escape his vice like grip, but he was too much for her.

The strong muscular athlete shook in rage, glared into her eyes, never blinking for one moment, while gritting his teeth, seemingly oblivious to her cries and timid protests. Resistance was futile against such a formidable opponent hell bent on doing her harm. Knowing she was no match against the power and might of her tough broad-shouldered antagonist, she resigned herself to her fate. Fortunately for her, David gradually calmed down, slowly released his hold on her bruised, thumb-marked throat. Francesca immediately jumped forward, coughing and gasping for air, before swallowing huge gulps of water from a nearby glass tumbler. Collapsing back onto the settee, holding her head in fear and gazing into his eyes, she wondered what was going to happen next, and whether she'd ever see another dawn.

The silly, misguided waitress had tried to besmirch David's good name and hard-fought reputation and was now in the firing line, facing the music as the painful consequences of her betrayal came home to roost. Curled up in the corner of the settee, she tried to make herself as small as possible, burying her head under umpteen soft floral cushions while her red-faced assailant continued berating her with every breath.

David's juvenile infatuation with Francesca had got him into hot water, made him vulnerable, open to ridicule and blackmail. He knew the slightest whiff, the merest hint of scandal would destroy, wipe out his Pedal Power Programme, like the flick of a switch, sending his wealthy sponsors and loyal benefactors into hiding.

Francesca was in a state of shock when she poured herself a whisky, coughed and spluttered again, then wiped her eyes with a bundle of damp tissues lying scattered across the cool marble floor.

"You must do what he says. He's a violent man; he's already put me in hospital earlier in the year with a broken wrist. He'll do the same to you if you cross him," she said with a wheezy, crackly sound in her voice.

David could see the deep yellow outline of earlier bruises on her exposed shoulders and upper arms which seemed to substantiate her story, giving some credence to her alleged brutality at the hands of her yobbish boyfriend. He continued to quieten down and compose himself, while pacing around the cluttered, tissue-strewn suite, like a wild cat, stalking its prey, thinking what to do next.

"When will he call me?" he barked.

"In the morning, about nine o'clock," she replied without hesitation, fearful of antagonising David any further. He wanted to believe her as the evidence of cruelty at the hands of the bully boy was clear to see, but he needed something more tangible, more convincing, than a fanciful story about a few dodgy bruises and some odd-looking scratches.

"So, why d'ya tell me the plan, put yourself in danger?" he shouted. "You could do what your boyfriend wants, be living the high life, enjoying yourself tomorrow all at my expense. Why the change of heart?"

She sipped some water, leant back cross-legged on the settee, then sniffed and wiped her sore nose with a couple of fresh paper hankies that she'd quickly retrieved from the adjacent bathroom when the millionaire's back was turned.

Fearful of his reaction, she said, "Because I like you very much. You're a very kind and caring man. That's why. You've got to believe me, it's true," she pleaded.

"Rubbish, that's not good enough," he ranted, hurtling his empty tumbler to the floor, sending small fragments of crystal glass everywhere. Cowering on the settee with her face in her hands, she took up a foetal position, trying to protect herself from his venomous tongue.

Fortunately, the phone rang. David grabbed it impatiently. "Yes?" he yelled. "No, there's no problem. I'm sorry, but I may have had the TV on too loud. My apologies. Sorry for the disturbance." He slammed the phone down without waiting for a reply.

"That's your boss," he smirked. "So, let's get this right. In the morning, your boyfriend will ring me, threaten blackmail unless I cough up 200,000 euros. You tell me you've had a change of heart and that you aren't going through with the deal anymore because you like me," he sniggered.

"That's laughable. You must think I'm stupid. I don't believe you, not one word. Not one blasted word. Do you realise something? I really trusted you. I misguidedly thought you were someone I could rely on, but you've betrayed me, sold me out for a few miserly euros," he screamed, then grabbed hold of a large sofa cushion and hurtled it across the lounge as his anger reached boiling point yet again.

In a quiet timid voice she mumbled, "I'm ever so sorry, I really am." She ripped another paper tissue from the Kleenex box and sobbed loudly, and stared at the floor with her head held firmly between her hands while her long black strands of hair hid her face from view.

"It seemed a good idea. Pinch a few hundred euros off a drippy millionaire with money to burn. It didn't seem too serious. After all, he wouldn't miss a few euros with all the money he's got. But things have changed. Now I've met you, seen what you do for other people and how kind you are. I wish I'd said no to the whole stupid idea. I've made a terrible mistake. But I'm also very frightened because if I don't do it, I'm going to get beaten to pulp by Midge. He's determined to go through with the plan come what may. He's made up his mind and his boss says it's foolproof. Please believe me, David, I didn't expect this to happen," she begged as floods of tears continued rolling down her face.

Suddenly, like an uncoiled spring she jumped up, dropped the damp soggy tissue on the floor and shouted. "I'll go to the police, give myself in. At least you'll be out of it and you can return home, no worse off, with your reputation intact. I'll have to face the music, put up with the consequences."

"No, you won't," he snapped. "You'll do exactly as I tell you. I want to catch Midge and his accomplices red-handed so keep the police out of it, leave that to me. D'ya hear? Go back to your room, tell Midge his plan is good to go and come back here at eight thirty in the morning. Tell no one, okay? Not a soul. I think you've been very stupid and you don't realise the serious damage you could cause me and my colleagues, not to mention the lives of the people who rely on us. My work is hanging in the balance, on a thread because of you and that blasted moron," he ranted. "I'll tell you what we're going to do. Betray me now and Midge's violence will seem like a walk in the park compared to what I shall do to you. Against my better judgment, against everything I believe in, I'm giving you a second chance, but let me down and you will pay for it," he yelled, sending a cold shiver shooting up her spine as the blood-curdling threat tripped off his tongue with conviction.

"I won't let you down," she replied, walking tentatively towards him, reaching out to the furniture for support, unsure how her antagonist might react. She then bent forward very gingerly and pecked him on the cheek. He didn't flinch, he didn't move a muscle.

"I'm sorry, I'm ever so sorry," Francesca said in a sad, forlorn voice.

"So am I," he retorted, pointing towards the exit in one swift movement. David then turned his back and walked towards the balcony, carefully tiptoeing between the tiny fragments of glass spread across the marble floor. Bending down, he grabbed hold of two upturned chairs and slid them under the badly scraped balcony table, before letting out a sigh of despondency as he exhaled the air from his bloated cheeks.

Still in shock after her contemptuous dismissal, Francesca collected up his cups and dirty plates and walked disconsolately along the brightly lit corridor. Here she accidently collided with two inebriated guests, who whispered goodnight in slurred unintelligible Italian before breaking into rowdy drunken laughter when, after umpteen failed attempts, they managed to open the door to their hotel room.

Chapter 42

David leaned on the balcony rail with an overwhelming sense of apprehension as a tugboat spluttered and spat somewhere in the gloom, with the familiar sound of waves gently licking the banks of the nearby quay. A deep red band of flaming ribbon filled the sky above the distant shoreline, promising much delight for any local shepherds out tending their flocks in the morning. Late-night holidaymakers could be heard in the black darkness, laughing and chatting, as goosepimples came to the fore, heralding a chilly treat for the good-humoured night owls after the day's tortuous temperatures that sapped the strength of even the youngest visitors to Italy's celebrated resort.

The visitor was livid, fuming, enraged, but most of all incensed with himself for being so damned gullible, so easily taken in by a silly, soppy girl. "I trusted that woman; I believed in her," he shouted angrily, glancing up to the pale moon stationed overhead, praying for some kind of divine intervention in his hour of need.

The clumsy amateurish attempt at extortion by Francesca and her stupid boyfriend highlighted his vulnerability to any lunatic with half a brain who fancied a bit of blackmail and a few extra bob in the bank. But the more he thought about it, the more surprised he was that it hadn't been attempted before, knowing how the Programme had been trumpeted with unbridled fanaticism across the whole of Europe by an obsessive media besotted by the antics of him and his mates. It showed how slack he'd been with the organisation's finances, never asking the right questions, always taking things on face value, always trusting people to do the right thing. He naively assumed everything was hunky-dory, when clearly that wasn't the case. An accusation of gross incompetence could be laid at his door for which he could offer very little defence. There he was, busily beating down the doors of the big wealthy corporations, pandering to the whims of the rich and famous, rubbing shoulders with the great and the good, when all the time he was being taken for a mug by a network of thieving toe rags who dipped their grubby hands in the till whenever they fancied.

With a glass of orange in his hand and the moon still staring down at him ominously, he reckoned Francesca's crude attempt at extortion was the tip of the iceberg; a smokescreen for a much more complex web of embezzlement that had flourished for some time under his very nose. Sure, Francesca had betrayed him, like others had done in their quest for a quick buck, but he'd hit the roof, not because of her boyfriend's crude attempts at blackmail, but because it laid bare his own shortcomings, showed the world that the enterprising David Lane was a soft touch, a joke and a buffoon when it came to matters of finance.

Elgar's *Enigma Variations* were playing on the BBC World Service offering temporary solace from the traumas of the day, with the heart-warming sounds of *Nimrod*. Its soothing melody and hypnotic strings soothed his frayed nerves, transported him to a place of quiet reflection and tranquillity thanks to the amazing musical talents bestowed on the late composer.

Sadly, the mood of the moment was brought to an abrupt end when David heard an annoying ping on his phone, just as the sweeping strings were reaching their symphonic crescendo. Frustrated by the interruption, he let out an irritable grunt while glancing out of the corner of his eye at the illuminated text message.

It read. "What the hell are you doing? Don't you realise the upset your selfish action will cause Louise? I'm sure you've gone mad. I implore you, please stay away. We can talk next week when you're back. Roger's fuming. I had to tell him the truth. Please do as I ask. Suzy."

Susan's text was predictably emotional, having little impact on David even with the oily rag on the rampage. He was too taken up with his daughter's forthcoming birthday to get embroiled in domestic trivia, as he called it. As his slim two-metre frame lay stretched out across the settee, with the misty white glow still stationed overhead, he quickly turned on the Bosch radio hoping to catch the last few bars of the maestro's celebrated concerto. His disappointment was quickly dispelled when his ears were treated to the mellow sound of Beethoven's celestial *Sonata*, and David's sanguine mood went up a further notch when he poured himself a small glass of a mature Scottish single malt.

Meanwhile, Midge was waiting in Francesca's pokey hotel room feeling rather pleased with himself, when Francesca strolled in, somewhat bleary eyed and unsteady on her feet. She wasn't expecting him, but with a half-hearted smile and a quick peck on his bristly cheek confirmed that David's plans hadn't changed and they'd be much richer this time tomorrow. He rewarded his tired and dejected girlfriend with a big kiss and a hug and said the meeting with the boss went well and he'd see her bright and breezy in the morning. With hair in the air, tattoos in abundance and a slight whiff of alcohol, Midge sneaked off the premises without anyone noticing, which wasn't surprising.

Midge's list of social deficiencies were as long as your arm. Garda's gormless goon didn't twig that his long-suffering girlfriend was traumatised following her terrifying ordeal in the hotel's Presidential Suite. Francesca was still shaking an hour later when she eventually crawled into bed, with a thumping headache and nursing a sore throat. Initially, the Glenfiddich came to the rescue, casting its warm soporific glow over the wilting rose, but as the night progressed, her sleep was disturbed more and more by the nightmare sound of David's bellowing voice reverberating inside her head.

Strangely enough, Francesca had always felt okay in Midge's company, even though he knocked her about from time to time, was very moody, drank too much and wallowed in self-pity with a big chip on his tattooed shoulder. In all honesty, she'd known little else since leaving school and imagined, from her limited exposure to the male population, that all men were self-opinionated bullies devoid of drive and ambition.

But that was until the impressionable young maiden crossed paths with the illustrious David Lane. He was kind and articulate with oodles of charm, towering effortlessly over his contempories, while his deep blue eyes made women go weak at the knees, captivated by his hypnotic smile.

"Bit like a Richard Gere, or a Johnny Depp," said Francesca to the hotel manager late the previous night, when they were clearing up the glasses after a rowdy wedding reception and a sixtieth birthday bash that limped on until the early hours.

Michel Rouen smiled to himself when she spoke warmly of her adoration for the English gent, but chose not to burst her romantic bubble knowing full well she was batting way outside her league. The likes of David Lane wouldn't give a second thought to a witless hotel waitress who bites her nails and attracts the attention of the local misfits, whose only ambition in life was to plaster themselves in gaudy tattoos and get blind drunk every Saturday night.

David's high standards of personal grooming, that began in Hastings many years earlier, had paid off handsomely, always outshining the scruffy competition. He looked immaculate whether dressed in a casual jacket, smart trousers with hand-stitched shoes, or suited and booted for a posh gala dinner at a glitzy West End Hotel. Of course, he had a head start. David was stinking rich; flushed with cash, very good-looking and a head turner even on a cold blustery day when umbrellas have a will of their own. Richmond's famous son was a magnet for the wandering eye of his many adoring female fans, seduced by his sharp intellect, quick wit and striking personality. He had it all.

The handsome charmer was going somewhere, was on the way up. He had a lot more fuel in the tank, there was no doubt about that. Many of his female fantasists would have traded their beautifully manicured nails, their expensive Radley handbags and exclusive designer dress wear, their precious club membership cards and probably their boring, predictable husbands to have joined him on his exciting, no-holds-barred journey to who knows where.

Chapter 43

At seven a.m., the early morning sun peeped through the hazy mist promising yet another day of wall-to-wall adventure in the sun-drenched paradise called Garda. The air-conditioning kicked in, kettles were on red alert, bubbling into action and early-risers could be heard some way off. The predictable routine of wash, shave and shower was in full swing as eager, enthusiastic visitors prepared for another day of self-indulgent pleasure in Italy's prestigious holiday resort. Shall we go to Venice, the Dolomites, or venture further afield to Florence, or perhaps take a leisurely ferry ride across to Salo, or Limone? These were the enchanting choices on the itinerary of the discerning traveller with time on their hands, factor thirty at the ready and credit cards biting at the bit.

Following the exhausting events on Sunday, David chose to relax in the comfort of his spacious suite with its splendid views of the surrounding countryside and guaranteed privacy from nosy prying eyes.

After a hot steamy bubble bath and a strong cup of black coffee, he rested back in a comfortable high-backed wicker chair on the balcony and treated himself to a cooked breakfast with fresh orange juice and several rounds of buttered brown toast. Even after his early morning pampering, his legs and lower back still felt stiff and achy and he knew it would be several days before he was fighting fit again. David was an impatient soul who relished excitement and new challenges, where charitable giving was the focus of his privileged life, so being out of sorts, however brief, was always at odds with his energetic, full-on lifestyle. But he'd have to put his personal discomfort to one side, ignore it for the time being, knowing his Programme was at risk and the actions he took in the next few hours would determine its survival as a beacon for good.

Being away from home and seeing young innocent teenage girls enjoying themselves was a seminal moment for David, reminding him of Louise and all those lost years. The abuse he'd suffered following his parent's death was bad enough, but the one saving grace, the one ray of hope that had kept him going for the last eighteen years was his beautiful daughter, the apple of his eye, whom he'd doted on from the moment of her birth and hoped and prayed one day, they'd be together at last.

But things were about to change. The teenager's up and coming birthday was the catalyst for a fresh start; a new beginning, when two complete strangers would get to know each other, share time together and the dark sinister cloak of secrecy would be swept away. His time had come and his patience and compliance would soon be rewarded when eighteen innocent candles wafted their plumes of white smoke skyward, burning brightly on an ornate birthday cake dedicated to the wonderful Louise Lane. Quietly reminiscing, he picked up his iPad, scrolled down several pages of notes before retrieving a poem he'd composed when relaxing one evening on his favourite park bench in the Imperial Gardens in the esteemed company of Gustav Holst. It's called, *Out of the Shadows*:

Never heard your first words, or saw you run and play,
Didn't catch you when you fell on a balmy summer's day,
Never saw that new pink dress, adorned with pretty lace,
Missed the sound of your thrill voice, your cheeky saucy face,
Never chased across a park, or pushed you on a swing,
Always hidden out of sight I've never seen a thing,
But now those days are in the past, my future is with you,
Doing things with my girl that a father loves to do,
Going out, having fun, laughing late at night,
Makes me wonder what I've missed, hidden out of sight.

Over the years David had become quite an accomplished poet, capable of quickly capturing his thoughts and emotions in simple, uncomplicated verse. So composing a piece of rhyme as a heart-felt tribute to his long-lost daughter, with all that evokes, was an easy thing to do.

Suddenly there was a knock at the door and Mr Parker-Wright strolled in looking refined and debonair, very much in the image of a suave A-listed Hollywood actor ready to deliver his lines on a busy film set. Dressed in white perfectly pressed trousers and matching belt, with an open-neck, blue floral shirt and expensive Armani sunglasses on his forehead, he looked self-confident, totally at ease with life while a provocative aroma of expensive French cologne followed discreetly in his wake.

"Good morning. Happy birthday," said Chris with a beaming white smile, having availed himself of the hotel's exclusive teeth-whitening service. He patted his best friend warmly on the back making him wince and take in a quick gasp of air.

"Thanks," replied David, looking jaded after a sleepless night, dabbing his slightly moist eyes with a fresh Kleenex tissue. Putting his iPad to one side, he said, "Chris, we've got a big, a big problem, it's much worse than we thought. Last night, Francesca, the pretty waitress in the hotel visited my room. You know the girl?"

"Oh yes," replied Chris, with a saucy smirk and wink of the eye while helping himself to a tumbler of water.

"No, it's not what you're thinking," snapped David. "We're not all like you, you know. She said her boyfriend, Midge, would be calling me at nine o'clock this morning saying I'd raped his girlfriend and he'd be telling the police if I didn't cough up 200,000 euros."

"What!" yelled Chris. "You must be joking. It can't be true. She's having you on, mate. It's a stupid Italian prank, isn't it?" asked Chris with a pronounced frown.

David shook his head in response. "No, it's deadly serious."

The smooth operator, long known for his quick wit, lively banter and cheeky off-the-cuff remarks was caught off guard. He didn't know what to say, slumping down onto the settee and thinking through the grim ramifications of what his best mate had just said.

"Oh my God, this is serious," Chris cried. "What do you intend to do? I know we suspected Francois' involvement in some kind of fraud and perhaps this is his handiwork as well. I wouldn't be surprised. I'll kill the bastard, I damn well will."

David was cool, calm and collected thinking methodically about the next steps while the well-dressed old Etonian was overheating, blowing a gasket at the thought of the damage such a scandal would cause. David leant on the mahogany drinks cabinet and stared across the beautiful iconic lake, with the sun still slowly rising in the distance. The quiet peaceful scene was at odds with the anger and bitterness raging through his visitor's troubled soul.

"I've always trusted Francois, thought he was a good man, always on our side. But it turns out, from my information, that he's a common thief who's been lining his own pockets for years. But Chris, the rape allegation is altogether different. It's more personal;

it's directed at me and smells of hatred, anger and jealousy. That really hurts," David said, gazing down at the swimming pool below.

He went on. "I suspect there are others involved. He must have a network of accomplices otherwise the embezzlement would have been exposed a long time ago. That I am sure."

He walked back into the lounge while Chris, who was now more composed, bent forward on the edge of the settee balancing a glass of orange in the palm of his hand.

"I tell you this, we can't allow anyone to undermine the Programme. I mean that," he growled, kicking the wooden base of the settee making PW jump with surprise and spill his drink. "It's been a power for good and no one, I mean no one is going to stop us.

"I shall do everything I can to protect our beloved project," said David, pacing around the room. PW didn't say a word, he knew it was more than his life's worth to interrupt Mr Lane when he was waxing lyrical on a subject close to his heart.

"Our Programme is a marriage made in heaven where like-minded people, with a benevolent streak in their veins, have joined forces to help eradicate suffering and disease. We, my friend, are only at the beginning of a campaign to revolutionise charitable giving. We are pioneers for good, a beacon for hope and that's why we can't allow the bad, the greedy, the corrupt to stop us in our tracks. Vulnerable people rely on us and we're not going to let them down. Just think about it for one moment," David cried. "We've helped cancer research on a number of fronts, built children's hospices, supported big-name charities across Europe, made vast donations to smaller projects that have made a difference to people's lives. Look what we've done for ME in the last twenty-four hours. An illness that wreaks havoc on so many innocent lives. We've filled their coffers with some much-needed cash, we've raised the profile of the illness, got people talking about it, made it newsworthy," he retorted, banging the top of the lounge table with his grazed fist.

"Sadly, and this is what distresses me most, the pot of gold that we've collected for ME/CFS should be much more, but for the conniving, money-grubbing activities of some of our trusted friends and supporters. I always thought we might be vulnerable to corruption, but I never imagined we were the target of such a disreputable campaign of greed and malice, orchestrated by the very people we held dear. They won't derail our efforts, not one jot, or undermine my resolve to fight the corner for those less fortunate, in need of a helping hand." Richmond's famous orphan spoke with great oratorical compassion. Every breath, every word, symbolised his obsession for good, whilst a sinister expression lay draped across his face when imagining the fate of those who had the audacity, the effrontery to try and do him harm. Even though Chris was slightly offended by his friend's brusque manner earlier on, he shared David's resentment at the corruption in their midst and was equally determined to protect the name of their revered Programme.

David's unrelenting, unwavering conviction was one of the many reasons why PW held his long-time friend in such high regard, feeling motivated, sometimes even inspired by his illustrious friend's enthusiasm and uncompromising dedication to the cause. David went on. "I don't think Francesca poses a threat even though her disloyalty is a bitter pill to swallow, a real blow for a number of reasons. But putting that aside, we must rout out everyone, the whole messy network, whatever it takes and then destroy them. I mean destroy them. That is imperative Chris, as I'm sure you'd agree?"

Not waiting for a response, the birthday boy carried on:

"Funny how your mind wanders and mine does a lot of that as you know. At this moment in time, when we're under the cosh, I can't help thinking of Mark Twain's famous quote. It sums up my feelings as I reflect on the opportunities I've been handed since the loss of my parents and how I've been preparing for this very day, this very one. This was always my destiny, Chris. I can see it clearly now. For the first time in my life, I know why I was spared an early grave and the plans my loving parents had carved out for me.

"When I was relaxing one day in the lounge of the Imperial Hotel, back in my days in Hastings, I read *The Prince and the Pauper* by the great Mark Twain. Obviously there's nothing unusual about that, he's a very famous nineteenth-century American writer after all. *Huckleberry Finn and the Adventures of Tom Sawyer* are also great reads, but it's his quotations that often resonated with me and there was one that stuck out from the rest. I remember it vividly. I made a note of it in one of my many folders back at the ranch. It's so relevant to today, even when we're under pressure, feeling angry, upset and a tad fearful for the future which is understandable." He coughed and cleared his throat to emphasise the importance of what was to follow.

"Mark Twain said, *The two most important days in your life are the day you were born and the day you find out why.*"

"How powerful is that? I now know why I was born, Chris. Why I was put on earth. The events of the last few days have brought it home to me. I'm here for a purpose. Nobody, I mean nobody, will stop me in my quest, I owe it to my Ma and Pa. Mark's words are so profound, so poignant it's as though they were written for me."

The solemn mood was suddenly dashed however, and the two highly emotional playboys were brought back down to earth with a solid thump. David's text from Claire brought a smile to his face. "Happy birthday. What's it like to be forty-four? Mr M has cleaned and polished Jordan, so she looks spick and span, ready for a good ride. If the Millins' are still alive on your return, you can no doubt thank him. A young girl called a couple of times wanting to talk to you. I told her you were away. Perhaps it's your mistress! Ha, ha, ha. Love, Claire." Chris peered over his shoulder, read the message and was still in a reflective mood following David's impassioned sermon on the mount.

"I wonder who that might be?" asked PW with a shake of his head.

David ignored him. "Right, we mustn't get distracted Chris. Concentrate. Time is of the essence, my friend," he barked, thumping the low-level coffee table with his fist, scattering the bowl of fresh fruit everywhere. Unperturbed, PW rose to his feet and checked his appearance in the full-length hall mirror, then smoothed his fringe off his tanned forehead, under the watchful gaze of his highly polished front set, before brushing his broad, upright shoulders with the palms of his manicured hands. Reaching into his back pocket, he opened a slim green box and placed a beautiful diamond-encrusted Rolex watch into David's hand.

"Happy birthday, David, glad to see you're catching me up! If you don't like it, you can always change the engraving on the back from DL to LL and give it to the offspring on her eighteenth birthday. Now, there's a money-saving idea for you. Worth thinking about, don't you agree?"

The birthday boy smiled, shook his head and thanked his partner warmly. PW was never renowned for his tact and diplomacy but his

239

wicked sense of humour was quite timely, helping to reduce the tension and inject a bit of light-hearted humour into the mix.

"Are you still going through with the challenge?" his friend asked hesitantly while chewing on a piece of cold brown toast and helping himself to a cup of black coffee from a Russell Hobbs silver flask. "Our supporters will understand if you withdraw, especially with this blasted fraud issue hanging over our heads and now this stupid rape thing. I studied the auditors' report again last night, which makes for pretty solemn reading. They don't pull any punches, do they? We can't afford any whiff of scandal, you know. It'll mean curtains for us, the end of everything."

"Yes, I know, you don't need to tell me the bloody obvious Chris," retorted David sternly. "But I'm going through with it. I've no choice in the matter. There's a lot of money riding on it, but more to the point, I'm not going to let a bunch of thieves derail my plans and put our hard-fought relationship, with our loyal benefactors, in jeopardy. I know it seems frivolous to go ahead in these circumstances, but the show must go on and that's the end of it."

Tradition had it that after the final ride in the season, there was always a lavish celebratory banquet for the gallant riders and their devoted sponsors and backers. It was a bit of a jolly, where everyone let their hair down and misbehaved rather badly. As a finale to the year, a six-inch silver-plated trophy of a Victorian penny-farthing, bought from a market stall on the Portobello Road, was awarded with great pomp and gusto to the rider who was the stand-out team player during the year as voted by his peers. It was a light-hearted end of season bash where fine wines ran freely, champagne corks popped loudly and exaggerated stories of life in the saddle were on the menu. Towards the end of the evening, the chairman, Sir Anthony York, an eminent city gent and highly respected financier, briefly outlined the company accounts and explained the five European cycle venues for the next twelve months, before everyone retired to the bar for a nightcap, or two.

At the behest of the sponsors, for a bit of added spice and excitement, they always set a Daredevil Challenge for one rider to complete following the penultimate event in the forthcoming year. So, at the end of a lavish dinner, as the riders were languishing in their own glory, savouring their after-dinner cocktails and mints and boasting unabashed about their many conquests and achievements, the candidate for the next Daredevil Challenge was selected. Not surprisingly, at the 2013 bash in Lisbon, David's name popped out of the proverbial hat and the infamous gold envelope was handed to him on a silver platter by a sexy, glamour puss who kissed him on both cheeks, treated him to a friendly smile and offered a tantalising glimpse of her ample cleavage.

Details of the 2014 Challenge were quite explicit. They explained that the lucky rider was required to return home looking scruffy and badly dressed. The journey must include a private jet and a minimum of 250 miles in a taxi. The Daredevil event was to be recorded through a series of selfies and upon successful completion, a generous bounty of fifty thousand pounds would be paid to the ME Association by the sponsors as a goodwill gesture.

"Now then, Chris. Let's just walk through the plan again, make sure we haven't missed anything. According to Francesca, her boyfriend Midge will call me at nine a.m. threatening to call the police on a trumped-up rape charge if I don't pay 200,000 euros. I shall agree to meet him by the bureau de change to organise the money transfer. However, you'll meet him with your friend instead of me. Yes?"

Chris nodded and said, "Tiny knows exactly what he looks like. We'll hide outside the hotel. He's bound to be hanging around, thinking you might do a runner. It would seem very unlikely without your locket, but then he's a thick prick and probably doesn't realise its significance. Anyway, he's bound to stalk the hotel between nine and nine-thirty. What else would the dimwit do with his time? We'll then follow him to the rendezvous."

"Good, that sounds okay," replied David. "We know from our information that Midge is working for Francois, but we can't prove it. That's the problem. I want you to follow him with your friend. Grab him, threaten him, do whatever's necessary and carry out the money transfer from my account. According to Francesca, Midge has to call Francois once the deal has been struck and the monies are in his account. Under threat of death, get the little prick to make the call. He must say that 200,000 euros are in Francois' account. He mustn't say anymore, not a dickey bird. This is vital. Do you understand?"

Chris nodded in agreement.

"I don't care what happens to Midge afterwards. I leave his fate in your capable hands, but your mate must interrogate the little sod and find out who else is involved. We must discover the names of all of them. I mean all of them. They must be in key positions at Head Office. I want them all flushed out. No doubt your friend can get him to talk?"

Chris sneered as his head nodded up and down several times in quick succession. "No problem. He likes his work very much, does our Tiny. He always gets results. He's a nasty piece of work, you know, and I'm glad he's on our side, I can tell you."

David continued, "Now this part of the plan is the most important. You'll remember the Scandinavian riders gave me some money over the weekend? Well, I've arranged with the hotel manager for it to be held in their secure safe. Mr Rouen checked the envelopes with me and signed a receipt confirming there's 25,100 euros in one and 22,500 in the other. He knows Francois is collecting the money at ten-thirty when he drops off my locket to Sarah, the hotel receptionist. She'll then arrange for a courier to deliver it to my home in the UK. Okay so far?"

"Yes, but wouldn't you prefer me to collect it for you?" asked Chris quizzically. "It'll be much safer in my hands, surely."

"No thanks, Chris. You've got enough on your plate, leave that to me. I want you to follow Francois when he leaves the hotel with the cash. He'll definitely go to a bank to make sure the transfer has been made to his account and pay in some of the cash. But here's the rub. Hopefully, the greedy sod will steal some of the money from the two envelopes. That would be great. Whatever he does, though, we've got him and the police have been alerted to the sting and they can do the rest. I don't think he knows we're on to him, but he's a cunning old fox and we mustn't let him slip out of our grasp.

"Have I missed anything?"

"No, it seems straightforward to me," replied Chris, quietly mulling over the plan.

"There's only one flaw as I see it. Will Francois remember that I should be doing the Daredevil Challenge? I am going to send him a text reminding him that I can't leave the country without the heirloom and I've postponed the Daredevil Challenge until September. That should put him off the scent. I hope he believes me. I can't see why not. It's important, therefore, that you don't let Midge open his big mouth and tell Francois that I've left Garda. He'd smell a rat, do a runner and everything would be lost. Sorry to dump all this on you Chris, but I can't think of another way of doing it," David explained nervously. "It's imperative we expose all the criminals in the network, bring them all to book, otherwise the toe rags will only lie low and do it again in the future with some other unsuspecting organisation. We mustn't lose sight of that."

"It's not a problem, David. I've got as much invested in the Programme as you have. Over the years, we've built up an impressive network of influential, high-profile contacts across Europe. From boardrooms to government ministers, film directors to movie stars, sports personalities to TV celebrities, so there's no way I'm going to let a little French shit ruin everything I believe in and undermine what you and our dedicated colleagues have done for the last five years. It isn't a chore David, it's a privilege," replied Chris, with conviction.

David hadn't heard his chum talk with such enthusiasm before and was quite moved by his touching words of support. He was equally gratified to know he had a loyal lieutenant by his side who'd step up to the plate and do what was necessary. Finishing their drinks they shook hands, hugged each other warmly before going their separate ways, promising to keep in contact every step of the way. A few moments later, there was a soft, barely audible tap at the door. Francesca stood there, looking decidedly under par after her broken night's sleep, dressed in pale blue jeans, a cream cotton blouse and her customary flip-flops with long strands of unkempt black hair draped down her face and across her shoulders, crying out for a bit of urgent TLC.

Her tear-stained eyes, sullen cheeks and grey complexion spoke volumes. David was cold and business-like. Not wishing to show his true feelings, he got straight to the point, telling his uneasy visitor to keep out of sight for the next few hours, put as much distance as she could between her and the tattooed delinquent, suggesting things could turn out very nasty and she might be in the firing line. Francesca didn't say anything, she was too embarrassed to make eye contact after the previous evening's showdown let alone speak, but was reassured by his apparent concern for her welfare. It lifted her spirits, made her believe there was a way out of the unholy mess she'd got herself into. Speaking in a quiet whisper, she said, "I'm ever so sorry for what I've done. I'm very sorry." David was checking his phone, with his back turned, when she quickly slipped an envelope out of her back pocket and placed it on the lounge coffee table.

"I believe you," he replied, swinging round to face her. "Do as I say and you won't come to any harm. Now, off you go."

Standing there at the open door, not knowing how he might react, she moved forward tentatively and slung her long gangling arms around his neck. She kissed him on the cheek just as a pair of elderly white-haired guests sauntered past with eyebrows raised and saucy smiles, clutching a couple of rolled-up plastic macks, care of Primark – just in case.

In the meantime, David rested back in the quiet sanctuary of his top-floor suite as Francesca disappeared into a waiting lift rubbing her clammy hands together smiling anxiously. Flopping down on a wobbly balcony chair, being serenaded by *Mr Blue Sky* from the Cafe Lido below, he checked the arrangements for his long trek home. It's about 300 miles to Zurich and would take about six hours by taxi travelling on the Autostrada via Brescia and Milan and then north up the A2 to his final destination nestled at the top of the lake of the same name. That means I'll be there late afternoon, in time to catch the flight to Staverton. Good, that'll work fine, he decided.

After a couple of calls to finalise his plans, he sent a short text to Claire confirming some of the details. She replied with more gushing praise for Team 30's marvellous achievement on Sunday, saying the money was still pouring in thanks to their valiant efforts. The second part of her text was less serious, however, explaining that the live-in orang-utans, as she called them, were driving her mad. Their gruesome murder was very much on the cards, telling him to prepare for the shock of a heavily stained Wilton carpet on his return. David chuckled to himself, imagining the blood-curdling scene in the traditionally quiet, leafy suburbs of his adopted Cotswold town, the esteemed home of national hunt racing and famous the world over for its artistic festivals, and Regency architecture.

Chapter 44

Meanwhile in Hastings, Susan was slumped at the bottom of the stairs, clutching a damp handkerchief, sobbing and shaking with fear, glaring at the tear-stained screen, reading the text for the umpteenth time. She hadn't misread it, she was right. It was earth-shattering, her life had changed at the sound of an innocent ping that had winged its way from the shores of Lake Garda, over the snow-covered Alps, across the French countryside and into her secluded home in suburbia. She'd dreaded that day, hoped, prayed it would never happen, had had frequent sleepless nights and vivid nightmares as fear of the unknown gripped her, stalked her every step. Sometimes, it forced the forty-something to wonder, for the sake of her only child and her own sanity, which was cruelly tested, whether it was best to end it all. Call it a day.

At last, the rain stopped and the gales and storm-force winds abated as the dishevelled solicitor stood in the bay window, holding her soggy hanky, sniffing and coughing and wiping her bloodshot eyes. Susan was gratified to see the newly erected wooden border fences and fledgling trees were unscathed after their relentless battering from the deep low pressure that had swept across the southern counties, leaving a trail of widespread devastation in its wake.

Colonel Bogey made his presence felt and Susan shot out of the lounge, like a bullet out of a gun, opened the front door to be greeted by Lynn, her best friend and bridesmaid. The embrace was vicelike, pining her shocked visitor to the spot as she hugged Lynn's slender neck for all it was worth. After a few tense moments, her bewildered chum managed to disentangle herself from the tight clutches of her shy introverted friend, who was not known for her emotional outbursts.

"What the hell's the matter, what's wrong? Your phone message sounded serious. Sorry I was away last night, I only returned this morning. What's up? What the hell's happened?" Lynn yelled in fear and desperation.

"I don't know where to start," whispered Susan. "I've done a terrible thing. I don't know what to do. You don't know me very well, Lynn. You don't know me at all. I've got a terrible secret, I've kept it hidden for years and its now come to the surface and I don't know what to do. Oh God, what have I done? You'll hate me. I know you will. Oh God. Please help me."

"What are you talking about, Sue? You're not making any sense. I don't understand what you're saying. Are you unwell, do you want me to call a doctor?" asked her anxious friend, sliding her arm around her shoulder and brushing her damp untidy hair out of her tear-sodden eyes.

Susan sniffed, coughed and blew her nose which was bright red with bits of flaky skin around her nostrils. They looked very sore. A mop of unruly hair, badly chapped lips, chewed fingernails and a pale sullen complexion was the sight that greeted her friend on that damp dreary July morning. Susan slowly composed herself, snatched a glass of water off the hall table to soothe her dry, rasping throat before continuing.

"You see, I've known another man for a long time. It all started many years ago when I was much younger, very innocent and so was he. He was a client, you see, when I worked in Hastings and I foolishly seduced him when he was vulnerable and very innocent. I was so taken by his good looks and boyish charm and just couldn't help myself."

"A client," repeated Lynn, quizzically. "What do you mean, a client?"

"Watch out for bits of broken glass, I haven't had time to hoover them up yet," shouted Susan, kicking the front door shut with a resounding wallop.

Lynn was stunned, speechless and taking heed of her friend's warning, carefully guided Susan between the tiny glass fragments that led into the spacious modern kitchen at the rear of the house. Here the pair plonked themselves down on a couple of barstools, whilst the befuddled host poured them a glass of Merlot and carried on regaling her tale of woe.

"We were in love to begin with and spent hours in each other's company. We both enjoyed our time together, driven by raw sexual passion, which was quite overwhelming and unbelievable. I've not known passion like it since." Susan became excited, even animated reliving the memories of her illicit relationship at the hands of Mr

Lane. Lynn was traumatised, unable to move, sipping her wine on the wobbly barstool, trying to digest the enormity of her friend's salacious antics for which she was ill-prepared and especially at that unearthly hour of the day.

"But then things went downhill when I fell pregnant and our liaisons became less frequent and not so exciting, even though I was still madly in love with the guy. I still am. The pregnancy changed everything in more ways than one."

She blew her tender nose with a rough piece of kitchen paper roll and squirmed when it rubbed against her tender flaky skin.

"Pregnant!" gasped her agony aunt, trying her best to keep up with the unbelievable tale of middle-class decadence reminiscent of *Fifty Shades of Grey*, her current late-night read. "What do you mean pregnant? Louise is your pride and joy, the best thing that ever happened to you. A real ray of sunlight. Roger was overjoyed, I can tell you, when after all those torrid years of IVF, you became pregnant. He's always been a proud father. He'd do anything for his little Louise. You know that and so do I."

She peered into Susan's bleary eyes and swallowed a crunchy ginger nut in one mouthful and helped herself to another large glass of chilled Merlot, which disappeared as quickly as the savoury snack. Susan shrugged her shoulders, gazed into her empty wine glass, bit her lower lip and rested her sad forlorn face in the palms of her hands that shook uncontrollably on the kitchen table. The hot hussy gazed down at her sorry, battle-scarred reflection bouncing back at her only a few inches away and sobbed.

"You're not saying, no you're not, are you? You're not suggesting that Louise isn't Roger's daughter, are you?" Lynn shrieked at the top of her voice.

The silence was palpable. You could have heard a penny drop as Lynn's frayed nerves waited for a response. All you could hear was the kitchen clock ticking in the background and the sound of birds singing in the garden with the occasional drone as a vehicle trundled by. It seemed like hours, a lifetime, before her tired dejected friend plucked up courage and replied.

Susan glanced up and, biting her bottom lip nervously said, "Yes, I am, David Lane is her father, her proud father. The father of my child. What's more, he wants to meet his daughter this week for the first time. Have a little chat, get to know her, have some time together," she muttered sarcastically under her breath, hardly believing what she was saying, as a sinister sneer crawled over her face and a stream of tears trickled down to greet it.

Lynn was not sure what to say next, grabbing another biscuit from the barrel and shoving the whole thing into her mouth without even thinking. Table manners were the last thing on her mind. After all, she'd already drunk a couple of glasses of wine before ten o'clock in the morning so swallowing an innocent ginger nut in one piece was small beer in comparison. Lynn was trying to piece together the story quickly unfolding before her very eyes, while wondering, with some trepidation, what was coming next.

It was just unbelievable that her sweet, kind friend of many years who wouldn't say boo to a goose, rarely raised her voice in anger, could have done such a terrible thing, lived a life of lies and deceit for so long with the knowledge that one day, the truth would come out. She had to pinch herself to make sure she wasn't dreaming. Sadly, she wasn't. You only had to peer at the soulful wretch perched beside her to know that Susan's life was in absolute turmoil and Louise's big birthday bash had just taken a turn for the worse. Lynn reached across the table, picked up Susan's phone rather shakily and slowly scrolled down the text messages until the name David Lane appeared on the small finger-marked screen. There were several.

It read. "Hi Suzy, I'm in Garda for the big ride this weekend. Enjoyed our time together as always. I know we agreed that I wouldn't meet Louise yet, but as she's eighteen next week, I think it's only fair that, as her father, we get to know each other. I'll be in touch about the arrangements and will be travelling home via Zurich on Monday evening after paying my respects to the special ones. Glad you've brought the oily rag up to speed. See you and my daughter soon. Love, David."

Lynn couldn't believe what she'd read. She reached out, unsure what to do next, grabbed Susan's arm and tried to raise a smile. She was a tough resilient saleswoman, used to handling herself in a crisis, able to give as good as she got, but this was a different ball game altogether. It even had her reeling on the ropes, trying to think of a solution, a way out of the mess.

"Is he for real, this guy? Does he know the damage he'll cause you and Louise? He must be mad. What the heck is he trying to do? Don't worry, we'll think of something. I'm sure he won't go through with his threat, will he?"

"Yes, he will," snapped Susan. "You don't know him. He's very determined, extremely wealthy and capable of anything. He always gets what he wants. I have dreaded this day for years. I always knew he would come for his daughter and then my life, my marriage, would be totally destroyed."

She slumped across the badly smudged glass kitchen table, grabbed a couple of paper hankies and wiped her damp red beacon for the umpteenth time wondering what to do.

"I'll ring him, get the nasty swine to see sense," said Lynn, trying to comfort her distraught friend more in hope than expectation.

"No, you can't," snapped Susan. "You don't know him and the danger he presents. He wields enormous power, is well connected and will do anything to meet his daughter. The very people who could have influenced him, got him to see sense are now long gone. I'm on my own and I deserve whatever the gods decree. It's my fault, Lynn. I was very stupid. I corrupted a young man when he was vulnerable and quite innocent and I shall now have to face the music."

"Where's Roger?" queried Lynn, quickly changing the subject and looking around with a frantic expression glued to her face. "Does he know? He'll go mad when you tell him. Oh my God, what have you done?"

Susan slid off the stool and leaned on the kitchen table for support and said, "Roger knows. I told him yesterday evening when the first text came through. I said David's a wealthy man who seduced me when I was young, when I didn't know what I was doing. That he's blackmailed me over Louise ever since. In my blind panic, I even said he was visiting his parents at the St Rouen Cemetery in Zurich before flying home to Staverton following the Garda Challenge.

"I was stupid, I know, but I had to tell him something otherwise he'd have killed me, I'm sure of that. He shook me by the throat at one point and looked and sounded evil. I really feared for my life. He went mad. Shouting, swearing, throwing plates and cups everywhere. He thumped the walls with his bare fists, smashed the conservatory glass with a heavy chrome kitchen stool and ripped the new curtains and sashes off their wooden rails. I've never seen him like that before; it frightened me to death, I can tell you. I thought he was going to have a heart attack, as he charged around from room to room like a deranged lunatic. At one point, he pushed me to the ground, he's never done that before, then raced upstairs, banged and crashed around. I took refuge in the kitchen before he raced out of the front door, kicked my potted plants everywhere and drove off at breakneck speed. The disturbance was so bad that the nosy bat in number seven came across to make sure I was okay. He took an overnight bag and a pile of cash out of the safe and I haven't heard from him since."

Susan was nursing a thumping headache when she flung a handful of wet, soggy tissues into the chrome bin, perched next to the hot dishwasher, that had just completed its economy cycle.

"I wish my life was as simple as that," she said to herself. "You cram all your problems into a blessed machine, spin them all around for an hour or so and, at the end of the programme, hay presto, you pop out looking sparkling white, ready for another day.

"I don't feel too good, I'm going upstairs for a lie down. Please see yourself out, Lynn. Thanks for coming around at this unearthly time. You're a real friend. I'll call you later," said Susan.

The bedraggled solicitor staggered up the wobbly staircase that seemed to sway of its own accord. Feeling drunk, very drunk with her head threatening to explode and her stomach churning round and round, she gave a cursory wave to her agony aunt from the first-floor landing before snuggling down under her crumpled duvet, fully clothed. Dosing off to sleep under the soporific influence of Mr Merlot, she hoped the father of her daughter would return to the UK unscathed and that Roger would one day forgive her for her infidelity, and their lives would return to some resemblance of normality.

Chapter 45

Love is in the Air, by the legendary John Paul Young was ringing out around the bay thanks to the musically inclined Lido Garda Beach Cafe, when David's phone rang in the lounge. He knew who it was. David slid the balcony door shut and sadly JP's dulcet harmonies were no more. In contrast to the soft mellow crooning of the Scottish-born Australian singer, his ears were suddenly subjected to the bellowing voice of Garda's tattooed tearaway. He ranted on about the alleged rape, threatening to contact the police unless David did exactly what he was told. Unsurprisingly, the reprobate had a number of social misfits in his pocket who were more than happy to testify to David's vicious attack on his girlfriend. Raising the ante a few notches more, the callous simpleton said he'd rearrange Francesca's pretty face, with the aid of a blunt carving knife, if the millionaire tried any funny business. David was told to meet the blackmailer immediately outside the bureau de change to carry out the transfer of 200,000 euros. If he failed to comply with the thug's instructions, he'd alert the authorities to his crime and it would be curtains for the posh prick, as he called him. Trying to wrestle back the initiative, David explained he needed more time to organise such a large sum of money, particularly as he was outside the UK and he'd have to go through a myriad of security checks.

After much arguing and shouting, punctuated by a number of choice Italian expletives, the belligerent yob agreed to meet David at nine forty-five a.m.

"I shall be watching your hotel, making sure you don't sneak off. I can make life very difficult for you, Lane, so don't try being a smart arse," he yelled into the mouthpiece. Feeling pleased with himself for putting the posh prick in his place and making David Lane sing to his tune, Midge rested back with a confident sigh under the expansive awning of a lakeside tapas bar. His French mentor then patted him firmly on the back and handed him a fresh bottle of Peroni, as a reward, with the promise of much more to come.

David took the hotel lift down to reception where he settled his bill, ordered a taxi and reminded Sarah that Francois would be delivering a valuable item of jewellery at ten o'clock. In return, she was to hand him both sealed envelopes full of cash and ask the Frenchman to sign for them. That was very important. The thirty-year-old brunette with pale green eyes, a curvy slim figure and beautifully manicured fingernails would tell Francois of David's relief at hearing of his locket's safe return and he would be collecting the heirloom later in the morning. Sultry Sarah would text David once the jewellery was in her possession. A crisp 100-euro note was placed in her thin, shapely hand to seal the deal.

The playboy appeared reasonably composed running back up the stairs, two at a time, to collect his belongings and finish off his packing. He unzipped a suitcase lying on the king-size bed and removed the Stewart Davidson passport from the inside sleeve and gazed at the mugshot. This was the tricky bit; it called for a steady hand and an equally steady eye. He had to get this right, he knew that, but as he'd rehearsed the procedure several times before, he felt pretty confident he could pull it off and take on the convincing role of Mr Davidson.

So a dark grey wig was removed from its soft paper wrapping inside a small square cardboard box. He placed it carefully on his head, adjusted it slightly and then gently combed the top and sides of the relatively short-cropped hair, so it clung to his head, feeling and looking pretty natural. Staring in the hall mirror, he then smoothed the hair down with his slightly damp fingers, but allowing one or two loose strands to stick out around his ears, making it appear more real, more authentic. After a few fine touches the imposter nodded his head approvingly hoping, with fingers well and truly crossed, that his new identity would outwit even the shrewdest observer. Matching false eyebrows were then slowly slipped into position. This was a more intricate task to perform and after a few painstaking moments, with a pair of tweezers and a steady hand, the bushy grey hair was fixed in place. The next stage wasn't any easier when a thin beard was slowly attached to his face from the jawline to the tops of his ears. It was executed with intricate precision, just like a surgeon performing a delicate procedure. David's smooth deeply tanned contours disappeared behind a thin veneer of short bristly hair as he gently applied pressure to the beard so that the sticky backing strip gripped his skin firmly. A dark grey moustache was delicately removed from its paper wrapping and was the final piece in the impersonator's jigsaw. The cunning masquerade was nearly complete and very soon he would be ready to enter the fray. Next, thin layers of special artistic make-up were carefully applied to his exposed skin making him appear older, quite dour and as ordinary as possible. He didn't want to stand out in a crowd, attract unwarranted attention, knowing he had to have his wits about him and be alert at all times if he was to avoid detection on his trek north.

The ornate full-length mirror was the first to catch a glimpse of Mr D in all his glory, standing in his dark shiny trousers, white long-sleeved shirt, rather worn beige linen jacket and a pair of scruffy black shoes that were crying out for a clean and polish. David gazed at his reflection and, after a bit more tinkering to his facial hair and wig, stood back and admired his work. He was the spitting image of his passport photograph and that was all that mattered. But for reasons best known to David, he'd dramatically exceeded the remit for the Daredevil Challenge.

The stage was now set as the curtain rose for the elderly thespian. All he had to do was play his part, deliver his lines without wavering, impress the audiences at his many impromptu auditions while meandering his way back home. To satisfy the whims of his mischievous sponsors, he took a couple of selfies in front of the gold-plated clock hanging on the wall in the adjoining kitchen. The sixty-four-year-old bachelor, with a slight limp and appearing a little rough around the edges was at odds with the handsome, man about town that he'd consigned to history, for the time being anyway.

David Lane was nowhere to be seen. Stewart Davidson was his elderly replacement; the new kid on the block, charged with completing the Daredevil Challenge and claiming the £50,000 booty for the hardworking ME Association. The imposter grabbed hold of his luggage, checked the drawers and cupboards for the last time and gave a final cursory glance around the suite, making sure he hadn't forgotten anything. It was then he noticed a red envelope on the coffee table addressed to him. He picked it up and zipped it inside a pocket of one of his suitcases. With a degree of trepidation, like a fledgling actor walking the boards for the first time, he climbed into the vacant lift, strolled casually along the ground-floor corridor where he waved and smiled to a couple of familiar guests, who thankfully walked past, ignoring him completely.

To his relief, Sarah also blanked him as he sauntered towards the busy reception desk between the automatic glass doors that quickly swished open in their eagerness to guide him on his way. David stood outside in a car parking bay with his two suitcases and one small piece of hand luggage, resting at his feet, accompanied by the humming sound of nearby traffic with a tantalising glimpse of the famous blue lake glistening through a line of conifer trees.

So far so good, he thought. In the corner of his eye, through the reflection in the double glass doors, he caught a glimpse of a scruffy youth emblazoned in tattoos, leaning against a wall with a phone glued tightly to his ear. David's presence didn't alarm his adversary at all. At one point, Midge gawped open-mouthed in his direction on hearing the hotel's glass doors sliding open, but seeing nothing untoward carried on with his mindless jabbering. Studying the view for the last time, David was gratified to hear the reassuring sound of a Mercedes reversing up the steep gradient. Gregor, his taxi driver, jumped out from behind the wheel like a coiled spring, grabbed his luggage and slid it into the cavernous boot of his top of the range E-class motor. Resting back in the soft sumptuous leather, David caught the final bars of a legendary Beatles chart topping hit on the car radio. *All You Need is Love* brought fond memories to the surface, reminding him of his teenage years in Hastings; the luxurious Imperial Hotel, the Crawfords, who did so much for him when his life was at a low ebb, and how could he forget his initiation into raunchy sex and the breathless world of *Kama Sutra*, thanks to his mistress' insatiable sexual appetite?

"Stop the car," cried David as their quiet limousine glided effortlessly down the hill into Garda. "I want to have a final look around the place before going home."

Here bustling crowds of enthusiastic holidaymakers queued with ferry tickets in hand, waiting to be whisked away to their dream locations nestling on the shores of the beautiful unspoilt lake. La Rocca's white towering cliff face stood proudly on the headland shining down on Garda's attractive waterfront and sweeping shoreline stretching as far as the eye could see. Seeming bluer than ever, the awe-inspiring lake lay still and calm as shards of light darted freely across its unruffled surface.

Nearby was his old friend *Andromeda*, dressed in her bright white livery, looking majestic and serene as she moved effortlessly from her moorings and headed south towards Bardolino with her cargo of expectant tourists on board. Glancing around, David noticed with pride and some humility the many banners and colourful posters draped along the promenade proclaiming their undying support for the ME cause, reminding him of the tumultuous events the day before.

"I need five minutes so please stop here," said David, pointing to a vacant parking bay. Feeling confident with his disguise, even though Francois and his cohorts could be on the prowl, he quickly jumped out of the car. He'd already fooled umpteen people at the hotel and Gregor, who'd driven him on numerous occasions before, didn't have the faintest idea who he was. A manic scene greeted him as crowds of happy faces chatted and laughed, while sipping cool drinks and tucking into mouth-watering ice creams. For the next few minutes, he strolled up and down the waterfront, trying to see if Francesca was around anywhere. At one point, he thought he saw her browsing through some leather handbags hanging from a rotating metal frame outside a flashy designer shop, but the girl's rotund boyfriend, with several chins to his name, wasn't too pleased when David grabbed his girlfriend's bare arm and spun her around. The elderly gent apologised for his mistake, but the bulging blubber wasn't happy and kept looking back over his shoulder at David as he slowly sauntered away from the scene of the altercation. In the meantime, Gregor was waiting by his pride and joy with the diesel engine running when David, looking downcast, strolled into view. A hairy outstretched arm, holding a chilled bottle of Evian water greeted the wonderer after his futile walkabout. David smiled and grabbed it with both hands.

"Thank you, my friend, just what I need," said David. After a quick slurp, he jumped up onto a nearby concrete bench to survey the hectic scene, just like an inquisitive policeman on point duty watching the comings and goings of the people in his gaze. But it was hopeless, a complete waste of time and, feeling a little disconsolate, turned to his cheery-faced companion and said, "Right, home James. Let's be off." The Romanian cabby didn't understand what he meant, his English wasn't that good, but as his passenger slipped into the rear seat and checked his passport for the return journey, he quickly caught on. Moments later, the sleek silver machine sped south, towards the base of the lake. Driving towards the picturesque town of Lazise, he pictured in his mind the Ristorante Alla Grotta, a prominent landmark and most certainly a familiar background feature on many holiday snaps with its striking red-painted walls and bold white characters depicting the name of the lakeside restaurant.

All of a sudden, Beethoven's Fifth chimed out and hoping it was PW, David answered the call in a flash. To his surprise, it was Andrea, a new member of the support team who, after some brief pleasantries, said she had some bad news about Gary.

Sounding upset Andrea said, "Apparently, Gary returned to his hotel suite late Sunday afternoon complaining of feeling unwell and suffering from intermittent chest pains. But after a lie-down, he felt better and later on that evening he had a few drinks in the Riviera bar, where he chatted to a group of cycling enthusiasts before joining forces, later in the evening, with a bunch of journalists to watch the World Cup final in a local Cantonese restaurant." Andrea sniffed, blew her nose loudly and then continued, "Sadly, things went badly wrong during the night. At about two o'clock, Gary called reception, saying he was suffering from severe chest pains and wanted a doctor urgently. The young inexperienced receptionist had a hard job hearing his muffled voice over the constant whirring of the air-conditioning and her English wasn't too hot either, which didn't help. Anyway, after repeating his request a couple of times, she got the gist and Dr Veneto was summoned.

"When the GP entered the dimly lit room, with the anxious night duty receptionist holding onto his arm, they didn't know what to expect, but they soon discovered Gary lying in bed, dead to the world. I understand it was a heart attack," explained Andrea blowing her nose yet again.

David was shocked by the tragic news, offered his condolences and thanked Andrea for the call. "I'll call his wife on my return. I'm busy on other things at the moment so could you please ring the chairman straightaway? I can't use the mobile for long-distance calls as I keep losing the damn connection. Tell him what's happened, he'll want to talk to his wife to see what we can do to help. It's all very sad," David said disconsolately.

Meanwhile Gregor was listening to the car radio, humming along to a familiar Italian aria, not listening to their conversation; that was until his elderly passenger ended the call by saying he was on his way to the bureau de change in Garda and would text her later in the morning for an update.

Garda's prize-winning cabby peered inquisitively into the driver's mirror and, with a broad frown, looked straight at the OAP for an explanation. After all, Gregor had been booked to drive him to Zurich, or so he thought, and they were currently heading south towards Sirmione at the foot of the lake, in the opposite direction to Garda. Had his pregnant wife got the wrong end of the stick when the contract was agreed earlier in the day? He began to wonder. Seeing his driver's fraught expression, David explained that Andrea was a young attractive female guest he met at the hotel, who'd become a bit clingy and he wanted to put some distance between them, not get entangled in a serious relationship. Hence the little white lie. The affable cheeky faced driver accepted his off-the-cuff explanation and nodded with a saucy smirk. But then to David's surprise, the randy Romanian performed a number of frenetic gestures with his arms and fists, grunted several times with a pronounced grin and, for some reason, grabbed his crotch and yelled out a number of Italian expletives as a finale to his salaciously animated performance. I think he's got the drift, thought David, lounging back in the soft sumptuous leather, savouring the splendid views for the last time, wondering when the heck he'd hear some news from PW.

Chapter 46

As planned Chris and his friend followed their tattooed target into town after spotting the idiot lurking around near the Excelsior Hotel. Looking pleased with himself, no doubt planning how he'd spend his ill-gotten gains, Midge took a short cut down a narrow winding pathway towards the bureau de change. This was his undoing. To his surprise, PW and Tiny sneaked up behind him, grabbed an arm each and frogmarched the scruffy little irk towards a secluded concrete bench overlooking the bay and in the shade of some low-lying branches. It was the last thing the tattooed yob expected. The sight of PW's notoriously well-known friend made him quake in his flip-flops, wishing he was anywhere on earth, anywhere at all, rather than in the company of the mafia's number one hit man whose reputation went way before him. The mobster with the deadpan eyes rarely smiled, rarely showed any emotion at all. The only time you saw his glistening top set was when his taught muscular arms rippled and rolled and his huge bulging fists, the size of saucepan lids, were clenched ready for the fray. Tiny was well over six feet tall, boasting a wide bulging neck that never seemed to end, massive chunky shoulders like a heavyweight boxer, with legs the size of tree trunks and a couple of nasty scars stretching down both cheeks as trophies from previous conflicts.

Unless you had a death wish, Tiny's the last person you'd mess with. His name alone was synonymous with death and despair as the most hardened of criminals would quake in their boots, regret with everything that's holy that their paths ever crossed. So the outlook wasn't good for the miscreant; the cards were heavily stacked against him. Faced with such hopeless odds, Midge had little choice but to comply with the demands of his assailants, hoping his acquiescence would at least guarantee his survival. Subservience was his only hope. PW plonked his laptop down onto Midge's lap and the quivering wreck, fearing for his life, retrieved a scrappy piece of paper from the pocket of his grubby jeans and, after pressing several keys, the money transfer to a numbered account was complete. Still shaking and praying for a miracle, Midge called his boss to confirm the transaction.

In stark contrast to his beleaguered colleague, Francois whooped and cheered in celebration knowing he'd conned David Lane out of a cool 200,000 euros and it was nigh on impossible for anyone to trace it back to him. Midge's reward for his compliance was simple. Tiny and two of his equally unsavoury mates strung him upside down from the top of a thirty-foot tree leaving him dangling precariously by his legs, with masking tape stuck over his mouth and a black hood tied loosely around his head. Twisting, wriggling and gasping for air, the felon was left waiting for the local police to cut him down after being tipped off about his predicament by a melee of concerned onlookers armed with cameras and smartphones.

But once the carabinieri realised the aerial contortionist was none other than Midge, the well-known village idiot, the peacemakers weren't in too much of a hurry to turn the buffoon the right way up. They decided to let him hang loose for half an hour or so before rushing to his aid. Midge, for his part, didn't realise how close he'd come to meeting his maker that day as Tiny had preferred the concrete waistcoat in the middle of the lake for his final resting place, but eventually succumbed to PW's request and employed a less gruesome punishment as retribution for the idiot's thievery.

After what seemed an eternity, the call came. PW's dulcet tones were a welcome sound for the anxious traveller quietly listening to Handel's *Arrival of the Queen of Sheba* on the car radio accompanied by the swaying torso of his friendly driver clearly captivated by the maestro's musical masterpiece.

"Hi," said PW. "We got Midge to do the transfer to Francois' account so we've got sufficient evidence to link him to the blackmail. Tiny did a number on him, but sadly Midge doesn't know who else is involved and he's now entertaining the holidaymakers on the prom."

Kicking the back of the passenger seat with excitement, he cried, "Well done, Chris! That's fantastic. We've got something on him at last. Pity he can't help with any names, though. But where is Francois now?" asked David impatiently.

"We caught up with him at the Excelsior Hotel where he dropped off your locket and collected the two bundles of cash from Sarah," replied Chris.

"Thanks," said David impatiently. "That's good. Go on, go on."

"But then it was sod's law. A bloody fire alarm went off and all the hotel guests swarmed out of the building and fire engines arrived on the scene with a couple of ambulances. In the confusion that followed, Francois somehow sneaked away and I'm off into town now to try and find him."

"What?" yelled David. "How the hell did you lose him? All you had to do was follow him. Oh God, do I have to do everything? For heaven's sake, Chris, stop pissing about, find him and find him quickly," shouted David at the top of his voice while repeatedly smacking the back of the car seat with his fists and then thumping the passenger door for good measure. Frightened that his irritable highly-strung customer might turn his firepower on him, the anxious cabby slowly slouched down in his seat out of harm's way.

"The damned fire alarm was out of the blue. How could I have planned for that?" cried Chris defensively. "I'm sure the blasted frog had something to do with it. You can bet your bottom dollar. If you don't like it, why the hell don't you sort it out yourself rather than poncing about in drag like a big girl's blouse?

"Don't shout at me David, I'm doing my best here so get off my back," ranted Chris, feeling aggrieved by his partner's vitriolic attack.

"Well, it isn't good enough. Stop messing about, go and find him. He'll be on his way to a bank to pay the cash in and check the transfer, you can bet on that. Just go and find the sod and catch him in the act," retorted David, slamming the phone down. In his anger, he smacked the back of the front seat with so much force that it sent Gregor's packed lunch, of freshly cut sandwiches and two cherry-flavoured yogurts, flying through the air before disappearing out of sight into the deep recesses of the car's floor well. The rueful Romanian was having serious doubts about the sanity of his fellow traveller sitting just inches away, especially as one of his eyebrows appeared to be sticking up at the edge, just above his right eye. One minute the OAP was inconsolable, shouting and hollering in the back seat as though the world had come to an end, then the next he was peddling a far-fetched story about evading the clutches of a young woman, which judging by his downtrodden appearance seemed highly unlikely. Then, without warning, the lunatic was laughing and joking as though he'd won the lottery, but only moments later was ranting and raving again like a demented idiot, taking great chunks out of his precious leather interior, while making damn sure the hard working taxi driver would have to make other arrangements for his midday meal.

Chapter 47

On that sun-kissed morning in mid-July, as the intrepid duo were knocking nine bells out of each other, fate intervened in a mysterious way. Just below the hotel, off the main road into Garda, there's a steep stone pathway leading down to the lakeside quay. This is a much-favoured route for tourists, locals and late-night revellers. But a word of caution: this short cut had its pitfalls and had been the scene of much carnage over the summer months as many visitors could testify with nasty bruises, twisted ankles and broken bones to their name. The brief shower early that morning added to the risk of injury, making the smooth stone surface very slippery and quite treacherous for the unwary. According to an eyewitness, Francois lost his footing on the top step, tripped and fell headfirst down the steep shaded pathway, careering into the prickly thorns and stinging nettles bordering the precarious route, before crashing to the ground in a crumpled heap at the foot of the unforgiving concrete staircase. This was bad news for the Frenchman who'd hoped to play a low profile, keep well under the radar and not alert anyone to his whereabouts. His clumsy misfortune was made worse when a group of elderly holidaymakers, on a scenic coach trip from the UK, recognised him from the day before and rushed to his aid with much urgency and fuss.

After all, he was the smart, well-dressed Frenchman sounding like Sasha Distel, their sixties heart-throb. He'd organised the exciting cycle ride twenty-four hours earlier, when handsome hunky young men in tight-fitting outfits flaunted about by the ferry point, so the very least they could do was summon urgent medical assistance with as much haste as their arthritic limbs could muster. Struggling to his feet and brushing aside all offers of help, the ill-tempered thief limped off towards the town centre dragging his battered suitcase behind him. His filthy dirt-splattered knees hurt like hell having taken the full impact of the fall. His face hadn't faired much better either, plastered in mud and grime with some nasty deep cuts and scratches. Shaken by his ordeal, he knelt down by the awning of an ice-cream parlour where the chatty shop assistant was scooping great dollops into wafer-thin cones before handing her sauce-laden creations to eager-eyed youngsters busily licking their lips in anticipation. Surveying the scene like a wild animal stalking its prey, he decided to move along the quay, keeping very low, before crouching down against an uneven red-brick wall to get his breath back and take stock. At one point, he thought the coast was clear, no one was following, but his instinct told him otherwise so he didn't budge for several minutes, watching out for anything unusual, anything out of the norm. The paranoiac Parisian wasn't taking any chances, he'd got too much to lose so caution was very much his byword.

Okay, his stupid ham-fisted accident was a bit of a hiccup, but he knew he could outwit the authorities even if Midge got apprehended, and with the unexpected bonus of several thousand euros thanks to the witless silver spoons, things had come together quite well. Unfortunately for him, his battered body ached with every movement, with every painful step, but the charlatan had to keep moving if he was to catch his afternoon flight and get to Berlin in one piece. As a safeguard, his passport and airline ticket were under an assumed name and by the time the police worked it out, he'd be long gone. The much-vaunted Austrian ride in September was always a smokescreen, having decided earlier in the year that the Italian jaunt was his last throw of the dice. He knew the strong arm of the law was closing in and his days were numbered so the blackmail idea was his swansong, his parting gift to a pampered playboy. His soppy accomplices wouldn't see a penny of it. No one could link him to Midge, he'd made sure of that and Alison was too dim to catch on and anyway she'd served her purpose, she was dispensable. Team 30 didn't know what was going on under their very noses, they were too concerned with their latest conquests, or the design of their new limited edition supercars to pay much attention to him, or so he thought.

It was the time to bid farewell, sign off and start up again somewhere else, swop his subservient existence to a bunch of privileged egotists for the good life so easily taken for granted by the attention-seekers who he envied and despised in equal amounts. Francois knew with all the talk of fraud and corruption surrounding the Programme, as highlighted in the auditor's report, that he was beyond suspicion, was never in the frame. Nevertheless, the cautious conman didn't take any chances and had covered his back as much as possible. The fire alarm was an unexpected windfall, allowing him to sneak through the hotel grounds, climb over the perimeter wall and drop on to the adjacent main road. It was going well, very well indeed until his stupid mishap on the soggy concrete staircase.

Breaking cover, seeing nothing suspicious, he limped towards the bank, ignoring the excruciating pain across his shoulders and lower back. For some strange reason, a crowd of animated holidaymakers were busily peering up into the leaves of a large overhanging tree, pointing at something swinging from the upper branches close to the water's edge.

Feeling uneasy on his pins and very hot and sticky, Francois decided to leave the silly tourists to their childish pranks and aim for the bank with its promise of rich pickings and a new life in the fast lane, thanks to the generosity of Mr Lane and his cycling simpletons.

Concerned onlookers continued to report Midge's plight to the police, who were well versed in the 'dope on a rope' punishment meted out by the mafia and would release the infidel in their own time, whereupon he'd be charged with disturbing the peace and sentenced to a few hours community service. The outlook for Midge wasn't good. His long-term chances of survival were greatly reduced when the leading lights in the underworld discovered that the village idiot was involved in a plot to steal money from the ME coffers, a charity which they supported because one of their number had suffered from the debilitating illness for many years and they'd witnessed first-hand the damage it could do.

However, in all this confusion there was a silver lining for a solitary member of the crowd sat quietly savouring every moment of the bully's discomfort, buoyed by his misery and misfortune. Leaning on her arm and sucking a bright red cherry on a stick, she watched his frantic wriggling and writhing, witnessing the animated overhead display from her exclusive front row vantage point, as the cool summer air softly caressed her suntanned cheeks and long strands of flowing black hair.

Such was her sense of elation at her newfound freedom, she sent a text message to Sarah, at the Excelsior Hotel, asking her to thank David for erasing Midge from her life and asking, yet again, for his forgiveness.

A few moments later, still walking on cloud nine, she had a bit of a scare when a familiar face appeared on the horizon, looking agitated and uncommonly scruffy with great blobs of dirt and muck stuck to his light-coloured trousers and soiled shirt. He was bent down with his hand over his mouth, hugging the edge of the harbour front, clearly not wishing to attract any attention. Her pink chiffon scarf, floppy hat and dark sunglasses did the trick, offering a quick impromptu disguise from the Frenchman's wandering gaze. Undeterred, she continued reading *La Figaro* occasionally peeping over the broadsheet to savour Midge's agony as the energetic contortionist swung about from side to side between the branches of the tall leaf-laden tree accompanied by the sound of seagulls squawking in protest at his unwelcome presence in their territorial domain. "I'll call the police. Leave it to me," she called out to an anxious bystander clearly worried about Midge's predicament and in earshot of other concerned busybodies who were soon put at ease by her reassuring Italian accent and confident manner.

Francesca was convinced that the hooded man wriggled even more when he recognised her voice a mere thirty feet below. When a group of well-fed Americans sidled up to her with bulging stomachs and several chins to match, she explained that Midge was a renowned circus performer, took his training very seriously, often perfecting his stomach-churning high-wire act on a Monday morning away from the bright lights and crowds of adoring fans. Some were so taken in by Francesca's little ruse that they asked about tickets for his next matinee, whether they could book on-line and were the seagulls part of his daredevil act? With a beaming smile and a confident swish of her long black hair, Garda's hidden gem gazed skyward, took a deep breath, sipped the last remnants of her drink, threw her crumpled broadsheet newspaper into a nearby refuse bin and quietly slipped away, leaving her ex-boyfriend wrestling with his conscience.

Chapter 48

The bank was deserted when the dishevelled Frenchman plonked himself down behind a creaky wooden desk, wiped his brow with his silk handkerchief and reached for his phone. There was a short delay as he tried impatiently to get a signal, but eventually his luck was in and a sinister smirk appeared on his face when the tiny finger-marked screen confirmed his pension pot had just had a hefty top up. The fraudster glanced out of the window, still on his guard, all the time checking for anything unusual. After a few moments' careful surveillance, he was gratified to see nothing untoward; nothing out of the ordinary just the customary throng of boisterous holidaymakers milling about in the foreground lapping up the pleasant early morning sun. Feeling dirty, hot and uncomfortable, he shoved his smartphone back into his ripped trouser pocket and opened his badly battered suitcase that was covered in bits of grass and muck. On the top were two envelopes bulging with cash that Francois had collected earlier from the Excelsior Hotel when he delivered David's gold locket to Sarah for safekeeping. According to the yellow chits stuck on the outside, there was 25,100 euros in one envelope and 22,500 euros in the other.

Francois sniggered to himself when he read the white Post-it note stuck on the outside of one of the pristine white envelopes. It read. 'Please check the amounts and pay the money in as normal. Thanks as ever, David Lane.' "What a prat, what a bloody idiot," he mumbled under his breath, shaking his head from side to side. Moving over to the till, he ripped open an envelope and plonked the neat bundles of cash, secured by a series of elastic bands, onto the highly polished counter. According to the chit there was 22,500 euros and, not wishing to waste time checking the amount, he reached into his rear trouser pocket and took out a folded paying-in slip for the Pedal Power Committee which he duly completed in his capacity as communications director. A shy young girl with fair skin, auburn hair and large circular-framed reading glasses glanced up from behind the reinforced glass panel, closed her Mills & Boon paperback and smiled as he stood there nervously clutching the piece of paper.

"Good morning, sir," she said in a quiet whisper. "May I ask if you're all right as you appear to have had an accident. I hope you're not seriously hurt. Do you need anything?"

"No I'm okay, thanks. I fell down some stairs. I've taken a bit of a pasting, but I shall be okay once I've had a shower and a change of clothes."

"I hope you'll feel better soon," she replied sympathetically. "Anyway, how can I help you, sir?"

"I want to pay this into our company account please," replied Francois, carefully dropping the cash and the paying-in slip into the open tray. Mia grabbed the bundles, removed the elastic bands and placed the crisp new euro notes into the automatic counting machine in blocks of about a thousand at a time. Still on his guard, he peered around the small branch office with its dark-coloured wooden floor, that creaked underfoot, while a series of framed coloured prints of local landmarks hung indiscriminately on the panelled walls and a noisy air-conditioning unit rattled incessantly in the background. A rather gaudy rectangular clock hung in the corner of the room behind the two cashiers' tills, ticking very loudly and making a thumping sound every time the minute hand jumped forward. Gazing around, making sure no one was looking, he shoved the second envelope under his clothes in the bottom of the suitcase. For some reason, when turning the key in the lock, he felt strangely uncomfortable, ill at ease and very anxious to be on his way. After all, Berlin was beckoning from afar and he was eager to rekindle his relationship with the vibrant fun-loving city and begin the next exciting chapter in his life. Over the years his scurrilous activities had netted the fraudster a small fortune and he now planned to enjoy the benefits of his ill-gotten gains in a fit of uninhibited extravagance. Perhaps splash out on a dream home in some far-off haven or buy a brand new top of the range prancing horse, or he might even indulge his passion for the sea and buy a luxury multi-million pound motor launch with all the latest fancy gizmos. Needless to say, the choices were endless.

After a few tense moments, Mia peered at her computer screen and said, "It's a hot day today, sir. Thank heavens for the air-conditioning. I don't know what I'd do without it. Right, I'm nearly there. Can you please confirm Mr Dijon that the amount you're paying in is 22,500 euros?"

"Yes," he replied abruptly, flicking some bits of dirt from underneath his black fingernails. "How long is this going to take? I've a flight to catch," he snapped, frantically brushing some of the grime and mess off his handmade trousers and soiled designer shirt.

"Not long now, sir. I just need to make doubly sure as it's a large amount of cash you're paying into the company account. We don't want any mistakes, do we? I can then stamp your receipt and you can be on your way," Mia replied with a forced smile followed by a quick glance over her shoulder at the clock ticking loudly behind her.

"Doesn't that blasted ticking get on your nerves? It would drive me mad."

"No sir, not at all. I like to keep an eye on the time and it's particularly important today with so much going on."

Sat quietly, by an adjacent window, was an attractive young woman with soft unblemished skin and beautiful manicured fingernails. Her hair was tied in a neat bun and she was dressed in a white chiffon top, red pleated skirt and plain sandals. With an air of authority, she turned to face him as he leaned nervously against the counter waiting for his receipt, drumming his dirty soiled fingers impatiently on the polished mahogany surface.

"Excuse me. Did you enjoy the event yesterday?" she asked as Francois shuffled uncomfortably from one leg to the other, looking irritated and edgy and trying to ignore the stranger's unwelcome overtures.

"Yes," he snapped, quickly glancing over his shoulder, taking care not to catch her eye and enter into idle gossip with the local busybody. But then he wondered how she'd entered the branch without him noticing. There was only one entrance to the premises. He felt sure the squeaky, slightly warped solid green door had remained firmly shut, but then decided she must have entered the building when he was in conversation with Mia and the swishing sound of the euro notes passing through the counting machine, coupled with the din from the blasted air-conditioning unit, must have drowned out the sound of the creaky door.

The stranger, sensing his discomfort, slowly moved towards him and said in a soft engaging whisper. "Those brave young men did something rather special yesterday. They helped people who they'll never meet and showed what can be done if you're really determined to make a difference."

Turning to face her, he said. "Look I don't wish to be rude, but I'm in a hurry. I've got a plane to catch. I'm not really interested in the goings on of a bunch of high-rollers who've never worked a day in their lives, are on some kind of self-centred ego trip and pander to the limelight in every possible way. Those glory hunters spend a fortune on themselves, don't give a damn about others. They're all a bunch of dilettantes, in it for themselves," barked Francois irritated by her feckless ill-informed comments.

Ignoring his supercilious rebuttal, she carried on. "Those brave riders did something really special yesterday and didn't ask for any reward, no reward at all. They could have stayed at home enjoying themselves without a worry in the world, like so many of their wealthy contempories. But they chose not to. Instead, they did something really worthwhile. I believe you can achieve anything in life, anything at all, if you really put your mind to it."

Francois was becoming increasingly incensed by her constant babbling, wishing he could be on his way to the German capital, starting a new chapter in his life, when the woman sidled up to him and, without warning, grabbed his grazed right hand and glared motionless into his bleary eyes.

"One of the brave lads even made the ultimate sacrifice for the cause. You've become blinded by greed, Mr Dijon," she whispered in his ear, gripping his hand tighter and tighter, forcing a stream of blood to the surface between his dirty scratched fingers. He'd never known pain like it before. It was excruciating, attacking every nerve, every sinew, every muscle, making him feel lightheaded and nauseous, forcing him to hold onto the counter for support.

Dijon was paralysed, powerless, unable to move as his assailant increased her vicelike grip making him scream out in agony. Gazing into her cold unfeeling eyes, seemingly in a trance, he felt her sharp nails ripping through his soft skin, cutting into the flesh and bones, as small droplets of blood oozed to the surface before trickling across the counter and dripping onto the floor. Francois was frozen to the spot, unable to move, just staring in abject fear at his attacker whose blank expressionless face was unfazed by his weak cries of help. Drawing on what little strength he had, the distraught Frenchman stood bolt upright and breathing heavily cried out. "Get off me, you mad woman. Let go, for God's sake. I can't feel my hand any more. You're insane. For God's sake, let go."

Drained of energy, he slipped to his knees in a semi-conscious state, crashing against the wooden base of the counter with his hand bleeding and sweat pouring off his grey sullen face. "I'll call the police. I'll call the police."

"Now that's where I can help you, Mr Dijon," she remarked calmly. "I knew we were going to meet today; it was our destiny. You are a thief, a callous thief, someone who takes advantage of the kindness of others and you will pay for your crimes. That I am sure. Those who are close to me will see to that. Now, we've already called the police for you. In fact, I can see them coming this way with much speed and urgency. The loud ticking clock tells me they are on time."

Just then, Inspector Parry and two hot and bothered Italian law-enforcement officers rushed into the bank. Here they were greeted to the sight of Francois struggling to his feet, standing in a pool of blood and leaning on the counter for support with chunks of skin hanging loosely from his badly gouged right hand. As well as his serious injuries, Francois' posh Armani jacket, cream shirt and slim-fitting trousers were caked in blood and grime with bits of dirt, grass and muck spread liberally across his face. He was a mess.

Ignoring his predicament, the inspector said, "Can I see that paying in slip, Mr Dijon?" Snatching the piece of crumpled bloodstained paper out of his hand, he glared at his quarry and said with an expansive smile:

"Mr Dijon, I'm arresting you for fraud and embezzlement as our certified records confirm that the amount you were supposed to be paying in was 47,600 euros, but according to this bank slip, you only paid in 22,500 euros. So 25,100 is unaccounted for."

"Don't be so stupid. You've got the wrong end of the stick. I've been accosted by a deranged woman who's nearly ripped my hand off and you have the audacity, the nerve," he growled, "to accuse me, a highly respected business director, of theft. Just look at the sodding mess she's made," demanded the Frenchman, nursing his mauled right hand and removing a soggy, bloodstained hanky to reveal a mass of ripped skin and flesh. It made the senior policeman heave at the sight of his mutilated hand, knowing that type of injury was normally associated with a serious bar brawl, or a road accident, thinking that the prisoner must have come a real cropper on the concrete staircase to have done so much damage to his hand.

"I know that," he growled, struggling to stand upright. "I intend flying home to Paris and handing in the rest of the cash when I arrive back at head office later today."

"That's not good enough," retorted the inspector. "We shall check your travel documents and your phone and see what transactions you've made and if we discover, as I'm sure we will, that you're implicated in a major organised fraud then I can assure you, Mr Smoothy, that the inside of a dark, dank French prison awaits you and your thieving cohorts.

"Anyway, what woman?" asked the inspector. "We've been outside ever since you entered the building. The bank cashier and CCTV will confirm that you have been the only customer. You know darn well that your little accident by the Cafe Lido was where you sustained your injuries. Mia has served only one customer in the last half-hour and that was you. Isn't that the case Mia?" said Parry looking at her sat quietly behind the glass panel, trying to come to terms with what had happened in her normally quiet and sedate branch office. Mia was frozen to the spot, as if glued to the floor. The sight of a notorious criminal being arrested in her bank, was a real shock to the system, something she wasn't used to, but the timid teller plucked up courage, gave a limp smile and a half-hearted nod in response to the inspector's stern request.

Wait till I see my mum this evening, she thought to herself, closing her desk drawer with a solid resounding clunk, still reliving some of the highlights of the day when a ruthless mentally deranged villain entered her branch office, only to be dragged away screaming in irons by a team of crack undercover police officers. Mia hadn't had so much excitement since winning thirty-two euros on the lottery, earlier in the year, and that took some beating.

"Of course you saw the woman, she was sat over there by the window you stupid girl," shouted Francois, clutching hold of his hand as the river of blood continued to seep through his badly soiled hanky he'd borrowed from one of the Italian officers standing on point duty by the door.

"She attacked me as I stood at the counter paying the money into the company account," he cried.

"No one else has been in the branch. I can vouch for that and the CCTV will prove it, so don't shout at me. You're just a common run-of-the-mill thief, and a liar and you deserve whatever you get," Mia called out. She didn't like people yelling at her and decided to assert herself and let the middle-aged bully have both barrels.

Moments later, the dishevelled prisoner left the branch in police custody, holding his injured hand close to his chest and gazing disconsolately at the uneven pathway, all the time protesting his innocence. They passed throngs of open-mouthed day-trippers, bemused by the spectacle of a bedraggled criminal in handcuffs mumbling to himself in French and looking as though he'd come off the worst in a late-night drunken brawl.

"I was attacked by a demented lunatic in a bright red skirt, with matching sandals and long sharp fingernails, just like talons. She was vicious; vicious and heartless. Mia must have seen her. The lunatic grabbed hold of me as I stood at the counter gouging great chunks of flesh off my blasted hand. I'm crippled for life you know and I shall sue this bank for every penny it's worth. You've only got to look at my poor mangled fist and the great pools of blood on the floor to know something was up, unless you're as blind as her. The stupid girl must have been in on the act," he shouted.

"Shut up, shut up you fool. I've just about had enough of you and your constant whining," said the police officer. "Anyway, one of my colleagues here had a cursory glance at the CCTV, both inside and outside the building and it confirms Mia's explanation of events. I can assure you, my little French friend, that no living person entered or left the property during the time you were there. So shut up. I don't want to hear another word from you," the police inspector shouted while pushing his belligerent prisoner into the back seat of the waiting police car and slamming the door shut firmly behind him.

Out of the corner of his eye the distraught Frenchman, with a throbbing right hand, noticed a strange shape being lowered to the ground from a tall leafy tree by a couple of young policemen. They were laughing and joking as the hooded contortionist staggered to his feet and wobbled around from side to side, reaching out with both hands and looking very unsteady as he tried to regain his balance on terra firma.

What the hell's all that about? pondered Francois, gently removing some small bits of red fingernail lying lodged in a deep laceration, just above his swollen thumb.

Chapter 49

His phone rang. The bearded, stress-ridden passenger had been living on his nerves for the last hour, his chewed fingernails and worried frown were testament to that. "Yes," cried David impatiently, thumping the phone against his ear before Beethoven had time to catch his breath. The nervous tension emanating from the rear passenger seat was such that it nearly made the anxious cabby jump out of his skin. "We've done it, my friend, we've done it. The sting worked. Mr Dijon is under lock and key," announced Chris down the phone. "It's all over, we've caught the Frenchy with his grubby fingers in the honeypot. I followed Dijon to the bank and your mate Parry did the rest. Francois was in a sorry state, never seen him like that before, but that doesn't matter. We caught him red-handed and that's what we wanted."

"Fantastic," exclaimed David, hardly able to catch his breath, smacking the back of the driver's seat so hard that Gregor shot forward and smashed his stubbly, misshapen chin into the leather steering wheel with an almighty thump.

The startled Romanian was convinced he was sharing his car with a delusional lunatic who behaved most oddly every time Beethoven's fifth blared out on his cellphone. He was praying, to all that was holy, for the journey to end before his precious leather upholstery was reduced to shreds and his nerves in tatters.

"We got him at the bank. The greedy sod stole 25,100 euros there and then. I can't believe it. The toerag took the bait. He had the audacity, the gall to steal another pile of cash on his way home. The police have his phone, they've traced your money and it'll be returned to your account in due course. You'll be pleased to know Sarah has your locket safe and sound and will be forwarding it to you as arranged. Oh, one other thing. My friend is dealing with Midge in his own inimitable way so it's turned out for the best in the end."

"Well done, Chris. I never doubted you. Not for one moment. You've saved the day, we've beaten them. I shan't forget what you've done. You're a star mate, I'm very proud of you. Hello,

hello? Sorry, it's difficult to hear you, the line keeps crackling, you keep breaking up. I'll call you as soon as I can. I'll text you in the meantime. Thanks for all you've done. It's the best birthday present I've ever had." The line went dead.

David relaxed back in the comfortable soft leather, quietly reflecting on their success, hardly able to contain his feelings of elation and absolute joy. He knew Francois was no fool, no mug and that things could have gone horribly wrong, the consequences of which were quite unimaginable. David based his plan on the Frenchman's greed, knowing that 25,000 euros would be too much of a temptation, especially as it would be his last throw of the dice. But it was a calculated risk. If Dijon smelt a rat, suspected something was up, then he wouldn't have taken the bait, choosing to leave the sponsorship money at the hotel and going to ground, like the wily old fox that he was. But he didn't; that was the gamble. Greed had got the better of his traitorous colleague and that was his downfall.

The OAP, with a self-satisfied grin on his face, caught the last glimpse of the pale shimmering lake as his twitchy-eyed driver, wary of his dramatic mood-swings, drove passed Sirmione before joining the heavily congested autostrada en route to Milan some eighty miles to the west.

Feeling pleased with his day's work, David closed his eyes, slouched back and savoured the moment to the sound of *Nessun Dorma*, on Gregor's state of the art car radio, performed with great passion by Britain's number one tenor from Salford. It was not one of David's favourite pieces of music, often conjuring up embarrassing memories of England's ignominious defeats in the beautiful game, but as a grand musical piece with a rousing finale, it tugged at his heartstrings even though he was still living on cloud nine since PW's memorable telephone call, just moments earlier. Opening his leather wallet to check his flight details, he took out a small innocuous piece of paper, hidden behind his driving licence and read the handwritten quote. It was by W.H. Auden, someone he'd admired very much as a child and, strangely enough, it summed up the day, writing in a short poem that it was okay to do evil unto those that did evil unto you.

Smiling to himself, he slipped the wallet back into his creased jacket pocket, hanging from the coat hook over the passenger door and, feeling tired after the exertions of the day, with eyes getting heavier by the minute, decided to have a little nap. The soporific movement of the luxurious Mercedes E-class limousine soon seduced the middle-aged extravert into a deep sleep in the exalted company of *Nella Fantasia* which was much more to his liking.

Sometime later, he was woken from his dreams with a sudden jerk when their busy trunk road swept over a main railway line just as a high-speed TGV passenger train clattered past at breakneck speed. Rubbing his eyes and glancing down at his new Rolex, he was surprised to see how long he'd slept and, feeling parched, grabbed a bottle of chilled water from the centre console. Before he had time to acclimatise himself to the bustling highway, a text pinged through from Claire. With some anxiety, the passenger scrolled down the screen while his driver's head and shoulders bobbed from side to side to the hypnotic sound of the late Fontella Bass singing *Rescue Me* which seemed quite appropriate. Gregor smiled tentatively in the mirror when he caught David's eye realising, with some trepidation, that the eccentric Englishman had returned from the land of nod and was holding the dreaded phone firmly in his hand.

Apparently, Claire was at the end of her tether, pulling her hair out in giant clumps and seriously thinking about murdering the old wrinklies, whatever the consequences. Mrs Lane could be a real drama queen at the best of times and Mr and Mrs Millins definitely played their part in encouraging these extrovert qualities to flourish unfettered. It appears that Mr Millins had been on his best behaviour, to begin with anyway. He'd oiled Jordan's clanking chain and dodgy peddles so the trusty steed wouldn't squeak when the master of the house bounced up and down on her aging frame.

David's old bike had been with him through thick and thin and even though she was long in the tooth, beyond her sell-by date, the old romantic was reluctant to change her for a new, more sylphlike model. So Jordan's future was secure as long as she continued to treat him to a comfortable ride from time to time. The text went on. Because of his failing eyesight, the poor old chap managed to knock over a whole litre of Mobil oil, spreading a dark black gooey mess everywhere. Then the clumsy orang-utan traipsed the messy oil slick around the basement rooms, on the soles of his new Primark slippers, leaving a thin smear of high-grade gunk and grease in his wake. But that wasn't the end of it, not by a long chalk. He had more up his sleeve. Outside on the patio, he noticed a large piece of material lying draped across the back of a wicker chair and, because of his myopic condition, thought it had been discarded. So Mr Magoo, in his wisdom, decided to use it to mop up the nasty oil slick, after all it was big enough for such a task and so on bended knees he scrubbed and cleaned the floor with great care, hoping the lady of the house wouldn't be any the wiser as regards his messy misfortune. However, unbeknown to him, this discarded piece of material was Claire's precious handmade shawl that she'd ordered several weeks earlier from an exclusive Knightsbridge store and had been carefully hung on the back of the wicker chair to help lose some of its annoying creases. This was the catalyst for her murderous intent.

She intended flaunting the shawl at the big birthday bash on Monday evening when the great and the good would grace their Regency abode and she could impress their distinguished guests with her expensive eye-catching ensemble. Well that was the plan, but sadly it wasn't to be. Myopic man had put pay to that. The Millinses, had yet again scuppered her chances of raising her profile, stamping her mark on the spa town and moving out of the shadows of her celebrity husband.

Predictably, David's reply was curt and to the point, after all he was still revelling in their triumphant defeat of the Frenchman on the shores of Lake Garda to be interested in some mindless tittle-tattle back at base camp.

Claire slumped down disconsolately on the bottom rung of the staircase with phone in hand, agonising over her dour reflection that bounced back ad nauseam from the nearby china glass cabinet. Where did those wrinkles come from? They weren't there yesterday, she muttered to herself, staring at the rows of wavy tramlines gouged haphazardly across her forehead while drowning her sorrows in a glass of freshly opened Rioja, still pondering on the plight of the aging duo that had been foisted on her as punishment for some dreadful things she'd done in her dim and distant past.

"Should I drag them down to the local firing range, staple them to the target, so the blighters don't do a runner and shoot them? Better still, I could hang them over the top floor landing and let them dangle about for a few days on the end of a rope, or I could just simply drive the loonies into the Cotswolds and give them their freedom," she surmised. Mrs Lane, with chipped fingernails and a slight twitch, accepted that years of confinement in a women's prison would be a daunting prospect for someone of her social standing, but it was a price worth paying. She continued mulling over her plans and talking to herself out loud as the target of her murderous intent stood at the top of the spiral staircase, quivering in their new Primark slippers, fearing for their lives at the hands of the demented lady of the house.

"Yes, it would be worth it," she cried out as another drop of the red stuff slithered down her throat. "It would bring some degree of normality back to my shell-shocked life even if it means sharing a cell with a tattooed lesbian with a stapled tongue, sleeping in a creaky bunk bed and slopping out every morning with all the indignity that engenders. Oh God, it would be worth it!" she shouted at the top of her voice.

Leaning against the wooden banister rail for support, under the terrified gaze of her elderly helpers, she agreed it was a price worth paying to rid herself of the in-house hoodlums who dogged her every step, were determined to keep her firmly rooted to the bottom rung of the social ladder and were hell bent on reducing her to a jabbering wreck before the year was out. Mrs Lane believed that the Millinses were more of a risk to national security than any band of gun-toting terrorists armed to the teeth with every imaginable weapon and could inflict more damage in a single day than most fanatics could exact in a lifetime. They were that dangerous. So the scene was set; the die was cast. It was just a question of when.

Chapter 50

"Not far now sir," yelled Gregor, sounding rather demob happy with a confident bounce to his voice though still rubbing his chin after its bruising encounter with the Mercedes' solid leather steering wheel.

"Good," replied David, firing off a few quick text messages to his many supporters while gazing longingly at the mountainous scenery, the rolling green fields and the rich cultivated farmland laid out before him. One of the many rewards of travelling around Europe, at various times of the year, was being treated to some amazing views and awe-inspiring scenery. David often marvelled at nature's charm and seemingly magical powers, feeling captivated, even mystified by the many sights and sounds as the seasons came and went with predictable seamlessness.

But then, catching a cursory glimpse of his reflection in the driver's mirror, the daydreamer suddenly shot back in horror. Since waking from his long nap, he'd completely forgotten his disguise and the Daredevil Challenge and so the shock of his ungainly appearance gave him a real jolt. With eyes on extended stalks, Gregor stared in disbelief when Mr Davidson leaned forward towards the mirror, licked the ends of his fingers, dabbed his beard and moustache and then gently rubbed some cream into his cheeks and under his eyes, no doubt making sure he looked his best for the return flight home.

Is there no limit to the man's vanity?, he thought to himself, chewing on a crushed cheese and pickle sandwich that he'd managed to retrieve from the car's dusty floor well as the madman slept. Poor Gregor's stress-ridden journey was coming to a welcome close and it couldn't come soon enough as far as he was concerned. Brits were always viewed as an odd bunch, spending a small fortune on silly holiday tack, cheap local wine and soppy gifts, but he never thought they were as crazy as the madcap loopy who sat licking his lips and caressing his facial hair just a few inches away.

Nearing the outskirts of Zurich, the scenery changed and David's eyes were treated to an array of beautifully tended gardens boasting great splashes of colour and different eye-catching designs. The floral display reminded him of his visits to Hidcote and, in particular, the splendid red garden and its enchanting spectacle of fragrant fresh spring flowers that always filled him with hope and optimism. This brought back fond memories of Shirley and their times together, racing around the Cotswolds in the open-top sports, like a pair of love-struck adolescents, with her singing her favourite ABBA songs very badly and laughing at his daft jokes.

The sun would often set on their magical days together as they lay sprawled out on the Pump Room steps in Cheltenham's idyllic Pittville Park where they'd enjoy a soft vanilla ice cream, with crunchy chocolate flakes, as excited children screamed and hollered in the nearby adventure playground. They'd often stroll arm in arm, hardly uttering a word, with the pale blue sky for company and birds singing overhead, just revelling in their own innocence when life stood still for a short time and they didn't have a worry in the world. Not one. Croome Park, one of Capability Brown's great landscape achievements, was a favourite haunt. Here the young things spent many a day meandering through the open parklands with its majestic lake and uninterrupted views of the Worcestershire countryside. Standing proudly on top of the escarpment was the church of St Mary Magdalene. Here they'd offer a prayer or two in memory of his parents while Shirley would sit and sometimes weep, often nursing her head in her hands and gazing at the floor before lighting three wax candles in their name. One for luck, was her sombre throwaway remark, as she carefully dropped her donation into the church collection box and bowed her head in solemn reverence then gazed, with tear-stained eyes, towards the alter and the imposing cross of Christ.

Evoking memories of their all too brief time together, David could still hear her laughing and giggling and see her meandering through the long straggly grass with her slightly bent sunglasses hanging precariously on the end of her short stubbly nose, with the rolling Malvern hills standing tall on the far horizon.

Slipping his damp handkerchief back into his trouser pocket, he told his edgy companion to head for the St Rouen Cemetery on the east side of the city and, knowing a short cut, told Gregor the route to follow so they'd miss the busy rush-hour traffic with its endless queues and lengthy tailbacks. Gliding across the smooth tarmac surface, he never failed to be impressed by the striking architecture that greeted him with every turn of the wheel, every turn of the head, but sadly the very same place reminded him of his dearly departed parents who were laid to rest at a small community church in the shadows of the snow-capped mountains of the treacherous Alpine range.

Peering through the car's front window and the swirling afternoon mist, was a grand Gothic building standing as a monument, a tribute to the memory of his parents with its centuries-old brickwork, impressive bell tower and, thanks to David's generosity, a magnificent new roof of deep grey tiles with subtle terracotta edging.

David's wealthy globe-trotting grandparents had strong family ties in Zurich and were buried in the same graveyard and so it seemed appropriate to reunite Jeremy and Louise Lane with their loved ones. Mr Crawford, in his own inimitable way, had ensured their wishes were fulfilled and the family tradition was maintained, much to David's delight. The sultry air felt muggy, quite oppressive as he climbed out of the car and strode nervously towards their resting place. He'd walked this path many times before under an arbour of carefully tended trees providing a touching guard of honour for its parade of tearful visitors. He stopped momentarily, with just the humming sound of nearby traffic and small birds chirping overhead, before continuing past the cemetery's many grass-covered graves and weather-worn headstones. Then the lonely disconsolate figure stopped and stood head bowed, completely motionless, with just a light breeze fluffing up his dark trousers and cotton shirt. He looked down at the unobtrusive marble headstone, with its simple inscription immortalising the names of two people who meant so much to him. The reassuring smell of freshly mown grass wafted in the air and the beautifully tended borders of red carnations and white roses gave a sense of calm solemnity to their heart-wrenching reunion.

Sinking to his knees, David touched the damp earth with both hands as a line of tears trickled down his cheeks. When he stroked the cold headstone he often felt close to his beloved mother. He could sometimes smell her fragrant perfume lingering gently on the breeze, or hear her calm reassuring voice, but sometimes it was just too overwhelming, too much to bear as a desperate feeling of loss swept over his body, forcing him to cry uncontrollably. With head bowed and eyes closed, he sometimes imagined his mother gently tucking him into bed, kissing him goodnight, pushing the straggly curls off his forehead with her long, elegant fingers. The reunions were always raw, always painful and the agony of their demise never diminished, not one bit.

In the lighter moments, he recalled his childhood days sitting on Oddicombe Beach on a warm summer's afternoon, peering over his mother's shoulder, as she wrote the obligatory postcards home. His father always teased her, when she walked around and around the revolving metal card stand, trying to find the best views of Devon's famous landmarks.

His dad reckoned, as it was highly unlikely that the lucky recipients would ever meet to discuss their respective postcards, that Mum should just grab a bunch of the things, write the same two-line message for each one and be done with it. "Ten minutes tops," was what he always said. Mum would tell him off for being a grumpy old misery and not joining in the spirit of the holiday. David remembered glancing over her shoulder, as she perched on the edge of a wobbly deckchair with a battered copy of *Woman's Own* spread across her lap, writing her carefully chosen postcards to friends back home. It was then when he found out where they were going next, whether the family holiday was going well and, most important of all, whether he was behaving himself and not being a naughty boy.

He knelt there for some time, oblivious to his surroundings, immersed in his own private thoughts, but his mood was slightly different on that particular day. The famous Mark Twain quotation had really struck home. For the first time in years he felt more at ease with life, more relaxed, knowing his parents had defined his destiny, were setting the course and he was fulfilling his dear mother's dying wishes through the success of the Pedal Power Programme.

After a few moments' quiet reflection he struggled to his feet, brushed his knees, leaned forward, spoke a few words and kissed the headstone tenderly. Then with tears welling up in his eyes, he slowly retraced his steps back to the waiting vehicle, glancing back over his shoulder from time to time, as the solemn emblematic gravestone slowly disappeared in the swirling mist.

The young Romanian driver was leaning casually against the silver bonnet, smoking a cigarette with a plume of white smoke belching from the twin exhausts of his precious car, when he saw Mr Davidson ambling across the gravel pathway towards him blowing his nose and wiping his eyes with his white cotton handkerchief. Taking a quick last drag of his cigarette, he stubbed out the half-smoked Marlboro with his foot and swung open the rear door for his glum, crestfallen customer. With a forced smile David gazed into the eyes of his long-suffering driver, shivering in the gloom, looking pallid and white as a sheet.

"How are you feeling, my friend? You don't look so good," he asked.

"Oh I'm all right, thank you. The long ride has tired me, but I shall be okay after a sleep," he replied with a croaky voice. "This'll cheer you up. Here's a crisp 500-euro note for you," said David.

"Thank you very much," said Gregor gripping the note firmly in his gloved hand while wiping the droplets of perspiration from his forehead and resting back on the car's bonnet for support. Being concerned about his driver's state of health, David had a sudden brainwave and darted round to the rear of the car, opened the boot and unzipped one of his suitcases lodged in the far corner. With a jaunty grin, he handed his precious red and white lined jacket, with its striking gold leaf monogram and matching woollen scarf, to his bewildered driver with a runny nose.

Gregor didn't know what to say, wondering what the heck was going on, whether his client had finally taken leave of his senses. After all, he was now giving away his precious clothes, so whatever next?

"It's not very thick, but it's better than nothing, my friend. I hope it fits okay. Try it on. Why don't you use some of the money to pay for a room before driving home tomorrow? Anyway, here's another 200 euros as a contribution," said David. In his enthusiasm, the Londoner slammed the boot shut with such a hefty wallop that, unbeknown to Gregor, it sent his freshly opened large can of Diet Coke bouncing off the dashboard, spreading its fizzy contents all over the Mercedes' soft leather upholstery.

Grabbing the notes in his shaky hand, the man from Bucharest couldn't believe his good fortune and immediately forgave the OAP for his sustained assault on his precious silver machine and for keeping him on edge throughout the 300-mile ordeal. He was even prepared to overlook his bruised jawbone and badly inflamed chin that throbbed every time he sneezed. All was forgiven in a flash. It was as though it never happened as he embraced his impetuous passenger warmly, like a long lost brother, and shook his hand mercilessly. Standing proudly under the shaded arbour of the overhanging trees that bordered the church graveyard, Gregor slipped the jacket over his threadbare cardigan and quickly zipped up the front for protection from the unusually chilly afternoon breeze. Even though he was clearly under par and running a temperature, there was a great beaming smile etched on his face when he wrapped the brightly coloured red and white scarf around his neck several times for added warmth and comfort. This was a unique occasion in the history of the Lane family when a six-foot-two, thirty-five-year-old Romanian immigrant, draped in their well-known colours with a red nose to match, was seen prancing up and down the pavement proudly showing off his posh designer gear like a top-notch male model on a glitzy Parisian catwalk.

As the international airport was nearby, David decided to take the air and get a bit of exercise after sitting down for such a long time. He'd walk the short distance towards the city centre and then hail a cab for the rest of the journey. Before going their separate ways, David took a couple of selfies of the pair leaning against the glistening Mercedes with his new Rolex watch in full view. For the final snaps, Gregor kindly took some close-up pictures of his passenger's moustache and beard from three distinct angles.

After the antics of the last few hours, the fun-loving cabby thought nothing of it and wasn't fazed by the experience at all, putting it all down to British eccentricity. Not only had his elderly passenger overpaid the fare by quite a margin, but he'd even given him some of his own designer clothes which seemed very expensive even to the untrained eye. So a few innocent photographs, with the obligatory facial hair, was quite ordinary after the outrageous goings on he'd witnessed in the back seat of his luxury car since leaving the freshwater lake many hours earlier.

After the carefully choreographed photo shoot, the rest of David's luggage was retrieved from the cavernous boot. They then shook hands again, said their goodbyes and the plucky Romanian patted the bonnet of his trusty steed, and with a sigh of relief and a cigarette in hand, prepared for the off and a welcome return to the world of sanity. His head was brimming with anecdotes and stories to share with his beloved wife of the memorable day he spent with a barmy, madcap Englishman who tried to demolish his pride and joy at every opportunity and then shouted, laughed or just giggled every time his blessed phone rang and Beethoven strummed his stuff.

Meanwhile peering over the adjacent church wall, catching a final glimpse of his parent's gravestone someway off, David felt a deep sense of regret at having to leave their side after such a short visit in order to complete the Daredevil Challenge. He hoped they understood.

Suddenly, without warning, there was an almighty bang, like a car backfiring or a traffic accident, which gave him a bit of a start. Glancing back over his shoulder through the haze he saw a sight he'll never forget. To his horror, Gregor was lying slumped on the ground with streams of blood gushing from the side of his chest. He didn't move. "Oh my God!" David yelled, quickly taking cover behind the uneven cemetery wall, fearing for his own life, thinking it could be a lunatic terrorist on the loose taking pot-shots at innocent members of the public. Horrified motorists screeched to a grinding halt and traumatised faces gazed out of open car windows wondering what the hell was going on and why some poor soul was lying in the gutter in a large pool of blood. Peering through the gloom, David couldn't see anything untoward. He crouched down, stared across the open road with cars, vans and buses all parked up haphazardly. Doors were thrown wide open and mobile phones on hand while, in the mayhem, groups of tearful panic-stricken pedestrians ran around shouting and screaming fearing for their very lives. Undeterred by the panic and confusion in his midst, David kept peering from left to right like a windscreen wiper, until his patience was rewarded. His eyes fell on a shape, a strange motionless silhouette some hundred yards away partially hidden behind a line of trees bordering the main road and holding, what seemed to be, a firearm in his hand.

He ducked down even lower not wishing to attract any attention as the shooter, thinking the coast was clear, started walking briskly with his hood up towards the city centre. David sneaked along the damp pathway still crouching, but keeping the gunman in his sights. Glancing back quickly over his shoulder, he saw Gregor sitting upright against the front door of his blood-splattered car with half a dozen people helping him as best they could, as the reassuring sound of sirens could be heard blaring out in the distance. On seeing the gunman sneaking away, hoping to disappear into the milling crowds of afternoon shoppers, David knew he had to strike. The spritely-forty-four-year-old quickly gave chase, darting across the congested main road towards the bright neon lights in the neighbouring streets and was very soon closing in on his startled prey. General fitness and physical strength gave David the edge as he charged relentlessly through the hectic city centre, dodging between parked cars, heavily laden shoppers and the well-to-do suited and booted.

He was hardly breaking a sweat when he shot across a crowded pedestrian crossing, darted up a steep incline and, seeing his quarry only yards away, raced along the middle of the road while two lanes of stationary vehicles waited, with engines purring, for the traffic lights to change colour. In the swirling plume of diesel fumes, he was now only a matter of feet behind the madman who was no match for David Lane, clearly struggling with every stride to maintain the relentless pace set by his feisty elderly pursuer. The shooter's loose-fitting jacket was within his grasp. It was tantalisingly close.

Reaching out, ever closer with every step, David's fingertips were only inches away from his quarry. But then from nowhere a car raced past with a rear door wide open and, when it reached alongside the exhausted gunman, he jumped into the passenger seat and the getaway car sped off at high speed, leaving great tramlines of smouldering rubber on the tarmac. It was then when David recognised Gregor's attacker smirking back at him through the car's rear window. The face was familiar; very familiar, he knew it immediately. He'd gawped at his ugly mugshot several times over the years whilst entertaining his wife in numerous hotel suites on the famous Sussex downs.

He'd seen his harelip on many holiday snaps, in umpteen family videos and on numerous photographs at Christmas pantomimes and end of term school plays, but was horrified to come face to face with the oily rag in such bizarre circumstances. It was Roger Sands. Susan's husband, Louise's guardian, the protector of his only child. David shouted in frustration and waved his arms frantically in the air as the shiny silver Audi disappeared around the corner in a cloud of white smoke and a screech of tyres.

Feeling angry and incensed by the lunatic's assault on his harmless cabby, he limped across to the pavement, with his ankle throbbing thanks to Martin Conway, and David bent down with both hands on his knees, trying to get his breath back after his dramatic high-speed sprint. He couldn't understand why Roger was staring out of the car's rear window, not trying to disguise his appearance in any way, seemingly unfazed by the turn of events as though shooting someone in broad daylight was a normal everyday occurrence. But then it dawned on him, the penny dropped when he peered into the dimly lit Marks and Spencer's shop window and saw the tawdry reflection that greeted his tired eyes. I'm not David Lane. Of course I'm not. I'm Stewart Davidson, he hasn't the faintest idea who I am. He wouldn't know me from Adam. I'm a rather scruffy, bearded nobody with seemingly bad dress sense who's unlikely to remember his ugly mug in any future police identification parade.

David mastered the art of disguise from some impromptu lessons by Jamie, his long-standing friend whom he met in a rehabilitation clinic in his twenties and they've been mates ever since. His pal worked as a make-up artist at the nationally renowned Everyman Theatre in Cheltenham. When David explained the Daredevil Challenge to him over lunch, at the Café Rouge restaurant, he came to his aid providing all the make-up and special hairpieces to help with his clever disguise. It had to be really convincing if he was to con the eagle-eyed airport authorities who were always on their guard and particularly in such unpredictable times.

Still shocked by the violent unprovoked attack on his innocent driver, he slowly retraced his steps back to the scene of the altercation, where he collected his suitcases that he'd quickly hidden behind the church wall when all hell let loose. There was a horde of nosy onlookers milling about behind specially erected police cordons when the injured taxi driver was wheeled on a stretcher into the back of the waiting ambulance. Feeling somewhat jaded after his sudden exertions and traumatised by the sight of Gregor's bloodstained injuries, he hailed a cab and bade a hasty retreat knowing his intervention wouldn't help things and could seriously compromise his speedy return to Blighty.

Driving towards the airport lights and the promise of a quick ride home, he thought about his poor chum and how he'd taken the hit intended for him. David couldn't understand why the oily rag hated him so much to the extent that he'd followed him all the way across Europe in order to shoot him. It was unbelievable. Susan's obviously told him about me, which might be a bit of a shock, he agreed, but that's no reason to go around brandishing a shotgun like a cowboy in a cheap spaghetti western having a pop at every Tom, Dick and Harry. The man's taken leave of his senses, gone barking mad, thought David, as the bright neon lights of Zurich's international airport beckoned on the horizon. As the cabby looked in vain for somewhere to stop the car, he continued remonstrating with himself about the horror he'd just experienced. I've helped finance Louise's upbringing, made up for any shortfall in the family purse and provided for her in my will as a dutiful father. I've also compensated for the gunslinger's shortcomings in the trouser department which kept his sex-crazed wife satisfied and their dodgy marriage on the straight and narrow. The gormless goon with the funny lip should be shaking me by the hand, treating me as a chum, a best mate, rather than sneaking about, waving a shotgun, taking pot-shots at people for no apparent reason.

Eventually the aggrieved athlete climbed out of the back of the cab, feeling rather shaky after his close call. The sound of blaring horns and sirens could be heard in nearby streets while the news of the shooting in broad daylight, on Zurich's normally quiet peaceful streets, was already making the front pages in the local press and was quickly promoted to the lead story on all the regional radio networks. The myriad of airport television screens were full of it.

Strolling across the bustling airport concourse, which was a hive of frantic police activity, he decided to warn the Swiss authorities about the oily rag's well-known violent streak and his potential threat to public safety. It was his civic duty to blow the whistle and protect innocent people from the lunatic on the loose. It was the least he could do as a responsible father, benevolent fund-raiser, upright citizen and a prospective Member of the British Parliament.

Chapter 51

It was early evening when Susan heard *Colonel Bogey* chiming at the front door. She jumped out of bed as though her clothes were on fire, grabbed her crumpled red and white dressing gown and rushed down the stairs, two at a time. A couple of young fresh-faced police officers were standing in silence under the porch canopy with grim faces and warrant cards in their hands when she flung open the door in a blind panic.

"What's up?" yelled Susan. "It's not Louise, is it? Tell me it's not. Please say it isn't." The female officer was shocked by the unexpected appearance of a bedraggled homeowner with deep bags under her eyes, an unruly mop of blonde hair that hadn't seen a comb in ages and reeking of alcohol.

Christine replied with a startled expression on her face. "No, we're not here about Louise. It's something else. Can we come in, please? It's very important that we talk to you."

Sensing something was up, Susan quickly ushered them into the lounge and banged the front door closed with a hefty kick of her foot, sending the key-ring sliding across the stone-tiled floor before crashing into the chrome refuse bin in the kitchen at the rear of the house.

"It's Mrs Sands, isn't it?" asked Robert, with a reassuring smile and tilt of his head as though he was hosting a daytime quiz show. The two rookies graduated from Hendon a couple of years earlier and weren't looking forward to meeting Mrs Sands, knowing that bringing bad news of a family death was always a tricky thing to handle, made even worse when the person in question died in tragic circumstances. But the pair, who were normally assigned minor disturbances and petty crimes, were ill-prepared for the scene that greeted them on that warm summer's evening in July. The entrance to the lounge was covered in crumpled newspapers and ripped magazines with broken cups and saucers lying scattered across the chipped and scratched coffee table. A curtain rail had been pulled away from the wall and was licking the carpet under the bow window that was boasting two missing panes of glass and a bent frame. There were umpteen vertical blinds lying crumpled and ripped on the soiled cream carpet, with bits of coloured porcelain and glass fragments scattered everywhere, some of which were firmly embedded in the material. The Panasonic television hadn't fared any better. The forty-inch screen was smashed to smithereens exposing numerous bare wires and odd-looking cables that would be a challenge for even the most talented electrician.

The glass cabinet, a treasured wedding gift from her parents, hadn't escaped the violent onslaught either and was reduced to a pile of rubble in the corner of the room with shards of broken glass and mangled wood strewn everywhere. An upturned leather sofa and a three-legged chair were piled on top of each other across the arched entrance to the adjoining kitchen.

"Yes," replied Susan sternly. "I'm sorry about the room, but we had a little domestic issue yesterday and I haven't had time to clear things up yet. It's not a break-in, if that's what you're thinking. Just a minor skirmish. A quick hoover round should do the trick. Shouldn't take too long at all."

The fledgling officers, still slightly damp behind the ears, didn't know what to think. Nothing had escaped the violent onslaught as far as they could see. Every item of furniture had been totally trashed, or damaged beyond repair. They'd never seen anything like it before. If that was a little domestic, they'd hate to think what a full-blown dispute would look like.

"Well, I'm sorry to say we've some grave news for you, Mrs Sands. Is there someone who could come and sit with you?" asked Christine hesitantly.

"No," snapped Susan. "What is it? What the hell's this all about?" she shouted, rubbing her face with both hands while prowling around the room between broken pieces of furniture and ripped magazines and newspapers.

Robert, the young freckle-faced officer chirped up and took the lead, saying, "Last night, a man of your husband's description was seen firing a gun at another male near a cemetery in Zurich in Switzerland."

"I know where Zurich is, you buffoon," shouted Susan over the sound of his crackly radio. "What are you talking about? Are you mad? My husband's never been to Zurich in his damn life. You've got me muddled up with someone else, you idiot."

The officer continued undeterred and grabbed hold of two easy chairs that were lying upside down in the fireplace and plonked himself down opposite Mrs Sands who was perched on a chromium barstool looking tearful and very hung over.

"Your husband arrived in Zurich yesterday evening following a flight from Gatwick Airport. According to eyewitnesses, the gunman answering to your husband's description shot a man and ran off. An anonymous call from a member of the public also verified this. Several police officers tried to apprehend Mr Sands who was a passenger in a getaway vehicle which refused to stop following repeated requests by the Swiss police and the security forces.

"Then, following a frantic pursuit on foot, I'm sorry to say Mr Sands tripped and fell in front of a local authority refuse truck and died from his injuries at the scene of the accident. I'm very sorry Mrs Sands, to be the bearer of such bad news."

Susan went pale, and staring down at the dingy high-pile carpet covering her bare feet, wondered what the hell was going on. Was it a dream? Will I wake up in a moment? "Please let it be a dream," she prayed to herself.

"There is more unfortunately, Mrs Sands," said Christine tentatively.

"What do you mean, more?" shouted Susan, still trying to come to terms with the tragic circumstances of her husband's death on foreign soil, struggling to imagine what further bad news could befall her.

"I'm sorry to say the victim of the shooting is seriously injured and even though the information we have is quite scant, at this stage, it appears to have been a random shooting, with no apparent motive. Obviously, these are early days and we won't know the full facts until the Swiss authorities have completed their detailed investigations."

Susan blew her nose and wiped her doleful eyes with a handful of damp soggy tissues when the two baby-faced officers stood up to take their leave, promising to be in touch as soon as they had further information.

"Oh, there is something I'd like to ask," said Christine, griping her notebook for all it was worth. "I'm sorry to have to bother you further, but I need to ask you one final thing. We've only got limited information on the injured man so far, but I understand from the

Swiss police that he was dressed in a striking red and white jacket with a gold monogram sewn on the breast pocket and a matching scarf." Christine turned the pages of her notebook.

She fumbled about nervously for a few seconds. "Yes, here it is. On the jacket there are two initials. The initials are, wait a minute, just a second. I need to check my notes. Here it is. They are DL, yes DL. Do you happen by any chance to know a man who fits that description with those initials, Mrs Sands?" asked the police officer quite innocently.

By the time the paramedics had revived Susan and put her to bed, Louise had arrived home from her weekend away and was sat anxiously waiting for her mother to wake up. She wanted to know what was happening. Why two young police officers were in the kitchen helping themselves to tea and ginger nut biscuits and why some local hacks were camped out on their front lawn with stepladders and cameras at the ready. After all she'd only been away a couple of days and it seemed as though World War Three had broken out in her absence.

Louise was slim, blue-eyed with slender shoulders, boasting an hourglass figure and striking auburn hair. She was gratified to see Lynn, a familiar face, resting in an armchair alongside the unkempt double bed that was strewn with various items of clothing, while her mother looked as though she'd been on a bender for the last few days judging by her dull complexion and the strong smell of alcohol lingering on her breath.

"What's been going on, Mum?" asked Louise quizzically, while gripping her chin with both hands, fearful of what she might say. At this juncture, Lynn thought it politic to make a speedy exit before the s...t hit the proverbial fan.

"I'll get off, if you don't mind," said Lynn, gently kissing Susan on her forehead and squeezing her hand. "I'll give you a call tomorrow. Don't be too hard on your mum Louise, eh?"

After Lynn had manoeuvred her way between the unwelcome house guests, she drove off into the sunset pondering on Susan's dilemma. How would the timid, straight-laced solicitor explain the serious gunshot wounds to Louise's real father at the hands of the man she'd called daddy for the last eighteen years, who incidentally was now lying flat out on a cold slab in a Swiss mortuary having been crushed by a local authority dump truck? It was a storyline more at home in a cheesy daytime soap than in the leafy-laned world

291

of middle-class suburbia. What I'd give to be a fly on the wall, she thought to herself, listening to the news of Roger Sands' tragic death on the car radio. Lynn was in tears when she opened the door to her one-bedroom ground-floor apartment, just around the corner from the exclusive Imperial Hotel, knowing that her boss and long-time lover wouldn't be coming to see her anymore. Thursday afternoons would never be the same again. Charlie, her ginger tabby cat, jumped on her lap and greeted her with his usual soft gentle purring when she slumped down on the two-seater settee, holding a framed photograph of Roger Sands in her hands.

No longer would she share romantic candlelit dinners with him in posh top-notch restaurants, or enjoy occasional business trips to exotic European locations where they'd chat about their future plans and how they intended swopping their dull uneventful lives in Hastings for pastures new. But his tragic death put paid to all that. All she had now were just memories, cherished memories of their happy times together and stolen moments of passion locked in each other's arms, away from the humdrum of everyday life. Helping herself to a large gin and tonic and stroking Charlie for comfort, she wondered who might take over the car dealership and whether she needed to travel to Switzerland to rekindle some old flames. Obviously she'd have to give it a few days, out of respect for her dead lover, but after then she'd start thinking seriously about her future, seeing where her special talents could be put to good use, yet again.

Chapter 52

Claire wanted Number One Pavilion Avenue to look spick and span for David's big birthday bash and gave her ungainly employees the task of cleaning, hoovering and polishing the surfaces in the downstairs rooms where her important guests would be milling about during the evening's celebrations. She thought twice about asking Mr M to put up the flags and bunting, fearful of the damage he would do to himself and, more importantly, to the Regency property and its expensive decor. Instead, she roped in next door's spotty-faced teenager with the promise of a front-seat ride in the birthday boy's new Bentley Continental that would adorn the gravel driveway later that week. She missed her husband very much and hoped things would improve after their silly bickering and petty arguments of the last few months. Claire knew his obsession with the Pedal Power Programme, and his other benevolent pursuits, had taken its toll on their relationship and was undermining their future happiness together. He was a driven man, who she admired greatly and she wouldn't do anything to stand in his way, but she hoped her charitable husband, with all of his altruistic qualities, would at least share some of his precious time with her, give her the attention she so craved for before it was too late.

The Millinses had always been a thorn in her side and she couldn't understand why David was so enamoured with them, blind to the damage they were doing to his reputation and standing in the local community. The cheap tacky gifts for her wealthy sophisticated husband, sitting on show in his prestigious first-floor office with its hand-crafted redwood furniture and highly polished surfaces, were a constant source of annoyance, making him a laughing stock in her eyes. During her frequent periods of frustration with the resident wrinklies, she often toyed with the idea of slinging the tawdry gifts out with the rubbish and to hell with the consequences, but having been in the firing line of David's anger in the past, decided against it.

The bottom shelf of the three-tier bookcase in his office housed a quartet of bulky lever-arch-files with dates on the spines from

1988-1991. She carefully slid one from its moorings, as she'd done umpteen times before, and like a cheeky adolescent took a crafty peek inside. There were various sections in the file with handwritten notes and simple jottings on historical landmarks, world geography, international politics, economics and modern history, all fairly dry subjects of little interest to the social climber.

She flicked through the pages of the other bulky files covering uninteresting subjects on business management, corporate finance and international affairs. David made great play of social etiquette and a section in the third file was dedicated to this single topic, going into great detail about dress codes and styles, different types of wines, fitness regimes, healthy eating, personal grooming and so on. It also included a copious list of some do's and don'ts. The lady of the house gained a valuable insight into her husband's secret world, quietly leafing through the many pages and dipping into the archives dating back to his youth when the ambitious youngster had an unquenchable thirst for knowledge. The modest library next door was home to a wide diversity of classical and modern literature collected by the avid bookworm over many years. Shakespeare, Keats and Shelley adorned the shelves sharing the limelight with twenty-first century novelists such as Clive Cussler, James Patterson, Lee Childs and Sebastian Faulks. It offered the self-educated wordsmith a rich variety of reading materials. To her surprise, there was a raunchy book by Jilly Cooper and a well-thumbed copy of *Fifty Shades of Grey* hidden in a corner. Predictably, Tom Sharpe's paperbacks occupied a prominent position in the middle of a bookshelf and the legendary titles brought a cheeky smile to the face of anyone conversant with his rude, witty and salacious tales.

Claire always knew these notes, comprehensive records and newspaper cuttings, all carefully indexed, formed the basis of his early days and shaped David into the man he was today. She pushed the leather upright chair to one side and, leaning on his beautifully polished desk, read some very poignant phrases in the social etiquette section. It read, 'Chardonnay is a popular white wine. Rioja is Spanish and tastes nice with steak and fish meals. Champagne is often called bubbly. Start from the outside when faced with a lot of cutlery. Always stand when a lady greets you.' And so it went on. These uncluttered notes were recorded in 1988 when he was just eighteen and starting out in life. Of all his many little anecdotes and famous quotations, these simple vignettes were the ones she liked most. They captured a moment in time, a piece of history when the orphan was immature and innocent, unsure about the future, and the congenial Mr and Mrs Crawford were acting as his moral compass and unofficial adopted parents.

Just then the house phone rang, which made her jump up as though she'd been scolded, but before she had time to pick up the receiver the redoubtable Mr Millins did the honours in the downstairs hallway.

"Hello!" he yelled. "You'll have to speak up. I'm 'aving me yers syringed on Wednesday so you'll 'ave to talk louder otherwise I shan't ear a word yer saying. Sir who?" he yelled. "What d'ya mean, sir?"

Claire darted down the stairs, two at a time, like a hungry wild beast bearing down on its prey, snatched hold of the phone from a quivering Mr Millins who retreated hastily from the scene. She said, while struggling to get her breath, "Hi it's Claire Lane here, who is that, please?"

"Oh good day Claire, it's Anthony York here. Just calling to say we may be a little late this evening as my wife's having lunch in town with the Home Secretary and we might be delayed somewhat. I do apologise."

"Oh, that's okay, Sir Anthony," explained Claire, with due deference to the respected knight of the realm, seeming to almost curtsy when her well-chosen words tripped off her tongue. "Thank you for letting me know, very kind of you sir," she whispered in a soft unobtrusive way.

"Oh I'm pleased to hear David and his colleagues did so well in Italy, but I'm sorry that one of his companions died. Very sad indeed. Deeply upsetting. I think the ME cause was a brilliant choice. I'm sure you must be very proud of your husband.

"I'm looking forward to catching up with him and hearing about his adventures first hand. I do hope your father's better soon. Earwax can be most distressing, I know. Give my regards to David. Look forward to seeing you later. Goodbye for now." The phone went dead.

"Father?" she yelled. "Father, oh my God."

She slammed the phone down, glared at her housekeeper, who was now busily dusting the ornaments in the lounge, cowering behind the fifty-inch TV, trying to keep a low profile judging by the pronounced curvature of his back. At the same time his arthritic wife was hoovering in the kitchen, listening to the incorrigible sound of Eric Idle on Radio 2 singing, *Always Look on the Bright Side of Life.*

"I wish I could nail you to a cross in the middle of a bloody desert," she mumbled under her breath, staring in the direction of her male tormentor, who was looking very sheepish, very disconsolate, polishing the dainty porcelain figurines on the lounge coffee table with increased vigour.

Looking dejected, Claire stumbled back up the staircase, holding onto the banister for support, feeling embarrassed by yet another social faux pas, thanks to the unwelcome intervention by the king of wax. Mrs Millins broke off from her chores in the kitchen to catch a glimpse of Claire disappearing up the spiral staircase, wondering what she might do to reduce the tension in the house and put matters right, once and for all. Like an old worn record life had conspired, yet again, to undermine Claire's efforts to move up the greasy pole. This latest humiliating episode, in the long-running saga of social chaos, convinced her that Mr Smooth had to sort it out. They had to go and go quickly. That was the unequivocal message she left on David's phone, while leaning over the first-floor balcony so everyone could hear her vitriolic rantings up and down the Avenue, let alone the occupants of the salubrious Regency abode.

"It's like juggling bloody chainsaws living here," she yelled down the phone. "With this belligerent pair of nobodies blotting our copybook at every turn, thwarting our every attempt to establish the Lane family name as a beacon for style and panache."

David's nervy, highly-strung wife could really wax lyrical when she was annoyed and that day was no exception. The blood-curdling message, left simmering on her husband's voicemail nearly syringed his ears when he had the misfortune to play it back on loudspeaker.

In her haste to answer the downstairs phone and stop Mr Millins in his tracks, Claire had inadvertently knocked over one of the lever-arch files, sending it crashing onto the beige carpet at the foot of the master's handcrafted desk. As she bundled up the cumbersome folder, making sure nothing had fallen out, she noticed there was another less bulky file hiding at the back of the cabinet which she'd never seen before. Smiling to herself, she read about Hastings and some of the haunts David frequented as a young tearaway. She wondered who Susan James was, no doubt a teenage crush, she surmised. Being inquisitive, she delved further. To her surprise the file included a series of poems penned years earlier. His collection covered many of Cheltenham's famous landmarks and historic places, but it was his solemn well-crafted tribute to the boys who died in the First World War that really pulled at her heartstrings, giving her a tantalising glimpse into the person she'd grown to love and admire so very much. It read:

Come Home Jack

Jack stands against a mighty foe, defies their battle cry,
He knows his task that dark, dull day, it is to do, or die.
The sound of guns as whistles blow, men charge for all their might,
Across an acrid smoke-filled land, hell's murderous torrid sight.

He is so young, he's still a child, Jack's classroom is a trench,
Where he will stand in filth and grime, smell mans' unholy stench.
Hear young men scream out in pain, sharp bullets tear their skin,
Jack stands aside his young comrades, as battle sounds begin.

They charge across in no man's land, dead bodies all around,
They hear the cries of men in pain, red poppies do abound.
Then the end it comes at last, loud guns go off to sleep,
So we can weep at our sad loss, but won't accept defeat.

Those brave young souls they grit their teeth, fought with all their might,
Against a foe that was so strong, so eager for the fight.
Their eyes were damp with cheeks so grey, and nails of dust and dirt,
And so they died beside brave chums draped in a khaki shirt.

He lost his youth for a just cause, of which he wasn't sure,
Saw his life just melt away, as the fighting was no more.
He left scarred fields and drifted home, Jack's memories didn't
fade,
As nightmares haunt his very soul, Somme's death toll was man-
made.

Lines of tears were streaming down her cheeks and her flimsy cotton hanky did its best to quell the tide as the tough confident businesswoman, known for her steely nerves and forthright manner, was overcome with emotion. Claire knew her husband was a talented self-made man, with a generous caring streak as wide as the English Channel, but she never imagined in her wildest dreams that the reformed drunk and renowned playboy was capable of penning such a wonderful piece of rhyme. Still wiping her eyes on her hand, she noticed a piece of paper carefully tucked into the sleeve at the back of the file. Being nosy, she opened the neatly folded page and read the contents.

'Dear Mum,
I miss you very much and love you lots. I clean my teeth every night without fail and always brush my hair even when I'm cold and tired. I am scared and very lonely and never have much to eat. I wish you were here to kiss me goodnight. Love David xxx.'

Claire sat slumped on the floor, unable to move, holding the piece of paper in her shaky hand, and with head bowed wept uncontrollably. It was a painful heart-wrenching insight into David's traumatic early years at the hands of his cruel vindictive cousin who made his life a living hell. Eventually, after several minutes, she composed herself and dried her cheeks and eyes as best she could. It was when Claire gently pushed the file back into its slot that she noticed a slim folder in a recess at the rear of the bookcase with what looked like the initials LL firmly stamped along the narrow spine.

Just at that moment, much to Claire's irritation, she heard her elderly housekeeper yelling at the bottom of the stairs:

"Mrs Lane! Yahoo, yahoo. Mrs Lane, yahoo. Can I have a word, please?"

I'll have a look at that file later, she promised, carefully sliding it back in its little hidey hole. What the hell does the wizened old witch want now? mumbled Claire. She stood up, checked her stress-ridden face in the office mirror before wandering down the sweeping staircase still thinking about David's literary talents and his tear-jerking note to his mother all those years earlier. No doubt the pair of miscreants will try to worm their way back into my good books, show their indispensability, try to put off the day when they'll be cast to the wind, she imagined, with a sinister smirk, as Mrs Millins' annoying bird impressions still hung in the air.

Chapter 53

David sauntered across the loud unruly concourse in search of his flight home, but first of all he needed a fresh set of clothes after the rigours of the day. So, following a brief pit-stop in the men's department at M&S, David emerged dressed in a plain white shirt, an uninspiring tweed jacket, with its obligatory brown patches on the elbows and a cheap pair of black polyester trousers. He knew his dowdy off-the-peg ensemble would allow him to merge into the background, not attract any untoward attention from the authorities, but he also realised that his unfashionable get-up, even though it was clean and tidy, had a short shelf life and would no doubt end up in a charity shop on the Bath Road if his fussy cellmate had anything to do with it.

Deciding to have a quick wash and brush-up, he made his way towards the nearest gent's toilets. However, after his tiring, eventful journey, he wasn't prepared for the shock at seeing this rather craggy bearded gent, dressed in some dodgy clothes, glaring back at him in the full-length mirror. David hadn't got used to his unsightly appearance, even after all that time, and was caught off guard, yet again, causing him to jerk sideways in surprise and collide with the infamous ten-second Dyson hand-dryer.

Then, much to the annoyance of a well-dressed fellow traveller, he knocked a wooden basket brimming full of linen hand towels and neatly wrapped bars of soap onto the black and white tiled floor. Thinking David was probably having a fit, or had overdone the vino at one of many bars and bistros, the snooty gent peered over his bifocals in disgust and bade a hasty retreat, leaving the ham-fisted pensioner to clear up the mess. David stared into the mirror and was amazed to see his disguise had fared so well, remained intact after all he'd been through. The bushy eyebrows hadn't moved, the carefully applied make-up on his face and around his eyes hadn't smudged and the deep lines and extra shading across his cheeks and jawline were perfect. Even the grey beard with white strands of hair was still most convincing, giving the impression of an elderly gent. Just the ticket.

The hairpiece was still fixed to his head and little strands of grey hair were sprouting over his ears and shirt collar, giving a slightly unkempt appearance. So after a bit of cosmetic tinkering and some final touches to his facial hair, the fledgling actor was ready for the next test. This was the big one, the big audition, there were no second chances. He had to get it right. He couldn't cock it up.

Checking his phone for any messages, he chuckled at PW's text saying he was en route to Barcelona to see his parents and doting sister who were longing for their hero's triumphant return, promising a red carpet, no-holds-barred ticker tape reception on his arrival at the country's second city. In equally gushing terms, PW also explained that once he'd finished his extensive media commitments and satisfied the demands of his adoring fans, he'd fly post-haste to the UK to celebrate another candle on the cake. David, in his wisdom, decided not to tell Chris about the antics in Zurich, it would be too complicated, thinking he'd bring him up to speed with events next time they met. Shoving his phone into his inside pocket, he gazed skywards hoping for some kind of divine intervention and, after taking a couple of deep breaths, walked with a confident air towards passport control.

Jostling between crowds of people on the bustling concourse, with its booming tannoy system and occasional blasts of loud music, he became increasingly nervous at the daunting prospect ahead. The Daredevil Challenge sounded like a bit of fun at a drink-fuelled dinner party when he'd sunk a few glasses of wine and port and was laughing with his mates, but the cold reality of his mission was altogether different as his churning stomach and damp clammy hands would readily testify.

There was Gregor fighting for his life in a hospital bed, the oily rag lying on a cold mortuary slab, if the news bulletins were to be believed, and there was David travelling incognito, trying to evade the clutches of the eagle-eyed police who were on red alert following the city centre shooting. You couldn't have written the script if you'd tried. It was too unbelievable for words; like a fictional scene from a John le Carré thriller. Arriving at the desk feeling hot and sticky, hoping his make-up hadn't run, he showed his flight details to the glum-faced officer as his luggage was placed on the conveyor belt and scanned for their contents. He was then asked some straightforward questions as his fake passport was checked, and carefully scrutinised. The tension was palpable, jumping up a few more notches when Cheltenham's finest noticed the two heavily armed police officers standing nearby carefully surveying the scene for anything out of the ordinary. But then after what seemed like a lifetime, he was given the green light and, with a huge sense of relief, David walked briskly in the direction of his flight, not looking back for one second, not tempting fate, just aiming straight for the exit doors and his flight to safety. Salvation was firmly in his sights, the gods had come to his rescue; they'd answered his prayers. But then it happened.

It was his worst nightmare; the thing he'd dreaded most. There was no mistaking it. He heard someone calling out his name, forcing him to stop dead in his tracks. Rooted to the spot, praying to the gods and anyone else that knew him, he glanced tentatively over his shoulder, not sure what he might see.

"Mr Davidson? Excuse me, sir. This way please." A short rather rotund female customs official was beckoning him with her index finger as two grim police officers stood motionless on either side, glaring in his direction, eyeing him up and down as he walked towards them. This is it. I've been rumbled. I'm for the high jump. I'll have to face the music. It's curtains for me, he decided reluctantly. Gurder, for her part, looked very officious wearing a peaked hat with rows of gold braiding while bright sparkling epaulettes adorned her broad upright shoulders. Not knowing what destiny had in store, his face took on a red complexion, his mouth dried up in sympathy and his palms sprang a leak.

"I can explain everything. It's a bit of fun. I know it sounds crazy, you'll think I'm daft doing something silly like this, but at the end of the day it's all about the money and helping others," he blurted out unthinking, not knowing what he was saying, such was his confused state of mind.

"I understand. I know you could get home much cheaper if you took a scheduled flight, but that's up to you sir. No, the reason why I've stopped you Mr Davidson is because you didn't pick up your boarding pass. You won't get very far without it," Gurder explained with a saucy wink. "Have a good trip, sir," she whispered, gently touching his outstretched fingers as she handed him his pass, bit her bottom lip and shook her head rather provocatively.

"Thank you," said David, wondering what that was all about. The inscrutable traveller, with a sweaty brow and a parched mouth, then walked assuredly towards the glass concourse doors that swished open to greet him, all the time under the watchful gaze of his middle-aged admirer. Still in a daze, but with a welcome breeze on his face, he marched briskly over the shiny black tarmac towards the gleaming silver jet sat patiently on its stand.

David forced a mild grin when the pretty young air hostess, with the whitest teeth he'd ever seen, gave his boarding details a cursory glance before welcoming him aboard flight 104 to Staverton Airport. In the meantime, his luggage was whisked away by an eager baggage handler who shuffled off towards the rear of the aircraft, with a badly bent spine and a pronounced limp, reminding him of a strange hunchback character he'd read about in his early childhood.

So after a couple of quick selfies with Miss Colgate, who for some reason insisted on pouting her lips and standing on one leg, he gripped hold of the rail and climbed aboard the salubrious executive jet just as the twin Rolls-Royce engines fired up. The narrow cabin in the Cessna had four pairs of comfortable high-backed reclining seats with a walkway down the middle. The subtle white-painted walls and beige carpet offered a relaxing atmosphere that would have appealed to even the most hard-nosed seasoned traveller. A middle-aged couple were locked in deep conversation at the front of the aircraft, oblivious to his presence, as he manoeuvred his way towards his reserved seat at the rear of the cabin. David wiped the beads of sweat off his forehead and slouched back in his comfy cream leather chair just as Lou Reed's husky voice hit the airwaves. Yes, it'll be a perfect day once I'm safely home, the charlatan thought, gazing out onto the runway with its line of passenger aircraft sat waiting as mounds of luggage were unloaded into deep cavernous aircraft holds. A few moments later, with his ears popping, he glanced out of the small circular window, pleased to see they were airborne, homeward bound, powering at speed towards the imposing white-crested Alpine range.

Once they'd levelled out and set their route for the north-west, the youthful trolley dolly, with the halogen torch stuck in her mouth, offered him a much needed drink from the mobile cocktail bar. He gulped down the glass of Merlot Reserve in one swig and asked for a refill before the pretty hostess, with long auburn hair and a bright blue jacket and pleated skirt, had chance to open his folding table and present her guest with the food and drinks menus.

David sent a text to Claire explaining he was on his way. There'd been a bit of trouble in Zurich, but he was safe and sound and should arrive at Staverton in a couple of hours. There was no reply. He sent a longer, more convoluted message to Sarah at the Excelsior Hotel in Garda thanking her for her help and asking the receptionist to check on Gregor's medical condition and let him have an update as soon as possible. He also apologised for his busy schedule, promising to spend more time with her when he was next in the resort. A short time later, cruising effortlessly over the Alps, a tray of mixed sandwiches and piping hot coffee was brought to David's seat. He quietly munched his way through the egg and cress fingers and warm freshly baked scones, which reminded him of Mrs Millins's culinary skills back home. As a special treat, the athlete sampled some of the mouth-watering dark Belgian chocolates on offer, with their soft gooey centres and marzipan topping, knowing that a frenetic half-hour ride on Jordan would soon burn off any excess calories.

Then, without warning, to the sound of loud gasps inside the cabin, the jet lost height dropping several hundred feet in just a few short seconds. An unexpected downdraft was the culprit and the reassuring pilot, with a deep gravelly voice like Huey Lewis, explained that turbulence was a common occurrence near high mountain ranges and that erratic unpredictable weather conditions were par for the course at any time of the year. But the sudden unexpected shock reminded David of his parents' ill-fated flight all those years earlier, making the palms of his hands sweat as the imposing Alpine range loomed large through the tiny window, with its white snow-covered peaks and ice-laden slopes glistening innocently in the late afternoon sun. The pilot's remedy was simple. Jeremy suggested they relax back and recline in their soft comfortable seats. Treat themselves to a drink from the well-stocked bar, order any food and snacks from Elsie, their friendly air hostess and enjoy their short flight back to the UK, where the weather was warm and rather muggy, following a recent storm.

It's commonly known that the slightest turbulence would normally have Cheltenham's adopted son reaching for the sick bag, sweating like a cornered nun, holding his six-pack in a vice-like grip, preventing his internal organs from exploding everywhere.

But not that day, the frequent flyer had other things on his mind. He was immersed in his own private thoughts.

David was tormented at the thought of Roger Sands' attempt on his life, for which there was no reason. Equally, he was agonising over Susan's cruel betrayal and deception and her downright duplicity in the whole sordid affair, ending in his innocent cabby's life hanging in the balance through no fault of his own. He tried to suppress his anger by concentrating on other issues and sent a short text to his colleagues on the Garda 150 thanking them again for their stellar performance in exceeding the five million pound target, explaining he was well on his way with the Daredevil Challenge and looking forward to their reunion in September. At David's request, the light meal was finished off with a plate of neatly sliced pieces of cheddar cheese and Crawford cream crackers complemented by a dainty glass china bowl bursting with fresh grapes and orange slices. After the banquet in the sky, and his little tasty titbits, the revitalised millionaire thought long and hard before dialling the number following his earlier text.

"Hello Susan, it's me." It was quiet for a moment then she spoke in a whisper.

"I got your text. Thank God, you're alive. What the hell's going on, David?"

David explained the turn of events to his agitated mistress and then said, "But you know all this. There's a dead man on a slab and badly injured driver lying prostrate in a Zurich hospital ward.

"You sent him after me, didn't you? I can't believe you'd tried to hurt me after all we've meant to each other. I never thought you'd stoop so low to protect your little world." Raising his voice, he said, "Please tell me you're not behind all this. Tell me I'm being paranoiac. Tell me, Suzy." The phone went dead.

He flopped back in shock as the trolley dolly poured a refill in his china coffee cup and handed him a malt whisky and dry ginger on a silver salver. His errant mistress had confirmed what he already suspected, knew in his heart of hearts, but to hear it from the horse's mouth, so to speak, was a difficult pill to swallow even for someone as tough and streetwise as the redoubtable David Lane.

Closing his eyes, he relaxed back and thought about the different women in his life. How treachery, betrayal and disloyalty had forged a destructive alliance, forming a common theme of greed and

305

deception going back many years. He'd been duped, cheated, hoodwinked, made a fool of by those he loved, those who meant so much to him, the very people he trusted with his life. He'd learnt a painful, salutary lesson.

Chapter 54

The bumpy landing at Staverton, due to strong crosswinds, woke the playboy with a hefty jolt. He squinted out of the tinted window into the early evening gloom as the Cessna taxied along the runway, swaying from side to side on the uneven surface. Still half asleep and rubbing his eyes, he saw a familiar black BMW parked several hundred yards away, no doubt waiting for him. A combination of alcohol and broken sleep made David feel drowsy, and it was not until he plonked his size tens on terra firma and had his last poignant glimpse of Elsie's halogen lamps that he realised his predicament. Graham, his diminutive driver and a retired customs official was striding briskly across the open ground in the direction of passport control. Taking to his heels, the phony forty-something ran as fast as he could towards the brightly lit two-storey office standing at the end of the runway like a beacon welcoming him home. Now, the grim-faced official, with a bulging stomach and several chins to his name, wasn't in a hurry and took what seemed like an inordinate amount of time to process his paperwork.

Not surprisingly, David berated himself for being too blasé, for taking his eye off the ball and not thinking ahead. His casual indifference had seriously jeopardised his plan, put his carefully crafted scheme at risk. But thankfully, his prayers were answered, the gods came to his rescue and, after a few tense moments, the well-fed official with the garlic aftershave did his bit with a rubber stamp and a self-satisfied grin crawled across the weary traveller's face. He'd done it, he was back on home turf, safe and sound. But there wasn't a moment to lose, no time to celebrate. The champagne would have to remain on ice. Grabbing his luggage and rubbing his ankle, that for some reason had started to throb, he aimed towards the neon sign flickering on and off near the entrance to the customs office. To his surprise, Graham suddenly pushed the double doors wide open looking flushed and rather agitated with his phone firmly glued to his ear. Fortunately he didn't notice David, he didn't give him a second glance dressed in his tweedy ensemble and hiding under Jamie's cunning disguise.

"Yes, Mrs Lane. I'm at the airport now but I can't see him anywhere. I'll have a word with my mates. Don't worry, I'll find him. He's around here somewhere."

Scratching his bald head and rubbing his stubbly chin, the bewildered cabby peered on tiptoe around the spacious customs office like a meerkat surveying its territory. He couldn't understand it. Where the hell was he?

David saw his chance and shot into the gent's toilets. A young fair-skinned guy with long strands of wild curly hair, was standing po-faced in front of the full-length mirror brushing his unruly locks, trying to get them to behave. Recognising David from passport control, he nodded his head. But then glancing out of the corner of his eye, Bob got rather nervous when the elderly gent leant against the toilet wall in a rather provocative way and started taking selfies of himself and his facial hair from different angles. Slightly anxious, not knowing what might happen next, he continued gazing into the mirror, while David filled the sink to the top, then submerged his face into the hot soapy water before frantically pulling at his beard with his fingers and thumbs. He then gently dabbed his face on a bundle of Kleenex tissues before moving to the next stage of his routine. To the amazement of his nervy onlooker, David then removed his beard in one simple flick of his wrist. The shock made Bob jump back in surprise, splashing the front of his light-green trousers in hot soapy water that then dripped onto the floor from the overflowing sink.

"Could you shove it in the lid of my case, please?" asked David, frantically scrubbing the layers of make-up off his face. "Quick as you can please. I haven't got much time. I'm in a real hurry."

Bob duly obliged, but he couldn't understand why. There he was visiting the gents, minding his own business, trying to look his best before meeting the girl of his dreams on his much-vaunted blind date. So why had he got involved with an elderly lunatic in drag? After all, he could end up being an accessory to some terrible crime, caught up in a web of criminality, drawn unknowingly into a world where false beards, eyeliners and imitation hairpieces were the order of the day. This was bad news, very bad news for the nervous Romeo with a worrying tic that got worse the more fretful he became. Bob wanted to make a good first impression. That was the advice given to him after meeting girl number twenty-nine earlier in the week which, following his litany of failed liaisons, turned out to be another pitiful disaster in the romantic stakes. Leave her wanting more, was the smooth-talking adviser's passing shot when he quickly processed his credit card for another six months' exclusive gold card membership. Now in Bob's long-running association with the website, 'we can match anyone, yes anyone.com', his track record with the fairer sex was lamentable; a desperate saga of abject failure.

But in his torrid world of unrequited love, he had one saving grace, one solitary claim to fame that he held onto like a barnacle on the bottom of a boat. His date had never done a runner, never disappeared in a cloud of dust before the simple formality of the introductory handshake. That was a nightmare scenario from which he'd never recover. So, with his tainted reputation hanging by a thin thread, he knew his unkempt appearance and nervous tic didn't bode well, as the humiliating prospect of rejection was looming large, seeming an odds-on bet for the deflated love machine.

"Quickly, pass me a handful of tissues from that Kleenex box over there," said David, pointing impatiently to the back of the sink. "Thanks. Now, here's the tricky bit. Hold your hands out flat and stop shaking 'cause that doesn't help."

Again, his assistant did as he was told, looking on in surprise when the grey moustache was slowly peeled away from his upper lip, making David wince as the glue stubbornly resisted the tug of his impatient fingers and thumbs. The trickster then wiped the remaining layers of make-up from his face and neck before peeling off his fake lifelike eyebrows and pulling little clumps of grey hair from inside his ears. The voyeur watched open-mouthed, glued to the spot, firmly stapled to the floor, unsure what the unmasking would reveal as the transformation continued unabated.

"Now, put all the bits of hair into the lid as quick as you can. Come on, stop messing about, you'll have to be quicker than that," said David sternly. Cupid was becoming increasingly agitated by the whole affair and, in between acting as David's assistant, continued frantically rubbing his soaking wet crotch with a handful of paper tissues in an attempt to soak up the moisture and dry the damp unsightly patch as best he could. Sadly, poor Bob was unready for the next stage in the thespian's repertoire as David raised his left arm skyward and, with an assured flick of his wrist, removed his hairpiece in one slick movement. It was just like a matador swishing his flowing cape through the air and happened in a split second. It was cheerio to Mr Davidson, the hairy OAP with a pallid complexion and miles too much hair and hello to Mr Lane, a smooth skinned forty-four-year-old, boasting an impish grin and a raucous laugh. Well this was the last straw, it was too much for lover boy, too much of a shock to his fragile nervous system. There standing before him, gazing into the innocuous full-length toilet mirror with a smile to match Simon Cowell's ego, was the bronze charismatic face of the legendary David Lane. As if on cue, Romeo's nose started twitching up and down like a rabbit and, in a state of shock, David's bewildered assistant tossed his damp soggy tissues in the air and took to his heels, never looking back for one second.

Outside in the fresh air, Bob took a deep breath and tried to compose himself, hoping the light breeze would carry on drying his damp trousers. Looking along the runway, he noticed the Swiss flight had landed and, with fingers crossed and a glance towards the heavens, he hoped girl thirty, famous for her bright sparkling smile, would be the new love of his life and that she'd never forget their first few moments together.

Seconds later, David pushed open the toilet door, checked whether the coast was clear, then sneaked out of the building and shot across the deserted airport runway as fast as he could towards the parked BMW. Thankfully there was no one there. Leaning across the polished black bonnet, panting very slightly, he caught sight of his bemused driver ambling towards him with his phone stuck to his ear.

"Hello, Mr Lane. Where did you come from? I must have missed you, sir!" he said, shaking David's hand with a vice-like grip.

"I've been waiting here for some time," he replied. "Don't worry. I'm just pleased to be home. It's good to see you. How are things?"

Graham slid the luggage into the boot of the BMW, wondering why his wealthy passenger was wearing a boring tweed jacket that was more suited to someone older and down on their luck. It was most strange.

"I'm okay thank you, sir. Happy birthday by the way and congratulations on your achievement yesterday. My wife and I watched your progress on television. To ride 150 kilometres in that kind of heat was something else. I don't know how you did it. I understand you collected over five-million pounds for the ME charity. Glad you put it on the map, made people talk about it. I'm sure the money will help a lot."

Driving towards the town centre, resting back in the soft leather, Graham's passenger was captivated by the musical eloquence of Elton John singing *Your Song*. The poignant lyrics lifted his spirits for a few moments, but still feeling very upset and betrayed after his conversation with Susan, he thought about Shirley, the first love of his life, and how much he missed her, wondering whether he'd ever find true love and a real sense of belonging.

"Yes, Graham. We put the spotlight on ME. We lifted it out of the shadows and shone a light on the illness, but how long will it stay on? It's like your daily newspaper. Can you remember yesterday's headlines, let alone last week's? I can't let the illness slip back into the gloom. It can't be a one-hit wonder, it's got to stay in the charts for months and years to come. I've got to keep it on the front page and that, my friend, is the big challenge for me going forward."

"I totally agree. Oh, I'd like to ask you something if I may, sir?"

"Yes," replied David, closing his eyes as Elton tickled the ivories for the last few chords.

"Is there any reason why you're wearing make-up, sir?"

David jerked upright, looked straight into the car mirror and was startled to see he had some hideous streaks of make-up smudged on his neck and under his chin which he'd obviously overlooked during his antics in the gent's loo. Thinking on his feet he replied, "The sun was very hot when I left Garda this morning and it looks as though I overdid the sun cream. Thanks for letting me know. I'll clean up when I get home."

David thought the story sounded plausible and, as Graham seemed relaxed with the explanation, he grabbed his phone and sent a quick text to Claire, reminding her to contact the sponsors, saying he'd completed the Daredevil Challenge and looked forward to receiving a cheque for £50k for the ME charity. A selection of selfies, as proof of his exploits, would be posted on Facebook in due course. She didn't reply. As they entered the outskirts of the town past GCHQ and the leafy suburbs, Graham piped up again, much to David's annoyance. The birthday boy was hoping to grab a bit of shut-eye before the evening celebrations which promised to be a boisterous, drink-fuelled affair lasting into the small hours.

"If I may be so bold, sir. I think you've got an eyebrow, or a sideburn lodged in the collar of your shirt. I expect you stuck it there sir, as additional protection from the blazing sun," he suggested sarcastically.

"Thank you," replied David, climbing out of the car and grabbing hold of his suitcases from Graham, who was quietly chuckling to himself as he slammed the boot closed.

"Have a good time tonight sir, but before you rush off, I heard a funny story from Charlie on passport control. He's the one with lots of chins and smells like garlic. Got a very good memory, has our Charlie. Strange thing is, he couldn't remember seeing you, from the description I gave him, amongst the arrivals when you landed from Zurich. What's more, your name didn't even appear on the passenger list. But here's the funny thing. He can recall an older-looking gentleman with a beard, deep-set eyes, dark sullen complexion and a tweed jacket, similar to the one you're wearing, but he couldn't remember you. Anyway, don't forget the make-up sir and well you're at it, there's a bit of grey hair sticking out of your right ear which looks a bit unsightly for a man of your standing," said Graham, with a wry smile and a nonchalant shake of the head.

David ignored his churlish comments and waved his hand half-heartedly as the BMW's Pirelli tyres crunched noisily over the uneven gravel surface.

Chapter 55

The party was in full swing, judging by the racket greeting the returning hero on pushing open the side door and peering in. His friends were all drinking, joking and talking loudly in the capacious lounge at the front of the house with David Bowie raving on about his little china girl.

Leaving his luggage in the vestibule, he crept up the spiral staircase, keeping low and out of sight, not wishing to attract any attention. He felt hot and sweaty and was looking forward to a cool refreshing shower after what had been a truly unforgettable day even by his standards. Smiling to himself, he recalled his antics in the airport toilet with the nervy guy who'd wet his trousers, hoping he hadn't spoilt his evening too much. Still rebuking himself for making so many infantile errors at the airport, after all his meticulous planning, he climbed out of his clothes to the mellow sound of Sam Smith's falsetto voice greeting him through the Bosch wall-to-wall sound system. Then thinking back to Graham's fatuous remarks, David knew he'd been rumbled by the cunning old fox, but was grateful to him for keeping his counsel, not asking any embarrassing questions which could have got him into deep water with the authorities.

He quickly grabbed a pair of boxer shorts and his cream dressing gown and sneaked down the back passage at the rear of the house, hoping to have a quick ride on Jordan to inject some much-needed energy into his weary limbs and stop his body stiffening up. Nipping down the stairs two at a time, he noticed the party food on display in the palatial high-tech kitchen and pinched a couple of dainty sausage rolls and a thin slice of Mrs Millins's famous homemade flan. He saw a mouth-watering trifle in a crystal glass bowl with piles of juicy red cherries spread liberally across its sumptuous cream topping. Licking his lips, it was very tempting for the man with a sweet tooth, sat on its own in the middle of the solid oak table begging to be eaten. There were trays of sandwiches covered in clingfilm and a wide selection of cheeses and dips and other savoury treats to tease and tantalise the taste buds. The side tables were home to umpteen cases of red and white wine and an exotic collection of cocktails he'd never heard of, while a choice selection of spirits and French champagne stood in line, like soldiers on parade, all for the delectation of the specially invited guests.

The spacious ultra-modern kitchen with its beautifully handcrafted sleek sideboards, elegant decor and its array of state-of-the-art sophisticated gadgets and appliances, would have had Nigella Lawson, and any Michelin star chef, swooning in delight at the culinary facilities at their fingertips. But casting his eyes to the floor, the man of the house quickly lost interest in the fancy foods and expensive drinks on offer and was horrified to see an empty peanut bag lying discarded near the base of the chrome refuse bin.

Now Claire had suffered from a serious nut allergy since her childhood days and even the smallest morsel could prove fatal, so he had every reason to be concerned for her health and would raise the issue with her as soon as he could.

Forty minutes later, feeling fully rejuvenated, the birthday boy strolled into the downstairs front room, like a Hollywood star on the red carpet, with a broad grin stamped on his face and dressed in a deep blue lounge suit with an open-neck white shirt and button-down collar. His enthusiastic guests shrieked and hollered when he appeared in the doorway, singing happy birthday with great enthusiasm while treating the tanned specimen to lots of hugs, many firm handshakes and untold kisses. Everyone wanted to share in the maestro's big day and join in the celebrations such was the warm friendly atmosphere pervading throughout the posh Regency house.

Claire raced forward, as the dutiful wife, embraced her husband and kissed him passionately on the lips while the sound of three cheers echoed around the room that was decorated in flags, paper chains and colourful streamers and full to bursting with cheery-eyed well-wishers. Bryan Ferry didn't stand a chance, not a prayer, as the sultry rhythmic chords of *Avalon* were drowned out by the rowdy behaviour of his exuberant, highly charged guests. With tears in her eyes and, in earshot of their excitable friends, she told her husband how much she loved him. The birthday party got its second breath, its second lease of life once the star of the show arrived on the scene, and the adulation of his many loyal chums and colleagues soon reached fever pitch as the champagne corks popped and the wines and cocktails flowed freely.

Gazing about, with a glass of chilled bubbly in his hand, he saw Jamie and his partner from the local theatre chatting to Mike, his party agent, leaning rather precariously on his wife for support. Mohammed and Clara, members of his political campaign team, were busily chatting to each other and pointing enviously at some of the expensive fine art paintings on show around the room acquired over many years from exclusive galleries in Chelsea and nearby Broadway. David was gratified to see Colin and Steve, two reformed alcoholics, had made the cut. They were in deep conversation with Amanda, of all people, showing off their usual down to earth rustic charm and quirky take on life.

Smiling to himself, he remembered one occasion when Steve was so drunk that he found himself chatting up a partly dressed female mannequin in M&S's Ladies' Wear. Not wishing to upset other customers, a big burly female security guard, with a faint moustache, ushered the inebriate to the nearest exit telling him that the nice lady wasn't prepared to let him have her mobile number whatever the pretext. To appease the sozzled old soak Sandra promised to apologise to the one-armed mannequin for any offence he may have caused and she'd pass the message on as soon as she re-entered the store. Cross my heart and hope to die was the promise she made to Steve as he stumbled off towards the nearest pub like a yacht tacking through waves on a windy day.

Amanda, the sophisticated socialite, was a renowned snob. She talked with a huge plum in her mouth, putting the Queen in the shade when it came to posh cultivated accents. Sadly the pair of ill-equipped Casanovas were batting way outside their league, judging by the pained expression on the investment banker's face as she nibbled on a dainty cucumber sandwich and sipped a glass of Evian water in order to preserve her size-ten figure. Once the comedy duo sensed they weren't making any headway with frilly knickers, there was only one thing for it. It was time to introduce her to Rupert.

He was their secret weapon, their pièce de résistance, their party trick who was only brought out of cold storage for the chosen few. So the scene was set and the jovial jousters from Gloucester stood either side of their elegant victim waxing lyrical about the plight of poor Rupert. Initially frilly knickers wasn't interested, kept yawning behind her hand, but the lovable rogues weren't deflected in their mission and decided to raise the stakes, give her both barrels from their well-rehearsed script. Steve explained quite eloquently how Rupert's tragic disability made even the simplest household chores difficult to perform. Posh pants slowly took the bait, seemingly intrigued by their tear-jerking tale of woe while Colin started plying her with glasses of pink bubbly, which she downed with great haste as the enthralling story of domestic tragedy pulled at her heartstrings. Steve went on to explain that Rupert's luxurious five-bedroom house had lots and lots of lights, hanging from room to room, along the sweeping corridors and up and down narrow winding staircases. This posed a very serious problem for the poor lad particularly as he lived on his own.

"What do you mean, problem?" asked Amanda, struggling to keep upright.

At this point, Colin took over. He told their victim that Rupert only had one hand and that was a distinct problem when it came to changing a light bulb. "What was he to do? It was a real nightmare," he explained, charging her glass and handing Amanda a couple of fresh tissues.

Sounding very squiffy after downing yet another glass of champers, Amanda interrupted Colin. "But surely you can't change a light bulb if you've only got one hand. It's obvious, isn't it?" she blurted out in slurred speech, punctuated by three rapid hiccups and another noise which is best left unsaid.

The rogues knew they'd got her; she was well and truly hooked. So with broad beaming smiles, the two reprobates peered into her bloodshot eyes and said, in unison, "But yes you can, Amanda. You can always change a light bulb so long as you've still got the receipt."

Well Amanda's reaction was completely unexpected, totally out of character for a lady often featured in the gossip columns of *Tattler* and the *Horse and Groom*. She started laughing hysterically, snorting at the same time, gripping hold of Steve's tattooed arm for support. Guests were mystified to see the renowned socialite, a pillar of respectable society, laughing and sniggering and repeating the punch line with her slim index finger pressed firmly against her upper lip.

"So long as you've got a receipt," she kept mumbling. "So long as you've got a receipt." When Freddie, a respected jump jockey, joined his inebriated girlfriend, she was still repeating the same strapline and giggling out of the corner of her mouth and working hard to keep upright.

Some of the guests couldn't resist the temptation, pointing their smartphones in her direction, guaranteeing the socialite's embarrassing appearance on YouTube for days to come. By this time, she'd discarded her cumbersome five-inch heels and was hanging onto the mantelpiece with tears of joy streaming down her face, with black mascara smeared under her eyes and red lipstick smudged around her mouth and chin. Just as the floorshow was coming to a climax, Claire grabbed hold of David's arm.

"I didn't know you'd arrived home," she remarked with a sinister smirk. "You're not walking too well. Is that because of your accident in Torbole?"

"Yes, how did you know about that? I got in a short time ago, gave Jordan a bit of a go and here I am fully refreshed and ready for the fray."

Claire didn't reply, but turned to her guests, clinked the side of her champagne glass for attention and yelled at the top of her voice. "Listen up everybody! Not only has my gallant husband ridden around the infamous Lake Garda in the most gruelling conditions, but he did it the day before his forty-fourth birthday, well done my darling."

Fluted glasses were raised skyward, all saluting the man of the moment as an outpouring of love and adoration swept through the room, spontaneously. They loved him and he knew it.

David was overcome with emotion, feeling quite tearful, and even though he was worn out after the events of the last three days, he wouldn't have missed the evening for the world. He cherished the company of his many kind caring and loyal friends who meant a great deal to him. Piles of colourfully wrapped presents, in all shapes and sizes, and numerous unopened birthday cards, spread out on the corner table in the elegant bow window, were testimony to their affection for the charitable benefactor and smooth-talking socialite.

"Speech, speech!" was the clarion call from his slightly intoxicated guests, standing in awe of the great man. "Speech, speech!"

"Okay, I'll say a few words, I'll keep it brief," said David, smiling and waving his hands energetically in the air. "Thank you for coming this evening and for the wonderful gifts. So very kind. I do appreciate it very much. I must say the Italian ride was more challenging than any of us had imagined. Even though we were constantly battling the intense heat, my compatriots and I were driven by a single cause which my dear friend Anthony York will fully appreciate," he remarked, nodding in his direction and raising his glass in acknowledgment of the Programme's distinguished chairman.

"I don't intend to preach, particularly at such a happy time, but my friends, my dear friends, please bear with me for just a couple of moments. Do you know there are over 250,000 people suffering from a debilitating illness in the UK without a cure and the worse sufferers are confined to bed for long periods? I'm talking about ME/CFS. It's a Cinderella illness, ignored and overlooked by the authorities and the forgotten sufferers are invisible to the naked eye, left to their own devices. They don't exist; they're nowhere on the radar. They're the submerged minority. Many rely on various forms of support which is patchy, scant and limited to say the least. This isn't good enough, not good enough at all. Something has to be done. So my valiant chums and I got on our bikes and peddled for 150 kilometres to raise the profile of the illness, get people talking about it and fill the coffers of the charity that does so much good work across the UK. I'm pleased to say we made over six-million pounds on Sunday, which wasn't bad for a bunch of oldies and I'm proud to say we're definitely on the cusp of something very, very special."

His guests cheered and clapped at David's triumph, but as the applause slowly subsided he grabbed a glass of orange and carried on:

"The person who motivated me to nominate ME as the chosen charity for the Garda 150 is a young woman who lives here in the town, in Cheltenham.

"Lucy is truly remarkable and has given a great deal over the years in helping fellow sufferers combat the illness. It's quite amazing considering she herself is blighted by ME and has lived with it for over twenty-five years, all of her adult life. Just imagine that for one moment. I'm hoping to visit her in the next couple of days."

His friends looked on spellbound while David, the orator, the philanthropist, captured their imagination with his carefully crafted words, seduced them by his compelling story of life under the spell of ME. Even the most hardnosed guest was left reaching for the Kleenex, such was the emotion in his voice.

"Regrettably, one of our number paid the ultimate price. This has drawn a dark cloud over the event and has affected us all, as you would imagine."

There were gasps and sideways glances. No one realised that amongst the excitement of the famous Italian ride, featured with such razzmatazz in the press and on social media, that one of David's number, one of the brave audacious riders had lost his life.

"Yes I'm sorry to say one of our colleagues is no longer with us. But I know Gary would be pleased to hear of our success, that his tragic death was not in vain. I would therefore ask you to raise your glasses in memory of our fallen hero. A man to whom we owe so much. To Gary."

With glasses held aloft, everyone called out his name and glanced at one another with stern expressions, bloodshot eyes and crumpled handkerchiefs at the ready.

"Thank you again for coming along this evening and for the wonderful gifts and goodwill messages. I love you all." David wiped his eyes, kissed Claire on the cheek and sipped a glass of Pinot Noir handed to him by Jamie his resourceful make-up artist.

"Where are the Millinses?" asked David, peering around the room hoping to catch a glimpse of his loyal companions going about their business, but his live-in helpers were conspicuous by their absence.

"You don't read your texts, do you, Mr L?" said Claire sarcastically. "I killed them earlier today, buried them in the garden under a great pile of silage. A fitting end for a pair of dopey old duffers, don't you think?" David stared at his wife. He wasn't amused by Claire's infantile attitude towards his trusted housekeepers who had a very special place in his heart, showing him devotion and loyalty since day one, something which was sadly lacking from the various women in his life.

"Okay, the orang-utans are in their room," she snapped. "I told them not to come out until our guests had left and the coast's clear. I bought them another couple of DVDs of *Downton Abbey* which will keep the idle ne'er-do-wells occupied and they've also got a tray of sandwiches and a selection of party food, plus an expensive bottle of chilled Chablis. That'll keep them quiet, don't you think?"

Claire helped herself to another glass of champagne, swigged it down in one mouthful and, leaning on the drinks' cabinet to steady herself, took a sharp intake of air while an angry expression slowly rolled over her face. "Oh, I was in your office, your inner sanctum earlier today tidying up, making sure your precious files weren't harbouring any dust or dirt. But then guess what happened my home-grown hero? Guess what I found buried in one of your little cubby holes in your private world? Who the hell is Louise?" she whispered in his ear. Just then, Amanda waved in his direction, treated him to a display of her bright shiny teeth before collapsing back onto the settee in the foetal position with a number of smartphones in hot pursuit.

"This better be good, lover boy," Claire shrieked in his ear, her hands shaking in anger as rows of deep furrowed lines wriggled across her forehead. She was ready to explode, spill her molten lava, just like the famous Vesuvius, promising equally devastating results for anyone in close proximity.

David was caught on the wrong foot. After all, his files were his own personal property, his own affair and he didn't expect his wife to snoop about behind his back, delving into his private papers and personal records. He always intended speaking to Claire about his daughter, but at a moment of his choosing and definitely not in an emotionally charged atmosphere where temperatures were at boiling point and alcohol had been flowing freely for some time.

"We'll talk later when the guests have gone and we've got time to have an intelligent adult conversation. It's not what you think," he replied, composing himself as best he could, trying to buy some time to collect his thoughts.

Just then his chairman came to his rescue, patted him on the shoulder and shook his hand. Claire saw her opportunity to make a speedy exit, not wishing to embarrass herself in such exalted company, but promising to return to the subject later that evening when all hell would let loose. She was quietly fuming, ready to lynch her deceitful two-timing husband from the nearest tree in Pavilion Avenue, but her day would be complete, the answer to all of her prayers, if the Millinses were also dangling by their scrawny necks on either side of the womanising philanderer. That would be perfect.

"So according to your email, the whole network of thieves have been uncovered and arrested is that correct?" Sir Anthony asked impatiently.

"Yes," replied David. "The Programme is safe and secure and will carry on from strength to strength now that the criminals have been apprehended. We've lost some funds, but Inspector Parry thinks we have a good chance of recovering a sizeable amount and I'm seeing him soon to discuss the matter. As we said before, our new accountants and auditors will set up a watertight system to ensure we aren't the target of thieves and embezzlers in the future. On a lighter note, as you know I successfully completed the Daredevil Challenge and managed to evade detection by the authorities so the sponsors will have to cough up £50k for the ME cause."

"I don't want to know the details, but I'm sure it was all legal and above board?" Sir Anthony asked quizzically, not expecting a reply.

"Now, let's have another look at those selfies you took in the gents. My favourite is that one," explained Sir Anthony, peering over David's shoulder and pointing to the screen. "That poor guy's expression when you peeled off your beard. Just look at his face, his eyes were ready to pop out at any moment. But look at this one when you removed your wig, he nearly had a heart attack. They're fantastic," said the chairman, laughing and patting David on the shoulder. "I don't know how you managed to take them, but they're great. You're a remarkable man, David Lane, and your parents would be very proud of you. It's fitting that when I retire this year that you take over the reins. After all, it's your baby."

"I'll have to think about it, if I may," replied David, wondering how best to handle Claire now that Louise was on the scene and his long-standing relationship with Susan was out of the bag.

Sir Anthony grinned as he sipped his Bloody Mary. "Let's not talk shop anymore now. Perhaps we can catch up later in the week. Now let me go and have another slice of that Victoria sponge before it all disappears. I think your Mrs Millins is a gem, if you ever tire of her, send her my way.

"Do you hear?"

"There's no danger of that," replied David. "She'll always be welcome in my home whatever happens."

Chapter 56

Later that evening, when the last of the guests had staggered past the front door and negotiated the steps onto the gravel drive as though it was the north face of the Eiger, Claire was taken ill and rushed to hospital. The initial tests showed she'd eaten peanuts at some stage during the party and was the reason for her drifting in and out of consciousness, and her irregular heartbeat and shallow breathing also caused some concern among the medical team. The prognosis wasn't good and the next twenty-four hours were seen as critical. So on Tuesday morning, just after dawn and following many night-time telephone calls to the BUPA hospital, David arrived to check on the patient's progress and was pleased to see his wife sat in an easy chair watching TV and sipping a glass of crushed orange juice. Her favourite tipple. Apparently she'd only consumed a very small morsel and, as her symptoms were treated quickly, the danger to her health had been averted. "She should be as good as new in a couple of days," explained Dr Hussein with a huge grin and a hearty tug on his stethoscope hanging loosely around his neck.

Text messages and emails flooded in from anxious friends and relatives all expressing their best wishes for a speedy recovery. Many of whom had their own pet theories as to how their dear friend had fallen ill in such strange circumstances and the harbingers of doom had a field day spreading rumours and mischief wherever they went.

Because of Claire's ingrained animosity towards the Millinses, her husband thought it unwise to let them loose in the hospital, particularly as the bad blood between the warring parties had worsened of late and now Claire's unexplained illness merely added to the tension. Needless to say, the finger of suspicion pointed at Mrs Millins, the resident cook and chief bottle washer, but David pooh-poohed the whole idea, laughed it off without a second thought, saying it was a tragic accident caused by the caterers who'd cocked up the food order. There was no doubt in his mind as to who should carry the can.

Claire's husband spent most of the morning catching up on the local news and talking to the medical staff about his wife's improving condition while dipping into the odd chapter in Tom Sharpe's novel, *Riotous Assembly*, which appealed to his sense of humour often forcing him to laugh out loud at some of the author's lewd jokes and irreverent storylines. But then during the afternoon, she dropped the bombshell just after the opening credits for *Silent Witness* and following his first glimpse of the delectable Emilia Fox. He was quietly relaxing in a comfy leather armchair without a care in the world, with a refreshing cup of freshly brewed Earl Grey tea in his hand and his favourite novelist resting on his lap, when all of a sudden Claire piped up.

"I've been thinking about it all day and I've decided to leave you David. I want a divorce. I thought there was some hope of reconciliation even though we've grown apart in recent months, but now I discover you've had a mistress in Hastings for twenty years and have a grown-up teenage daughter. A daughter. It's unbelievable. I can't believe it," she shouted. "Well, it's just too much. Surely you can understand that? You've led a double life for years. You've betrayed my trust. I don't want to hear your weak excuses, your clever explanations. You can't worm your way out of this one. Anyway, I've found someone else. Someone who takes an interest in me, spends time with me and doesn't have lots of skeletons hiding in the cupboard. You've spoilt everything, David." Her eyes filled up and her voice quaked as she spoke. Claire reached for a tissue from her bedside table and gently dabbed her red blotchy cheeks and blew her nose while coughing into her hands that insisted on shaking.

Emma, a young trainee nurse, entered the room to check her patient's blood pressure and pulse and tidy up after the constant stream of visitors, but she quickly sensed all was not well in suite number four. There was a distinct atmosphere of nervous tension pervading throughout the room. Both adults were sat in perfect silence staring at the floor, motionless as though something terrible had happened, making Emma feel very uneasy and eager to make tracks.

Hardly able to control his anger, David glared at his wife slumped on the end of her bed holding a crumpled copy of *Hello* magazine with a pile of soggy paper tissues by her side.

"So you've betrayed me behind my back with some low-life, some toe rag that spends a bit more time with you than I do. You've brought humiliation on my family name and shown utter contempt and disregard for me and what I stand for. I know things haven't been so good lately and we need to spend more time together, but I hoped we could have sorted things out like adults. Instead you betray me. So how long's this sordid little affair been going on?"

"That doesn't matter now," she barked. "It's irrelevant. I won't be coming home. I've had enough, David. This is the last straw so kindly send my stuff onto my mother's in Ross. She's expecting it. She's amazed I've put up with you for so long."

David got up, rubbed his right leg and stared straight into Claire's swollen eyes.

"Think what you're saying for one moment. One moment. Do you really mean it? You've decided what to do without getting my side of the story; you've made up your mind without hearing my version of events. You're telling me here and now that you want a divorce, is that correct?" he yelled.

She stood upright and scowled at her husband while clutching hold of her crumpled *Hello* magazine. Without a moment's hesitation, Claire replied in a calm measured tone. "Yes, yes I want a divorce. I want you out of my life for good, forever. I've had enough."

David was surprised by her confident steely-eyed reply, sounding cold and calculated and devoid of any emotion. Turning away, he paced around her first-floor room, like an animal on the prowl, gazing towards the rolling Leckhampton Hills stretching up towards blue cloudless skies as a mood of gloomy inevitability made its mark. Looking upset, he remembered visiting the very same hospital some twenty-odd years earlier when Shirley, the first love of his life, lay on her deathbed, resigned to her fate, knowing her short life was coming to an end, was slowly ebbing away. A feeling of helplessness swept over him, yet again, as life dealt him another duff set of cards for which the man from Richmond had no answer, no real solution. One thing he did know, however, one thing was painfully clear. The very people he loved, the very people who meant so much to him had schemed, lied and betrayed his trust at every turn, every opportunity, using his wealth and influence for their own personal gain. Looking forlorn, he helped himself to a handful of green grapes and a shiny Cox's Orange Pippin from her wooden hamper brimming full of exotic fruits.

Facing Claire, he said. "In the last few days, my colleagues and I have sweat blood and tears for a good cause. We've safeguarded the Programme, achieved the unachievable, helped a number of people enjoy a better life, with one of us sadly paying the ultimate price and all you can do is think about yourself. You should be ashamed for behaving in this shabby selfish way, but I can promise you one thing. Mark my words, you'll regret your decision. I can assure you of that."

This was no flight of fancy. Claire had thought long and hard before reaching her verdict. She still held a candle for her errant husband and wished things could have turned out differently, but she'd made her bed and now she was going to lie in it. He was a kind generous man, caring and thoughtful, always fighting for the underdog, trying to put the world to rights. But there was a downside to this mercurial character. He was an incorrigible womaniser, a philanderer, an adulterer, devoid of any moral fortitude, with a ruthless, uncompromising streak that came to the fore whenever challenged, or pushed into a corner. The Frenchman in her life wasn't as charming, nor as dashing and definitely wasn't as witty as David Lane, but at least she could live a more sedate life, not be forever looking over her shoulder, waiting for the next revelation in her husband's roller-coaster world.

Life with David was always conducted flat out in the fast lane with the briefest of periods spent recharging batteries and taking on fuel. Her wild extrovert husband with his boundless energy and unbelievable qualities of drive and perseverance, accomplished more in five years than most normal people did in a lifetime. But that frenetic, no-holds-barred existence, with all the uncertainties it evoked was not for her anymore. She'd done her time. Claire wanted to enjoy refined dinner parties and social occasions in the company of the great and the good, taste the finer things of life, not live on her nerves at the beck and call of her salacious husband and his madcap deluded housemates. Sure, she'd miss his unpredictable behaviour, his childish antics, his unbridled passion and his wicked sense of humour that got him into hot water on many occasions. It was these endearing qualities that singled him out from the crowd. Made him the man that he was.

Claire sobbed into her hanky as he walked silently across the room, closing the door quietly behind him, not saying a word. She wondered what the future had in store; what life would be like without the dangerous unscrupulous David Lane who, with all of his failings and shortcomings, made her feel valued, very important, an essential part of his colourful, often unpredictable life.

David walked briskly down the corridor, towards the quiet reception desk where two fresh-faced nurses sat holding phones close to their ears. Their eyes followed him, without blinking, as he sauntered out into the cool air towards the Aston lying in wait for its master in a nearby parking space. His mind had moved on. David was thinking about his meeting with Inspector Parry when he'd get the heads up on developments since leaving Garda.

Being a sensitive type, he chose not to tell Claire about Francois' arrest, knowing it could compromise the ongoing police inquiry and also undermine her recovery to full health. For some time, David suspected Claire's infidelity and, to add credence to his misgivings, Mrs Millins told him on several occasions that a jaunty Frenchman telephoned in his absence, usually late in the evening, when his adulterous wife was preparing for bed. He had no reason to distrust her, knowing she was merely showing loyalty towards her employer, which was to be commended. So the unsolicited comments from his faithful housekeeper added fuel to the fire, created an atmosphere of suspicion and doubt that festered and rankled between the one-time doting couple. Putting two and two together, it wasn't hard to work out who Claire had been seeing behind his back. But, unbeknown to her, their secret love tryst had already hit the buffers, died a death, like a sad Shakespearian tragedy, with the spineless Frenchman lying banged up in a foreign jail miles away, unable to rekindle their adulterous affair for many, many years to come.

Chapter 57

Later that day Inspector Parry came to the house to bring David up to speed with the news following Francois' arrest in Garda on Monday. The self-assured policeman was in a convivial mood, sounding very upbeat and clearly enjoying his host's quick wit and strange quirky take on life. David loved taking a pop at life's socially inept, bringing a smile to the copper's face when he unleashed his acerbic razor-sharp tongue on those that applauded mediocrity, giving vent to the talentless numpties that cluttered the TV stations and radio airwaves with their mindless chitter chatter. Also in his sights were the narcissistic egotists who proudly flaunted their ignorance on mind-numbing quiz programmes and tedious reality shows that could only appeal to the brain dead and those for whom original thought was a bridge too far. The well-dressed senior officer from the Met, nicknamed Lanky by his irreverent colleagues, was relaxed and quite pleased with himself. His wide-ranging enquiries were at an end, the case was closed and he was the bearer of good news. Slouching back in a comfortable armchair, alongside a highly polished redwood coffee table, he never failed to be amazed by the lavish, opulent lifestyle David Lane enjoyed. It was out of the reach of your everyday common-or-garden copper who worked hard to pay the mortgage, keep the family clothed and fed while putting something aside for life's little extras.

"How things are different since those days when I came to your hotel room to tell you about your cousin's tragic death," he said with a little twinkle in his eye. "We were both much younger then. A lot of water has gone under the bridge in the meantime. But you've done all right for yourself. Now that I'm based at Scotland Yard, I concentrate on major corporate crimes of fraud and embezzlement. So when I heard of your concerns, I looked into the matter knowing that you weren't the kind of guy to make a fuss for no apparent reason. As you know, our investigations soon revealed a complex web of wrongdoing, but it's only now, thanks to you, that we're able to identify the ringleader; the brains behind the fraud that has sadly gone on in your company, undetected for a number of years," he pointed out rather sheepishly, fearful of David's reaction. Then changing the subject, he said:

"I don't wish to be rude David, but I think your house is fantastic. It must have set you back a pretty penny," joked the good-humoured policeman, gazing enviously around the exquisitely furnished room with its impressive collection of antique ornaments and fine art paintings. It was the kind of house he could only dream of.

"You're right, it's not cheap. But you'll remember I inherited considerable wealth when my dear parents died and some of this funded the purchase of this grand property. It goes without saying that I would give it all away tomorrow to spend time with my beloved Ma and Pa who meant so much to me and are never out of my thoughts, not for one minute," replied David abruptly, making his guest feel very ill at ease.

Parry had inadvertently struck a nerve, ventured into dangerous territory and had become the target of the playboy's venomous tongue. The Met's main man looked embarrassed and, reaching nervously for his handkerchief, felt as though he'd been admonished like a small child for his churlish impudence. He thought it prudent to quickly change the subject again, not wishing to attract David's wrath any further.

"We had our suspicions," Parry went on with a frog in his throat. "But we weren't totally sure who was the mastermind, but the Frenchy was always in pole position, always at the top of the leader board, so we weren't surprised when he took centre stage in Garda. I'm pleased to report that he's been charged with fraud and embezzlement and is facing a lengthy prison sentence for his serious wrongdoing. He was definitely the ringleader; the brains behind the deceit, establishing a network of accomplices that operated undetected in the accounts department in Paris, and elsewhere, siphoning off large sums of money, mainly cash, over a five-year period then depositing it into a series of complex bogus accounts, that only they had access to. It was very clever actually," he carried on. "These are respected individuals in positions of trust, who took advantage of the sloppy accounting procedures that sadly had been endemic since your Programme was established in 2009. The greedy devils lined their own pockets without a thought for anyone else and the harm they were doing.

"It's hard to say how much they've stolen, David, but at a rough estimate, it must be around ten million pounds. Don't forget, cash pours into your head office throughout the year and is in addition to the monies collected at the time of the rides, so it's very difficult to be precise about the scale of the fraud, but according to our clever number crunchers, it's got to be around that figure."

David slumped back as the size of their losses hit home. He never imagined it would be so great. At that moment, Mrs Millins entered the room with two cups of freshly brewed coffee on a silver tray, with a plate of homemade biscuits and some warm scones that she'd just taken out of the oven. They looked very inviting and smelt absolutely delicious.

"You're spoilt, David Lane, you know that. This charming lady treats you too well, you know."

David grinned, then sipped his warm drink and mulled over the figures.

His housekeeper was embarrassed by the unexpected praise and quickly picked up the tray and made her exit with a jaunty smile and what looked like a modest curtsy as the solid oak door creaked closed behind her.

"Can we get some of the money back?" enquired David impatiently, cutting the soft-textured scone in half and smearing a thin layer of butter over the crumbly surface.

"Hopefully, but it's early days. These things take much longer than you think," replied the inspector with a cup of coffee in his hand and a half-eaten biscuit in the saucer.

"I warned the chairman that our losses could be high, but he won't be expecting anything as bad as this. I shall have to tread very carefully, not alarm the old chap unnecessarily."

Parry went on. "I'm pleased to say all the culprits have been identified and one has already been charged following Dijon's capture. Alison, the Programme's nurse, and her husband were last seen boarding an easyJet flight to Spain, where according to Francois, who's turned Queen's Evidence by the way, they own a second home at Tossa de Mar. It's only a matter of time before they'll be brought to book and stand trial for their heinous crimes. Apparently, Alison was often handed cash by some of your compatriots, but sadly most of it never saw the light of day."

David was staggered, shocked by this revelation and couldn't understand why Alison, of all people, could have betrayed him and his colleagues in such a cold, calculated way.

"I can't believe it," he shouted, holding his head between his hands and staring down at the floor with his eyes filling up and teeth firmly clenched.

"I trusted Alison. I trusted her, you know. I thought she was my friend and ally, committed to the cause, someone I could rely on. But how wrong was I? God, I've been so stupid. She took me for a bloody mug.

"You see my mates are a great bunch of guys who wouldn't have imagined, for one moment, that the people we worked with, we trusted, were stealing money behind our backs. Our attention is focused on completing the ride, bringing home the prize, helping others, not checking the cash and asking for receipts. That wouldn't have occurred to them or me," David protested with a shake of the head and hefty thump on the polished coffee table.

"I've learnt a salutary lesson during this sordid affair. I can't trust anyone, anyone at all. But no one will turn me over again, I can tell you. I hope the full force of the law comes down on these lowlife's who've striven to undermine my efforts!" yelled David at the top of his voice, suddenly jumping to his feet and kicking the handcrafted coffee table across the room with one almighty wallop. Half full cups of coffee, delicate china saucers that hadn't done anyone any harm, were sent flying through the air creating an unholy mess at the base of the mantelpiece and all over the recently painted magnolia wall. Amanda's sophisticated birthday present didn't fare too well either. The once beautiful oil painting, specially commissioned from an exclusive Knightsbridge gallery, was now covered in coffee stains and bits of fruit and pastry with a smearing of low-fat butter for good measure, all thanks to David's uncontrollable temper.

Parry shot out of his chair, gazing on in horror. "David, calm down! Calm down, for God's sake, man," he shouted. "I can assure you that they will suffer for their crimes. Trust me. I won't let you down. Now take it easy. You'll have a heart attack, or a stroke if you carry on like this. Now sit down, please."

The strong arm of the law came into play and the petulant playboy did as he was told, plonking himself down on the wing of an easy chair, looking red-faced, very angry and sweating buckets.

After a few moments' silence, Parry chirped up. "Trust me. They will pay for their crimes, sir. Trust me. I promise you. Now please quieten down. Okay? Now there is something I must mention to you before I leave. Dijon kept babbling on about a mad woman attacking him in the bank just before we arrived on the scene. I think he's nuts. Gone bonkers. We checked the CCTV and interviewed the young cashier, but there was no evidence to support his outlandish claim. Any ideas?"

"Did he describe the woman?" replied David with a pained expression, unsure why he was being asked such an inane question.

"Yes. She was dressed in red and white clothes, looked about thirty years old and spoke with an English accent and sounded well educated. According to the frog, she attacked him, ripping his hand to threads. How daft is that?

"The woman told him everyone who took part in your ride, were heroes in her eyes. Then, according to Dijon, she repeated a line several times, ad nauseam. I made a note of it." Flicking through the pages of his black book he suddenly stopped. "Here it is. *I believe you can achieve anything in life, anything at all, if you really put your mind to it*. That was it. She also said she was expecting to meet someone very special later that day, many miles away. It all sounds daft to me, but do you have any ideas, David?"

"No, I'm sorry, I can't be of any help," replied David standing up rather abruptly, seemingly eager to get rid of his guest as quickly as possible.

"I must get off now and please try and calm down," said the officer, taking the hint and walking briskly towards the front door, promising to be in touch when he had something further to report. They shook hands. Then David slammed the door shut and charged up the stairs, losing his footing several times on the low-pile carpet in his frantic effort to reach his first-floor office. Stephen Parry's throwaway comments at the end of their conversation reminded him of something he'd seen many years earlier. His deranged cousin had destroyed most of his family memorabilia, but fortunately the quick-thinking Mr Crawford had managed to salvage some stuff and handed it to him for safekeeping when he moved to Cheltenham in 1991.

It included death certificates and wills with an impressive portfolio of investments together with umpteen letters and postcards between his parents which had a special place in his heart. Since moving to the town, he'd often read their love letters, imagining they were still alive and would soon appear arm in arm in the door giggling like a pair of lovestruck teenagers. But sadly, it wasn't to be.

And then he found it. He held the picture with both hands, lurched back in his leather chair as the palms of his hands sprang a leak. Shaking, he grabbed a hankie from his trouser pocket, wiped his cheeks and neck with it before discarding the crumpled mess onto the floor. Tear-stained eyes gazed unblinkingly at the old photograph of his mother taken in the seventies sat on Oddicombe Beach with her hair tied loosely up in a bun. She was dressed in a white chiffon top and a red pleated skirt with plain flat sandals on her feet and holding a gold locket in her hand with a small posy of red roses resting on her lap. Turning the photograph over, he read the inscription and gasped. *I believe you can achieve anything in life, anything at all, if you really put your mind to it.*

David couldn't believe it. It was exactly as Parry described. The words were the same. But what did it mean? He felt elated, excited and nauseous, all at the same time. But before he had time to think things through, he was distracted by the sound of Mrs Millins' dulcet bird impressions calling from afar. Tripping down the stairs two at a time, he decided to put his mind at rest by confronting Francois in prison. He suspected it was a cruel jealous joke cooked up by the Frenchman. A nasty vindictive way of getting his own back, hitting him where it hurts, after being caught with his grubby fingers in the till and his clean-cut reputation lying in tatters. The sneaky sods obviously looked through my things when Claire invited him to the house and that was when he hatched the plan. That was the only logical answer, he thought to himself.

His amiable housekeeper took her duties very seriously and wanted David to cast an eye over the proposed menu for Wednesday evening's gala dinner which he did. It was then that David had a short succinct text from Chris saying that he would be joining him the following day. He just needed to clear up a couple of pressing issues.

PW's many varied contacts never failed to amaze David. His business partner seemed to have his fingers in many pies, being on speaking terms with the rich and famous, and many of the most powerful and influential movers and shakers in Europe. He was on first-name terms with many Hollywood stars, industrialists, business tycoons and political leaders of every complexion. His gallery of top-notch contacts seemed inexhaustible and, as well as including the great and the good, also featured some rather seedy characters from the underworld, whose unique services he'd call upon from time to time. Of course his parents' vast global connections were at his disposal and, as David had learned over many years, PW was not just a pretty face, or a committed playboy with a passion for the finer things of life; he also made things happen, such was the power and influence he exerted. He was a good mate and a valuable friend who David felt relieved to have by his side especially after the disingenuous behaviour of the women in his life who'd failed miserably on all fronts, treating him with disloyalty at every turn, at every opportunity.

Suddenly, without warning, Mr Millins burst into the hallway looking flustered and on edge with his arthritic hands flapping by his side, like a bird preparing for flight, while his better half could be heard hoovering in the nearby front room oblivious to his distress.

"Mr Lane, Mr Lane! I'm sorry to bother you, but would you mind coming into the TV room please, sir?"

The elderly gent was quite stocky, pimply-faced with a slight stoop which isn't uncommon for men in their eighties. He'd lost most of his hair, due to the passage of time, with just a few determined white tufts sticking up in protest on top of his wrinkled scalp. Even though his hearing and eyesight weren't so good and his contribution to the smooth running of the household was probably zilch, David had a soft spot for the old boy and liked him being around. He was good company and a trusted ally.

"There's a man on spike who wants to talk to you. Apparently you left a message with Sarah at the Hotel Excalibur asking Trevor to contact you," Mr Millins explained anxiously.

"Okay," replied David, trying to work out the message, who the hell spike was and then it dawned on him. The poor old guy meant Skype! There on the forty-inch screen was Gregor's suntanned face smiling at him, leaning on a desk with his tattooed arm lying in a sling.

"Oh I'm sorry," said Gregor recognising the famous Mr Lane peering back at him. "I was trying to get hold of the gentleman I gave a lift to on Monday. I was told to call this number. I'm sorry sir I must have got it wrong. My mistake."

"No, you didn't. I'm that man, Gregor. I was in disguise. I couldn't let on, even to you. You'll remember the ME slogans and banners around the lake? Well, I did a little something extra for a big wad of cash for a charity. I had to dress in disguise, you see." Gregor's open mouth, with eyes blinking in rapid succession, said it all.

"But Mr Lane, the man was totally different to you. It seems unbelievable."

"Right," said David. "Let me tell you about our journey to Zurich. We stopped in Garda where I wondered around trying to find someone if you recall. I also told you about a girl I met the night before and you made some strange noises. I kept hitting your precious leather upholstery with my fist and I seem to remember sending your lunchbox flying in the air. I did a lot of shouting and yelling in the back of your car, for which I'm very sorry, and I gave you my red and white jacket and matching scarf at the end of the journey and sadly, you got shot. I'm sorry about that, too. I really am."

"Okay, sir. I know it must be you, but your disguise was so convincing, you really had me fooled," replied the cabby with a deep frown plastered along his forehead wondering what the hell was going on, why someone of Mr Lane's stature felt the need to behave in such a strange way.

"How are you, Gregor? I'm sorry about your misfortune. I expect you know that the man responsible for shooting you is now dead."

"Yes," said Gregor, with a grimace.

"Well I'm sorry about everything that happened and that you got hurt. I understand from Sarah that your car is impounded and it'll be sometime before it's returned to you?"

"Yes, sir. I can't drive until my arm's mended either and it could be weeks before I see my lovely car again."

"Well Gregor, I have a surprise for you. I'd like you to go to the Hotel Excelsior and ask to see the manager. He's expecting you. He'll take you to the underground car park where there's a brand new E-class Mercedes waiting for you. It's silver with black leather upholstery and the 3.2 litre engine will give all the poke you need. In the glove compartment, there's 25,000 euros to help you until you're back on your feet again," explained David, grinning.

The bewildered taxi driver, still convinced he was talking to a madman, slumped forward on the desk as the news of his good fortune sunk in.

"I don't know what to say, sir. You're so kind. Thank you so much. I'm lost for words," replied Gregor rubbing his shoulder vigorously, a painful reminder of the gunshot wound sustained earlier in the week.

"It's the least I can do after everything you've been through. I'll keep in touch and we can catch up next time I'm in Garda. Bye for now, my friend. Take care."

Gregor explained the unbelievable turn of events to his pregnant wife whilst sauntering towards their new pride and joy sat gleaming brightly in the dimly lit basement car park of the prestigious four-star hotel. "One thing, my love. If Mr Lane ever rings you to book a taxi, tell him I'm away. I'm ill. I've left the country. I've retired. I've joined the Taliban. I've been captured by aliens. Tell him anything, anything you like, but I don't want the lunatic anywhere near me and my car ever again. After all, it's the least we can do for our little Gregor still fermenting there in your fat bloated stomach."

Martina chuckled under her breath, struggling to manoeuvre her balloon-shaped torso into the front seat of the luxurious limousine. Reaching into the glove compartment, she retrieved the envelope full of cash and stuffed it into her frayed shopping bag, while inhaling great gulps of air and gripping her huge stomach with both hands as the contractions became increasingly more regular.

Chapter 58

It was Wednesday morning in the middle of summer. A day like any other for the Cotswolds' premier town lying proudly under an endless deep blue sky with a gentle breeze and the warm inviting sun for company. A car horn blew when the lights changed to red and the line of traffic came to a grinding halt. David raised his arm to acknowledge Graham, his good-humoured cabby, who waved his hand out of the open car window as David Furnish's extrovert partner mourned the demise of Norma Jeane on his car radio.

The solitary figure ambled across the road absorbed in his own private thoughts, seemingly unaware of his surroundings. It was like a soap opera, too unbelievable for words when he recalled the dramatic, life-changing events that had occurred over the previous seventy-two hours. Dabbing his face with a cotton handkerchief, he looked at his reflection in a brightly lit jeweller's shop window and, as he did, he could almost hear Carly Simon reprimanding him for being so vain. The Promenade, by this time, was milling with eagle-eyed shoppers heavily laden with parcels and carrier bags of all shapes and sizes, obviously out picking a bargain or two in the much-publicised summer sales.

The thought of a life without Claire upset him as he remembered fondly some of their happy times together. She'd been his stalwart, a rock, helping him through the dark days when drink was his best friend. Stood by him through hell and high water particularly when he slipped back and his unpredictable character came to the fore. Her strong business brain and well-honed organisational skills were a big factor in the success of the Pedal Power Programme. David owed her a lot and he knew that. The unexpected arrival of Susan and Louise on the scene was obviously a difficult pill to swallow and their turbulent, up and down marriage hit the buffers as a result. He felt confident, however, that once she'd thought things through, without all the emotional hang-ups and feelings of jealousy, that she'd come to her senses. She'd return to the fold as his dutiful wife, especially once she learned that her villainous French lover was in clink, on the other side of the Channel, with no hope of rekindling their adulterous relationship anytime soon.

I miss this place, he thought, strolling towards Neptune's Fountain with its frenetic spray gushing freely in the air, then passed Gustav Holst in the Imperial Gardens proudly conducting proceedings with his baton raised on high, before continuing towards the imposing Queen's Hotel looking down the Promenade from its celebrated vantage point at the top of the slope.

The beautifully laid out Imperial Gardens were a treat for the eyes with their carefully manicured beds bursting with an array of colourful flowers and ornate plants, offering a warm welcome for anyone out enjoying a quiet stroll or a little solitude from the hectic hurly-burly of everyday life. David didn't know much about horticulture. In fact he hadn't the faintest idea. He selected flowers by their colour and fragrance, that was the simple criteria and was good enough for him. Claire was never hot on flowers, couldn't see the point, so he took the lead. With the help of Mrs Millins's arthritic green fingers, they placed yellow and blue ones in the secondary rooms of the house with red, purple and magenta taking centre stage along the wide expansive hallway, the lounge and the adjacent dining room. At one time, the duo put flowers in the kitchen, but because myopic man kept knocking them over, they were quickly removed before Mrs Lane blew a fuse and resorted to defrosting his brain inside their sleek German microwave as she'd often threatened to do. The monthly bill from the local Montpellier florist was eye-watering, more than most people spent on food, but David didn't care. He wanted to impress his many friends and business associates, believing that freshly cut flowers were a living embodiment of style and elegance, reflecting the soft, subtle side of his character, something he was keen to project.

So, no price was too high for the ambitious playboy, with an eye on the future and the prospect of electoral success at the polls, hoping his unique talents would mark him out from the crowd and propel him to the front benches without too much delay. Feeling weary, he flopped down on his usual wooden park bench, under an overarching horse chestnut tree, where he'd often sit to collect his thoughts, write some poetry, or just relax on his own away from public gaze and scrutiny. Tom Sharpe was a familiar companion. His dry edgy wit had a special appeal with its outrageous blend of farce and deeply cutting satire often shoving two fingers up to authority and challenging the status quo. Sitting there in the failing sunlight, a menacing dour expression appeared on his face when he thought about Francois. How much he'd trusted him as a friend and ally, believing in his unflinching loyalty when in fact greed and jealousy had corrupted his mind, so much that he was reduced to peddling fanciful half-baked stories in a sordid attempt to besmirch his mother's fine name and memory. Just then a couple of drops of water landed on his open book and there was a rumble of thunder in the distance with a sharp flash of lightning, perhaps the forerunner to a July shower, he surmised. Glancing towards the heavens, with some dark menacing clouds slowly drifting past, he wondered whether ignoring Mrs Millins's wise words, about taking an umbrella, was a good decision after all.

In the past, when the weather was bad, he'd get her husband to come to his rescue, but now with the old boy's eyesight failing, the risk to the precious Aston and human life was just too much to contemplate as the only survivors in the picturesque Imperial Gardens would be those who could climb trees.

While massaging his thighs and grazed arms, his fingers rubbed across some of the many bumps and bruises lying in wait on his tortured body. These unsightly trophies would remain with him for days and weeks to come, a painful reminder of his adventurous 150-kilometre ride. Putting the beige and greys to shame, and looking as smart as ever, he was dressed in a blue linen jacket, a white silk shirt, black trousers and highly polished shoes, thanks to Mr Millins. Female admirers were infatuated by his striking good looks, turning their heads in adulation while sauntering near his shaded vantage point. The erudite figure, with the provocative persona, had achieved celebrity status, often appearing in the national press and featuring regularly on social media as his many daring pursuits captured the public's imagination, making him a hero, someone to admire. Richmond's finest was relaxed and at ease on his favourite park bench, albeit a little frayed around the edges. The suave philanthropist leaned back and started reading chapter five of *Porterhouse Blue*.

It was a cool fresh day with a light breeze and was the first chance he'd had, since returning home, to take the air and savour the town's Regency charm. Unexpectedly, as the orange glow dipped behind the passing clouds and the gentle warmth of the midsummer's day ebbed away, he felt a soft hand on his shoulder and before he could turn around, a gold locket and chain was dropped onto his open book. Looking up, he was staggered to see Francesca's beaming smile bearing down on him. David staggered to his feet with his jaw hanging down as if it was broken and, with arms outstretched hugged her tenderly. He hadn't expected to see Italy's finest senorita in Cheltenham and leaning on his favourite park bench of all places. His bone dry mouth became even more parched and, with a will of its own, started bleating out question after question like a nineteenth-century Gatling gun.

"When did you land? How did you get here? How did you remember?" So followed a myriad of disjointed questions rattling off his arid tongue. He was overjoyed, ecstatic to see her on home turf, looking beautiful, radiant, as gorgeous as ever.

"Thank you for returning my precious locket. It means so much to me. It's wonderful," he remarked as he walked around the bench several times, unable to contain his emotions.

Grasping the precious piece of jewellery in both hands, he slid it inside his linen jacket pocket. But as always, things with Mr Lane weren't necessarily straightforward, or as they appeared. In fact the locket was a replica; a very good replica. The handiwork of Jamie from the Everyman Theatre, incorporating poor quality photographs of his parents displayed in an imitation heart-shaped piece of jewellery with the original family heirloom back home, safely under lock and key. If truth were known, David always intended having an accident during the Garda 150 and using the famous locket to draw out the fraudsters from their lair, he'd then exploit their greed further by tempting them with two envelopes full of notes. This would ensure their arrest was a simple affair, with very little fuss and no adverse publicity.

Obviously he didn't want to spook their many sponsors and devoted benefactors by putting the spotlight on their sloppy accounting methods, so having a tumble in Torbole was a price worth paying to protect his beloved Programme. Who knows, one day David might tell her the truth, give her the lowdown, but then again he might not.

Francesca's shiny black shoulder-length hair rested gently on her shoulders while her plain green dress was splattered with tiny cream polka dots and finished off with a trim leather belt fastened round her slim hourglass waist. A small discrete handbag was firmly pressed under her suntanned arm and a simple silver bracelet hung gracefully on her lightly freckled wrist, completing the elegant, yet simple, ensemble. She was easy to talk to, no airs and graces, just a gorgeously attractive woman who captivated her suitor with every move, every breath, every shake of her head. Francesca seemed surprisingly unruffled considering the journey she'd just made and didn't appear fazed by her unfamiliar surroundings and the overwhelming reception she'd received from her gallant admirer. Their conversation was disjointed, jumping from topic to topic, like little kids at a noisy children's party, trying not to miss anything out in their eagerness, their haste, to share their random thoughts, however insignificant.

"I used the cash you left with Sarah to get a flight to Bristol and I put the rest in my bank account. She took 500 euros for herself as you said in your note. I then decided to bring the locket to you as I thought it would be a nice surprise. Hope that's all right?"

"Yes, of course it is," said David, appearing a little more composed after the shock of their meeting. "It's a wonderful surprise seeing you safe and sound and out of harm's way."

They carried on chatting on his precious park bench for some time like a couple of immature teenagers and the eloquent Mr Sharpe was put to one side for the time being. Tom's witty story lines and saucy plots would have to wait for another day as the incorrigible David Lane had other things on his mind.

"Now here's an important question for you. What colour would you choose for a Bentley Continental?" he asked, rubbing the end of his grazed chin and grinning provocatively at a group of young girls strolling by with their smartphones held aloft.

She thought for a moment, pondering on this all-important question, trying to adjust to a world where issues of this nature were of great significance to the super rich. Knowing her admirer quite well, she turned and stared into his blue eyes and suggested with a confident air. "Red of course, there's no alternative, Mr Lane."

"Well done, good choice," he retorted. Just then, some tiny drops of rain dripped onto their foreheads with the promise of a refreshing shower and temporary respite from the oppressive humidity that had been a feature of the weather for a number of days in the UK.

"Do you feel hungry?" he enquired.

"Yes, I'm ravenous," she replied.

"Right, let's go and taste the delights of the Brassiere Blanc."

During the lunch, he apologised several times for his aggressive behaviour in Garda, but explained that his Programme and reputation were of paramount importance and he wouldn't allow anyone to jeopardise his work whoever they were. To her embarrassment, he reminded her, quite forcefully, that she'd been very foolish and his actions were fully justified in the circumstances. Towards the end of the meal, drinking his small cappuccino, he leaned forward and said. "I have a surprise. It's what all this is about. It's nothing to do with me at all, but the capital letters ME symbolise something very important. Sorry if it sounds vague but everything I've done over the last few days, over the last few weeks in fact, has been a prelude to this moment in time. It is fortuitous that you are here sharing it with me."

Judging by the expression on her face, Francesca hadn't the faintest idea what he was talking about, but she knew from experience it was best to go with the flow, not resist the wishes of the main man. After settling the bill, they exchanged the clamour of the busy modern restaurant for the glare of the afternoon sun and a warm comforting light wind. To her surprise, David wound his arm round her waist. Things were really looking up, she thought, a far cry from the deranged madman who tried to throttle her in his suite only a few days earlier, with the threat of an early grave if she ever betrayed him again. She'd thought long and hard about the incident and, having talked to Sarah and Mr Rouen at the Excelsior Hotel, she realised his actions, even though extreme, were somehow warranted, bearing in mind the long-lasting damage she and her belligerent boyfriend could have inflicted on his revered Pedal Power Programme.

Strolling through the entrance to Montpellier Gardens, without a care in the world, David's eyes suddenly fell on a familiar figure in the distance. PW had taken on a regal stance, a magisterial pose, leaning against the historic William IV statue and attracting their attention with a series of flamboyant waves of his white handkerchief like a modern day King Louis. The inveterate playboys hugged each other, shook hands vigorously, were clearly pleased to be reunited after the dramatic events of recent days.

David patted his partner several times on the back, draped his arm across his shoulder showing his warm appreciation and gratitude for everything Chris had done. PW had risen to the challenge; he'd stood up to the plate, he'd safeguarded the future of their illustrious Programme and the founder couldn't have asked for any more.

"We did it. We caught Francois and his gang of miscreants thanks to you. Well done PW, you're a real star. I always knew you'd do it. Never in doubt. Oh, forgive me. How rude. This is Francesca, who I've talked about, but you haven't yet met."

"Hello, Francesca. Nice to meet you." PW kissed her on both cheeks and rewarded her with a beaming smile that any dentist would have been proud of.

"How different it is meeting up in Cheltenham rather than the stifling heat of northern Italy. I've just flown into Staverton from Barcelona where the weather's hot, clammy and quite unbearable. Glad to be out of the oven," retorted Chris, checking the time on his Gucci watch.

Francesca was embarrassed by the attention lavished on her by the legendary fund-raisers. Her palms were damp and clammy and her complexion was bright red, brought on by the sense of occasion, but then her esteemed admirer, seeing all was not well, wound his strong arm around her waist and, as if by magic, she felt self-assured and more at ease with the world. With a flock of seagulls squabbling over a crust of bread, she slumped down on a nearby wooden bench, next to the park's Regency bandstand and started reading the first chapter of *Porterhouse Blue*.

Chris took David to one side. He explained the reason for his delay and outlined the circumstances leading up to Alison's death with her thieving husband when, according to an eyewitness their light aircraft plummeted into the Mediterranean Sea some twenty miles off the Spanish coast.

"How sad," smirked David sarcastically, still remonstrating with himself over their acts of deceit and betrayal. "They got their comeuppance, my friend. They're now languishing in a watery grave at the bottom of the sea with the hungry crabs for company. It's like déjà vu to me, you know. It's just like déjà vu."

"Oh, I'm sorry to hear Claire has gone walkabout," said Chris. "But it's a difficult pill to swallow when your husband has a teenage daughter and a long-standing mistress who's still in her prime, but then if Claire's been up to no good with the greedy frog, then perhaps it's turned out for the best. Silver lining and all that, eh!"

David shook his head at PW's insensitive remarks, wondering whether his best mate ever took anything seriously. "But you seem to have handled your grief remarkably well," he went on, nudging David in the arm and pointing to the new girl on the block. "Looks younger and no doubt fitter than the previous model, so what's the problem, eh?" David refused to get drawn into an infantile conversation about his estranged wife and quickly changed the subject.

"The Daredevil Challenge was great fun. I got away with the disguise. I had a few dodgy moments, I can tell you, but thankfully it worked out okay. It's another £50,000 for the ME charity, which makes it all worthwhile. I went to see Ma and Pa in Zurich which was sad as always. As you know from my earlier text, Francois' looking at spending a lot of time behind bars. Good result, eh! I'll fill you in on the details later, as well as explaining some of the things I got up to during the Challenge. You won't believe it, Chris. You won't believe it. It's your turn next year, so I understand!"

Chapter 59

"Now we're going to do something really special, my friends," said David, grabbing their arms. "It's the highlight of the day. Remember Mark Twain's famous quote? *There's two important days in your life. The day you were born and the day you understand why.* Well, the creation of the Pedal Power Programme is my reason why. We're now going to meet an extraordinary woman, the person who inspired me to ride the Garda 150 last Sunday and drag along twenty-nine other lunatics at the same time. This is the courageous woman, I told you about, who's battled ME/CFS for many years. Her plucky determination drove me to raise the profile of the illness. My research reveals some disturbing statistics. Very little progress has been made in finding a cure. Unlike the major high-profile killers that we all know about, it remains very much a Cinderella illness, hiding in the shadows of the big boys and that's not good enough and we, my friends, are going to do something about it."

The trio walked purposefully through Montpellier Gardens, into a pleasant residential area at the top of the town where quaint terraced houses, art galleries and posh eateries lived together in blissful harmony. David stood bolt upright, composed himself and knocked purposefully on the door of a modern semi-detached house. A chain clanked loose from its mooring and the door creaked open.

"Hi, it's Lucy, isn't it? I'm sorry to bother you. My name is David Lane, this is Francesca and this is my dear friend, Chris. We'd like to have a chat, if we may. I apologise for appearing on your doorstep unannounced. I know it's rather remiss, but it's important that we talk to you."

Lucy was bemused, clearly surprised to see three total strangers with gleaming smiles and deep bronze suntans standing at her modest front door. After a few tense moments, she asked them in. She had striking brown eyes, fair complexion, shiny auburn hair and was wearing a pink blouse, dainty silk neck scarf, a knee-length floral skirt and a rather worn pair of flip-flops that had seen better days. The trio followed Lucy along a narrow corridor into a large spacious lounge-diner where they plonked themselves down on individual high-backed chairs around a low-level wooden coffee table covered in an array of magazines and newspapers. The open double doors led onto an enchanting courtyard where narrow gravel pathways meandered between grassed areas and flowerbeds. Well-kept borders were brimming with summer plants in full bloom while a series of colourful baskets hung haphazardly on the perimeter wall at the foot of the garden.

"I'm sorry to barge in on you unannounced," explained David again. He turned his phone off and gazed towards the attractive thirty-something who was everything he'd imagined, sat nervously on the edge of her two-seater settee looking perplexed by their presence, but seemingly reassured by Francesca's warm amiable smile.

"I like your garden. It's very neat and tidy. I see you've got some red and pink ones and I'm sure I've got a few yellow ones like yours myself," he remarked, pointing towards the hanging baskets suspended on the adjacent garden wall that were dripping onto the ground after a recent watering. "My housekeeper, bless her, has got green fingers, or so she says, but I think she's killed all my favourite blue and green ones with over watering, but only time will tell. Forgive me, I'm sorry to witter on. I do when I'm excited. This might sound strange, but I was most impressed by your many blogs about ME and in particular, your charity work. I've read quite extensively about the illness you've bravely endured together with a lot of your fellow sufferers. I'm surprised how much you've done over the years for your charity and it's this enduring kindness that I most admire. I'm sorry, but I hope that doesn't sound patronising, or in any way condescending. I can assure you I am most sincere in my motives."

Looking red-faced, Lucy felt embarrassed by the compliments being showered on her by complete strangers; people she'd never met before and, staring at the carpeted floor, wondered on reflection whether it was such a good idea inviting them into her home.

Shuffling in her seat and rubbing her hands together nervously, she said, "How can I help you? What's all this about, please?"

David chirped up. "Let me explain what we've been up to. Chris and I and a number of other guys do various charity cycle rides each year and last weekend we completed a challenge in Italy which garnered over six-million pounds. I don't know whether you saw it on social media or whatever?"

Lucy shook her head. "No, I haven't. I've been in bed for the last few days and I haven't seen any news at all."

"Oh, I'm sorry to hear that. Let me cut to the chase. We were all inspired by your dedication to the cause and my colleagues agreed that the monies we collected on Sunday would be donated to ME research as a token of our support."

Lucy didn't know where to look, didn't know what to say, covering her face with her hands and dabbing her eyes with a damp Kleenex tissue.

Chris leaned forward with his signature grin, gently rubbing the glass of his Gucci watch with his silk handkerchief. His blue-rimmed Armani sunglasses rested on the top of his head, and his blue short-sleeved shirt was tucked neatly into a pair of freshly ironed cream trousers. With dark blue handmade shoes adorning his feet and his hair groomed to perfection, he portrayed a man very much at ease with himself and life as a whole.

"You see, we rode about 150 kilometres around Lake Garda which was gruelling, I can tell you. If you look on my iPad, you'll see the view from my helmet," said Chris, with a deep raspy tone, making him sound very sexy. He reached for the tablet nestling in his jacket pocket and Lucy seemed more relaxed as she peered inquisitively through her glasses at the small screen in PW's hand.

"It covers hours of riding, but it's been edited into highlights and downloaded as you can see. The bunting, the flags, the cheering faces speak volumes. Just look at the crowds. It was an amazing experience which I shall never forget and, thanks to this man here, I'm very proud to have taken part.

"All thirty riders threw themselves into the challenge and I'm here as their emissary to tell you how we got on. You inspired us all that day, you made us fight for a cause, you gave us a purpose."

Lucy gazed at the screen, hardly able to contain herself, mesmerised by a stream of magical scenes and sounds darting before her eyes. People she'd never met, she'd never know, living miles away in another country, were frantically waving flags, were smiling, clapping and cheering for ME. They were standing three or four deep on pavements and along narrow pathways, jostling for position to see the meandering snake-like peloton. Restaurants, shops and bars, leaf-laden trees, flagpoles, cars and foreign coaches were swathed in flags and bunting, proudly boasting their support for the red and white slogan: *Just for ME*. Not wishing to miss out on the pageantry, she giggled behind her hand at the sight of a passing police car and private ambulance draped in the striking emblematic colours for all to see. It was wonderful; truly wonderful. She'd never seen anything like it before. It was like a dream. Her chin trembled and her pale flushed cheeks turned red as lines of tears slowly trickled down her face. Francesca, seeing it might be too much for the young girl, put a reassuring arm around her shoulders and wiped her forehead with a handkerchief borrowed from PW, who seemed to have an endless supply.

"It's true, Lucy. This bunch of reprobates charged around a lake in the gruelling heat as a tribute to you and your bravery," remarked David Lane with a distinctive croak in his voice.

"I hope this hasn't been too much for you. I hope you feel we've helped your cause and now I think it's best if we take our leave," he explained, gently stroking his eyes with the back of his grazed hand.

"We've enjoyed meeting you today. You're the highlight of our week. Apologies again for the intrusion. As I say, your charity will be the beneficiary of a sizeable chunk of money for further research into ME and hopefully this'll lead to a cure before too long."

"If you're free this evening, the boys would like you to join us for dinner. It should be fun," joked Francesca, picking up her handbag off the floor and admiring the collection of Cath Kidston crockery displayed so lovingly on the polished mahogany dining room table.

David reached into his red leather wallet, a gift from Garda, patted his happy-go-lucky female companion on the shoulder and handed Lucy his business card.

"Bring your lucky boyfriend," interjected Chris, when his eyes fell on a black and white photograph, in a glass china cabinet, of a young good-looking guy standing with his arms around Lucy's waist on the steps of the town's prestigious Pump Rooms. David smiled when he saw the scene reminding him momentarily of dear Shirley and their precious, all too brief, time together.

"Thank you," said Lucy smiling nervously, still trying to come to terms with what was going on, convinced it was all a wonderful dream and sadly she'd soon wake up.

"Excuse me, but is that your sister over there?" remarked Francesca, pointing at a coloured photograph of a young woman with blonde hair, beautifully manicured nails and dressed in a distinctive panelled dress of orange, brown and beige."

"Yes," she replied gently blowing her nose on PW's soft silk handkerchief that, judging by its crumpled state, had lost most of its powers of absorption.

"Keep it," PW said with a muted smile and here's the tablet to go with it so you can show your friends what we've been up to."

Lucy didn't know what to say; how to respond. It was all too much for the suburban homeowner used to the quiet life away from the hurly-burly, the bright neon lights and the town's celebrated club scene. Chris kissed her on both cheeks, making her blush again, before leading the trio quietly along the narrow corridor and out into the bright daylight.

"Nice to have met you. See you soon," said David. "I'd like you to come and help with my garden, if you would. I need some new purple and red ones soon and a bit of TLC for my drooping greens, thanks to my overzealous housekeeper, who unfortunately sees her domestic duties extending way beyond the confines of bricks and mortar. Many's the day you'll catch her polishing the plants, yes I mean polishing, with the help of her husband. Creating a floral haven that only a myopic eighty-year-old and a fussy old biddy, with a can of Pledge, could conjure up. We can talk about it tonight. I'm really looking forward to seeing you again. I'll send a car for you at eight p.m. It's casual dress, no fuss. Bring your attractive sister along too, if she's free. Oh, I'd be interested to know who Reg is, by the way."

The door creaked shut. The key was turned and the chain was jangled back into place. Lucy stood still, completely motionless, glued to the wood-tiled floor. Her legs refused to move. They weren't going anywhere.

But then all of a sudden she raced down the corridor, threw herself onto the two-seater settee, which creaked in protest, as a huge grin lit up her face, quickly followed by a raucous high-pitched scream of sheer joy and excitement.

Meanwhile the well-dressed trio, who wouldn't have looked out of place at a top-notch wedding reception or on a Hollywood film set, sauntered towards Montpellier and its long strip of exclusive shops and eateries followed by a welcome breeze blowing on their backs.

Now it was common knowledge that Lucy was a devoted fan of the BBC's *Woman's Hour*, an avid listener to the morning programme, always looking forward to her daily fix. It was the highlight of her day, after all, but the events of the last hour trumped everything in her life. Alas that included Jenni Murray who was relegated to the backburner, for the foreseeable future anyway, with David Lane occupying pole position in her heart and mind.

Lucy was bubbling with excitement, elated, happy, euphoric and emotionally drained all at the same time. That was the gist of the garbled text message that her mother read while gasping for air during a welcome break from her energetic zumba dance routine at a nearby church hall, aptly called The Sisters' of Mercy.

Meeting Mr Lane and his glitzy chums was a turning point for Lucy, something she'd never forget. She sat spellbound with eyes transfixed, gazing unflinchingly at the wonderful sights and sounds of the beautiful iconic Lake Garda. It was true to say that Lucy was mesmerised by the flamboyant red and white ME slogans waving freely in the wind, with the cacophony of Italian chitter chatter bombarding her ears from all directions. 'If this is a dream then I hope I never wake up', whispered Lucy under her breath, toasting herself with a small glass of chilled Prosecco, and gripping hold of PW's sodden silk handkerchief for good luck.

The normally gregarious couple were tight-lipped, uttering not a word as they slowly ambled down the Promenade back to base camp. They even ignored the cheeky catcalls from a group of female admirers holding smartphones in the air, as their scruffy boyfriends, dressed in moth-eaten jeans at half-mast, sharing a family-sized packet of Walkers crisps, were oblivious to the saucy antics of their two-timing girlfriends.

Emotions were high following the memorable meeting with Lucy which had certainly lived up to its billing, exceeded expectations judging by the self-satisfied expressions stuck to their motionless faces. Eventually PW broke the silence when the party dived across the road, between a line of parked cars, towards a crowded newsagent.

"See you've made it on the front page of the *Gloucestershire Echo*, well done. Sir Anthony tells me that you're on the *One Show* next week, lounging on the green sofa opposite the lovely Alex Jones with those long extendable legs that never seem to end. You lucky boy. You definitely won't be short of anything to say. Miss

Wales will have her work cut out trying to get a word in edgeways if you have anything to do with it," he chuckled, quickly grabbing a copy of the local rag. David's mind was elsewhere. I don't think he even heard his friend's churlish remarks judging by the glazed expression printed on his face.

Francesca had already had her fair share of surprises for her first day on English soil, but she wasn't prepared for the big one. The Italian visitor, who'd lived a relatively sheltered life on the shores of a famous Italian lake, was lost for words when she strolled over the threshold of David's palatial pad. She'd only seen houses like that in Hollywood films and lavish period dramas and, even though she knew David had a few bob in the bank, she didn't think it stretched that far.

Her eye was drawn like a magnet towards the end of the long hallway where a distinctive Howard Miller grandfather clock stood on duty, housed inside a beautifully handcrafted wooden case that enhanced the exquisite nature of the highly prized timepiece. This was a wedding present from PW at the time of David's marriage to Claire as a sign of his devotion to the couple and heartfelt wishes for their future happiness, but with the proviso that in the event of a marital break-up, or death, that the cherished gift be returned to him in good working order. The insensitive rogue, who loved playing to the gallery, included this tasteless caveat in his witty, rude and irreverent best man's speech, to hoots of laughter and hilarity from some guests, with words of predictable derision from those unfamiliar with PW's unique blend of caustic humour.

Francesca stood spellbound, looking on in awe at the expensive ornaments and dramatic landscape paintings hanging from the tall magnolia walls in the spacious ground-floor rooms while a series of ornate pear-shaped chandeliers glistened brightly in the reflected artificial light. It was magic, real magic. The swirling staircase was the august centrepiece to the grand imposing property leaving her speechless. It took her breath away just gazing up towards the pale blue ceiling with its massive globe-shaped light shining down on its humble subjects, casting its uninterrupted florescent charm everywhere.

An array of tall-stemmed fresh flowers, arranged in colourful china vases, bedecked the elegant hallway, the capacious well-lit rooms and the majestic staircase. The fragrant scent filled the air injecting a cosy, homespun feeling to the place. The warmth and general grandeur said much about the man of the house, his take on life and, most importantly of all, the image he wanted to project to the wider world.

"I'm going to freshen up my friends. I'll show you to your rooms, if you'll follow me. Spare clothes are hanging up in your wardrobes, thanks to Mrs Millins, who thinks of everything. Let's meet in the garden for drinks in, say, an hour? That gives us time to shower, change and have a bit of a rest. Okay?"

Nodding their approval, his two house guests sprinted up the stairs behind their enigmatic host, still thinking about their conversation with Lucy and her amazing courage and charm. As the master of the house slumped on the end of his bed, listening to John Paul Young, he thought about Claire, how much he was missing her, wondering whether love was still in the air. She'd been his rock for many years, the true love of his life. He accepted that things had gone a bit pear-shaped in recent months, for which they were both responsible. David was confident she'd come to her senses, realising she'd over reacted to what was a little local difficulty, recognising her future was best served by his side. After all they'd come through worse patches in the past and their marriage was the stronger for it.

Francesca however was a different kettle of fish all together. The two women were like chalk and cheese. She'd lived much of her adult life at the hands of a feckless bully, being abused and manipulated and forced to do things against her will. This reminded him of his own early years in Hastings and the trauma he suffered at the hands of his cruel cousin. Initially he had strong reservations about her, wondering where her true loyalty and allegiance actually lay. The jury was still out, but thanks to PW he'd learn more about her motives and intentions in the days to come.

David hoped Lucy would make an appearance during the evening. After all, she was the catalyst for their cycling adventure some 800 miles south. He'd asked Francesca to do the honours, invite her to the dinner, knowing it would sound friendlier, less formal, from someone of a similar age.

Thinking ahead, David had arranged to visit Hastings in the next few days to check on number 5 Dewhurst Road and see how the tenants were getting on. Over the years he'd splashed out on similar properties as safe havens for abused and battered women and he'd be meeting Mr Barma, his long-standing solicitor, to get an update and discuss his future expansion plans.

Now the dust was settled following Roger's untimely death, he intended visiting Susan for what promised to be a frosty confrontation following her cold-hearted complicity in the shooting of Gregor who took a bullet intended for him. On a lighter note, he'd meet his daughter for the first time and deliver her birthday present in person. It still gave him goosepimples and a dry mouth just thinking about it. After years of cruel denial he would at last reap the rewards of his painful isolation. He couldn't wait until the big day when he'd hug and hold Louise in his arms, tell her how much he loved her and start catching up on all those lost years.

Having funded Louise's record-breaking number of driving lessons, with four different schools over the last twelve months, he thought it a good idea to buy her a spanking new car, with a modest engine, to celebrate her coming of age. The blazing red Fiat 500 with cream leather interior and a sporty soft top seemed to fit the bill. It had all the latest gadgets that any young girl worth her salt would be proud of, so said the pretty blonde saleswoman at the local dealership when David ventured out, under the cloak of darkness, for a test drive in their pink demonstration car.

Over coffee one morning, Mr Millins volunteered to drive the Fiat to Hastings and, not wishing to upset the old chap, David reluctantly agreed to his request. To cover his back, he roped in Jamie from the Everyman Theatre as a driver just in case myopic man started behaving like Mr Magoo ploughing up the Sussex fields and making short work of anyone foolish enough to stand in his way. During his stay at the Imperial Hotel in Hastings, he'd visit Martin Conway at his south coast construction site located just out of town on the road to Rye. He wanted to talk over old times, explain his overriding fear of bicycle sheds and introduce his old school chum to one of PW's less savoury characters who, by coincidence, also has an unhealthy interest in people's ankles.

Standing in his hot steamy shower, gazing up at the large chromium nozzle, rubbing dollops of shampoo into his scalp, he pondered on the dramatic events of the last few days. Susan had shown her true colours and would have to face the music for her treachery, and the oily rag hadn't fared any better, ending his days under a Swiss dump truck. Alison and her thieving husband were wallowing in a watery grave and, unbeknown to his adulterous wife, Francois was languishing in a French jail awaiting trial.

Needless to say, Midge's days were numbered and who knows what sorry fate awaited Martin Conway on the Sussex coast when Tiny's twin brother came calling.

Strangely enough, in this web of greed and betrayal there was one steady unwavering presence that projected a warm reassuring glow throughout the Regency house, making it feel snug, calm and very homely. That honour was bestowed on the redoubtable Mr and Mrs Millins; the loyal couple who got on with their duties, never made a fuss, kept themselves to themselves and enriched his life in so many different ways. Wandering into his office, drying his short cropped hair on a large fluffy towel and dressed in a soft white bathrobe, he glanced at their unforgettable gifts bought all those years ago, when they interviewed him for their positions and promptly moved in. The simple presents from Primark were still in pride of place, sitting reverently on the polished mahogany desk with the enchanting Cotswold hills providing a cinematic backcloth to their kind, heartfelt generosity.

Alongside was a photograph of dear Shirley encased in a solid-gold picture frame taken at Croome Park, one of her favourite haunts. She was wearing a big floppy hat, a pretty blue floral blouse, white jeans and red casual shoes.

Shirley loved having tea in a period café with its black and white posters and memorabilia of a bygone age when the nation lived under the dark clouds of war and food was in short supply. David often treated his girlfriend to a pot of her beloved Earl Grey tea with a couple of 'jackflaps' as she called them. The dainty slices reminded Shirley of her early childhood when her mother would bake several trays of goodies as special treats on birthdays and family occasions, but sadly David heard that she died of a broken heart within a matter of weeks of her daughter's untimely death. Munching her way through her mouth-watering treat, Shirley would keep bleating on about how many calories she was consuming, saying it wouldn't do her figure any good, threatening to spend the rest of the day in the gym, pumping iron and running the treadmill into the ground. It made David laugh, smiling fondly at her hourglass figure with perfectly toned arms and legs and not an ounce of fat to her name. He missed Shirley, he missed her very much. There wasn't a day that went by that he didn't think about her and their all too brief time together. David often visited her grave in Prestbury, alongside her dearly departed mother, nursing a bouquet of freshly cut flowers in one hand and a couple of 'jackflaps' in the other. He wished he could turn the clock back and tell Elgar's top saleswoman how much he really loved her, wishing, with tears in his eyes, she was by his side and remain with him forever.

Chapter 60

Mr and Mrs Millins were in their palatial first-floor apartment, having a well-earned break, drinking cups of freshly brewed tea with a plate of Hobnobs before getting ready for the gala dinner. Their room was light, airy and spacious, well laid out with a large double bed, built-in wardrobes and eye-catching en suite bathroom with his and hers sinks, a corner shower and the impressive Jacuzzi. Over the last few days, the good-humoured pensioners had kept a low profile, not wishing to bring attention to themselves following Claire's unexplained illness. But it was definitely crocodile tears that they shed when David sat them down in the television room, with a couple of glasses of Madeira sherry to steady their nerves, and broke the grim news of his failed marriage, explaining that Mrs Lane wouldn't be returning to Pavilion Avenue any time soon. If it wasn't for her lack of agility and advancing years, Mrs Millins would have gladly danced the Highland fling up and down the Avenue in celebration of the good news, shortly followed by a series of daring pirouettes, such was the sense of euphoria radiating throughout her frail arthritic body.

As private quarters go, the couple were in dreamland thanks to the kind generosity of their employer. The spacious half-circular balcony, with its stunning eye-catching views of the rolling hills and Cotswold countryside was the centrepiece of their luxurious accommodation. It's where they often sat and sorted out the problems of the world before relaxing in their cosy lounge beside their Chippendale coffee table draped in a pure white tablecloth with matching doilies. Rumour had it that when the expensive handcrafted piece of furniture was delivered by one of the town's exclusive stores, she was heard to say, "Not only can those young lads dance pretty well, but they can also make darn good furniture too." The television, DVD player and music centre were housed in the adjoining room which comprised a sleek double-seater settee, a couple of material easy chairs with a smart cocktail bar in the far corner. The specially installed lift was a blessing for the elderly couple suffering from ill-health, allowing them to move freely between the kitchen and their own private apartment without any fuss.

"Apparently on the day of the party last Monday, Mrs Lane wasn't happy with next door's tearaway. He knocked over one of her precious porcelain ornaments, blotted his copybook all right," Mrs Millins explained. "She really let rip. She can be really nasty sometimes. I felt sorry for the spotty little irk. But then I gave him a piece of my mind when I saw the wretch helping himself to some trifle in the kitchen, cheeky blighter. Sent him packing with a flea in his ear. Young people today, eh!

"I picked up a half empty bag of KP nuts left lying on the floor and shoved it in the bin. Wonder where they came from? We all know they're banned because of snooty drawers' allergy. God forbid that she gets ill, what a terrible thought," she said sarcastically.

"I've got to drive Mr Lane's car to Hastings shortly," said her husband, with a nonchalant shake of the head. "It's the least I can do to help him out. He relies on me you know, and I can't let him down."

"She's always threatening to kill us that woman, but now she's had some of her own medicine, perhaps she'll think twice before harassing us again. If she ever does, we know what we can do don't we? What's good for the goose, is good for the gander, I always say," his wife replied sternly.

"I agree," he said. "Mr Lane's a lot different to snooty drawers, he's friendly and very kind to us. I feel happier now I mentioned it to that nice inspector when I was at the front, doing the weeding. I said the verbal abuse had gone on for years. He said he'd look into it, but now she's gone it doesn't matter, but who knows she might try and worm her way back into his good books? I hate people who connive behind your back. But of course, we've got a trick up our sleeve if the wicked witch tries to hurt us," he explained with a menacing sneer as his mischievous wife giggled like a naughty young schoolgirl, behind her vein ridden hands.

Chapter 61

A short time later, David was relaxing quietly in the garden, with Chris and Francesca, chatting and laughing about their exploits over the last few days with the hypnotic sound of Mozart's 9th Symphony playing in the lounge. It's common knowledge that David's mood could go up and down without warning, just like a bride's nightie, but while his cheery companions were giggling and chuckling at Midge's expense, he was subdued and reflective, still thinking about his remarkable meeting with Lucy earlier in the day.

Suddenly, Chris broke off his conversation with Francesca and turned to face David, quietly relaxing on his recliner with his eyes half-closed and a James Patterson novel resting on his lap.

"Do you know something? You could write a book about your exploits. Just think of the eventful life you've led, the people you've known and some of the things you've got up to. You could write volumes about your colourful antics, puts the rest of us in the shade, I can tell you. There's enough stuff to keep the tabloids' printing presses turning for weeks without even exploring some of your dodgy skeletons. Just think of it, you'd be a box office sensation, an overnight success when some of your salacious activities hit the newspaper stands.

"God, we haven't even talked about social media and the explosive opportunities that offers. It makes you think, doesn't it?" said PW, jumping to his feet and shaking his head from side to side with enthusiasm as another glass of his favourite tipple trickled down his throat.

David quickly dismissed his friend's outrageous idea. "Oh, I'm not sure about that. No one's interested in my life and times. After all, I'm just an ordinary guy whose got a few bob in the bank and has tried his best to help others on the way through. In return, I ask for loyalty and trust, that's the deal," he replied sounding slightly wheezy and looking a little hot and flushed. David wasn't interested in such trivia. His energy and drive was focused elsewhere. His beloved Pedal Power Programme had gone from strength to strength, garnering huge sums of money on the way. The high profile Garda 150 was the pinnacle to the year's philanthropic push and that evening's gala dinner was an opportunity to press the flesh with the great and the good and present a cheque to the ME Association. The chairman would announce that for the first time in the history of the Programme one charity would feature on two occasions in the same season. The beneficiary of this unique accolade would fall to the ME Association.

All the money generated for the Austrian ride in September would be donated to that cause and the prestigious end of season event in Vienna would be christened 'Gary's Ride' as a fitting tribute to a fallen hero; a fellow rider whose contribution to the team would be sadly missed.

"Did Tiny really want to stuff Midge in a concrete waistcoat?" asked Francesca with a glass of white wine in her hand and resting back in Claire's infamous wooden wicker chair.

"Yes," replied Chris with a smirk. "He took some convincing, I can tell you. Apparently, a close relative of his suffers from ME and he's seen first hand the affect the illness has on people, so when he heard what your ex has been up to it was like a red rag to a bull. He went mad, ballistic. I can't see Midge surviving very long now I'm out of the picture, but that's not my problem. I don't really care."

"So the only way he can stay alive is by getting away from Garda, putting as much distance as possible between him and the place of his birth," replied Francesca.

"I guess so," said PW, with a strange quizzical slant of his head, trying to understand why she'd be interested in Midge's life expectancy, bearing in mind their torrid relationship and the yob's seedy role in the attempted blackmail.

The *Colonel Bogey* doorbell made its presence known in the hallway and Mrs Millins quickly made her way towards the front door wondering why people were arriving so early in the evening, hoping they hadn't misread their invitations, or even worse, that her beloved husband hadn't cocked up the arrangements. It wouldn't be the first time. She was holding the guest list in her hand trying to fathom out why one person in particular had made the cut. There was the guest of honour from the ME Association, Sir Anthony York and his wife, the local MP, a number of people from the world of business and commerce, plus Mike, his agent, PW, Francesca, Lucy and two others and Claire. Yes Claire. The housekeeper was puzzled.

Meanwhile back in the garden at the rear of the house, Chris was in full flow describing the bottom-clenching acceleration of his beloved Lamborghini, stressing its heart-pounding cornering powers and its top line speed to Francesca, who was trying to suppress a succession of yawns as PW became more and more animated with every mechanical detail that tripped off his tongue.

Suddenly, the housekeeper appeared on the garden patio, looking flustered, holding a drying-up cloth in her quivering hand with a crumpled copy of the guest list sticking out of her pinny.

"Mr Lane, Mr Lane? I'm sorry to disturb you. I do apologise for the intrusion, but I have a young lady at the door who insists on seeing you, sir. She's quite adamant. She won't take no for an answer."

"Okay, ask her to come through, please," remarked David, flopping back on his recliner with his badly grazed arms folded behind his head and gazing skyward just as the sun did a runner behind some dark threatening clouds. In the meantime PW was on a roll, showing his vast knowledge of the internal combustion engine to a bored Italian senorita whose mind was elsewhere, wondering who her host's surprise guest might be.

The young attractive woman who sauntered confidently towards the gazebo, gently flapping in the breeze, was suntanned and very slim, wearing a pale green dress and matching belt with a red Radley handbag clutched tightly under her arm. She looked gorgeous and somehow familiar, as the inquisitive host shuffled forward using his hand to shield his eyes from a sudden shaft of light. Peering tentatively in her direction, he stood up to greet her feeling unusually hot, sweaty and unsteady on his feet.

"Hi, Daddy. It's nice to see you at long last. I've heard so much about you," said Louise, with an impish smile and a saucy wink of her soft blue eyes. Her father couldn't believe it. He staggered forward to greet his long lost daughter with open arms, then hugged her close to his chest so she could hardly breathe. He smelt her fragrant perfume, kissed her soft rosy cheeks and felt her long strands of hair on his face, something he'd wanted to do for years. At last he could hug the love of his life, his sweet beautiful daughter whose affection he'd been so cruelly denied for so long. The emotion, the shock, was overwhelming. Tears of joy trickled down his flushed face, making her mascara smudge. His precious daughter was safely in his arms and there she was going to stay. But then without warning, with just the sound of the gazebo fluttering freely in the air, a sudden stabbing pain darted up his arm and across his chest as lines of perspiration streamed down his colourless face. Struggling to remain upright, he bent forward, grabbed hold of his stomach and stumbled into the wrought-iron table sending glasses flying everywhere, before slumping to the ground with the sound of screaming in his ears and PWs outstretched arms tugging frantically at his waist. Then the lights, the bright lights slowly dimed and David Lane's world was no more. It had ended.

Chapter 62

It was July, the sun was at its hottest and there wasn't a cloud in the sky. The mood in the church was sombre, which was only to be expected. All you could hear was subdued whispering and the occasional obligatory cough with the constant creaking of the old wooden pews as the congregation shuffled about in their less than comfortable seats.

Father Jenkins, a rotund pockmarked priest with a distinct fondness for communion wine, stood patiently by the altar waiting for the uplifting sound of *Jesu Joy of Man's Desiring* to conclude before addressing the mourners with his well-thumbed Bible in hand. The choice of organist was strange judging by the many raised eyebrows, but PW was the obvious candidate owing to his close association with the deceased and his lifelong passion for Bach's famous *Cantata*. But a word of caution before we shower the musical maestro with too many plaudits. PW's artistic prowess was not as it appeared. Realising, over the years, there were many routes to a lady's heart, he set about perfecting a famous piece of music on a number of different instruments. *Fields of Gold* is a case in point. A guaranteed prize-winner in the love stakes, always had the fairer sex swooning at his feet as the pin-up boy gently caressed the strings of his trusty Spanish guitar and looked on at his prey with his dreamy eyes and a seductive white smile.

The Last Post, on his father's bugle had most self-respecting people jumping to attention in admiration and was a guaranteed crowd pleaser whatever the occasion. But his heart-warming rendition of Handel's rousing melody, *The Arrival of the Queen of Sheba* was to die for, had even the most musically inept cheering to the rafters, pleading for more, when PW glided his elegant handcrafted bow across the fine taut strings, demonstrating to the world his mastery of the fiddle, if only for one memorable tune. Not resting on his laurels, and following a series of intensive piano lessons by his hairdresser, Elena, his repertoire had been extended. *Yesterday* by the Beatles was now polished, perfected and ready for its first public performance. John Lennon would be impressed by his delicate touch on the Steinway, if you believed the many tributes and rave reviews lavished on PW by the highly respected musical fraternity back home.

While the priest spoke from the altar, PW took his seat at the front alongside Sir Anthony York. He acknowledged his crestfallen colleagues in Team 30 dressed in their bright colourful skin suits as a fitting tribute to a fellow cyclist. Louise and Claire were sat motionless, glum-faced, surrounded by close friends dressed in dark traditional clothes, with red and white 'Just for ME' badges in their buttonholes.

As the sheet music was closed, the keys and stops came to rest, the resident organist stood to attention while the coffin, garnished in family flowers, was carefully lifted onto the shoulders of the bearers and carried out of the church while David Bowie proudly proclaimed that we can be heroes, if just for one day. With the sun glaring down through blue cloudless skies and tuneful skylarks bidding the hero goodbye, the melancholic line of mourners vacated the sanctity of the Church of the Holy Virgin and reconvened for a light meal at the nearby Red Lion Hotel.

It was a tense, cheerless car journey back to Pavilion Avenue for PW, Claire and Louise sat nursing their own private thoughts, reflecting on their tragic loss while a shaft of bright sunlight lit up the back seat promoting hope and optimism and better days to come, a vision that was sadly at odds with the unimaginable mood of loss and despair.

"I thought you played the organ very well Chris," said Claire blowing her nose. "I didn't know you had it in you. You're a real dark horse."

"Thanks, I did my best Claire, but I lost my way a bit when Friar Tuck wobbled about and slurred his words. I think it was either the heat or the drink that got to him. I could see myself conducting the service if the fat man collapsed. Now that would have been a treat, wouldn't it?"

"I didn't even get to know him. Do you know that? I never even heard him speak. One minute you're here, next minute you're not," Louise sobbed, with more tears welling up in her eyes.

Predictably, as if on cue, Mrs Millins was there at the door ready to greet them on their return. Cool cordial drinks were laid out on the coffee table in the lounge accompanied by a selection of dainty finger sandwiches on a shiny silver tray. No one spoke. They just quenched their thirsts after the journey, walked around aimlessly, eating the warm soft biscuits and freshly baked fruit scones.

"Can't drop our standards Mr Parker-Wright, even on such a gloomy cheerless day," explained the elderly housekeeper, wiping away the crumbs with her dishcloth and topping up the contents of the solid silver ice bucket. "Mr Lane wouldn't be pleased, I can tell you." Chris nodded.

A few minutes later, there was a firm knock at the door. Dr Pierre Sharon was standing there in blue faded jeans and a crumpled tartan shirt, ready to take Claire home. A grey dour face and glazed expression gave a clue as to his mood. Mrs Millins and PW looked at each other surprised to see that the latest man in Claire's volatile life was another surly Frenchman.

"Are you thinking what I'm thinking, Mrs Millins?" whispered PW in her ear.

She shook her head in bewilderment, wondering why Mrs Lane was so obsessed with the French, when there was a surfeit of eligible men in the town who'd be only too pleased to take her on, as long as they remembered to hide a handgun under their pillow and keep all sharp implements safely under lock and key.

"I must check to make sure everything's okay upstairs, sir, if you'll excuse me?"

"Of course," he replied, with a frown and gentle tug on his chin.

"Cheerio, everyone," cried Claire, walking down the steps, waving her hand nonchalantly in the air. She stopped, glanced back at the house momentarily before chatting to Louise and then strolling arm in arm towards the estate car where her latest flame was drumming his fingers impatiently on the dashboard with Elvis Presley crooning away on the car radio. Then with swollen tear-filled eyes, Claire hugged her several times before sliding into the front seat and leaning against the passenger door with her head held firmly between her hands. Judging by the raised voices, emanating from their open car window as they sidled off, the couple were building up to another unholy row, the prelude to much crockery throwing, and separate rooms for days to come.

Still unsure what was going on in Claire's topsy-turvy world, PW stood at the door as the dreary love boat departed the scene, leaving a plume of white diesel fumes in its wake, while PW offered a less than subtle two-fingered salute to the diminutive carpet hugger when his angry contorted face stared out of the open car window.

Later that evening, when the mood was less sombre, Louise and PW shuffled into the dining room after catching the last fleeting remnants of the sun before it performed its usual vanishing act behind the Leckhampton Hills. Here PW entertained the teenager with a segue of funny stories and anecdotes about her father, keeping well clear of anything contentious, or untoward. He didn't want to besmirch the old boy's reputation after all.

They shared a bottle of Rioja, from David's extensive wine cellar, happily singing along to the *Sultans of Swing* blaring out unabashed on the state-of-the-art sound system next door.

"We owe it to the dearly departed to keep our pecker up. I love that guitar rift, those smooth chord changes and that pulsating rhythm, it makes me tap my feet, bite my bottom lip and shake my head from side to side, or so the lady in my life tells me," said Chris, smiling.

"Will you ever get married, Chris, if you don't mind me asking?"

"No, that's okay. I'm not like your father, I'm not able to commit myself to anyone. I'm probably too immature for that, but I'll tell you a secret. Keep it to yourself. Very soon I'm going to ask Elena, the light of my life, to move in permanently. She's not just a good concert pianist with bright teeth and a talent for hairdressing, you know. There's a lot more under the bonnet."

Before Louise had time to say anything, they heard the droning murmur of the Millinses' private lift and the sound of muffled voices some way off. Meanwhile Mark Knopfler's *Walk of Life* had Chris' head bobbing from side to side, reminding the aging juvenile of his misspent youth. Those lazy sultry days on Barcelona's golden beaches sharing the sand dunes with pretty young girls, wondering which of the lovelies should make the cut and join him on his father's lavish motor launch moored close by.

"Now, let's have a look at that order," said Chris, grabbing hold of his reading glasses. "I'll ring the Chinese restaurant, get them to deliver our takeaway in the next half-hour or so. I've got everybody's order except for two people. We haven't heard from them for some time. I wonder what they'd like? Perhaps we ought to go up and find out, unless that was them in the lift and they're hiding in the kitchen."

"We'll have the house special chow mein with chips, twice!" yelled David Lane standing at the door, leaning on Francesca for support and using a walking stick, borrowed from Mr Millins, to steady himself. "Sorry I couldn't join you today. I feel real guilty, but sadly it wasn't to be. I'm still feeling quite groggy."

From his pale, weak and shaky countenance, you could see David was still under par, not his normal energetic self, having been laid low since Wednesday by a bout of pneumonia. Dressed in a pair of well-pressed black trousers, white open-neck shirt and blue casual shoes, he clearly hadn't lost his dress sense even though he appeared rather frayed around the edges. His fresh-faced companion was in pink jeans, white see-through blouse with her black hair tied in a bow. Smiling to himself, PW thought as entrances go, it was pretty darn impressive especially for someone unsure on their pins. But as always, like his partner in arms, David's neatly combed hair and immaculate appearance made him stand out in the crowd, towering over the badly dressed beige and greys, pushing them into the shadows, where they rightly belonged.

"How are you, Daddy?" asked Louise, hugging the invalid tightly. "I was going to pop up to see you, but Chris kept telling me stories of your times together and some of the things you got up to, so I lost all track of time. It's his fault," she said, pointing at PW with a bold grin and huge big eyes.

"Oh yes," said David inquisitively, glancing over at his partner pouting his lips and shaking his head innocently.

"Oh I'm okay darling, thank you," he replied, taking his customary seat at the head of the table. "Hi Chris, thanks for sorting things out today and for looking after the ladies and thanks again for stepping in at the gala dinner and for doing the honours. I understand the evening went really well. I see social media and the press reports have been very positive, pushing ME right to the fore. Just what I wanted. That's great news and with the next ride coming up soon we should really put ME/CFS on the map. I see the money is still coming in. Head office reckons we should hit seven million pounds by close of business today. In between sleeping over the last couple of days and dosing myself up with drugs thanks to Dr Bircher, I've been chatting to my lovely daughter here about lots of stuff. I think we're okay, aren't we?"

She grinned and hugged him tightly around the neck making him wince.

"Before we eat, I suggest we raise our glasses to Gary, our friend and compatriot, someone who will be greatly missed, but whose memory will always live on.

"To Gary the Wink," he cried, standing up to attention, gently wobbling to and fro on his dodgy walking stick.

"To Gary the Wink," they all replied with glasses held aloft and frowning as they did.

"I telephoned his wife again today. She's doing okay in the circumstances, but I said I'd come to Surbiton in the next week to see what I could do. She's been very brave you know. He's a big loss. It was only his first ride."

"Is that wise, darling?" asked Francesca with a worried expression on her face. "I don't think you should go anywhere until you're fully recovered."

"Thank you for your concern, but I think I'm the best judge of that, don't you?"

"Ouch! Your dad's getting better. What a tongue. Boy, can he be stubborn," whispered PW in Louise's ear, making her snigger, as he reached for his glass of red wine and grabbed a handful of salted peanuts. Chris then draped his arm around David's shoulders and said, "I've asked the Millinses to join us for our Chinese supper, if that's okay with you, maestro?"

"Of course it's okay, it's a great idea Chris."

So the evening was spent tucking into a local takeaway, drinking lager and champagne, seemingly a strange concoction, but judging by the laughter and joviality emanating throughout the house, everyone enjoyed themselves celebrating the welcome return of David to the fold, but with a tinge of sadness for a dear absent friend. The live-in helpers felt uncomfortable to begin with, like ducks out of water, but after a few generous glasses of Madeira, thanks to PW, they soon let their hair down. The highlight of the evening was a memorable duet between Chris and Mr Millins performing an impromptu two-man conga around the downstairs rooms singing *All You Need is Love*, much to his wife's embarrassment, if her crimson red complexion and stern grimace were anything to go by.

David took a back seat for most of the evening, not saying much, just sitting in the lounge with his eyes partially closed, listening intently to his daughter's dulcet tones. Every so often he peered towards the bow window making sure she was there, that it wasn't a dream. He would then close his eyes, listen in admiration as the beautiful young woman chatted freely to his house guests as though she'd known them for years. With mixed emotions, the curtain finally came down on the evening's little shindig as PW stood under the gazebo holding his trumpet to his lips and performing *The Last Post* with great passion. Everyone agreed it was a fitting tribute to Gary which the local canines took to heart, howling and yelping in ear-piercing harmony throughout the recital, right up until Chris's last triumphant blast.

At about ten o'clock, feeling tired and ready for his bed, David asked everyone to listen up before retiring. He had an important announcement to make. "The Pedal Power Ride in September will be the last outing for Chris and myself and Louise is joining the team and she'll occupy Gary's seat as the ME mascot. Anthony is hanging up his boots and I'm going to succeed him. In response to our recent troubles, my close friend here will be responsible for overseeing the company's finances in the short term. Making sure everything is hunky-dory. Louise has agreed to move in and we'll be visiting Hastings shortly to sort things out with her mother.

"Right I'm off to catch my lift. Oh, before I go. Claire asked me for a divorce when she was in hospital, but because of her state of mind, I wasn't prepared to grant it. In fact we've agreed to join Relate, would you believe. Our first meeting is next Friday so we'll see how it goes. It was Claire who brought the ME/CFS issue to my attention. Found out about Lucy and her selfless determination. Many sufferers are indebted to my wife for her hard work and resolve. Don't be surprised to hear a knock at the door as I understand Claire will be explaining her plans to Dr Sharon some time this evening. Fly on a wall, eh? I hope Francesca agrees to stay on. She's been a real rock the last few days and I'm indebted to her in so many ways."

There was a deep intake of air with many open mouths. Everyone looked aghast. It was like a bolt out of the blue, was the last thing anyone expected. Mr and Mrs Millins took a quick gulp of their sherry to steady their frail nerves, fearing their lives could be in jeopardy with the wicked witch on the prowl, and Francesca's sullen pose said it all. Chris and Louise just glanced at each other out of the corner of their eye, heads shaking in unison. This was a seminal moment in the life of David Lane.

"Welcome to the world of uncertainty, Miss Lane. If nothing else your father always keeps us on our toes. Separate rooms for the love birds tonight, no doubt," suggested PW. Chuckling to herself, Louise smiled in response and then gazed at the gravel drive with its well-tended borders and clipped conifer trees wondering what stories it could tell, what things it had seen.

The idea of a biography about her father's life had really captured her imagination, made her think and, at PW's behest, she'd keep it to herself; never breathe a word and then present him with a signed copy of the book on the day of its publication.

That would be a wonderful present, a real surprise that he'd never forget, thought PW, covering his mouth with both hands and gazing towards the heavens, praying for absolution. Unbeknown to Chris, David's talented teenage daughter had been working on the idea for the last couple of days. Taking a leaf out of her father's book, she'd already captured some thoughts in rhyme demonstrating, in the best traditions of the family name, that she also had a penchant for the English language. It read:

You speak for those in trouble, standing up for what is right,
Never falter in your mission, always ready for the fight,
A beacon and supporter of the poor and those in need,
Striving for the best in life, you always take the lead,
Brave spokesman and cheerleader, I'm proud to call a friend,
The hero of the ME cause, always toiling to the end,
A father in a million, smooth charmer through and through,
Someone I just admire for the things you say and do.

Complaining of a headache, Francesca slept alone that night not wanting to disturb the invalid, saying she'd be off early in the morning back to work, at the Excelsior Hotel, for the rest of the summer season. Closing the bedroom door she explained, with tissues in hand, that she might return at a later date, but she couldn't be sure as her elderly parents relied heavily on her. David was surprised by the news, thinking they were getting on well together, but as he still had reservations about her loyalty, following his chat with PW, he agreed it was probably best to part ways before things got too serious.

Everyone retired, feeling a little shell-shocked at David's unexpected announcement. As always, the charmer with the sylphlike tongue had the last word, leaving everyone on the back foot trying to digest what he'd said and the implications to them. No one expected in their wildest dreams that Claire would be darkening the doors of number one Pavilion Avenue any time soon, least of all the Millinses. Very soon the elegant Regency house was quiet and subdued except for the handsome timepiece ticking loudly in the downstairs hallway with its melodic musical chime ringing out every hour, on the hour. Now Chris was a light sleeper. The slightest sound had him reaching for the earplugs, hiding under the duvet with arms clasped firmly around his head counting as many sheep as he could muster.

For that reason, the housekeeper shouldn't have been too surprised, at sunup, to see a piece of Wilton carpet draped over the long case clock muffling its repetitive chimes, allowing the old Etonian to grab some much needed shut-eye.

Chris was billeted in the main guest room at the front of the house and, leaning against the velvet headboard, he noticed the two suitcases used by David on his recent trip neatly stacked on top of each other in an adjacent cupboard. Now PW's luggage was rather battered, in urgent need of replacement, so he decided to unzip them, have a peek inside and see how much space was available before ordering replacements for the 2015 season.

But then quite by accident, while feeling inside one of the pockets, his hand brushed across a piece of paper. Curious, he peered inside and was surprised to see a bright red envelope. Grabbing it with his fingertips, he noticed David's name written on the outside and quickly realised it had been overlooked with all the fuss and palaver of the last few days. Fortunately it wasn't stuck down so the nosy house guest opened it. Inside was a red and white birthday card, with a corny poem wishing him a happy day: nothing unusual there, he thought. However the message on the opposite page was more illuminating. It read:

'Sorry we couldn't spend much time together. I miss you so very much. Good news about the scan. Love you forever,
    Sarah xxx.'

Chris was in a quandary, what was he to do? So as to get his brain into gear at such a late hour, he decided to sneak downstairs for a quick nightcap and, after two large malts and a slice of Victoria sponge, he came up with the solution, the only sensible way forward. Without a second thought he tore up the birthday card, ripped it to shreds, forgot it ever existed. It was as simple as that. Job done. To be perfectly honest PW had much more important things on his mind than silly suitcases, out of date birthday cards and soppy love trysts. Elena, the love of his life, had replied to his earlier two-line text saying she'd love to move in, but did the invitation extend to the Steinway, the pink Fiat 500 and the two little PWs she'd got fermenting in her stomach?

While PW was planning his future, David had an email from Inspector Parry explaining that the French media had ripped into Francois like mad dogs showing no quarter, no mercy. Charlatan, villain, trickster and thief were just some of the words plastered across the front pages of the unforgiving press in their vitriolic attack on the Parisian parasite. The one-time hero of the Republic, a champion for the poor and needy was now a target of ridicule and abuse from a bloodthirsty press baying for revenge and his head on a spike. David was gratified to see he'd got his comeuppance and thanked the copper for his hard work, saying he'd sleep better knowing his erstwhile colleague was safely under lock and key, languishing in a Parisian *oubliette*.

Dozing on his king-size bed with Huey Lewis's gravel voice *Flying to the Moon*, he decided to keep quiet about his health problems, not wishing to alarm his nearest and dearest. With Claire's imminent return he'd put the Millinses out to grass, but let them remain in the house on the same terms for as long as they wished. Claire was right. She needed some younger blood around the place and with Mrs M safely out of the kitchen, that should protect my wife from any future mishaps, he chuckled to himself, picking up his worn copy of *Porterhouse Blue*, hoping to finish the final chapter before the dreaded medication kicked in.

It was Louise's eighteenth birthday on Sunday. It promised to be a great affair, a wonderful surprise. He smiled at the prospect of pre-lunch drinks around his favourite park bench with umbrellas at the ready, just in case, before popping over the road to the Queen's Hotel for a slap-up do. He glanced warmly at the family locket lying at his bedside while the miniature 'Just for ME' flag stood proudly next to his cherished photographs of Shirley and Claire, sat alongside a recently framed picture of his beloved daughter, Louise.

Feeling tired, with a faint smile on his face, he read out loud his latest piece of poetic rhyme:

You are my light, my life, my love,
My breath, my prayers, the skies above,
You are my spring, my summer sun,
The autumn breeze, my winter fun,
You are the stars, that shine on high,
The morning dew, late evening sky,
You are the air between the trees,
The rolling waves on tranquil seas,
You are my dream, my friend for life,
My darling bride, my gorgeous wife.

Closing Tom Sharpe for the night, he smelt the aroma of his mother's perfume filling the quiet night-time air. "I'm in heaven, I'm at peace with the world," he muttered, slowly succumbing to the medication and drifting off to sleep with just his mother's warm smile for company.